# THE FORBIDDEN TRILOGY

## THE FORBIDDEN SERIES

### TRACY LORRAINE

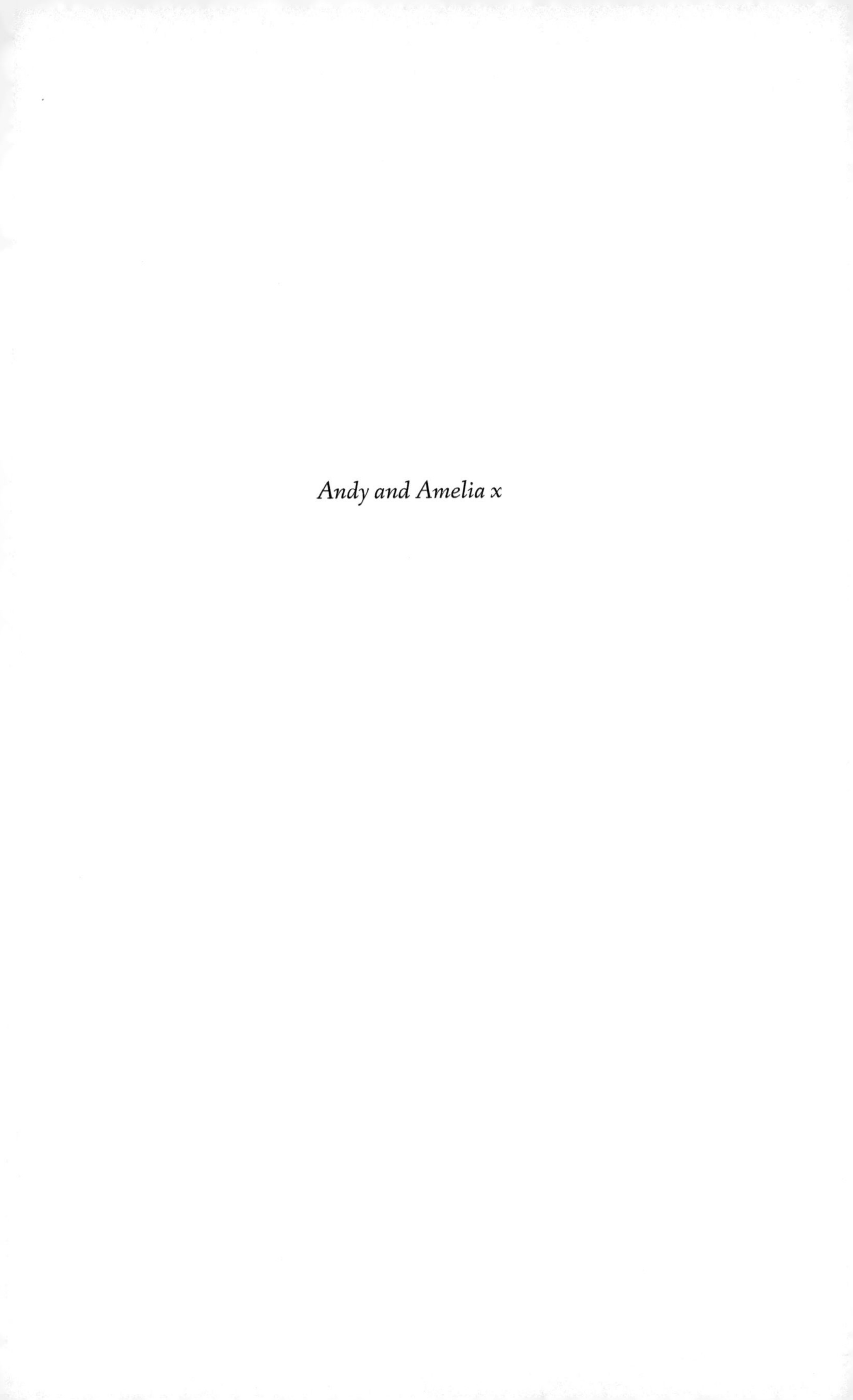

*Andy and Amelia x*

# A NOTE

The Forbidden trilogy is written in British English and contains British spelling and grammar. This may appear incorrect to some readers when compared to US English books.

# FALLING FOR THE FORBIDDEN

# CHAPTER ONE

F alling down on my bed, I blow out a long breath and tell myself that everything will be okay.

I had plans for this summer—a few weeks of fun before uni starts. The girls and I had been looking at last-minute holiday deals, and we had tickets for a music festival...but then my dad swooped in, in that way that he does, and ruined everything.

I knew it was coming.

I just wasn't expecting it quite yet.

I'd hoped agreeing to study what he wanted me to and working for him was enough—apparently not.

I decided a few years ago that I wasn't going to move away to study. I mostly love my life in London, and I loved living with Mum. I'm not ashamed to admit that she's one of my best friends. It was only as I started looking at universities that my dad piped up and told me that I would be studying accountancy and finance at The London School of Economics. He'd done his research and decided it was the best place for me to learn my trade so I could enter the family business.

I just about managed to contain my laughter when he emphasised the word *family*.

I've no idea how long I lie on my bed trying to convince myself that moving into his house with his new wife and her son isn't the worst thing to ever happen to me, but eventually my stomach rumbling has me moving. I sit on the edge of the bed and take in all my half-unpacked boxes. A large sigh falls from my lips. If I don't find everything a home, maybe I won't have to stay. I know it's wishful thinking. This is it for me now.

Disappointment floods me as I make my way through the silent house. It's not that I was expecting a welcome party or anything, but someone being here would have been nice. Someone to help me carry everything up to my room would have been even nicer. Since Dad moved in with Jenny a few years ago, I've been told to treat this place like my home.

It will never be.

It's just a house, a show home, a shell in which I'm scared to touch anything for fear of making a mess. Home is a place with character, with mess from day-to-day living, with people who love and care for you.

My dad isn't a bad man, per se, but he's not exactly what you'd describe as a doting father. Everything he does is for his own gain—if it happens to help others in the process, that's just a bonus.

My step mum, Jenny, is lovely. She really is, but I can't help feeling like she's just a little bit...broken. She makes all the right comments and does all the right things. She's a great mum. But there's such sadness in her eyes.

The fridge is full, as usual. It's strange, because I've never witnessed anyone eating more than a slice of toast or an apple in this kitchen.

I fix myself a salad with the unopened packets of fruit and vegetables, but it doesn't really have the effect I needed it to have. Being here makes me feel kind of empty, and no amount of lettuce leaves is going to fill the void after moving out of the flat Mum and I shared for the past few years.

Rummaging through the cupboards, I can't help smiling when I find a stash of naughty stuff hiding at the back.

Pulling my hair back into a messy bun, I put my thoughts to the side and set about making something that will make me feel just a little bit better.

The sun's just about to set, casting an orange glow throughout the kitchen. It almost makes it feel warm and inviting—almost. My mouth waters as I pour melted chocolate over the crushed biscuits and marshmallows I've managed not to eat already. Standing in only a vest and a small pair of hot pants, I decide to make myself a hot chocolate, grab a blanket, and enjoy my bowl of goodness out on the deck with a magazine. Chocolate makes everything that little bit better. If I eat enough, it might make me forget what this summer's actually going to be like for me.

I'm just waiting for the kettle to boil when a shiver runs down my spine. I'm sure it's just the size of the house that freaks me out. I've seen enough horror films to know there are plenty of hiding places in a place this big.

I'm still for a second, but when I don't hear anything, I continue with what I was doing. That is, until a deep rumbling voice has every nerve in my body on alert.

"Wow, step daddy sure is attracting the young ones these days." His voice is slurred, his anger palpable. It makes goosebumps prick my skin and a giant lump form in my throat. "You look too pure. Too innocent to be with that prick," he spits.

There's no love lost between my dad and my stepbrother, that's not news to me, but the viciousness of his voice right now makes me wonder what their relationship is really like. My dad might be many things, but he wouldn't cheat on Jenny—he loves her too much.

I can't remember the last time I saw him, but there's no way he can't know it's me. Who the hell else would be cooking in his kitchen? Deciding he's just trying to rile me up, I go to collect my stuff and get out of his way. Unfortunately, he seems to have other ideas.

His breath tickles up my neck moments before the heat of his body warms my back.

"You came here for the wrong man. I can put that right, though." The alcohol on his breath surrounds me. It's a reminder that there's a good chance he has no idea what he's doing right now.

The softness of his nose running up the length of my neck has tingles racing through my traitorous body. I don't realise he's smelling me until he blows out a long breath and the scent of alcohol hits me once again. I turn to leave, but his hands slam on the counter behind me and cage me in.

"Look at me," he demands.

"Let me go, Ben."

If he's surprised to discover it's me, he doesn't show it. If anything, his eyes shine with delight as he takes in every inch of my face before focusing on my lips. My stomach flips, knowing where his thoughts are.

Something passes over his face but it's gone too quickly to be able to identify. He pushes himself from the counter and away from me. No more words are said, but when he gets to the door, he looks back over his shoulder and runs his eyes over my body. They hold a warning I don't really understand.

Once he's disappeared from sight, I sag back against the counter. What the hell was that?

After putting half of the rocky road on a tray in the fridge, I forgo sitting outside and instead take my spoils to my room to hide. There's stuff everywhere in my room and, unlike the rest of this house, it makes me feel a little more relaxed.

Since the day Ben and I were introduced by our parents, we've not really had any kind of relationship. He's pretty much stayed out of my way and, in turn, I've done the same. It's not all that much of a task. When I'm here, he spends almost every minute somewhere else.

When he's home, he's moody, arrogant, and generally a prick, so I'm more than happy to stay out of his way.

It's just a shame he's so damn pretty to look at. As the years have passed, he's only become more attractive, too. I've no idea if it's just his job or if he works out as well because every inch of him seems to be toned to perfection.

Jenny spends most of her time apologising for his attitude and trying to explain that he's got a lot going on. I'm yet to discover what that is. As far as I can tell, he seems to be your average twenty-year-old guy who'd rather be off his arse drunk or with a woman than spending time at home with his parents.

By the time I've dug my way to the bottom of the bowl, I feel pretty sick. There's still no sign of my dad or Jenny, but the music pounding from Ben's room across the hallway leaves no doubt as to what kind of mood he's in.

# CHAPTER TWO

The steady beat of Ben's music must have eventually sent me to sleep, because the next thing I know, the sun is streaming in through the crack in the curtains and everything's silent once again.

After freshening myself up, I drag the hoodie I stole from my ex over my head, suddenly aware of just how much skin I had on display last night, and go in search of a cup of tea.

Just like the night before, everything is silent. There are no signs of them returning home late last night...no shoes by the door or a dirty glass in the kitchen sink like normal people. The whole place is, once again, perfect. Even the mess I made in the kitchen is gone, like I never existed.

Dad and Jenny eventually show their faces, going directly for the coffee machine. Dad mutters a good morning before disappearing into his office. I know that his argument for me living here was so I could be close for both work and uni, but I've not even been here twenty-four hours yet, and I'm pretty sure no one would have noticed if I hadn't bothered. I shouldn't really be shocked that Dad just wants me to fall neatly into his perfectly planned-out life, but I guess I am. When he originally suggested it, I was ready to point-blank refuse, but Mum seemed to think it was an excellent idea. I must remember to thank her for pushing this on me the next time I speak to her.

"Can you make sure you're free Sunday night? The four of us are going out to celebrate you moving in and officially starting at Johnson & Sons," Jenny asks once she's had a sip of her coffee.

The idea fills me with dread, but I agree before she also disappears. I hear her talking to someone before the house goes silent once again.

I'm still poking cereal around in a bowl when the atmosphere in the room changes. I don't need to look up to know why, but I do, nonetheless.

My breath catches at the sight of him. His dark hair sticks up in all directions, and his eyes are red and bloodshot, dark circles surrounding them.

"Morning," I sing politely.

All I get in response is a grunt and an angry glance as he follows in the steps of our parents and kicks the coffee machine into action. The scent of the beans once again fills the room and, just like always, I turn my nose up. I've no idea how anyone can drink that vile stuff.

<br>

AFTER FLICKING through the channels on my TV, I let out a long sigh. It's the first day of what should be my summer holiday, and I'm fed up already.

Grabbing my phone, I send a message to my best friend, Danni, who took me under her wing on my first day of sixth form and showed me the ropes. We hit it off instantly and have been close ever since, despite our obvious differences. She lives in an incredible house in Chelsea with her parents, whereas I was on the outskirts of the city in a small two-bedroom flat with Mum. Thankfully, her family don't see money quite the way Dad does. They're the most down-to-earth people I've ever met, despite the millions they've made from their antiques business.

It doesn't take much convincing for Danni to persuade me to stay at her place and go out for cocktails. I've only been here one night and I already can't wait to get out.

---

"SO, HOW'S THE SHOW HOME?" she asks as we're getting ready.

"About a fun as expected." Dropping my eyeliner pencil, I glance at Danni, sitting on her bed with a cocktail at her lips, her eyes filled with sympathy. "I'm sure it'll only get better once I start work on Monday."

"I can't believe you've got to work *all* summer. Zante won't be the same without you." My heart drops at her words. Our group of friends has spent months planning our first holiday without our parents—not to mention that I saved my arse off to be able to afford to go. But Dad put pay to any plans I had the moment he told me what my summer would consist of.

"You'll have an amazing time." I try to put as much excitement into my voice as possible, but I don't think I really manage it.

"I guess," she says sadly. "Anyway, how is it, living with Ben?" Her eyebrows wiggle in interest. It's no secret that not a single one of my friends would say no to a night with my stepbrother. His reputation still preceded him when I started at the same school he went to. It helped me fit in, in a sense, but it also made me a target for any girls brave enough to want to find out more about the elusive bad boy.

"He's..." The couple of interactions I've had with him run through my mind as I try to come up with a suitable answer. "Interesting."

"Interesting? That's all you've got?" Shrugging, I go back to finishing off my make-up.

The night is exactly as it should be. We drink, dance, and flirt with a group of guys who spend most of the night buying us drinks. I forget about what's on the horizon and just enjoy being eighteen while I still can.

We don't stumble back to Danni's house until almost dawn, and we sleep until well past lunch.

Her mum takes pity on our fragile states when we eventually emerge from Danni's bedroom and makes us bacon sandwiches to help cure our hangovers. Sadly, it doesn't even take the edge off mine.

I'm still feeling the effects of the previous night's over-indulgence and lack of sleep when I push the key into the lock of my new home later that day. The driveway's empty when the taxi drops me off, aside from my car, and the house is empty. Rolling my eyes, I slip my flip-flops off then carry them and my overnight bag up to my room.

---

I SPEND what's left of the day hiding in my room, watching films. I've no desire to venture downstairs and put on the act everyone else seems to. I can hear Dad and Jenny talking in the distance and eventually they come up to bed before the sound of their voices fades away.

I just start to drift off when the sound of the doorbell startles me. I wait to hear if there's going to be any movement, but other than the echo from the ringing, it stays silent.

My curiosity gets the better of me and I walk to the window to see if they're still at the door.

When I don't see anyone, I go to drop the curtain and get back in bed, but something catches my eye at the last minute. Someone is slumped in front of the house. I don't need to use too much brainpower to figure out that it's Ben.

Grabbing the hoodie I left hanging over the chair by the window, I pull it on and make my way down to rescue him.

"Ben?" He doesn't move or show any signs that he's aware of my presence. "Ben?" I say a little louder, but it's not until I bend down and give his shoulder a shake that I get any response.

"Yeah? What?" His voice is slurred and rough.

"Let's get you inside. Can you stand?"

"Of course I can fucking stand. I don't need your help," he snaps, trying to push himself up from the floor and falling straight back down.

"Oh, really?" I can't help but laugh at him. When he looks up at me, his face is hard, but his eyes show his own amusement. Maybe he's not quite as drunk as I first thought.

With the help of the wall, he stands to his full height. He towers above me at well over six feet tall, making me feel tiny. I'm not sure how much help I'll be, but I wrap my arm around his waist anyway.

A jolt of electricity shoots through me at our contact, and I immediately feel his eyes staring down at me.

Refusing to look up and acknowledge whatever just sparked between us, I focus on getting him inside.

"I really am okay," he says, his voice suddenly sounding much steadier than only moments ago. "You don't need to look after me."

"I'm just looking out for you."

"Why? No one else bothers."

My heart drops at his words. I'm saddened that what I experience in this house is his life. At least I have my mum at the other end of the phone if I need an ear to listen or a shoulder to cry on.

"I—"

Ben places large hands on my shoulders and turns me to look at him. A similar sensation rushes through me as it did when I first touched him.

I expect him to snap again. It seems to be his go-to defence mechanism whenever I've attempted to get close to him in the past, so I'm surprised when his eyes soften. "Thank you," he whispers.

Just when I think that maybe we're getting somewhere, his features harden once again, his mask goes back on, and he turns away from me.

He only makes it up two stairs before he falls flat on his face.

Silently laughing at his drunken state, I once again go to help him. To my surprise, he allows me to attempt to get him up the stairs, although I'm pretty sure he's just humouring me.

We come to a stop at his bedroom door. I remove my arm from around his waist and go to step away, but my breath comes out in a rush when I'm forcefully pulled back to him. My breasts press against his chest, and his heat burns through the fabric between us.

"Is that hoodie your boyfriend's?"

"Huh?"

"That hoodie you're wearing. It's a guy's."

"Oh. Yeah."

"Boyfriend?" he repeats.

"No. It's...it's my ex's," I stutter. The look he's giving me makes me nervous.

"Ex?"

"We weren't a very good match." His eyebrow lifts and I can't help more falling from my lips. "He wanted things I...wasn't ready for."

"Fuck," he barks, his features hardening as understanding dawns. I expect him to push me away but he only pulls me tighter against him. My heart thunders in my chest as his eyes continue to bore down into mine. He must be able to feel my body trembling against his, but he doesn't react.

"Ben?" I ask when the silence continues to stretch between us.

His eyes flick down to my lips when his name falls from them. I'm powerless to stop my tongue running along my bottom lip in anticipation. When he does eventually move, I find myself stumbling across the hallway.

The slam of his door vibrates through the entire house. I feel it in the wall at my back. It's the only evidence I have that what just happened wasn't my imagination. My racing heart and quivering body sure point towards it all being real.

He was going to kiss me, I'm sure of it.

Why me, and why now? He's gone out of his way to avoid me since our parents forced us on each other. He's been nothing but an arsehole.

After a few seconds of confusion, the sound of another door closing has me moving. I push myself from the wall and make my way back to my room.

---

"LAUREN? BEN? ARE YOU READY?" Dad hollers up the stairs.

I've no idea where we're going for this meal, but I'm assuming it's somewhere pretentious to make Dad look good. I'm wearing a pencil skirt and a blouse instead of the jeans and vest I really want to be in.

"Just coming," I call back before swiping some gloss over my lips and smoothing down my hair.

"You look beautiful, sweetheart," Dad says when I get to the bottom step. Seeing him in a suit and Jenny in a floral summer dress makes me think my assumption might be spot on. He's much less impressed when Ben eventually makes an appearance. "What the fuck is that?" he barks, making both Jenny and I turn towards the stairs.

He's wearing a pair of ripped jeans and a white V-neck, skin-tight t-shirt. "What?"

"Go and put some decent clothes on."

"These *are* decent."

The two of them stare at each other, a silent argument raging between them.

"Ben, please," Jenny begs, stepping in before things kick off. "Just go and put a shirt on, at least."

"This is a fucking joke," he mutters as he disappears up the stairs. I can't help but agree with him. This whole 'let's be a family' thing all of a sudden is a bit much. I'm actually surprised he even agreed to it in the first place. He usually avoids any family event at all costs.

The drive towards the restaurant is silent and awkward as fuck as

Ben and I sit beside each other in the back. His words from the night before and the feel of his body pressed against mine are still at the forefront of my mind, but now we're out as a *family*, it makes everything I'm still feeling seem very, very wrong.

From the moment we sit down at our table, Dad has his phone out. He's totally oblivious to the death stares he keeps getting from Jenny.

"So, Lauren, are you looking forward to starting work tomorrow?"

"Uh...yeah, I think so. I'm a little nervous."

"Aww, no need for that. Everyone's lovely. Right, Ben?"

"Yeah, great. The boss is a bit of a dick, though." I can't help but snort a laugh.

"Ben, don't," Jenny snaps, but Dad's too focused on whatever he's doing to have heard.

The waiter comes over to take our orders and Dad actually looks surprised when we prompt him to say what he wants. His eyes scan the menu quickly before ordering a steak and being pissed off when he's asked how he'd like it cooked.

"Who in their right mind would order it any way other than rare in a place like this?" he grumbles once the waiter's left us to it.

"Let's just enjoy our evening. Work keeps us busy all week."

"This won't wait. Unless you want to deal with it?" Dad snaps at Jenny, who pales at his outburst.

"No, no. You know what you're doing. Just don't spend all night on that thing." The glare she receives would make most people cower, but somehow, she manages to hold her own.

Looking back to the two of us, she continues with her earlier small talk. I don't need to see him; I can sense the tension radiating from Ben because of the way my dad talks to his mum. Thankfully, he has enough self-control to keep his disapproval to himself—for now, at least.

Dad's phone rings and he immediately answers it before getting up and walking out of the restaurant to deal with whatever is so important on a Sunday night.

"I'm just going to use the bathroom before the food arrives," Jenny whispers, watching her husband disappear from sight.

"Well, this is fun," Ben says once we're alone.

"That's one way to describe it. I'm surprised you turned up."

"There's...suddenly something worth making the effort for." His eyes drop from mine, to my lips, and then lower. My whole body heats under his gaze and I squirm in my seat. "You're fucking trouble." It's the last thing he says before Dad reappears, looking pissed off. Ben goes back to sitting mutely beside me for the rest of the meal, but I don't miss the odd glance my way when Dad's distracted.

Once the bill's paid, we rush out of there like the place is on fire. Jenny looks upset, and I feel bad for her...but I fear she's trying to turn us all into something we're never going to be.

A perfect family.

# CHAPTER THREE

I've no idea why, but as I walk into the office for my first day, I'm nervous as hell. I've been here many times, and I've met every single person, but still, butterflies continue to riot in my belly. I put it down to the fact my dad's about to become my boss, and I know exactly what everyone around here thinks of him. I don't expect special treatment because I'm his daughter, but I do hope for a little reprieve from him.

I follow Dad as he barks instructions at Betty and Erica, who are sitting at their desks, ready to start the week. Betty immediately jumps up and rushes towards the kitchen to make Dad his morning coffee.

"Would you like anything, sweetheart?" she asks when she spots me.

"Uh...tea would be great. Thank you."

Betty has been working for Johnson & Sons for so long that she's practically part of the furniture. I think before my dad took up residence in the office and started throwing his weight around, she was probably classed as one of the family. But Dad's done a stellar job of turning this friendly family business into something more corporate. His desire to be the best knows no bounds, and the second he could get his teeth into this place, he did.

Pushing the nagging feeling that this business is the only reason Dad married Jenny to the back of my mind, I walk over to my desk. I worked here for a few weeks last summer so I know my way around. I mostly spent those weeks doing menial tasks like shredding, but this time, I'm an actual employee with actual responsibilities. I'm not sure whether I should be excited or scared.

"Are you ready for this?" Erica asks. We hit it off immediately last year. She'd just dropped out of uni and found herself an admin job here. Thankfully, she's got plenty of backbone and can handle herself around my dad.

"Honestly, I've no idea."

"It'll be fine. You're up for tonight, right?"

"What's happening tonight?"

Rolling her eyes at me like I shouldn't even need to ask, she says, "Your new job drinks."

"Oh...uh...it's okay."

"No, no it's not. It's tradition for any new staff—*under the age of about...thirty-five*," she whispers, "to go out for drinks on their first day."

"Even on a Monday?"

"This is London, hon. Every night is Friday night."

I grin. "Okay, then. When and where?"

"The Olive Branch. Eight o'clock. To start with."

"To start with?"

"Oh, honey, you've no idea."

My first day is exhausting, and not just because I only had a few hours sleep the night before. My hopes for being eased in gently were dashed the second I was given accounts to go over, customers to contact, and invoices to process. Being a member of the 'family' means I get access to everything.

Dad's mentioned the day I take over the company more than once since I moved in. To begin with, I corrected him, saying that

Ben was the one who would one day own it, seeing as it's actually *his* family business, but I was soon put in my place. He seems to think that, by marrying Jenny, he's entitled to everything. Which I guess is true. Once again, I question his intentions, but I push the thoughts aside every time they pop up because, although my dad might not be winning any parenting awards anytime soon, I like to believe he's pretty genuine and just wants to be successful.

***

WALKING INTO THE OLIVE BRANCH, I pull at my dress, questioning my choice when I see that most people around me are still in their work clothes. I look around for Erica or any of the others I might recognise from work, but I before I find them, I hear my name being shouted.

Following the sound, I find Erica waving like a loon from her spot by the bar. As I walk over, I get a better view of what she's wearing. Her silver dress sits high on her thighs and the back is completely missing. Suddenly, I don't feel self-conscious at all about my slightly revealing red wrap dress.

"Wow, Lauren. Look at you. The guys are going to trip over themselves!"

"I'm sure that'll go down well with my Dad," I say with a laugh I don't really feel.

The bar soon fills up, and it's not long before the sounds of a large group of guys filter through to us.

"Oh, they're here. Are you ready for this?"

My stomach drops. I hadn't realised when Erica invited me earlier that we'd be the only females, but I guess it was obvious seeing as we work for a building company and all the other women in the office are above her thirty-five age limit to be invited. We're pretty outnumbered.

The second they get to us, Erica is pulled into Will's arms before he spins her around, getting a good look at her exposed skin. "Looking good tonight, gorgeous," he growls, his pupils growing darker by the second. Until he looks up and spots me. "Wait a fucking minute. Is this little Lauren?" My cheeks heat and my skin prickles as he runs his eyes over every inch of me. My hands clench with the need to do something to put an end to his molestation. I've no idea what it is, but something about Will creeps me out.

"Dude," a familiar voice barks before Will lifts his hand to rub his head where he was just slapped.

"What? Just fucking look at her." Something erupts inside me when Ben appears from behind him. His eyes run the length of me and, unlike the unwelcome feeling of Will's attention, my body erupts in goosebumps. "Anyway, it's not like she's your actual sister."

Ben has Will's shirt in his fist in seconds, their noses almost touching. He drops his voice so low, I have no chance of hearing what he says. But whatever it is, it works, because Will does apologise to me the minute he's released.

Thankfully, he turns his attention back to Erica. Once we've all got a drink, I'm introduced to some of the guys I've yet to meet. I get hungry eyes from a few of them, but the moment Erica reveals who my father is, they soon lose interest. I can understand why.

Ben says nothing to me. Instead, he stays with some of the guys at the other side of our group. That doesn't mean I don't feel his eyes burning into me every few minutes. I fight the need to look up, too afraid of my body's reaction if I catch him staring.

We have a couple of rounds of drinks before Erica rounds everyone up to head towards a club.

"It's a Monday night," I complain when she links arms with me and steers me towards the exit.

"And?"

I guess if I'm going to be starting uni in a few weeks, I'd better get used to this kind of nightlife. "Nothing. Where are we going?"

"Just wait, you're going to love it!"

The club, Erica's favourite, is called Fire, and it's insane. I've no idea how many floors there are, but we came up at least three sets of stairs to get to the bar we're currently stood at, waiting for drinks.

"Two rum and Cokes, six pints, and eight shots of...Apple Sourz, please," Erica shouts at the bartender.

In minutes, I'm holding a drink in each hand as I watch all the others down their shots. I follow suit and wince when the sour liquid makes my mouth water.

"And that one, hon," Erica says, nodding to my rum and Coke. "It's time to dance."

Draining the glass as quickly as I can, I allow Erica to pull me towards the crowded dance floor. We're only alone for one song before a few of the guys join us. Jon pulls Erica to him and they start grinding against one another before I feel hands on my waist.

My skin prickles, so I'm not surprised to find Will when I turn around and remove myself from his grip. Pouting, he tries to grab me again but, before he reaches me, his hands are slapped away and another body blocks him from me.

"We're leaving," Ben barks, grabbing my forearm to pull me away.

"Why?" I stand firm. I already have to follow Dad's orders. I refuse to have another man trying to control my life.

"Because you're drunk, and Will's a dick."

"And you're not? You're the one ruining my fun."

"Lauren," he growls.

"Don't *Lauren* me. I'm having fun. How about you dance with me instead?" I step into his personal space, his body heat burning the front of me. He stills, his eyes boring down into mine. "What? You don't dance?"

"I can dance just fine. Let's go." With his hands on my waist, he guides me from the dance floor and then the club.

Once we step outside and the coldness of the night hits me, I realise I'm too drunk and exhausted to start arguing with him. With his hand still resting on my lower back, he finds us a taxi and we head for home.

The house is in darkness when we enter. Leaving Ben in the hallway, I start to weave my way up the stairs, knowing I really need to get to sleep if I'm ever going to make it to day two of my job.

"Lauren, wait," he calls when I'm halfway up. "Let me help you."

With his arm wrapped around my waist, he helps guide me towards my room. I might be tipsy, but I'm not too drunk to manage myself. The feeling of his solid body pressed up against mine is too good, though, so I allow him to continue. I guess he owes me, anyway, after the other night.

Pushing my bedroom door open, he comes to a stop. "You okay from here?"

When I look up at him, I find dark, hungry eyes staring down at me. His lips are pressed into a thin line and there's a rapid pulse throbbing in his neck.

Finding his eyes once again, the silence between us stretches out. That is, until the sound of the toilet flushing from the other end of the house reaches us.

"Fuck. I need to...Damn it."

I don't get a chance to question him, because he's gone and his bedroom door is closed behind him.

---

THE WEEK FLIES by once I manage to rid myself of Monday night's hangover. As Friday comes towards an end, I can't wait for the weekend to start. I have no plans as of yet, but that's fine, because right now, all I want to do is sleep.

I'm just finishing up going through last month's invoices when I spot something. Dad's already been through them once, and he told me there was no need for me to do so as well, but it helps me understand the process. Now, I'm here, and I might as well make the most of the opportunity, even if I'm not sure I want to spend the rest of my life working with numbers like he assumes.

Everyone else in the office has left for the day, so when I come across something that looks wrong and doesn't add up, I've got no one to ask. I go over it again and again, but I can't figure it out.

Where the hell could fifty thousand pounds have gone?

Eventually, I shut my computer down for the night in frustration. I hate not knowing everything, but with only a few days under my belt, I've got a lot to learn and the answer is probably staring me right in the face.

Unsurprisingly, the house is deserted when I get home. Ben's probably out getting pissed like he is most weekends. I've no idea where Dad and Jenny are, but they seem to make a hobby out of trying to spend as little time at home as possible.

I've barely seen Ben since the night he helped me up to my room. That makes it easier to pretend that what happened between us is just a very vivid part of my imagination.

Seeing as it's Friday night, I run myself a bath and order a takeaway for when I get out. I'd hoped to spend tonight catching up with Mum, but when I rang her yesterday to make plans, she excitedly reminded me about her weekend away with her sister. We still talk almost daily, but damn, I miss her.

The discrepancy on the accounts still nags at me while I lie surrounded by bubbles. I do my best to push it aside and relax. Turning up my favourite playlist on my phone, I sink down into the warm water.

I FEEL REFRESHED when I wake up late Saturday morning. As I lie in bed, considering what I want to spend the day doing, I'm amazed that I can hear chatting in the house. My curiosity has me getting out of bed and dressed to find out if this family could be doing something as normal as having breakfast together.

I'm wrong, of course. As I get closer to the kitchen, I realise that what I thought was light chitchat is actually a heated argument. Jenny sits at the island, mute, while Dad and Ben argue about responsibilities and appropriate behaviour. The second I join them, they stop what they're doing. Jenny looks at me and apologies for the noise—I swear all she does is apologise for other people. Dad and Ben continue staring daggers at each other until Ben storms from the room and out the back door.

"He'll come to his senses, love," Jenny says softly, placing her arm on Dad's forearm, but it does little to calm the fire raging in his eyes.

"You keep saying that, but all he does is disobey the rules."

"He's just struggling at the moment."

"He's a twenty-year-old man, Jenny. He needs to grow up," Dad spits out. If Jenny is surprised by his outburst, she doesn't show it.

They take their seats around the table and silently sip on their coffees. The tension surrounding them is almost palpable, and I consider turning on my heels and walking straight out of the house to get away from it all. Mum's flat is empty. I could spend the weekend there in peace.

I'm starting to fully understand why Ben's never home.

"Would you like some breakfast, darling?" Jenny asks me, her voice sickly sweet. I know she's trying to make up for my dad's attitude, but it's really not necessary. His temper isn't news to me.

I agree and sit myself beside Dad, who's still tense, while Jenny floats around the kitchen. I watch them both, trying to figure them out. I never noticed before, but since moving in with them, the cracks in their relationship are obvious. I still think they genuinely love each other, but there's some strange kind of tension between them, almost like they're trying too hard.

Thinking it might take Dad's mind off whatever was going on with Ben, I bring up what I thought I found with the accounts yesterday.

"You're wrong," Dad barks the second I suggest I couldn't account for fifty grand.

"Probably," I admit, "but I'd really like to go over it with you so I can—"

"Enough, Lauren. I didn't give you a job so you could question everything I do. I just need you to do your damn job. Is that too much to ask?" A lump forms in my throat and tears sting my eyes. I feel like a child under his intense, angry stare. "What the hell is wrong with the kids in this house? You've both had everything you could ever desire, yet you're totally incapable of doing the most simple of tasks."

My lip trembles and I'm about to interrupt to apologise when warm fingers circle my wrist. Sucking in a breath, I'm pulled up and into a solid wall of man. I recognise his scent immediately.

Before I know what's happening, I find myself in the passenger seat of his BMW with him jogging around to the driver's side.

As he reverses off the drive, I get my first chance to look at him. Sweat beads his brow, his hair's a little damp and curling out from his neck, his skin's flushed, and his chest is heaving. His black t-shirt clings to his body like a second skin, showing off every muscle covering his solid frame.

"Stop it," he snaps, startling me.

"Stop what?"

"Running your eyes over me like that."

"Wh—I...uh...was wondering what's going on."

"Do you always let him talk to you like that?"

"No. He—"

"Do not make excuses for him, Lauren." The way my name sounds coming from his lips has my insides clenching. He's angry, his white-knuckle grip on the wheel shows that, but his voice is also deeper, rougher than usual.

"I...uh...I wasn't," I argue, and he gives me a look, casting a glance over at me that tells me he knows I'm lying. "What? I shouldn't have questioned him."

"Why not?"

"Because he's right. I don't really know what I'm talking about."

"Says who?"

"Him and everyone who's worked for Johnson & Sons for longer than me, I would imagine."

"It doesn't mean you're wrong. Trust your gut, Lauren. If you think something's wrong, it probably is."

"Just like being alone with you feels dangerous?"

His eyes flash with something. Excitement, shock, I'm not sure. It's not until I see his reaction that I realise I said those words out loud.

"Dangerous?" he repeats, intrigue filling his voice.

"Uh...yeah...anyone ever tell you you're a shit driver?"

His laugh lightens the atmosphere in the car. It's like I can breathe properly for the first time since being pushed inside it. "No, no one's ever told me that."

"First time for everything," I mutter quietly. I'm not expecting an answer, so I jump a little when I hear his voice.

"I guess there is."

I've no idea if it's meant to be, but it feels like a promise. My thighs clench and my cheeks flush with embarrassment. "You okay?" When I risk a look, he's got a sexy little smirk playing on his lips.

Damn him.

"Yeah. I'm good. Thanks. What were you and my dad arguing about?"

Blowing out a long breath, he considers his answer. "It would probably be quicker to go through the things we don't argue about."

"Oh?" I knew they didn't really see eye-to-eye, but I didn't realise things between them were that bad.

"It's nothing you need to worry about."

"No, but you can tell me anyway."

"He just...doesn't agree with my choices."

"What choices?"

"All of them." Pulling the car to a stop, he looks over at me. His face is softer than I'm used to seeing, but it's clear his walls are built right up. There's no way I'm breaking them down anytime soon, if ever. Not that I'm sure I want to. "No one deserves to be dragged into my life."

"You're forgetting something."

"I am?"

"Like it or not, I'm part of your life. I'm already in it. So what's the harm in sharing the load?"

"Motherfucker," he mutters, but it's with a smile twitching at the corners of his mouth. "Things aren't always what they appear to be. Let's just leave it at that."

I open my mouth to question his cryptic statement, but before I get a chance to say anything, he's out of the car and shutting his door behind him.

For the first time since he came to a stop, I look out the window and focus on where he's brought us. The park.

"Ben, what are—oh!" I can't help but laugh as I watch him lift a picnic basket from the boot of his car. It's wicker and has red and white gingham fabric poking out from the edge. It's the last thing I think I ever expected to see him carrying.

With my eyebrows raised in surprise, I look up at him.

"I was meant to be meeting friends for a picnic," he says with a shrug.

"Y—you should go. Don't change your plans for me."

"Lauren," he says, stopping and turning his angry eyes on me. I suck in a breath at their intensity, but I know it isn't directed at me. "There isn't anywhere else I'd rather be."

My lips form an O and I fall into step beside him.

With the basket in one hand and a blanket tucked under his arm, he places his other hand at the small of my back and guides me towards the vast expanse of grass beyond.

We come to a stop under a huge oak tree and Ben shakes out the blanket before placing the basket in the middle and lying down next to it.

"I won't bite," he says when he looks up and sees I'm still standing.

"I'm not sure I believe that." My voice comes out as an unsure whisper and he doesn't miss it.

"Remember what I said about trusting your gut." He winks at me and I fall down onto my back, allowing the sun peeking through the leaves to warm my skin.

I feel heat coming from somewhere else, and when I turn my head and crack one eye open, I find Ben staring down at me.

"You're really beautiful."

Propping myself up on my elbows, I look around to see who he's talking to. We're still alone, and heat blooms from my cheeks, warming down my neck. Slowly, I look over to find him staring right at me.

"You're talking to me?"

"No, that tree over there. Of course I'm talking to you." I fight to keep my eyes on his, but his stare gets too intense and I have to look away. "Hey..." His warm fingertips connect with my jaw and my head is gently turned so I have no choice but to look back up at him. His deep blue eyes hold a sincerity I don't think I've ever seen before.

He's silent for the longest time. When he does speak, it's not to say any of the things I imagined might fall from his mouth.

"Fancy a sausage roll?"

# CHAPTER FOUR

Once I stop laughing, our conversation takes a bit of a lighter note. We steer clear of bringing up anything to do with work or our parents.

I never thought I'd say it, but I end up having an amazing day with Ben. He's still intense and brooding, but as time goes on, he manages to let go of some of the anger that seems to follow him around and, for the first time since we were introduced, I feel like I've actually got to know him a little. He's not nearly as scary as I once thought he was. That fear has been replaced by another feeling, one I'm not all that comfortable thinking about.

The way he looks at me, the gentleness of his touch—he awakens things within me that I've not experienced before, and that can't be a good thing.

I had a semi-serious boyfriend last year. I enjoyed my time with him, but I didn't feel the pull I do when I'm with Ben. The more time I spend with him, the more I seem to crave his attention...and his touch.

"Lauren, is that you?" Dad calls out the second we step foot inside the house.

"Yeah, Dad. I'll be right there."

"Don't take any of his bullshit. I'll be upstairs if you need me." Ben's fingers brush against mine and he squeezes quickly before disappearing up the stairs, leaving me with the tingles kickstarted by his caress.

"Lauren?" Dad snaps.

Following the sound of his voice, I find him in his office, staring at a spreadsheet.

"I wanted to go through what you thought you saw yesterday so we don't have the same misunderstanding again."

"Oh. Yeah, sure." Pulling up a chair, I silently listen as Dad talks through the spreadsheet and the figures on it. He does the same calculation I did the previous day...and the total is fifty thousand pounds more than what I worked out.

"See, everything's fine. You must have missed something."

"Yeah. I guess so."

"Happy now?"

I mumble my agreement, but Ben's words linger in my mind. *Trust your gut, Lauren. If you think something's wrong, then it probably is.*

As I walk out of Dad's office, I put it all to the back of my mind. I haven't even started uni yet and I'm questioning my dad's accounts. He was right this morning. I don't know what I'm talking about.

Something feels weird as I walk towards my bedroom door. It's not shut like I left it, just pulled flush. I live in Dad and Jenny's house, so I guess it's their right to go into their own rooms, but that doesn't stop it feeling like an invasion of privacy. As I push the door open, I realise immediately who's been in here and suddenly I feel uncomfortable for an entirely different reason. Laid out on my bed, in the exact spot I left my ex's black hoodie this morning, is a navy Johnson & Sons one.

I stand frozen, not knowing what to do. I should give it back. Accepting it and wearing it are wrong. It's pushing boundaries that we shouldn't be anywhere near. But it's just a hoodie, right? His actions and words today come back to me, and I fear we might have already blurred a couple of those lines.

In the end, I push my door closed and walk over to the neatly laid-out fabric. In a moment of madness, I swipe it up and bring it to my nose. I'm taken back to the enclosed space of his car when the only thing I was aware of was him sitting next to me. The fullness of his parted lips as he concentrated on where he was going. The gentle rise and fall of his strong chest and the tense muscles as he held onto the steering wheel.

Sitting down on the end of the bed, I try telling myself that the flutters of excitement I feel in my belly are wrong, but it does little to dispel them. In fact, the more I think about our day together, the stronger they get. The need to go and see him nags at me, but I fight it. Putting his hoodie down on my chair, I attempt to distract myself with the TV.

I can only assume that Dad wants to make amends for this morning, because when I venture downstairs a while later for a glass of water, I find him and Jenny in the kitchen, surrounded by food.

"Ah, there you are. We were just going to shout up. Dinner's ready," Jenny sings as if being called down for a family meal is the norm around here.

"I'll go and tell Ben," Dad says, getting up from his stool.

"It's okay, I'll go." I see something flash in Dad's eyes at my suggestion, but when he doesn't say anything, I spin and head back in the direction I came from.

Pausing for a second outside his bedroom door, I suck in a deep breath in preparation for seeing him again. Anticipation engulfs me and I feel like a schoolgirl waiting for her crush to walk into class.

After giving myself a little talking to, I lift my hand and knock. I'm expecting to hear movement from inside, so when I don't, I'm a little disappointed.

"Ben?" I call, and after a few seconds, I push the door handle down. As expected, the room is empty. I guess he's on his usual Saturday night out with his mates. My stomach drops. I stay where I am for a couple of seconds and take in his room. It's tidier than I would have imagined. Stacks of CDs surround his player and a few items of clothing are thrown on a chair, but other than that, it's tidy. The bed's even made.

Closing the door behind me, I make my way back downstairs to embark on what's going to be the most awkward family meal I think I've ever experienced.

***

BEFORE I GET into bed some time before midnight, I pull the curtains back just to make sure he's not warming the doorstep once again, but there's no sign of him.

I've never really put all that much thought into where he goes and what he does, but suddenly I'm lying here, worrying about him. What if he gets too drunk and one of his friends isn't there to help get him home? What if some other guy starts a fight? All these stupid thoughts run rampant through my head and I end up getting frustrated with myself.

My entire body is tense. Sleep is the last thing on my mind when I eventually hear footsteps creeping up the stairs. My heart races erratically as I picture him getting himself ready for bed.

When I hear a door click much closer than I was expecting, I sit bolt upright in bed. Light filters into my room and I squint as I try to focus on his silhouette in the doorway. My heart pounds in every part of my body as I wait for him to do something.

"Fuck. I shouldn't be here."

I watch, enthralled, as he brings his hands up and scrubs them over his shadowy face.

Expecting him to leave as quickly as he entered, I'm shocked when he reaches out and pushes the door closed. The small amount of light disappears and I'm left with hardly any vision. My other senses are immediately heightened, and the second he steps a foot forward, I stop breathing.

His manly scent gets stronger and goosebumps prick my skin as I wait for what he's going to do.

When he reaches the bed, it dips as he puts his knee on the edge. I'm shocked when he lies down beside me. Reaching for my hand, he encourages me to join him.

We lie with only the sounds of our increased breaths filling the room. My head spins with the knowledge that he's right here, next to me, on my bed.

The pillow rustles as he turns to look at me. I fight to keep my eyes on the darkness in front of me, but eventually the pull to look at him is too strong.

I can just make out his features. His eyes sparkle, reflecting the tiny bit of moonlight seeping in around the curtains.

He searches my face. I've no clue what he's looking for.

I start to think that maybe this is it. That he's come in here just to lie with me and hold my hand. It's not unwelcome. It actually feels pretty incredible, but I'm confused, anxious, and desperate to find out what's really going on in his head.

He rolls onto his side and I follow his lead. The heat from his body burns into me and my fingers twitch to reach out and touch him.

I suck in a breath when his face moves closer to mine. Our eyes stay locked, but, instead of doing what I'm expecting, he rests his forehead against mine. I swear he's trying to tell me something, but my brain's not exactly functioning correctly with him this close to me.

"Fuck," he whispers, nudging his nose against mine. I can almost hear his internal argument. "I can't stop thinking about you," he admits. His honesty forces all the air from my lungs. "Tell me to stop. Tell me to fucking leave. Right now."

I can't. I'm powerless to do anything but lie there and wait. Time seems to stand still as we stare at each other in the darkness.

"Fuck," is the last thing he says before I feel the softness of his lips against mine. His hand lands on my waist, the heat of his palm burning through my top.

He doesn't move to deepen the kiss, but my need for him has my lips parting. The second he feels the movement, he pulls back and stares at me. My eyes have adjusted to the dark enough now to see the tension lining his face.

"Please," I whisper. I can't think of anything worse than him walking out and leaving me alone right now, but it's not enough. No sooner does the word pass my lips, he's up on his feet and backing away from the bed.

"I'm sorry. I shouldn't be here." His voice is full of regret as he stares at me. Eventually, he turns and disappears from my sight. His footsteps thunder down the stairs and the sound of the front door slamming shakes the entire house.

---

BEN NEVER CAME BACK HOME that night, or the next day. Once I knew he'd really left the house that night, I let all my frustration out. I cried for longer than I'm willing to admit. My tears were full of disappointment, regret...and desire. I want to be able to say there was some shame in there, but there wasn't. And in a way, I'm ashamed for not feeling it. Nothing about that kiss and his touch felt shameful. Every moment since he walked out of my room, I've been craving more. More of his kiss. More of his touch. More of everything. He's taking over my thoughts.

It's not until the following Wednesday that I get to lay my eyes on him again since that dark night. I'm sitting, staring at my computer screen, trying to look busy, when the door to the office is pulled open.

I look up. I don't usually bother because no one's ever looking for me, but somehow, my body knows it's him.

Instead of the shirt he should be wearing as he meets with customers, he's clad in a hi-vis jacket and dirty work clothes. Dirt is smeared across both cheeks and his hands are mostly black. Every muscle in my body tenses.

Swallowing, I try to get some moisture back in my mouth and drag my eyes away from him before he notices my attention.

I keep an eye on him over the top of my monitor as he walks in and has a very short and sharp conversation with my dad. I can sense the tension between them from here. I don't miss the tightness of Ben's muscles, the pulsing in his neck, or his clenched fists as he stands just inside the door to the office.

After a few short words, he turns to leave, but at the last minute, he looks up. Our gazes lock and something sparks between us. His eyes brighten but he shows no other signs that he feels the same pull between us that I do.

Our connection only lasts for a couple of seconds, but when he pulls his eyes away and walks out of the office, it's with his shoulders sagging in defeat.

My fingers curl around the base of my chair as I fight my need to follow him, to find out what's going on and why he looks so sad.

"Lauren," Dad barks. "Are you going to answer that or just let it annoy the shit out of all of us?" It's not until Dad's finished talking that I even realise the phone on my desk is ringing. I take a deep breath in an attempt to compose myself before lifting the handset to my ear.

Just like almost every other time it's rung this morning, the caller asks for Jenny or Dad. Most days, I don't feel like I'm needed or really wanted here to do anything with the accounts. Instead, I seem to be becoming Dad's personal PA.

"I'm sorry, but Jenny is out of the office today. I can put you through to Nick." Dad glares at me from his desk. He told me earlier to put off any callers, but after watching the way he was with Ben, I've no real desire to do as I'm told.

Thankfully, after he's taken the phone call he didn't want, Dad leaves the office. The atmosphere immediately lightens and Erica even puts the radio on, which is banned while the boss is around.

The day goes on forever, my thoughts consumed by the look on Ben's face as he dragged his gaze away from me earlier. Every time I hear the main door to the office squeak, my heart jumps into my throat, but he never reappears. I can only hope he might make it home tonight so at least I can find out if he's okay.

"We're going out tonight," Erica announces after following me into the kitchen to get her lunch from the fridge.

"Tonight?"

"Yeah. Wednesday's the new Friday."

"I thought every night was a Friday night in London," I grin.

"Exactly." She winks at me, throwing her tub of leftovers into the microwave. "You've been moping for days. You need a good blow out. I'll shoot a message out to the guys. They'll be on board."

I know it's pointless arguing, but to be honest, a night out and letting loose does sound like a good idea. I almost ask her not to tell the guys because the last thing I need is Ben ruining another night for me, but I bite the words back, knowing it'll only invite unwanted questions.

"Yeah, okay."

"I'm going to have to work a little late, though. How about you go home and grab your stuff, then we'll get ready together at mine? I've already got tequila in the fridge."

"Sounds good."

The more I think about it as the afternoon wears on, the more I'm looking forward to it. Erica keeps me informed about who's coming, and when I don't hear that Ben's presence is confirmed, I feel even better about it. The last thing I need is him trying to ruin my evening by telling me what I should and shouldn't be doing.

"Girl! You look hot," Erica sings when I step into the kitchen in the house she shares with her sister. She runs her eyes up and down my body, nodding in approval. I'm wearing a black leather skirt and a gold sequined cami with an open back. "I'm going to have to pry the men off you tonight."

"What if I don't want you to?" I ask with a wink.

"Ooh, are you planning on hooking up?"

I make a non-committal noise because I'm fully aware that I'm not hooking up with some random guy in a club, but Erica doesn't need to know that. It seems to be what she does every weekend, so I may as well look like I fit in. I also have no intention of mentioning that I'm still a virgin.

"Here, drink this. My sister's going to drop us off in a minute."

With the tequila flowing through my system, I manage to put everything with Ben to one side and just enjoy myself. We meet some of the guys, but thankfully both Will and Ben are noticeably absent. I try not to look too relieved about it.

After a round of drinks, we head out onto the dance floor. Erica and I dance with James and Stewart, two of the builders from work. The four of us let loose, not worrying about what we look like or who's watching us making fools of ourselves. The dancing is mostly innocent, but there's the occasional bump and grind when the song commands it.

Leaning into Erica, I shout in her ear that I'm heading to the toilet and she waves me off. Weaving my way through the packed dance floor, I eventually make it to the to the other side of the room to where I need to be.

After fighting with the women trying to touch up their make-up in the mirrors, it seems like forever when I eventually make it out again.

I'm about to walk down the corridor to re-join the main room when someone wraps their hand around my wrist. I fight to free myself, simultaneously turning to see who it is. My breath catches and the fight leaves me as I stare into the blue eyes of my stepbrother.

His stare holds mine for a beat before he pulls me towards the stairs. We go down one flight and then he continues moving towards the dance floor. The music's different on this level—the bass is louder, the tempo sexy and seductive.

As he drags me in front of him, his hands land on my waist and he pulls me back against his body. A loud sigh leaves me when our bodies align and I feel him move against me.

His fingers tickle at my shoulder as he moves my hair, exposing my skin. Dropping his head, his nose runs up the length of my neck before I feel his lips at my ear.

"I couldn't watch you dancing with someone else any longer," he growls, pulling us even closer. I gasp when I feel his length against my arse.

He grinds his hips with mine, keeping perfect time with the song booming through the speakers, but I barely hear any of it. My focus is solely on the connection of our bodies.

His lips trail down my neck, his tongue sneaking out to taste my skin, and something inside me explodes. Heat blooms between my legs and the only thing I want is to be in a room alone with him, not in a club full of sweaty strangers.

"Jesus fucking Christ, Lauren. I shouldn't need you this much."

Turning in his arms, I look up at him. His pupils are dilated and his lips parted, his chest heaving. His tongue runs across the bottom lip and I'm just about to close the distance between us when he looks up.

His eyes widen before he lets me go and disappears into the crowd. My body aches for him the second he leaves.

"There you are," Erica shouts, walking up to me and immediately breaking out some moves like the most erotic moment of my life didn't just happen where we're standing. "Are you okay?"

"Yeah. Sorry, I bumped into someone I knew."

"That's okay. Just let me know next time you want to disappear, yeah?"

"Sure. I...uh...actually, I think I'm going to head home."

"What? It's still early."

"I know, but I'm wiped. I'll see you in the morning?"

"Sure. Text me when you get home."

Waving, I get the hell out of that club as fast as I can. Every single part of me is desperate to hunt through the entire place to find Ben. Just how badly I need him is enough to make me go home. Nothing good can come of the strength of my feelings.

Thanks to my long day and night, I crash the second my head hits my pillow. That doesn't mean my dreams aren't full of *him* and how differently the night could have ended if we weren't interrupted.

---

WHEN I WAKE the next morning, I'm feeling much fresher than I deserve to be after a night out. I can't say the same for Erica when she shows up to work almost an hour late. She looks like she's just fallen straight out the club...or maybe some guy's bed. The day's crazy and the phone doesn't stop ringing, so I don't get the opportunity to hear about the rest of her night. From the look of the love bite on her neck, I'm pretty sure I don't want the details, anyway.

I'm becoming used to the silence, and it's no different when I let myself into the house after work that evening. Jenny's car is in the driveway, but there's no sign of her once again.

After making myself a drink, I head up to my room to change into something more comfortable. I decide to have a shower and wash my hair because the one I had this morning was way too quick to properly wash last night off me. I strip out of my work clothes and step under the hot spray.

I stand there for the longest time with my head tipped forward, allowing the powerful jets of water to massage my tense shoulders. I knew moving here and living with Dad wasn't going to be a walk in the park, but I never imagined it would be quite like this.

I've no idea how much time's passed when I eventually stand in front of the mirror and remove what's left of today's make-up. My usually light blue eyes seem to have much more grey in them as I stare at myself. I might be trying to put Ben and this thing between us to the back of my mind, but I'd be kidding myself if I thought I was being successful.

I'm lost in my own head as I walk from the ensuite wrapped in only a towel. I'm not expecting to have company, so a little squeal passes my lips when I find Ben sat on the edge of my bed, waiting for me. His hair's still damp from his own shower and he's wearing a dark pair of slim-fit jeans with a white t-shirt that looks like it's been painted on his skin.

I freeze just inside the room and my stomach knots. His eyes widen and I watch them darken as he runs them leisurely around my almost bare, and still slightly wet, body.

"Well, my day's sure looking up."

Pulling the towel around me tighter, I walk over to my dresser.

"What's up?"

"Plenty," he says after clearing his throat. "I just wanted to make sure you were okay."

"Yeah, I'm good. Why?" I can only assume he's asking about what happened last night.

"No reason." He's lying. I can see it in his eyes. "You hungry?"

"I am."

"Have dinner with me?"

"Uh...sure. Can you cook?"

"I wasn't thinking of that kind of dinner." I swear I see a little colour rise to his cheeks, but I must be mistaken because there's no way the brooding, cocky man stood in front of me gets embarrassed. Ever.

"You mean, go out?" *Like a date?* I want to ask, but I manage to keep the question in. I could be interpreting this so incredibly wrong, which would mean asking my stepbrother if he wants to take me out on a date is a very bad idea.

"Yeah. As much as I hate to suggest it, get dressed and we'll go." His eyes run the length of me once again and tingles follow their movement around my body. Biting down on my bottom lip, I refrain from suggesting getting takeout and not leaving this room. There's no way I should be having these thoughts, and he definitely shouldn't be looking at me like he is right now.

I start to think he's not going to leave, but after another lap around my body, he gets himself up and walks to the door. "I'll wait in the car," he says over his shoulder before pulling it closed behind him.

"WHAT WAS wrong with waiting in the house?" I ask when I fall down onto his passenger seat a little over thirty minutes later. I tried to be as fast as I could, but there was no way I was going out with him looking like he does, and me with wet hair and no make-up.

"You've probably noticed that it isn't my favourite place to be," he says, casting a glance towards the mini-mansion we both call home before looking over at me. "And your dad's d—Whoa." His lips curl up in sexy smile and his eyes darken as he takes me in.

I had no idea where we were going, and I wasn't given a lot of time to make a decision about what to wear. In the end, I slid my favourite white skirt up my legs, teamed it with a black and white striped vest and a pair of wedges. My blonde hair is loosely hanging around my shoulders and my make-up is light. I thought I looked okay when I gave myself a once-over in the mirror before I left the room, but seeing the look on Ben's face makes me feel like a million dollars.

"You look..." He trails off and I watch the muscles in his neck ripple as he swallows. "Incredible."

"Thank you," I whisper, suddenly feeling nervous about our impending evening together. When his eyes come back up to mine, something sparks between us and my skin tingles with awareness.

"I shouldn't be doing this," he says, but it seems to be more to himself than me.

"We're just going for dinner."

His dark stare turns my way, and a shiver runs down my spine. "Just dinner," he repeats. "But what about all the other things I want to do?"

My mouth waters as thoughts of what he could be suggesting run through my head.

"Shit." His sudden outburst has me flinching before I reach for the seatbelt and strap myself in as Ben slams his foot to the floor and speeds away from the house.

"What the hell was that?" I ask, seeing Dad's car turn into the driveway after us.

"It's probably best he doesn't see us together."

"What? Why?"

"You're his little girl, Lauren. He wants to protect you."

"I don't need protecting from you."

"You sure about that?"

# CHAPTER FIVE

Something changed with Ben after he saw my dad. He shut himself down like he's too scared to show me who he really is. I hate the idea that I could have given him any indication that he can't be himself with me.

The pub he brought me to is one I've not been to before. It looks like an old London boozer from the outside, but inside it's modern and bright, and the food is out of this world. It's nowhere near what I pictured when Ben mentioned dinner. I may have decided against suggesting it was a date, but that's very much what it feels like—aside from his weirdness where our parents are concerned.

"I guess we should get back," I say regretfully once he's insisted on paying the bill.

"Do we have to?"

"Why do you hate it so much?"

"You like living there?"

"Uh..." I try to come up with something diplomatic, but my silence must say it all.

"Exactly."

"Why don't you move out? You must earn good money from the business. You don't need to stay."

"I have my reasons." Raising my eyebrows, I wait for him to continue. "Not today," he says, standing from his chair and holding his hand out for me.

Sparks shoot up my arm the second our skin connects, and his eyes flash to mine. He felt it, too.

Together, we walk out of the pub and towards his car. "Do you mind if we just drive for a bit? I'm not ready for this to end yet."

"Of course." The sadness in his voice ensures I'll do whatever he wants. "You know you can tell me anything, right?"

"Trust me when I tell you that you don't want to know."

"But—"

"Lauren, please. Don't."

"Okay, okay. But I'm here, if you need me." Reaching my hand out, I hesitate a few inches from him. Sensing what I'm going to do, he threads our fingers together and places our joined hands on his lap.

He blows out a long breath, and when he glances over at me, I see some of his earlier tension has vanished. It's as if looking into my eyes calms him somehow.

"Thank you," he whispers before turning back to the road.

"For what?"

"This. Everything. For just being here."

I lose track of the direction we go in, and it's not long until I've no clue where we are. Ben seems to know, though, and eventually he pulls the car to a stop in a deserted car park.

"Wow," I breathe, taking in the bright lights of the city in the distance.

"I spend a lot of time here."

"And there I was, thinking you were out getting drunk every night."

"Oh, I do that, too," he chuckles.

It warms me from the inside out, knowing that I can make him laugh. It's not something he seems to do very often, and it only makes me want to make him do it more. His bad boy image lessens when he laughs and he looks more his age. "I've never brought anyone here before." His voice suddenly takes on a more sombre tone.

"Thank you for sharing it with me."

Dropping his hands from the wheel, he reaches over and once again entwines our fingers.

"Things haven't been easy for me in that house, Lauren. I won't taint you with the details, but it was my dad's dream home. He and my granddad build it with their bare hands. Every day, it's a reminder of everything I've lost."

"I'm so sorry." Bringing his hand up, I press my lips against his rough knuckles.

"I know I'm not the easiest person to get on with or even to share a house with, but Mum needs me."

I want to tell him that she's not his responsibility, that she's got my dad to do that now, but I know it's not what he needs to hear. And I've spent years keeping an eye out for my mum, so I do understand what he's saying. "What about what you need? Who supports you?"

He shrugs. My heart breaks for him. I've heard stories about how close he was to both his dad and granddad. I can only imagine how their deaths have affected him.

His phone vibrating in his pocket ends our little moment. He lets go of my hand to slide his phone out. Groaning when he looks at the illuminated screen, he cancels the call and throws it down into one of the cup holders between us.

"So...what do you want to do now?" I ask when a tense silence descends around us.

"You want the truth?" Turning his head, he stares at me. The darkness in his eyes is almost a warning and my stomach turns over, although I'm pretty sure it's only excitement I'm feeling.

"Always," I whisper eventually.

Reaching over, he takes my cheek in his warm hand and leans

forward. I find myself doing the same and, in seconds, our lips are almost touching.

"I shouldn't have done that the other night. It was wrong—"

"But…" I say, sensing there's more.

"I can't stop thinking about it. About you."

"Me, either," I admit quietly.

"Fuck, Lauren. We shouldn't be doing this."

"Says who? As far as I can tell, the only two people who matter are—" My words are cut off when he closes the tiny amount of space between us. His lips part and his tongue finds its way in. His taste explodes in my mouth, my tongue running along his, eager to explore.

His hand cups my other cheek and he tilts my head to the side with his fingers in my hair to deepen the kiss.

I've been kissed a couple of times in the past, but never like this. It's intense. Explosive. Consuming. Everything I previously had in my head vanishes, and the only thing on my mind is getting more of Ben.

Reaching out, I place my hands on his solid chest. I need to feel him. I need more than his lips. Every inch of my body aches for him, for his touch. So, when his hands slide down to my waist and he lifts me, I eagerly help to climb over the centre console until I'm sitting across his lap.

With his large hands around my waist, I settle myself into the kiss, but it's not long before even feeling him beneath me isn't enough. My head might not know what I should be doing in this situation, but it seems that my body is fully on board.

Needing more, I lift the hem of his t-shirt and go to run my hands up the taut skin of his stomach. But the second our skin connects, he rips his lips from mine.

"Shit. Fuck, Lauren. What the hell are we doing?" he pants, his eyes wide and his lips swollen.

Pressing his forehead to mine, his breath tickles across my face as I try to get control of my breathing. With his hands still on me and his solid thighs between my legs, it's not all that easy.

Ben's phone vibrates in the cup holder once again. After letting out a long breath, he breaks the connection between us and lifts me back into the passenger seat.

"I'm sor—"

"Don't," I snap.

"Let's go home." The sadness in his voice has me almost jumping back onto his lap. My fingers grip the leather beneath me to make me stay put as Ben starts the car.

Before putting it into reverse, he looks over at me. I open my mouth to say something, anything to take the pained look from his face, but he beats me to it.

"This is for the best." I'm not sure who he's trying to convince because I'm pretty sure neither of us truly believes that.

I never would have thought it, but the brooding boy who's avoided me at all costs in the past makes me feel alive in a way I never have before. I know he's trying to do the right thing, but damn if the only thing I want to do right now is break all the rules.

There's no way we should be doing this. No one, other than us, will understand this pull, this incredible connection. The thought makes my heart drop. I could have found the one person most people spend most of their lives looking for...and he's the one person I never should have looked twice at.

"ARE YOU READY?" Ben asks after we've sat in the driveway in darkness and silence for a few minutes.

I desperately want to say no, that I'm not ready for our time together to be over, but he doesn't need to hear it. His entire body is tense. I know he's struggling with this just as much as I am.

"Maybe we should run away." I suggest it as a joke, but when he turns to look at me, his eyes are deadly serious.

"Do not tempt me, Lauren," he warns. The deepness of his voice hits me and I swallow a ball of emotion that threatens to form in my throat. He really hates it here. I wish he'd open up. I just want to understand, to help in any way I can.

"Come on, let's get this over with."

I don't understand the concern in his tone. All we're doing is going home. What's he got to be so concerned about?

Everything starts to make a little more sense the second the front door clicks shut. Suddenly, all Ben's ignored phone calls and his worry about coming back make sense.

"Get in here right now," Dad booms from the living room.

Dread fills me. Looking over at Ben, his lips are pressed into a thin line, his eyes hard and angry.

I squeeze his forearm and make him look down at me. "It's okay. I've got this."

"I'm not leaving you with him."

Ben doesn't get to say any more because Dad staggers into the doorway, leaning against the frame for support. He's drunk.

"What the fuck do you think you're doing?" he hollers, his angry eyes focused on Ben. I immediately drop my arm and step in front of him. He shouldn't have to deal with Dad like this.

Dad's eyes don't move from Ben, even with me trying to distract him.

"Go upstairs, Lauren," Ben says behind me.

"No."

"Lauren," Ben growls. "You don't need to be in the middle of this."

"But—"

"Do as you're fucking told for once, kid," Dad barks. Tears sting my eyes at his belittling tone. With a quick glance at Ben, I run from the room and up the stairs.

"Shut your door and put some music on," Ben says when my foot hits the first step, but I don't respond.

My heart pounds and my hands tremble as I sit on the top step and wait for the shouting to start.

I'm not disappointed, and suddenly I understand why Ben hates it here so much. My dad really doesn't like him. I just don't understand why. So what if he's a little moody and comes in late, drunk? He's a twenty-year-old guy—that's fairly normal. It's probably no different to what he did at that age.

I can't make out all of Dad's words from up here. He's too drunk and most are so slurred that I doubt even Ben has a clue what he's saying. But I hear his warning loud and clear. "I told you to stay the hell away from her. If I find out you've so much as laid a finger on her, I'll fucking kill you."

My stomach knots. I've never heard my dad talk like that before. Never heard him so vicious. I've hidden myself away from plenty of arguments between him and Mum in the past, even him and Jenny on a very rare occasion, but he's never threatened either of them like that.

The second I hear footsteps, I jump up and run to my room, not wanting either of them to know I was listening.

Sitting on the end of my bed, I try to figure out what I'm going to say to Dad when he's sobered up. There's no way that Ben and I won't be spending any more time together. The connection between us will make that physically impossible, especially when he sleeps just across the hallway.

# CHAPTER SIX

My mind races and my heart pounds as I wait to hear Ben come home. Dad crashed his way up to bed not so long ago; he's probably passed out by now, so I know the coast is clear.

Grabbing my phone, I quickly type him a message.

Lauren: Come back. Please. It's safe.

I stare at the screen for ages, but it never shows that the message has been read and I get no response.

Breathing out a frustrated sigh, I turn over once again, trying to figure out what the hell my dad's issue with him is. As far as I'm concerned, Ben's done nothing wrong since the day they were first introduced, but then I'm always kept in the dark. Even living here, I feel like everything important is discussed when I'm out of earshot. It's frustrating as hell.

I've almost given up hope that he's going to reappear when I hear his footsteps creaking on the stairs. Holding my breath, I wait, hoping he'll come to me like he did last time. But when a door clicks open, it's not mine.

I force myself to wait a whole minute before throwing my legs over the side of the bed and getting up.

I knock on his door just to be polite, because what I really want to do is storm in and demand some answers.

When he doesn't answer, I push the handle down and invite myself in. The second my eyes land on him, I panic. He's too focused on filling a bag full of his stuff to notice my arrival. My heart picks up pace at the thought of him leaving.

Wasting no time, I race over and place my hand on his forearm. He flinches before dragging his eyes over to me. He looks exhausted, the deep frown line between his brows showing how much of a toll my dad's putting on his life.

"Ben, I—"

"I can't do this, Lauren. Just walk back out and pretend you didn't see this."

The sadness in his voice guts me.

"No. No way. I won't let him push you away like this. This is your home. It's where you belong. Your business is where you belong."

He casts his eyes over my shoulder, his expression dropping even more, if that's possible. "This isn't my home. It's just a place I stay to try to protect those I love. The business hasn't been mine in a long time. It never will be. It's time I accepted my life for what it is and try to do something about it."

"No, please," I beg, ducking under his arm that's still holding on to the bag on his bed. I slide up his body, and the spark that I'm becoming to expect when we're together crackles between us. "You're better than just running from this. You've got more here than you think. Can't you feel that?" I ask, my heart pounding with fear that I'm the only one with these crazy feelings.

His eyes flash with awareness and an acceptance that, even if he opens his mouth and denies it, I know he'd be lying.

"I can't, Lauren. You deserve so much better than what I can offer you."

"Bullshit," I bark. "Do not believe any of the crap my dad tells you. You are so much more than he thinks. Don't run from him. Prove who you are."

"Don't you think I've tried? I have, time and time again. I've done everything I thought was expected of me, but still...he's taken everything and turned everyone against me."

"No one's against you." I think of Jenny and everyone at work. Sure, they don't all sing about how wonderful he is, but they certainly like him well enough.

"You so sure about that?"

"Yeah, and my dad...he's just being protective."

Anger fills his eyes. "I told you to shut yourself in your room tonight."

"I don't always do what I'm told, Ben. It's time people started learning that I'm an adult who can make my own decisions. As soon as Dad's sobered up, I'm going to talk to him about tonight. I'm—"

"Don't even think about it. You coming to my defence isn't going to help my case."

"But—"

"There are no buts here, Lauren. He won't accept this." His eyes drop to where we're still pressed up against one another. "He'll never accept this."

"So, who gives a fuck what he thinks? Who made him God?"

"Lauren," he warns, but I can already tell I've won. The anger that was in his eyes has been replaced by something else entirely.

Lust.

His gaze stays on mine for a few more seconds before dropping to my lips. I wet them in preparation and I've barely got my tongue back in my mouth before he's on me. His lips press against mine and his tongue sweeps into my mouth. His hands slide up my waist and around my back, holding me tight and bringing us even closer together. My curves mould against his hard, muscular body and I melt under his touch.

Groaning into his kiss, I find the bottom of his t-shirt and run my fingers up the warm, smooth skin of his back. When I start to drag my nails down, he moans and starts to harden against my stomach.

Excitement flutters in my belly that I have this power over him. He's the bad boy that every woman I know lusts after. All my friends want him and the women at work wish they had the chance. But I'm here, in his arms, with his lips pressed against mine.

All the reasons why this really shouldn't be happening are far from my mind as I lose myself to his touch. My skin burns wherever he touches me, and my body aches for more.

Shifting his hands to my thighs, he grips and lifts me so I have no choice but to wrap my legs around his waist. His hardness presses against me. A wave of sensations I've not experienced before explode from my centre. Pulling my lips from his, I suck in a surprised breath. His hooded eyes lock on mine as he rolls his hips. The same thing happens again, only it's stronger this time. A sexy and determined smirk tugs at his lips, making something unfurl inside of me.

"Ben, please." I've no idea what I'm asking for, but whatever it is, I need it. I need it badly.

Dropping his lips to my neck, he kisses the sensitive skin below my ear. Goosebumps spread across my body and heat plumes in my belly.

*Holy shit, I want him* is the only thing I can think as he lowers me to the bed.

But instead of continuing, he stands and goes to walk away.

"What are you doing? Come back." My words come out in a rush. My need for him has heat hitting my cheeks and spreading down my neck.

"Patience," he says with a chuckle.

The second he flips the lock on his bedroom door, something heavy settles in my lower stomach. *Oh my God, this is happening.* I probably should be scared, but that's the last thing I'm feeling as I watch Ben cross the room, scroll through his phone, and then turn on his speaker. Before turning back to me, he reaches behind him and drags his t-shirt over his head.

"Holy cow," I whisper, more to myself than him, when he turns towards me. Not only are his eyes so dark they're almost black, but what I always knew to be a muscular body is so much more than I ever imagined. I didn't think bodies like that existed in real life. The dark tattoo I didn't know he had wraps around his ribs, a stark contrast to his lightly tanned skin.

"You know it's rude to stare." Amusement fills his voice as he slowly stalks back over to me, his eyes never leaving mine.

"S—sorry, I just..." I stutter, not really sure what I should be saying in this situation.

"I'm joking, Lauren. I don't want anyone else's eyes on me but yours."

I'm not stupid. I know he's been with plenty of women. I've even had the pleasure of bumping into a few after he's kicked them out. But it's easy to put all of that to one side when he's looking at me with longing in his eyes like he is right now.

"I shouldn't be doing this. I think we both know I don't have the right to take anything from you."

"I'll give you everything you want. I'm yours."

The muscles in his neck and shoulders tense, but his lips stay pressed into a hard line.

"You're not mine to take. But I can make you feel so fucking good." With those words, he wraps his fingers around the waistband of my shorts and drags them and my knickers down my legs.

I gasp, embarrassment filling me momentarily, but no sooner has he dropped them to the floor, he sits me up and pulls my lips to his. His kiss washes away any concern and embarrassment I have. And by the time he's kissing down my neck and curling his fingers around the bottom of the hoodie he gave me, I'm panting for more.

The sweatshirt joins the rest of my discarded clothes before he peels my vest from me. My breasts feel heavy, my nipples peaked painfully, and it only gets worse when his eyes drop to take them in.

"You're so fucking beautiful. Too fucking pure and innocent for the likes of me."

Pushing me back to the bed, he kisses across my collarbone and then down over the swell of one breast.

I'm not totally innocent. I've done things with guys in the past, but each encounter was a rush job just to get them off. I've never experienced anything like this—being adored and worshipped. Having my own pleasure matter.

My back arches as he sucks one of my sensitive nipples into his mouth.

"Oh God, Ben."

He looks up at me and another pool of lust explodes between my legs.

"Oh, please...oh...oh," I chant as he kisses lower.

The music in the background barely registers in my head, but as I continue whimpering, I understand why he put it on. This house might be massive, with our parents' bedroom at the other end of the L-shaped corridor, but neither of us needs to risk being heard. I tell myself to keep it together and get control of my volume, but the second I feel his tongue gently lick at me, I cry out in pleasure.

I fist the sheets beneath me when he adds a little more pressure before sliding a finger inside me. I've no idea if the words and cries falling from my lips are intelligible or not, but I don't really care. What he's doing has taken over ever inch of my body, and I never want him to stop.

My body coils tighter and tighter and I know that, at some point, something's got to give. When I feel him slide another finger into me, that something inside me snaps.

White light flashes behind my eyes as my entire body explodes with a sensation beyond anything I've felt before. I feel it in the tips of my fingers and all the way to my toes.

It feels like it lasts forever, but as I come down from my high and lock eyes with Ben, who's still between my thighs, I realise it wasn't nearly long enough.

There's pride in his eyes, but the overwhelming emotion is sadness. My initial thought is that I'm about to be sent on my way when all I really want is more of him.

When he sits up, I'm just about prepared for what's to come. Without words, I know that's as far as he's going to take this.

I prop myself up, ready to do the walk of shame back to my room, but, to my surprise, he doesn't say anything. Instead, he stands, drops his jeans to the floor, and pulls the covers back beside me. Sliding under, he looks at me with anticipation. There's a vulnerability oozing from him, something I'm sure he doesn't allow many people to see.

Jumping into action, I lift my arse and climb under the covers with him. The second I stretch my body out, he rolls onto his side and pulls me to him.

"Why did you—"

"Shh...I won't take any more from you than that. It's not my place," he says, repeating his earlier words.

"But I said—"

"That doesn't matter. I need to do what's right. Well...some of it, at least." A sad laugh passes his lips.

"Please, let me in." I press my hand to his chest, feeling the steady beat of his heart beneath. "Please, I could help make things better."

"It'll only make life harder for you. Promise me you won't say anything to your dad. Don't try to fight for me." The look on his face has me agreeing, even though it's the last thing I want to do.

I fall asleep in his arms.

When I wake the next morning, he's gone.

# CHAPTER SEVEN

The moment I realise I'm alone, I pick up my discarded clothes and run back to my room. I can still smell him on me and the last thing I want to do is wash it away, but I know I have to put last night behind me. I have a nagging feeling that last night was the beginning and the end of anything between us. The most sensible thing to do would be to put it behind me and try to move on.

"Lauren, is that you?" Dad asks the second I step foot downstairs.

"Yeah," I call as I make my way towards the kitchen.

"I'm sorry if I was angry last night. It's just that Ben isn't someone I think you should be spending time with." The vicious tone has gone, replaced by one that sounds a little like regret. "He's bad news. You've got plenty of other friends I'm sure you'd enjoy being with much more."

"He's not bad news, Dad. I think you've got him all wrong." Something darkens in his eyes, but it's gone again in a flash.

"Just trust me on this, okay?"

Ben's words from last night about not fighting for him come back to me. As much as I want to do just that, I trust him more than I do my dad right now, so I swallow the words on the tip of my tongue and instead whisper my agreement.

"Jenny and I are going away this weekend. I suggest you go and stay with your mother."

"Dad, I'm more than capable of staying here without you."

"This isn't up for discussion, Lauren. Don't you want to spend time with your mother?"

"Of course I do, but you can't just move me in and out when it suits you," I mutter.

"It's my house, young lady," he snaps, and I see a little of the person he was last night seeping in.

"No, Dad. It's Jenny's house. I'm nineteen in a few weeks. I'm more than capable of being home alone and not burning the place to the ground."

"*That* isn't what I'm concerned about."

"Oh, and what is it exactly that you're concerned about?" Raising an eyebrow, I wait for his response.

The silence stretches out between us before the noise of my phone going off sounds out like a siren. Ignoring it, I continue to stare at my dad.

"Give the girl a break, Nick. She's more than welcome to stay here while we're away," Jenny says, joining us out of nowhere.

Dad turns his stare on her, giving me a chance to look at my phone.

Ben: You are NOT going to your mum's this weekend.

Looking up, I glance around for him. My body is aware that he's looking at me, but I don't see him. That is, until a shadow catches my eye when it moves from the top of the stairs. He may not have been in bed when I woke this morning, but he's keeping a close eye on me—protecting me, just like he said he intended to do.

Once I know he's gone, I look back down at my message and

butterflies take flight in my stomach at the prospect of an entire weekend alone with him.

"You'd better be texting your mother," my dad grumbles, having finished his debate with Jenny, "Because if you don't arrange it, I will."

"Yeah, of course."

"I'll be checking," he warns, earning himself another look of disappointment from Jenny.

I want to argue with him, but the knowledge that everything he seems to be scared of happening probably will happen once the two of us are alone has the words dying on my tongue.

*A whole weekend with Ben in an empty house.* Some of the sensations he created in my body last night tingle within me, making me desperate for the weekend.

I DON'T GET a chance to make a plan to fool Dad into believing I'm with Mum this weekend, because the second I get to work, things go crazy. It's probably not helped by the fact that I've only had a few hours' sleep, and when I do get a quiet moment, my thoughts immediately transport me back to Ben's bed and how it felt to have his hands and lips on me.

I squirm in my seat once again and my face flames red when it doesn't go unnoticed by Erica.

"You okay, Lauren? You should book a doctor's appointment for that." She winks.

My cheeks have barely cooled down when my skin tingles and a shiver runs down my spine.

He's here.

It's only another two seconds before the door opens and Ben marches into the office. I look up, desperate to see him after everything that happened between us, but he doesn't even look my way.

Disappointment fills me.

I watch as he walks straight up to Laura at the other end of the office and starts asking about some delivery and hiring some lifters for the job he's working on.

The whole time I sit there, unable to take my eyes off him, willing him to look my way so that I know I didn't imagine what was between us. If the pull I feel is really there, surely he's fighting not to look my way right now.

As their conversation comes to an end, my heart starts to race. Surely now he'll acknowledge my presence?

Instead, he turns towards my dad's office, lets out a long breath and walks in—without knocking like everyone else does, of course.

With my frustration growing by the minute, I push my chair out behind me and mutter something about going to make tea before disappearing into our little kitchen and flicking the kettle on.

It takes forever to boil. Or, at least it feels that way as I fight to keep thoughts of him being in the other room from my mind. Being able to hear his deep rumbling voice through the thin wall doesn't help all that much.

I turn to start filling a mug when I sense someone join me. His unique scent mixed with hard work hits my nose. Lust rolls through me.

His heat warms my back before his hot lips land on my bare neck.

I moan as he tickles across my sensitive skin. "I missed you this morning."

"Sorry, I needed...a run," he stutters, like he isn't really telling the truth.

Movement from the office has him jumping back. His hand slides into mine and he pulls me into the ladies' toilets.

Once in the cubicle, he pins me back against the door with his hips. His lips land on mine and he gives me what I've been craving since waking up alone.

Him.

As the kiss deepens, my need for him grows and so does his

length against my stomach. I'm fully aware that he must have fallen asleep with the bluest balls known to man last night. It's something I'm keen to fix as soon as possible.

Slipping my hand down between us, I stroke him over the fabric of his trousers. The growl that rumbles up his throat only encourages me and I begin fiddling with the button so I can gain access, until his large hand wraps around my forearm and stops my movement.

"Lauren, not here." His voice is pained. Stopping is the last thing he wants right now.

But it's the sensible thing to do. We need to be careful. If last night and this morning with Dad taught me anything, it's that we cannot be caught. I've no idea what this thing is between us, but for now, whatever it is needs to be kept secret.

He steps back from me and I miss him the second our bodies part. It's crazy because he's stood right in front of me, but it's like my body needs his to be whole.

I take him in as he stands there with his chest heaving, his eyes dark and full of lust, his cock trying to break through his trousers.

I can't help but bite down on my bottom lip as I stare. Fuck, I want to see him with every piece of clothing gone. I want to give him the same treatment he gave me last night. I want to make him feel so damn good. My mouth waters at the thought of having him inside me. It's probably a good thing that he starts talking, distracting me from my sinful thoughts.

"Tell me you'll sort out this weekend. This might be the only chance we get to be properly alone for a long time."

"It'll be fine. I'll just tell Dad I've spoken to Mum and I'm staying there."

"He'll check, Lauren. I'd put money on it. You need to get your mum on side. Tell her whatever, but you need her to back you up."

What we're doing suddenly seems so real, and I panic. How are we going to keep this from Dad when it's happening under his roof? And even worse, what will happen when he finds out? I've no doubt he will, at some point.

"I will."

Excitement fills his eyes before he moves towards me once again and steals another knee-weakening kiss.

"Don't be surprised if you don't see me until they've gone. It's not because I don't want to be with you, I just don't want to raise any kind of suspicion," he whispers against my lips.

My stomach drops and suddenly tomorrow night feels like it's years away. "Okay."

"Hey," he says, tipping my chin up so I have no choice but to look at him. "There's no other way I want to spend my time than with you, but we need to be careful. One day, Lauren. One day, what we do will be up to us, but now's not that time. Tomorrow night can't come soon enough, and I promise to give you the best weekend of your life."

I nod against him and, with one last kiss, he slips out of the cubicle and he's gone. Gone until tomorrow night when all we have is each other. My stomach flutters with excitement.

When I walk back to finish the job I started, I find Erica stood in my place, filling the mugs. "I thought we were all going to die of dehydration," she says with a laugh when she sees me coming.

"Sorry, I...uh..."

"Got distracted?" she asks with a knowing smirk. My face must show my panic. "Hey, it's okay. Your secret's safe with me. I must warn you, though, it's not going to go down well with everyone." She casts a quick look over her shoulder to where my dad's office sits on the other side of the wall.

My lip trembles as everything that's happened in the past few weeks with Ben hits me all at once.

"Hey now," Erica shushes, pulling me in for a hug. I focus on my breathing to prevent myself from breaking down in her arms. Turning into an emotional wreck at work is the last thing I need right now. "Why don't you get out of here for the day? Go and treat yourself to something nice. I'll tell your dad you weren't feeling well."

"You don't need to do that." Pulling back from her, I look up into her kind eyes. Erica might only be two years older than me, but she's figured Dad out and somehow manages to get exactly what she wants.

"We're only young once, Lauren. And if I eavesdropped correctly, your dad and Jenny are out of town this weekend, right? You probably need time to get prepared," she says with a cheeky wink.

I can't help the laugh that falls from my lips before a more serious thought fills my mind. "You don't think..." I trail off, not knowing if I really want someone else's opinion on what I'm about to ask.

"I don't think what?"

"That it's...*wrong*?" I whisper, feeling a little ashamed for the first time.

"Lauren," she breathes. "The only thing stopping you is your own mind. People might frown upon it, but the reality is that you're not blood related. It's not illegal or whatever. None of us can help who we fall for. If he treats you right and makes you feel like a better version of yourself, then who is anyone to stop you? Plus, there's also his killer good looks and god-like body, so how were you ever going to say no?"

I know words are just that, *her* words, but they make me feel a hell of a lot better. "I knew there was something. The way he looks at you. I'd pay for a man to look at me with that kind of passion in his eyes. Now, get out of here. Go!"

Grabbing my stuff, I rush out of the office before anyone else spots me. I walk down to the tube station, intending to head home, but when I get to the bottom of the escalator, I turn left instead of right, deciding at the last minute to take Erica's advice and spend the afternoon getting prepared for the weekend.

***

WITH FRESHLY COLOURED hair and arms full of bags, I put the key in the door and step inside.

"Lauren, oh my God. I've missed you!" Mum calls the second she hears my arrival. "Wow, look at you." After taking in my new hair, she grabs my shoulders and pulls me into a tight hug. We talk most days, but being in her arms again has tears stinging my eyes.

"I hope you haven't eaten. I brought our favourite," I say, holding up a bag of Thai takeout.

"No, I haven't. Come on, I want to hear everything."

Following Mum down to our little kitchen, I sit myself at the table while she dishes up and makes us both a drink. All the while, I go over and over what I'm going to say to her to get her on board for this weekend. I've always told Mum everything, and I think the only way I'm going to get away with this is to be honest. Even if I have no idea what she's going to think.

"So..." she asks, once she's settled opposite me. "What's it really like living in the show home?"

"Pretty much what I expected. There's hardly ever anyone home, and when they are, they're not exactly what I consider welcoming and friendly. Other than the quick commute to work, I'm still wondering why you thought it was such a good idea." I quirk an eyebrow at her, hoping she'll give me more.

"It's good to get out of your comfort zone every now and then, Lauren. I know it's not where you'd probably choose to live, but it'll teach you a lot about life. Plus, your father can be very persuasive."

I fight to keep my cheeks flaming at the suggestion of everything that house will teach me.

I know the real reason Mum was so keen to agree to Dad's plans was the financial burden of putting me through university. This way, I might have to move in with them, but he's paying for everything plus giving me hands-on experience with the business. Most parents would have a hard time turning down that kind of opportunity for their child.

My life pretty much carried on normally when Dad met Jenny. It wasn't until they married that things started to change. Suddenly, Dad enrolled me into the same school Ben went to for sixth form, expressing their delight with Ben's education and that it would give me the best start in life despite the cost. I'd agreed because I hated my school and the thought of spending another two years there didn't really appeal to me. It was obvious I'd get more out of two years at a private school, and I was up for a new challenge. I wasn't aware that by agreeing, I basically gave him permission to control my education and life from there on out.

I can't really complain. I finished my two years with a whole set of As, acceptance into an incredible university, and my best friend.

"What's that look for?" Mum asks, noticing my slight embarrassment.

"I need to ask a massive favour of you. I'm not sure you're going to like it."

"Go on..." she encourages.

Blowing out a breath and casting my eyes to the other side of the kitchen, I prepare to tell Mum what's going on. "Dad and Jenny are going away this weekend and Dad wants me to stay with you, but..."

"But..."

"I've got plans that involve me staying there."

"Oh, have you met someone?" she asks excitedly.

"Yes...no—I don't really know."

"Lauren, you know I'd never stop you from having fun." The wink she gives me makes me want to curl up into a ball in embarrassment. "I don't understand the issue."

"He's already threatened to check up on me that I'm staying with you, so I need you to tell him I am."

"But why doesn't he want you staying there—"

I watch as the penny suddenly drops.

"Lauren, who's the boy you've met?"

Staring at her, I bite down on the inside of my lip. Once I say his name, I'm not going to be able to take it back. I'm terrified that Mum will think less of me, or won't approve—or worse, have the same opinion as Dad about Ben.

"It's..."

"It's..." she prompts, her eyebrows almost at her hairline.

"Ben," I whisper, looking down at the floor and cringing as I wait for her reaction.

"Jesus, Lauren," she breathes. When I look up, she's swallowing a giant gulp of wine. Her eyes find mine and I'm surprised when I see them crinkle with amusement at the sides. "*Now* I see your issue. Does your father know?"

"No. He already hates Ben. I overheard an argument between the two of them last night. I've never heard Dad like that before. He threatened to kill him if he so much as touched me."

Mum slouches back in her chair as she digests all this information and takes another sip of wine before she speaks. "Lauren, you're a bright young woman. I know you didn't come here for me to give you the *'but he's your stepbrother'* speech. I have every confidence that you've considered every angle of this situation and don't need a lecture from me. Having said that—" I can't help the groan that falls from my lips. "Are you sure he's worth it? Because I can guarantee you that when this gets out—and it will, you mark my words—all hell's going to break loose. I've no idea the goings-on in that house or their relationship, because I've tried my best to take a huge step back, but I do know there are issues, and I've no doubt your Dad's controlling streak is probably to blame. He wants what's best for you, and he's not afraid to bulldoze his way through others to make that happen." Mum's face saddens and I know all too well that she's talking from experience. "So, I'll ask again: Is he really worth the consequences of what happens when your father finds out what's been going on under his own roof?"

The silence stretches out between us as images of our time together run through my head. My insides flutter as I remember how he makes me feel when we're together, when he touches me. "Yes," I state. "He is."

"I remember what it was like to be young and in love," Mum says with a dreamy look on her face.

"I never said I was in love with him."

"No, but you're my daughter through and through, and looking into your eyes right now, it's like staring into a mirror and seeing the eighteen-year-old version of myself."

"What would you say to her now?" I ask, knowing exactly what happened with the man she fell in love with at only eighteen.

She chuckles to herself before trying to form her answer. "I'd love to tell her that she's young, foolish, and doesn't know what love is. But, in reality, your heart doesn't care how old you are, and it also doesn't have a crystal ball. So, the man I thought was my knight in shining armour turned out to be a cheating control freak, but I know plenty of people who are still very happily married to those they met as a teenager. My first love might not have turned out to be the man of my dreams, but he gave me many things, one of which I could never ever regret." Taking my hand, she stares at me through teary eyes. "If I had my time again, I think my advice would be to love as hard and as much as you can while you have it. Life is unpredictable and you never know when it might be taken away from you. You have to trust what your heart's telling you, Lauren. If you don't, you risk making a mistake you could regret for the rest of your life."

# CHAPTER EIGHT

**M**um's words run through my head all evening. It's almost a distraction from the fact that I know I'm not going to see Ben tonight. He told me earlier that he was going to stay away, and I've no reason to think he's changed his mind, as much as I might want him to.

After unpacking everything I bought earlier in the day, I run myself a bath, pour in the luxury bubbles I picked up, cover my face in a mask, and try to relax. Ben never said the words, but I'm assuming he's intending to go all the way this weekend, and I want to be as prepared as possible.

I scrub every inch of my body, shave and wax every hair I can find, and spend forever perfecting my eyebrows and nails. If I had more time, I'd get them done professionally, but this weekend has been kind of sprung on me so this will have to do.

It's long past midnight when I eventually get into bed. Just thinking about having a whole weekend alone with him has my heart pounding and excitement coursing through my veins.

I lie there, tossing and turning, but the anticipation of what the next few days might hold, plus listening for him to come home, stops any sleep I was hoping to get from coming. So much for being rejuvenated for tomorrow.

My body must have given up at some point because, when my alarm goes off the next morning, I almost jump out of bed in fright. I'm usually awake before it, so this is unusual.

It's not until I sit up that everything comes back to me. Butterflies take flight as I try to imagine what it's going to be like...Just the two of us doing whatever we want to do.

I sit there for way too long. I can't believe what time it is once I come back to myself, and I end up rushing around as I get ready to leave for work. It's only early, but already the heat of the summer morning has me melting as I run around, trying not to be late.

Dad's car has already gone when I look out the window. I debate driving myself so I can be home faster, but if I can't get parked, it'll be a nightmare. Deciding the best thing to do would be to get the tube, I slide on a pair of ballet pumps, pull my bag over my shoulder, and set about leaving the house. The next time I'm here, it's just going to be the two of us.

I get a knowing smile from Erica when I make it to the office, but thankfully the day passes without her saying anything. Dad spends a few hours locked away in his office before making a show of packing up while everyone else is busy. He can be a real arsehole when he wants to be. I've often wondered what my mum saw in him when she was only eighteen. Whatever it was, she clearly fell fast and hard if her words to me last night are anything to go by.

"Are you all set for the weekend?" he asks when he stops by my desk on the way out.

"Sure am." I smile sweetly at him, hoping it's enough to convince him that I won't be spending the weekend doing unspeakable things with his stepson. The reality of it almost has me laughing, but I manage to keep a lid on my emotions.

"I fully intend to check in with your mother later today to make sure."

"It's not necessary, Dad. We've got the weekend all planned." He stares at me for a few seconds as if he'll be able to see the evidence of my lie in my eyes. He must be happy with what's reflected back at him, because he wishes me a good weekend and marches from the office.

"Staying with your mum, my arse," Erica whispers when she comes to a stop in front of my desk to collect my mug.

I fight to keep my smile in, but the second I look up and see amusement dancing in her eyes, I can't help but let it slip.

"I hope you know what you're doing, Lauren, because you sure are playing with fire."

Her parting words hinder my excitement a bit, but I push it to one side. Nothing is going to ruin this weekend. Nothing.

---

WHEN I STEP foot outside the office later that afternoon, the last thing I expect to find is a guy getting out of a taxi, asking if I'm Lauren. I hesitate because wanting nothing to ruin this weekend includes not being abducted by a taxi driver.

"Ben booked me for you." He rattles off my home address and shows his ID when I still look a little sceptical. Eventually, I climb into the back of the car. I'm grateful the second the air conditioning hits me because the humidity today is through the roof.

The driver tries making polite conversation, but he soon learns that I'm really not in the mood. I just want to get home to find out if Ben's there waiting for me. I bloody hope so.

My stomach flips when I see his car parked alongside mine in the driveway as the taxi pulls to a stop.

"How much do I owe you?" I ask in a rush, impatient to get out.

"Nothing. He's already paid."

"Okay, well, thank you."

"Have a good weekend." I don't have time to return the sentiment because I slam the door before running towards the house.

I had this crazy fantasy of him sweeping me off my feet the

second I walk through the door, so when he's not there, a little disappointment threatens to take hold. That is, until I see a Post-It note stuck to the mirror.

*Go to your room x*

Plucking it from the glass, I follow the instructions and head upstairs. When I open the door, the first thing I spot is a bag on my bed with another Post-It stuck to it.

*Wear me x*

My hands shake as I pull the bag open and let the contents drop to the bed. Unfolding the fabric, I find a floral maxi dress, a man's zip-up hoodie, and a jewellery box.

Quickly stripping out of my work clothes, I have a very quick shower before smothering myself in my favourite moisturiser. I pull one set of the lingerie I bought yesterday from the drawer and wrap myself in the soft lace before sliding my new dress up my body. It fits perfectly and shows off just the right amount of cleavage—I assume that's on purpose. Finally, I slide my feet into a pair of flip-flops and pull the lid off the jewellery box. My breath catches when I see the two heart charms hanging from the dainty silver chain. I rush to put it on and hold the two hearts between my fingertips, taking a deep breath to prepare myself to go and find him.

When I get to the bottom of the stairs, the house is still in silence. Getting impatient, I begin checking each room downstairs, but I come up short. It's not until I get to the final room, the kitchen, that I start to understand.

Walking over to the sliding doors, I can't believe my eyes. It's still light out, but I can easily see all the fairy lights hanging from the trees over the garden. Candles cover the decking and table, and the scent of vanilla mixes with the barbeque and fills my nose, making my stomach rumble. The furniture is all set up with cushions and the giant swing seat has a blanket thrown over the back.

As I round the corner, I find the best sight in the world. Ben's stood in front of the barbeque wearing a pair of dark jeans and a white t-shirt. His feet are bare, his hair still damp from the shower.

Something inside me clenches at the sight and I stand, staring, trying to commit exactly how he looks right now to my memory.

"Feel free to take a picture," he says, when he realises I'm frozen.

"Sorry, you just look—"

"Nowhere near as good as you." His wide strides quickly eat the space between us and in seconds I'm in his arms, his lips on mine. My entire body sags against him. It's been too long.

His tongue sweeps into my mouth and he kisses me like he hasn't in months, not hours.

"Missed you," he mumbles against my jaw as he kisses a trail towards my neck. My response is just a moan of pleasure as he licks at the sensitive skin below my ear. My body melts under his touch and I want nothing more than to give myself over to him. I want him to completely own me.

Hearing a bang in the distance, I stiffen. "They've definitely gone, right?"

"Yep. It's just me and you, baby."

A thrill rushes through me and I reach for him again. Twisting the fabric of his t-shirt in my hands, I pull him flush against me, desperate to feel his hard body against mine.

We stand and kiss on the decking for the longest time. I can't get enough. When he pulls back, my lips are swollen and sore, but I can't think of anything better.

"We've got all weekend; we don't need to rush," he says with a laugh when I refuse to let him go. "I should feed you first, anyway. I've got a suspicion you're going to need sustenance." His eyes drop to my necklace and my exposed cleavage, and I watch them darken even further as his tongue comes out to wet his bottom lip. My entire body throbs with my need for him, but nowhere more than between my legs. It's bordering on uncomfortable.

"Stop looking at me like that or I'll forget all about the dinner."

"Would that be such a bad thing?"

"Lauren," he half moans, half laughs. "I'm trying to do this properly. Treat you right." For the first time ever, he seems so unsure of himself. It's just another reminder that the bad boy image he shows everyone is just an act. Underneath it all is a kind and gentle man who wants to be loved like everyone else.

"You're doing perfect," I say, dropping a kiss to the side of his neck. Intertwining our fingers, I pull him back over to the barbeque. "So, what are we cooking?"

"What *aren't* we cooking? I wasn't sure what you liked, so I went a little crazy." Lifting the lid, I see that he's not lying. Everything you could possibly want at a barbeque is laid on the bars beginning to cook. "And I made mojitos. That's what you drink, right?"

"Stop worrying. This is perfect. *You're* perfect."

Twisting us around, he pulls me in front of him and wraps his arms around my waist. I look out at the garden beyond as Ben breathes me in. "I'm far from that."

"Not to me." I feel his smile against my head and my heart beats that little bit faster. Mum's words from last night hit me. *"I remember what it was like to be young and in love."*

Was she right? Is this what falling in love feels like?

Turning me once again, he walks me backwards until my back bumps against the railing. His hips press against mine, and his arousal is impossible to miss. My eyes widen in surprise. I've barely touched him.

"You've no idea how badly I need you."

"I think I do. How long until dinner starts burning?"

"Probably ten minutes. Why?"

With the railing at my back and him at my front, I manage to lower myself to my knees. Ben's eyes follow my every move. The blue turns almost black and his lids hang heavy with lust.

"Lauren," he moans when I reach out and undo the button on his jeans. I've no idea if it was meant to be a demand to stop or words of encouragement, but now I've got the idea in my head, there's no way I'm not tasting him right now.

I feel his stare as I pull his jeans and boxers down his thighs, but I can't tear my eyes away from his cock as it springs free.

His body shudders as I wrap my hand around him. "Fucking hell," he groans. His pleasure spurs me on. I lean forward slightly and gently lick at the end of him. His hips thrust forward with his need for more, but I continue teasing him. "Jesus fucking Christ, Lauren. Shit. Argh," he moans when I suck him as far into my mouth as he'll go.

His taste fills my mouth as I pull back and slowly flick my tongue around him once more.

I start to smell burning coming from the barbeque behind us when I reach up and cup his balls in my hand. He moans loudly above me once again before his warning comes. Ignoring it, I suck him harder. His cock twitches and his entire body stills as his cum lands on my tongue.

Once he's finished, I sit back and lick my lips. I can still feel his stare burning the top of my head, and when I look up, my breath catches. The desire in his eyes, his parted lips as he pants out his increased breaths—it all has my thighs clenching.

"Our first time's going to be everything you deserve, but fuck if I don't want to bend you over that railing right this fucking second."

Standing back to full height, I allow my lips to brush his. "Ben..." His lids lower once again, expecting me to say something sexual, but instead I whisper, "Put your cock away. The dinner's burning."

Barking out a laugh that fills me with warmth, he quickly does as I suggest.

Sitting down on one of the chairs, I pour myself a mojito from the jug and enjoy watching him cook. Music softly plays on a speaker set up on the table, the birds sing in the trees above, and the evening sun warms my skin. I can't think of a better way to spend tonight.

"What?" Ben asks when I look over at him with a smile on my face.

"Thank you for this."

"You're more than welcome. Where does your dad think you're spending the weekend?" he asks as he brings over a plate piled high with food.

"At Mum's."

"I thought he said he'd ring to check?"

"He probably will. But Mum's on our side."

Pausing halfway through assembling his burger, he looks up at me, confusion filling his eyes. "You...told her? About us?"

"I did."

"What did she say?"

"That if I think you're important enough to risk it, she'll support my decision."

"Wow, that's..." He trails off, deep in thought, and I can only imagine he's wondering want Jenny would make of all of this.

"She's pretty incredible."

"She sounds it. It's a shame everyone doesn't think like her."

"Everything's going to be okay," I say when a sad expression falls over his face.

He opens his mouth to respond but must think better of it. "Let's forget about all of that for now and just enjoy our weekend."

"Sounds like a perfect plan."

Silence surrounds us as we eat, my concerns after that brief conversation at the forefront of my mind.

---

THE NIGHT GOES by all too quickly and, before I know it, we're sitting in the dark under the twinkling lights Ben strung up in the trees. Most of the candles have long burnt out and we've drunk our way through the mojito jug. I'm feeling suitably full from all of Ben's incredible cooking and buzzed from the slightly too strong cocktail.

"You're freezing. Shall we go in?" We've been cuddled up on the swing, under the blanket for ages, chatting away and just enjoying each other's company. Nerves and excitement for what's to come hit me all at once. "We don't have to do anything if you're not ready. As long as you're beside me, that's all I need."

Cupping his stubble-covered cheeks, I pull his lips to mine. "Liar," I say with a laugh. I go to kiss him to show him I want to give him everything, but he places his hands on my shoulders, stopping me.

"I'm deadly serious, Lauren. If you're not ready—"

"Shut up." Throwing my leg over his lap, I get settled and resume my earlier kiss. I've no intention of this night ending here. I've held on to my V card until I found the right guy, and I'm so bloody glad I did because I can't imagine anything more perfect than this.

"Go and get yourself comfortable upstairs. I'll be right up," he says between kisses to my neck.

I'm hesitant to move, too content to be sitting across his lap with his hands on me. When he realises I'm not going anywhere, he lifts me and places me on my feet. His biceps bulge as he takes my weight and the sight only increases my need to have his naked, hot, smooth skin pressed up against mine.

"Go," he says again with a tap to my arse.

Walking across the deck, I try to put as much sass into it as possible. I know his eyes are on me. I can feel them.

When I get to the sliding doors, I look back over my shoulder. Exactly as I expect, his eyes are focused on my arse. Realising I've stopped, he lifts his gaze and finds mine. The promise within his dark eyes has tingles racing through me.

I eventually manage to tear myself away from him and head towards my bedroom. Now that I'm moving, it hits me just how tipsy I actually am. My head spins as I wobble my way up the stairs. I'm too consumed with how Ben makes me feel when he's around to put much thought into the effects of the alcohol.

I've no idea how long I've got, so I quickly make use of the bathroom and brush my teeth. I feel like a different person when I look at myself in the mirror. My eyes are bright and sparkling and my skin has a glow I don't think I've ever seen on myself before.

Hearing a bang from downstairs brings me back to the here and now, and my heart thunders in my chest. This small amount of distance between us has allowed my nerves to creep in. They're easy to forget when Ben's got his hands on me. My body takes over and tells me exactly what I need. *Allowing me this alone time was dangerous,* I laugh to myself as I try to force my anxiety down.

I'm running a brush through my hair when I hear his footsteps pounding up the stairs. My body temperature spikes, my heart races, and my hands begin to tremble. But the second the door opens and my eyes find his, all of that vanishes.

It's just the two of us. No worries or concerns, no outside influences. Just me, him, and this explosive thing between us.

"Lauren," he breathes, running his eyes down the length of me. Tingles that had started to disappear suddenly hit me full force once again.

Stepping up to me, he takes my hand and pulls me over to the bed. I lie down and rest my head on my pillow at his encouragement. Our eyes meet and our breaths mingle, our bodies just inches apart.

I flinch when his warm hand lands on my cheek where I'm so lost in his eyes. I wasn't expecting this. I had visions of him stripping me bare the second he entered the room and doing wicked things to me. Instead, his face is full of emotion, almost to the point where I'm concerned.

"You make all of this so much easier, Lauren," he whispers, and my breath catches at the honesty in his words. "You make everything seem worthwhile again. I've been walking through life in a haze for a long time, but for the first time in years I'm suddenly seeing things clearly. I feel like I have a home again, I feel like I belong." Tears burn my eyes. Until now, I had no idea if this crazy connection I felt with him was one-sided, but, if anything, it seems like it means even more to him.

"You make me want to do something about this bullshit life I've been living. You give me a reason to fight. To fight for what's right. To fight for what I deserve." He pauses and his eyes run over every inch of my face. "I had no idea I was looking for something, and I really had no clue that I was going to find what I so desperately needed in my own house. But here you are, like a guardian fucking angel. I promise you, I'm going to do whatever it takes to prove I'm worthy of you, to protect you, to keep you...to be yours."

The strength behind his words renders me speechless. He must sense it because nothing more is said as he closes the space between us and presses his lips to mine.

He kisses me for hours, his hands running over every clothed inch of me, but he never pushes for more. I thought I'd be disappointed, but I can't have imagined anything more perfect. It was exactly what both of us needed after his confession.

# CHAPTER NINE

I wake up feeling hot. I soon understand why when I feel the soft brush of Ben's lips across my collarbone.

"Good morning," I whisper, but it comes out more like a breathy moan.

"It sure is, baby."

Tearing my eyes open, I find him staring down at me, lust filling his eyes. Gone is last night's emotion, only to be replaced by a hunger I recognise well. It causes my insides to clench.

I go to sit myself up but his hand on my ribs stops me. "Lie back. I've got things I want to do to you—and trust me, they can't wait."

"Okay," I breathe, but I'm not sure he hears as he drops his lips back to my skin. He kisses down my chest and over the swell of my breasts. When he gets to the fabric of the dress I'm still wearing, he tucks his finger under the edge and pulls it back.

"Jesus," he moans when he sees the lace bra I chose especially for him. Lifting his hands to my shoulders, he slips the straps of my dress down my arms before pulling it down my body. His eyes feast on every bit of skin he reveals.

After dropping the fabric to the floor, he stands back and stares.

Tingles follow his eyes as he runs them over every inch of me. My chest heaves, my breasts strain against the lace covering them, and my core aches.

"Sweet Jesus. You look fucking sinful. What are you doing to me?"

If he's waiting for a response, he doesn't show it. Instead, he pulls his t-shirt over his head and drops it to the floor, followed by his jeans and boxers, allowing me my first look at all of him. Suddenly, I understand his fascination with my body a few seconds ago, because my eyes are glued to him. I follow the definition of his abs, down his v lines to his hard cock bobbing in front of him. My mouth waters.

He doesn't allow me any longer to appreciate the view because, after dragging my knickers down, he crawls back onto the bed and starts kissing down my leg. My thighs quiver when he makes it to my core.

"So fucking sweet," he murmurs, running his nose against my sensitive skin.

"Please, Ben. I need—" My words are cut off when his tongue connects with my clit.

It's like he can read my body and knows exactly what's going to have me racing towards my release. He sucks hard on my clit before sliding one, then two, fingers inside me.

I pant and moan his name, my hands twisting in the sheet beneath me as I reach the point of no return. He does something with his fingers and I'm falling. I cry out as my orgasm races through me, every part of my body pulsing with pleasure.

He looks smug when he pulls back and stares at me. "I don't want to know how you got so good at that," I say with a laugh.

His face pales slightly before saying, "I'm only going to get better with all the practice I'm expecting to have."

My thighs clench despite the fact that he's just shattered me into a million pieces.

After reaching down to his discarded clothes, Ben drops a little silver square to the bed and kisses his way up my body.

"You ready for this?" I swallow my nerves and nod. He can see right through my act because his palm lands on my cheek and his soft eyes hold mine. "If you're not, just tell me. We don't have to."

"No. No, I want this. I want you. Please, Ben. Just be...just be gentle?" I feel ridiculous asking, but I can't help the words falling from my mouth.

"I promise to never be anything but, baby."

I watch as he rolls the condom over his length and settles himself between my thighs. He presses the tip against my clit, his eyes locked on mine. He's waiting for me to change my mind, but it won't happen.

"I want you, Ben. I want you to be my first." I swear my words make his chest puff out a little. He holds our connection as he finds my entrance and slowly pushes inside me. Thanks to his talented mouth, I'm ready for him.

He feels huge as he slides into me, and I shift my hips as I try to adjust to the alien sensation—until he seems to hit a brick wall and I know what's going to come next is going to hurt like hell.

Dropping forward, he nuzzles his face into my neck. "I hate to do this," he whispers, "but I promise to make it so worth it."

The heat of his body pressing down on mine feels out of this world. I need this. I need more of him.

"Do it," I say, sounding more confident than I feel. Running my hands down his back, I squeeze his arse to give him a little encouragement.

He sucks the sensitive skin below my ear into his mouth. I'm just enjoying the tingles it causes when he thrusts his hips forward.

He doesn't move again as I moan in pain. "I'm sorry, I'm sorry," he whispers. He sounds mortified to have hurt me.

Pulling his head from my neck, I force him to look at me. "Hey, it's okay." I go to run my thumb over his bottom lip, but he captures it and sucks it into his mouth. His earlier hunger seeps back into his features and I flex my hips, showing him that I'm okay. I'm actually better than okay; we're connected in the most intimate way possible, and I can't think of anything better.

"You sure?"

"Let me feel you. Please." He rolls his hips and the pain that was so strong only moments ago dissipates, the incredible feeling of him moving inside me taking over.

"Fucking hell, you're so tight. I hope you weren't expecting this to last long," he moans before dropping down to kiss me.

When his pace starts increasing, I know he's nearing the end and I'm desperate to experience it.

"Jesus, Lauren, I'm going to come so fucking hard," he grunts, the words filling me with warmth. Threading his fingers into my hair, his hips move fast, then faster. His other hand slips down until he presses his fingertips against my sensitive clit. My entire body arches from the bed at the contact. "Fuck."

With his fingers teasing my clit and his length hitting some magical place inside me, it's not long before he pushes me over the edge and I come with his name a soft moan on my lips. Seconds later, he growls above me before I feel his cock twitch violently inside me. He roars his release and the look on his face as he does is something I'll never forget. Everything that usually drags him down has gone, and he's lost to the pleasure. Pleasure that I am able to give him. My heart swells and I fear I'm falling way too hard, way too fast. I'm trying not to think about the future because I know that, no matter what, it's going to be a challenge.

"Holy shit, Lauren," he pants, falling down at my side, his breath rushing over my face as he tries to catch it.

"Good?" I hate the anxiety that creeps into my voice.

"Good?" He repeats with a laugh. "That was fucking mind-blowing. I'm already craving more." His lips meet mine as his warm hand slides around my back, tickling my hypersensitive skin before flicking the clasp on my bra. I'd totally forgotten I was still wearing it.

Pulling back from my lips, he ducks his head and pulls one of my nipples into his mouth. A sigh falls from my lips as another ball of sensation explodes within me.

"Stop it," he says with a laugh after releasing my nipple with a pop. "I don't need any encouragement to spend all day inside you."

"That doesn't sound like a bad way to spend today," I admit.

"No, but you need a rest before we go again." My heart swells once again at his thoughtfulness. "What? Why are you looking at me like that?"

"I like you." My cheeks heat at my admission, and if it wasn't for the incredible smile that erupts across Ben's face, I might have looked away.

"I like you too, Lauren. *A lot.*"

<hr>

"COME ON," he says, intertwining our hands and pulling me from the bed after kissing me breathless.

"You want me to..." I flick a glance down at his hard cock and raise an eyebrow.

"More than I probably should admit. But this is about you, not me."

I follow him into my ensuite, my mouth dropping open when I take in the flickering candles that cover every available surface. Walking straight up to the bath, he climbs in and encourages me to follow. In seconds, soothing bubbles and Ben's arms surround me. I lie back against his chest and sigh.

"I hope that's a good sigh."

"Mmm...it is. I don't think I've ever been this relaxed."

"Every morning should start with orgasms, don't you think?"

"As long as they're delivered by you."

He goes silent behind me. I can feel the sudden tension in his muscles. Sitting up, sloshing water everywhere, I turn and straddle him. I hate not being able to see his face.

"What's wrong?" He tries looking away, but I bring his face back to me. "Ben?"

"I'm sorry; it's nothing."

"It's not nothing. You can tell me, whatever it is." Sliding my hand around the back of his neck, I tilt and drop a quick kiss to his lips.

"It's just...this is so incredible." My breath catches when he places his hand over my heart. "You're so incredible. But..." He lets out a pained breath.

"What happens when we're caught?" I finish for him.

"Yeah," he agrees sadly.

"Enough," I snap, a little too harshly if his wide eyes are anything to go by. "We've got plenty of time to worry about that. But right now, we've got an empty house all to ourselves. The most important thing to worry about is what we're going to do for the next twenty-four hours."

"Or how many times I can make you come."

"Hmm...that, too. What did you have planned?"

"Nothing past last night. What did you want to do?"

"Nothing sounds perfect. Well, maybe not totally nothing." Sitting back between his legs, I slide my hand up his thigh, giggling to myself when it makes his cock twitch. Taking him in my hand, I slowly slide it up and down, all the while watching Ben's eyes roll back in pleasure. Yeah, I think this could be the perfect way to spend the weekend.

Once the water's cold, we both climb out of the bath and set about with whatever we're going to do. Ben walks over to the window and pulls the curtains back. "How about just chilling out in the garden? I've got plenty of food left over from last night. We could barbeque again later."

"Sounds perfect." Pulling open a drawer, I rummage around for a bikini.

"What's that for?" he asks, eyeing the small bit of red fabric in my hands.

"Sunbathing?" The look on his face as he stares at it makes the word come out like a question.

"Not necessary." The fabric is snatched from my hands and shoved back into the drawer.

"Ben, I'm not walking around all day naked."

"Why not? No one will see you but me." I try to come up with a reasonable argument other than I don't want to, but the moment I see the fire in his eyes, all thoughts leave my head. Running my eyes down the chiselled planes of his abs, I realise it's not such a bad idea. "And it means I can have you any time I want."

We don't leave my bedroom for at least another hour, and I have a feeling today is going to be exhausting in a very, very good way.

Thankfully, he relents on me wearing clothes, so as we walk hand in hand into the kitchen, I'm wearing my bikini and a pair of hot pants and he's looking like a freaking swimwear model in his low-hanging board shorts.

"What do you want for breakfast?" he asks after kick-starting both the kettle and the coffee machine.

"Hmm...cake."

"Cake?" he asks with a laugh.

"Why not? This weekend is about indulging, so what's more indulgent than cake for breakfast?"

"Good point. I'm pretty sure there's no cake in this house."

"There's stuff to make one, though." I know for a fact that there's everything we'll need at the back of the larder cupboard, because I bought it and put it there a couple of weeks ago.

"I haven't made a cake since Food Tech in year 9, and that was a disaster!"

"It's a good job you've got an excellent teacher, then."

"I'm sensing this lesson will be a little different than the one I'm remembering." His eyes drop to my barely clothed body, and he leisurely takes in every inch. "Definitely better," he mutters quietly while rearranging himself in his shorts.

"Come on, let's bake," I say, grabbing his hand and pulling him over to the counter. Finding the scales in the darkest part of the bottom cupboard, I give them a clean before instructing Ben to weigh out the correct amounts.

"Can't we just guess?"

"No. Baking is a science."

"I always preferred sex ed."

"You're a nightmare." I sit myself up on the island counter as Ben beats the eggs and folds in the flour exactly as instructed. "Don't forget the cocoa powder." I pop the top off and pull at the foil beneath. I put a little more force into it than necessary and, in seconds, almost a full tub of cocoa powder covers my boobs and thighs as well as the counter and the floor.

"You need a hand?" Ben asks, his eyes darkening as he looks at my dirty chest.

"No, I've got it." I go to dust it off but he captures my wrist before I get the chance.

"Let me." His head drops forward before his tongue licks the powder from my breast.

"That's going to be—"

"Ew, that tastes nothing like chocolate," he says, pulling back with his lips curled in disgust. "I know what will make it better."

"Ben, no!" I squeal when he reaches into the icing sugar and grabs a handful. The white dust is thrown just as I jump down from the counter. Icing sugar surrounds me. Every breath tastes sweet as it begins to settle on my skin. "I can't believe you just did that."

Before I have a chance to move, Ben's hands slide around my waist and I'm pulled against him. His lips go to my neck and he licks a trail down to the valley between my breasts. "So much better than cake," he mumbles as he continues licking.

My nipples pebble against the thin fabric of my bikini top and heat floods my core.

"Oh...I think you got a little bit..." Pulling the cup from my breast, I watch as Ben licks around my nipple before sucking it deep into his mouth. My head falls back as my clit starts to pound.

"Oh my God," I whimper as he swaps to the other side and gives it the same treatment.

"Don't move," he demands. The serious look in his eyes means I don't argue. I stand, surrounded by cocoa powder and icing sugar dust with my breasts on show while Ben adds all that's left of the cocoa powder into the cake mix. "Hey, I told you to stay there," he complains when I begin dragging my nails down his back. I can't help but smile when his skin pricks with goosebumps and his entire body shudders.

"Sorry, I couldn't help myself." I slide my hands around to his stomach as he begins pouring the mixture into the tins I lined earlier.

"Fuck, Lauren," he complains when I slip one hand under the waistband of his shorts and wrap my hand around him. He manages to flinch and miss the tin. Reaching out, I run my finger through the mixture and bring it up to his lips. "Suck," I demand, praying my voice sounds as sexy as I hope it does.

"Mmm," he moans as he laps at my finger, licking off every bit of the mixture. "I think I've got an idea for where I want to eat the rest of this from." My insides clench at the suggestion. "How...how long do these take?" he stutters when I start stroking him.

"About twenty minutes."

"That should be enough time."

"Enough time for what?" Slipping away from my grasp, be pulls the oven door open and slides the two tins inside. Then, he turns to me. His eyes are dark and hungry as they drop from mine and take in my curves. Reaching out, he pops the buttons on my shorts and pushes them down my thighs. Wiggling my hips, I get them to fall to my feet and step out while he pulls at the ties around my back and at my hips. In seconds, the fabric flutters to the floor and I'm stood bare before him, bar the cocoa powder and icing sugar clinging to my skin.

After dropping his own shorts, he grabs my waist and lifts. I have no choice but to sit on the edge of the counter.

"Lie back," he demands. I wince when my back hits the cold

marble beneath me, but it's soon forgotten when I feel Ben's breath tickle my sensitive skin.

Propping myself up on my elbows, I watch as Ben feasts on me. The fact that we're out in the open in the middle of our parents' house only helps push me closer to my orgasm.

His lids flutter open, and his intense eyes land on mine. My heart flips over. I'm totally consumed by this man.

He slides two fingers deep inside me, his tongue continuing to torture my clit, and I fall over the edge, my body twitching and convulsing on top of the counter.

Pulling back, Ben wipes his mouth with the back of his hand before taking himself in his hand. He teases my sensitive clit, then drops to find my entrance. "How sore are you?"

"Not sore enough to stop you."

In one quick thrust, he's inside me.

He grunts and stills for a beat. His eyes find mine and I swear I can see everything he's feeling inside them.

"I'm going to fuck you in every room of this house, Lauren." I'm not sure if it's a warning, a promise, or just a big *fuck you* to my dad, but in this moment I really don't care. I also don't have any argument because sex in every room sounds pretty incredible.

"What are you doing?" I ask the second he pulls out of me. I'm learning his body quickly and I know he's about to come.

"No...condom," he grunts before the heat of his cum lands on me.

*Fuck, that's hot*, I think as I watch the muscles in his neck and shoulders strain as he works his cock.

"It's okay. I'm on the pill," I admit once he's finished.

"We need to be safe," is all he says. I can't agree more. An accidental pregnancy is the last thing we need.

"I need a shower," I say with a laugh, looking down at my body.

"That sounds like a plan." In seconds, I'm in his arms and we're heading for the stairs.

My legs are still wrapped around his waist as he leans in and turns the water on. Once it's warm, he stands us under the powerful spray. Ben slides me down his body as the water begins to wash away the sticky mess covering both of us.

"Turn around," he whispers in my ear, and before I know what's happening, his hands are in my hair and the scent of my shampoo fills the small space around us.

"Oh my God. So good," I moan as he massages my scalp.

"You like my fingers, don't you, baby?"

"You're so cheesy," I laugh.

Once he's finished with my hair, his talented fingers skim over every inch of me, removing the evidence of our attempt at baking—

"Shit, the cake!"

"Fuck. I'll go." Quickly rinsing off the bubbles from his body, Ben jumps out of the shower, wraps a towel around his waist, and runs from the room.

I follow a few minutes after. The second I open the bathroom door, I can smell burning.

"Safe to say that's fucked," Ben says with a laugh when he reappears. Suddenly, I couldn't care less about the cake; he's still just got the towel wrapped around him and droplets of water running down his pecs and abs. I think it might be my favourite look on him.

"Keep looking at me like that and you might never leave this room."

"I can think of much worse things."

"Me too. But we'll save that for another day. Get dressed."

———

"WHERE ARE WE GOING?" I ask as we step out of the front door.

"You wanted cake, and we failed miserably at making one, so I thought I'd treat you instead."

Not being able to argue with his idea, I fall into step beside him as he walks us past both our cars and out onto the street.

"Oh my God, I love this place," I squeal as Ben leads me into the dessert-only restaurant not that far from home. The sweet smell has my mouth watering the second we enter.

"Will this fix your cake craving?"

"Just a little bit. The only problem is choosing."

Both of us indulge in way too many calories by the time we pay and make our way home...but I figure we've already exerted ourselves enough to get away with it.

# CHAPTER TEN

"Lauren, wake up." Ben's soft voice filters through my sleep-fogged brain and I pry my eyes open to look at him. The smile he greets me with melts my heart, but it doesn't stop me feeling like I should be fast asleep right now.

"What time is it?"

"Early. Come on, get up. There's something I want to show you."

Lifting my heavy head, I take in the numbers on my alarm clock. "Why the hell are you dragging me out of bed at three-thirty in the morning?"

"It'll be worth it, I promise." There are very few things that will make this worth it, but I refrain from voicing my concerns because Ben seems excited. "Here, get dressed." A pair of jeans and the hoodie he gave me gets thrown onto the bed, and after finding myself some underwear, I pull them on.

Once dressed, Ben takes my hand and leads me out to his car. It's still dark out and the street is in silence. As we drive through the city of London, it's quieter than I ever thought I'd experience—although there are still way too many people out at this hour, in my opinion.

"Where are we going?" I ask, desperately trying to keep my eyes open.

"Just wait."

I vaguely recognise parts of our journey, so when he pulls up into the deserted car park he brought me to after our first date, I'm not surprised.

"I should probably tell you now that I'm not really interested in any kinky shit that might go down in this place after dark."

Ben barks out a laugh. "Don't worry, I have no intention of allowing anyone to watch through the window. That's not why we're here."

"Why *are* we here?"

"For that," he says pointing to where the sun is just beginning to creep over the horizon in the distance.

"Oh." I'm gobsmacked that bad boy Ben has brought me to watch the sunrise. He really does put on a good show for everyone, and I suddenly feel so grateful to have been allowed to see the real him.

"Surprised?" he asks like he can read my mind.

"Yeah."

"It's just so peaceful. My dad first showed me this place. Just being here…" He pauses, and I can feel the emotion he's desperately trying to keep inside. His jaw pops where he grinds his teeth and his hands white-knuckle the steering wheel. "It just makes me feel close to him again."

He was only fourteen when his dad suddenly passed away. I can only imagine how he even began to deal with that. Having heard stories from back then, I know that Jenny totally fell apart, so not only was Ben trying to cope with losing his dad, but he was trying to support his mum at the same time. It's no surprise that, when my dad swooped in not all that long later, they didn't really hit it off. My dad had been working for Johnson & Sons, but as a builder. But it didn't seem to take all that long for him to move into their house and take over the business. It was almost like he was waiting, hoping for an opportunity to arise, and when it did, he swooped in like a knight in shining armour and saved the day.

"Let's get out."

Ben jumps from the car and I quickly follow suit, meeting him at the front. Resting back against the bonnet, he pulls me against him and places his chin on my shoulder.

We sit in a comfortable silence as we watch the sun rise over London. I feel so serene and secure in his arms as we take in one of the busiest cities coming to life.

I can't stop yawning as we head back into the centre.

"No sleeping yet. We've got more places to go."

"It's dawn on a Sunday morning. Where could we possibly need to go?" When he pulls up outside a McDonalds, I can't really argue. "Okay, yeah. This is a good plan."

We fill ourselves full of McMuffins and caffeine, and by the time we walk out, I'm feeling a little more awake.

To my surprise, Ben walks straight past his car and continues farther down the street.

"Where now?"

"I've got an appointment." I look over at him curiously but he doesn't elaborate. Things start to make sense when he comes to a stop in front of Just Ink, a tattoo studio. "Come on," he says, giving my arm a tug and encouraging me to follow him inside.

"Mornin'," a deep voice booms the second Ben opens the door. When I look up, I'm shocked to see Danni's older brother, Zach, with his arms out in an over-the-top greeting. "It's been too long, dude," He pulls Ben into a quick man hug and slaps him on the back.

"I know. Things have just been a little crazy. You know Lauren, right?"

"I do. Lookin' good, beautiful."

"Hey," I say, trying to keep my amusement hidden when Ben's muscles tense at Zach's greeting and the way he runs his eyes over me.

"Please tell me you've brought her because she's a blank canvas. I do love a virgin." My cheeks flush and I have to look away.

"She is, but you're not getting your hands on her." Ben says it with a laugh, but the warning in his voice is clear. Zach's eyes widen slightly in understanding before he nods and turns to Ben.

"I'm stuck with you, then, huh?"

"Sorry about that."

"I was hoping that if you were dragging me out of bed this early on Sunday, you might have something a little more exciting for me."

"Shut up and get ready, prick."

The banter between them continues as Zach sets up and Ben gets himself comfortable on the leather reclining chair in the back room. It's clear that these two are closer than I first thought. I knew they were friends in school, but I've never heard either mention the other since.

"What are we adding today?"

"I want a sunrise on my shoulder." I watch as Ben points out exactly what he wants and where.

"Sure thing. We'll have this sleeve done in no time."

I watch Zach ink Ben's skin with fascination. I'm in awe of his talent. He makes it look so easy, but I'm not stupid enough to believe that's actually the case.

"Are you sure I can't tempt you?" Zach asks once he's finished working on Ben. "There's nothing like being a woman's first."

"Enough, Zach," Ben snaps, clearly fed up with his blatant flirting.

Zach puts his hands up in defence as he starts clearing up.

"Maybe another day." Both heads turn towards me. Zach's eyes light up whereas Ben's eyebrows draw together, causing a deep line to form.

"You don't want this arsehole's hands on you, b—"

"You're probably right," I interrupt before he says something he won't be able to take back. I'm not sure it helps when I see the look

Zach gives us. "I'll just be out there." Turning on my heel, I walk out of the room to wait in reception.

"Promise me you won't let him put his hands on you," Ben says the second we're back inside his car.

"You do know he's already touched me, right?"

"He's fucking *what?*" Ben's face reddens, the muscles in his shoulders bunch, and his lips press into a thin line.

I have to bite back a smile before I can respond. "Calm down, caveman. He's Danni's brother and caught me when I fell down their stairs once, that's all."

Ben blows out a huge breath and sags back against the seat. "Thank fuck for that."

"I thought you were friends. He's a good guy."

"We are. Doesn't mean I trust him, though."

"But you trust me?"

"Of course. Zach's just...a dog."

I can't help laughing. "And you're not?"

He shoots me a look, but his eyes are full of amusement. "Okay, yeah, I deserve that."

Any reference of him being with plenty of girls before me always has nerves fluttering in my belly, but the moment he reaches over and entwines his fingers with mine, I forget all about the outside world and just focus on this—on us.

---

AS THE CLOCK TICKS AROUND, I feel Ben starting to pull away from me. The whole weekend has been beyond incredible, but we're both well aware that our time is coming to an end. Dad said they wouldn't be back until this afternoon, but it's barely lunchtime and we're both already on edge.

"Let's watch a film," I suggest in an attempt to take our minds off the inevitable. I've tried to push any thoughts of our reality to the back of my mind as we've enjoyed each other this weekend, but it's never really that far away. What we're doing might feel like the most natural thing in the world to us but, to the outside world, what we're doing is forbidden. As far as most people believe, a relationship between us is wrong.

But is it?

"Lauren, are you even watching?" I flinch when Ben's hand lands on my thigh.

"Sorry, yeah. I just zoned out for a minute."

"Do I need to ask what you were thinking about?"

"No. I just don't know what—"

"We'll figure it out." With his hands on my cheeks and confidence shining from his eyes, I almost believe him.

"How?"

"Honestly, I've no idea. But what I do know is that I'm not letting anyone get between us. I'm not letting you go, Lauren. You make everything so much lighter. I won't go back into the dark. I can't."

His body looming over me forces me to lie back on the sofa. He presses me into the cushions, his lips landing on mine and his hands trailing over my body.

Everything falls away—our surroundings, my concerns, everything but how I feel for him. It's exciting. It's overwhelming. It's scary as hell. But everything he just said is true, because I'm not giving him up, either.

"Honey, we're home." Jenny's voice rings out through the house loud and clear. Ben jumps into action, scrambling off me and practically flying to the chair at the other end of the room. I watch as he looks around in panic, running his hands through his hair, trying to smooth it down.

"Lauren," he prompts when he spots that I haven't moved.

Pulling myself to a sitting position on the sofa, I also attempt to sort out my hair and calm my racing heart. Dread fills me. I've never heard Jenny shout, let alone loud enough to wake the dead like that.

She knows.

"Did you have a good weekend?" Ben asks when she walks into the living room, looking between the two of us.

"Yes, it was love—"

"Lauren, what are you doing here?" Dad barks when he eventually follows her into the room.

"I...uh...came back this morning."

"Your mum said you were staying for lunch."

"I was, but I had some things that needed doing before work tomorrow, so I came back a little early. Problem?" I ask, jutting my chin out. Fire burns within me; I'm ready to start an argument if he wants to.

Turning towards Ben, his stare holds for a few seconds before he looks back at me. "I really hope not," he mutters before storming from the room.

The three of us stay silent as the sounds of him crashing about in the kitchen filter through. Jenny looks between us once more before muttering her excuse and racing from the room.

"This is bullshit," Ben barks.

Looking up at him, I see all the happiness and relaxation from our time together has gone. He's once again full of anger, and as always, it's directed straight at my dad. Frustration fills me that I have no clue what the issue is, but Ben's made it very clear that he's not going to share. I decide there and then that I need to start working on Dad. I need to get to the bottom of this if there's even a slim chance of this working between us.

"I know but—"

"But what? You have some master plan that you haven't shared that will magically make all of this okay?"

"No, but—"

"I can't do this. I can't sit around and watch you from a distance. I'm outta here."

I don't get the chance to respond, because he's gone. The front door slams and his car squeals out of the driveway.

"Oh, has Ben gone?" Jenny asks, walking in with two mugs in her hand.

"I'm sorry, I've got things I need to do." Biting down on my bottom lip so she can't see it trembling, I race past her and up to my room.

The second I enter, his smell hits me and I'm reminded of every thoughtful and gentle thing he did this weekend. My eyes sting and a lump forms in my throat. It was all so perfect for those few hours. Falling onto my bed, I silently cry for what could be. For what Ben and I could have if the situation was different.

---

"WHAT'S WRONG?" Dad snaps when the three of us are sat around the dining table later that evening. Ben still hasn't reappeared, and the messages I've sent him to ask if he's okay have gone unread. I feel sick. How can things go from being so perfect to so fucked up so quickly?

"Nothing," I mutter, shovelling some rice into my mouth.

"Could you at least sound a little grateful, Lauren? Not every kid has it as easy as you."

"I'm not a kid." My eyes find Dad's hard and angry ones across the table, but they do little to douse the fire raging inside me. "I'm not a fucking kid."

"Lauren, do not use—"

"What? Are you going to march me to my room and ground me like a child? I'm an adult. I can make my own choices and live my own life."

"You're eighteen. You don't know what you want, let alone what's right," he roars.

"And you do? How could you possibly know what I want and need? You're too busy controlling everything and everyone around you to have time to notice anything I do." Throwing my fork down on the plate, I push my chair out behind me and race to the door.

"Oh, I notice, Lauren. I fucking notice everything," he seethes as I round the corner.

I'm panting when I lean back against my bedroom door. I can probably count on one hand the number of times I've stood up to my dad, and most of those have been since I moved in.

"Fucking hell," I mutter to myself, pacing back and forth across my room. Knowing I can't sit here stewing, I grab my phone. I've got two options.

---

"OVER HERE," I hear my best friend shout the second I step foot in our favourite bar.

Looking over, I see she's got our favourite booth and there's already a cocktail pitcher in the centre. "So, you want to tell me what this impromptu drinking session is about?"

"Not really." Grabbing myself a glass, I fill it to the top and allow the cold, sweet margarita to slide down my throat.

"In my experience, it can only be two things. Your parents, or a boy. Now, knowing what your dad's like, it's probably him, but for argument's sake, let's say it's a boy. Give me all the details. Make it up if you have to. I need juicy details to make up for my lack of a boyfriend." My cheeks heat and Danni doesn't miss it. "You're blushing. So there *is* a boy!" she squeals in excitement, clapping her hands together.

Groaning, I fold my arms on the table and drop my head down onto them. "Yes, no...maybe. I don't know."

"Tell. Me. Everything."

I do—well the beginning, anyway, because the second she sees where I'm going, she stops me.

"Wait...please don't tell me you're fucking Ben. Oh my God, you are. You're fucking Ben. Ben, your stepbrother. Ben!"

"A little louder, please? The bartender in the staff room didn't quite hear you."

"Shit, fuck. I'm sorry. But fuck, Lauren. You're shagging your stepbrother? Do you have any idea how hot that is? Forbidden. But still, hot as fuck!"

I bite my tongue to stop myself agreeing.

Question after question falls from my best friend's mouth as she tries to piece together how I ended up sat here a broken mess.

"So is it over?"

"What? No. Well, I don't think so. I hope not." Panic at the thought alone crawls up my throat and I know that I'm in way too deep with this. No matter what happens next, this thing with Ben is going to shatter me.

"Maybe you'll get another nocturnal visit. He might sneak into your room, into your bed—"

"Stop, please," I beg, not needing the images in my head.

---

THE HOUSE IS in darkness when the taxi pulls up later that evening. It's way too late to be out on a school night, and I'm equally too pissed. It seems to be becoming a habit that I really need to get myself out of.

After shoving some money at the driver, I stagger my way towards the house. Leaning against the front door, I fumble with the key when it suddenly opens. As I fall forwards, I prepare for the pain that's surely going to follow, but instead of the solid stone floor, I hit a warm, hard, and very familiar body.

"Ben?" I ask, trying to get my eyes to focus so that I can see him.

"Where the fuck have you been?"

"Out," I snap, not liking the tone of his voice. It's too similar to Dad's—always demanding answers.

"Whoa, okay. I'm sorry," he soothes when I start fighting to get out of his arms. "It wasn't meant to come out like that. I was just worried when you weren't here and I couldn't get a hold of you."

"Sorry," I whisper, mortified that for even a moment I put him and my dad in the same box. "I just needed to get out of this house."

"Trust me, I understand that more than you could know."

He guides me towards the kitchen and, once he's happy I'm safe on the chair he's placed me on, he sets about getting me a glass of water and some tablets.

"I'm fine," I say when he hands them over.

"Now you are. In a few hours when you have to get ready for work, it's going to be another story."

Groaning, I swallow down the tablets.

Once he's cleared up any evidence we were here, Ben sweeps me up into his arms and carries me up the stairs.

"I can walk, you know."

"Sure you can, baby. I just love having you in my arms." I've no idea if the first part is meant to be sarcastic or not, but I let it go, enjoying the feeling of being pressed up against his hard body.

I don't realise I fall asleep in his arms, but the next thing I know I'm perched on the edge of my bed while Ben pulls my shirt over my head. Once my clothes are off, he stands and pulls his own t-shirt off before covering me with it. His scent surrounds me.

"Mmm, it smells like you," I mumble as he laughs at my drunken state.

"Strange, that. Do I need to get a bucket?" His words pass me by as I watch him take care of me. He's so kind and gentle with me that tears sting my eyes.

"I think I'm falling in love with you." It's not until his face pales in front of me that I realise I said it out loud. "Shit," I whisper.

"No, Lauren. It's just the excitement, the thrill of being caught." He might be saying the words, but there's no strength behind them, and as I drift off, I wonder who he's trying to convince. Him or me?

# CHAPTER ELEVEN

I feel like death when I wake up the next morning. It's not until I pry my eyes open that I realise it's not as bad as I first thought, because my head is resting on Ben's chest.

"Morning, baby. How are you feeling?" He laughs when I grunt and roll onto my back.

He goes to kiss me but must think better of it when I bite down on my lips. My mouth feels like the bottom of a bird's cage; I don't need to share it with anyone. His lips go to my neck instead, and almost immediately my hangover is put to one side.

---

"GOOD MORNING," Erica sings when she sees me walking into the office. "Did you have a good weekend? Wait, don't answer that...I can see it written all over your green face."

"I need tea," I mutter, walking past her desk and going straight to the kitchen.

"Sooo..." she purrs behind me. "Was it everything you thought it would be, even with the hangover from hell?"

I can't keep the smile from my face, and Erica squeals like a teenage girl. "It was...incredible. But the hangover is courtesy of my best friend. Dad and Jenny came home and things went to shit pretty quickly. I needed to get out and she was more than willing to ply me with cocktails if it meant she got the gossip."

"Sounds like a smart girl. Does your dad know?" Erica suddenly drops her voice and whispers the last bit.

"I'm still alive, aren't I?"

"Yeah, but the verdict's still out on Ben."

The memory of his hangover cure this morning makes my cheeks heat. "I'll take that blush as him still being alive, too...for now."

"I don't know what I'm going to do," I admit.

"I wish I had the answer for you, I really do. But in all honesty, I've no idea what advice to give you aside from enjoy yourself while you can."

My mood quickly depletes. The look Dad gives me when he eventually appears from his office is one that would melt a weaker person, but I'm fed up with letting him run my life. I'm nearly nineteen, and it's about time he realised that his control-freak nature won't roll with me. Jenny might bend over backwards to make him happy, but I won't. It's bad enough I agreed to live with him, although I can't really regret that decision anymore because it brought me Ben.

I'm thoroughly pissed off when I march through the house later that evening. My hangover has long disappeared and I'm just about ready to start drinking all over again if it means forgetting my shitty day.

Aside from a tense few minutes in the kitchen with Dad and Jenny while I find myself some dinner, I hide out in my room, silently hoping I'll get a surprise visitor, but he never comes.

---

"LAUREN, GET IN HERE," Dad barks from his seat behind his desk.

"Sure thing, *boss*," I mutter under my breath as I push my chair out and follow his demands.

"I need you to work late tonight."

"Great." The sarcasm in my voice causes his lips to press into a thin line.

"I need all the customer details from these," he says, pushing a massive stack of paper towards me. "Put into a spreadsheet."

"We've already got—"

"Are you questioning me?" he snaps, his eyes darkening with frustration.

"No. Whatever you need."

"What I need is for you to do your job without questioning everything. Can you do that?"

"Sure, but—"

"No buts, Lauren. Just go and do your damn job."

I walk out of his office with the stack of papers in my arms, tears stinging my eyes.

As I watch everyone else leave for the night, I'm still setting up the bloody spreadsheet Dad had drawn out for me on a scrap of paper. Spreadsheets are *not* my forte, so it takes much longer than it should.

I'm just making a start on inputting everything when the buzzer for the main door to the building rings out loud around the silent space around me. I glance at my phone, but I've got no messages or missed calls.

When it rings again, I make my way over and press the button to see who's at the door.

My heart turns over when I find Ben looking back at me. "Are you going to let me in anytime soon?" he asks into the speaker.

"Yeah, sorry. Hang on." Pressing the button down, I give him time to enter the building before going over the office door to wait for him. "Mmm...this is a nice surprise," I say once he's released my lips.

"I got this really weird message from Mum telling me that she and your dad were going out to meet a client tonight and that you were working late. She never usually tells me shit like that—"

"She knows about us."

His eyes widen in panic. "She does?"

"I don't know for sure, but I've got a feeling."

"That would make sense," he says with a nod. "Anyway, I've come to help, and I've ordered pizza."

"My saviour," I sigh dramatically. "Surely you've got something better to do tonight than help me with this bullshit?"

"What are you doing?"

I walk over to my desk and explain.

"This is *bullshit*. This spreadsheet already exists." He clicks around in the server and pulls up a replica of what I'm creating.

"He just wanted me out of the house. I can't believe it." The frustration I was already feeling starts to morph into anger.

"I can."

"He's not going to get away with this." Grabbing my phone, I unlock it and go to call his number, but it's snatched from my hands.

"Think about this, Lauren. I'd love for you to call him up and rip him a new one, but do you want to make him any more suspicious than he already is? He thinks that, by giving you such a pointless task, he's keeping us apart. You can hardly tell him that I turned up to fuck you in his office and pointed this out."

I stare at him. The anger coursing through my veins suddenly turns into something else. "You came to fuck me on his desk?"

"Well, I came to help. I was just hopeful for more."

Stepping up to him, I press my lips to his. His hands start on my waist but are soon tangled in my hair as he deepens the kiss.

The buzzer going off again forces us to break apart. "I hope you like pizza."

"Who doesn't like pizza?"

He shrugs before walking over to the buzzer and letting the delivery guy in while I smooth my hair down.

"How did you know that spreadsheet exists?"

"I'm more involved in this business than everyone believes."

"Oh."

"This is my legacy. My future. I need to know that there's going to be something left for me when my time comes."

"Why wouldn't there be anything left? As far as I can see, the profits are only increasing year after year and our reputation is sky high."

"Things aren't always as they seem." It's not the first time he's said those words to me.

"So, what are they, then? What are you trying to say?"

He's silent for a few seconds as he tries to come up with an answer. "I don't want to drag you into it. Just be aware, is all."

Narrowing my eyes at him, I wait for him to elaborate, but it soon becomes clear that he's not going to say any more on the matter.

"Now, copy and paste that stuff into a new spreadsheet so it looks like you've made a start, and then meet me in your dad's office." He winks at me as he tidies up the pizza boxes and a rush of heat fills my body.

I shouldn't be fucking my stepbrother. I really shouldn't be fucking him on my dad's desk. And I really, *really* shouldn't be this excited about it.

I do what I need to do in case Dad starts asking questions first thing. I've no idea what Ben's doing, but I can hear him crashing about in Dad's office. My pulse thunders in my veins as I think about what's waiting for me on the other side of that door.

This is so very wrong, but I can't think of anything I want more right now.

By the time I hit save, my entire body is aching with anticipation for what's to come.

After shutting down the computer, I comb my fingers through my hair and wipe away any smudged makeup from under my eyes. It's crazy because he's been sitting here right next to me for the last hour, but I'm nervous.

My legs feel like jelly as I walk over to the door. I should just turn the handle and walk in, but something stops me.

With excitement and anticipation filling me, I lift my hand and gently knock the solid wood.

"Come in." His voice is deep and has tingles racing down my spine.

The door clicks as I turn the handle, then I push it open and walk in. I find Ben sitting in Dad's chair with his feet propped up on the edge of the desk like he owns the place.

If it wasn't for the pulsing muscle in his neck, I'd say he was totally unaffected by this situation, but I know it's not the case.

He's just as excited as I am right now.

"Strip," he demands. His fingers entwine across his stomach as he rests back in the chair like he's about to watch TV—only his sole focus in on my body.

My hands tremble a little as I lift them to the top button on my blouse, but I never move my eyes from his.

With each button I undo, his blue eyes darken and the muscle in his neck pulses faster. He's fighting to keep himself in that chair right now, and the knowledge that it's me causing that has fire burning in my belly and my confidence soaring.

Turning my back to him, I allow the fabric to fall from my shoulders and slowly drop down my arms, exposing my back. It flutters to the floor and I look over my shoulder just in time to watch him follow its journey.

When his attention comes back to me, his impatience is clear on his face. "More."

Nodding at his request, I unclip my bra. I make quick work of toeing off my shoes and unzipping and dropping my skirt, revealing my thong-clad arse to him. His groan of approval spurs me on.

"Fucking hell," he breathes when I turn. His eyes drop from mine in favour of my body. Heat burns a trail where his gaze roams my skin. My nipples pucker as if he's touching them and even more heat descends to my core.

"Come here. I want you on this desk."

Nerves find their way in when I notice a photo of Dad and Jenny on the sideboard, but knowing he's the sole reason I'm here working late in the first place helps me push the concern aside. As I walk past, I lie the frame face down so I don't have to look at them again.

There's just enough space between Ben and the desk, so after climbing over his leg, I settle myself with my arse on the edge.

Feeling brazen under his intense stare, I lift one leg at a time and place my foot on the armrest of the chair, exposing myself to him.

He swallows and shifts a little in his seat as he stares at the tiny bit of lace stopping him from seeing every part of me.

I rest back on my elbows, my chest heaving with my increased breaths, my breasts rising and falling at a rapid rate.

He rips his eyes from my centre and runs them up my body. My nipples tighten and my stomach clenches with the desire and need to be touched.

"What are you waiting for?" I moan. My voice doesn't even sound like my own.

"Just making sure I commit this to memory. I might need it one day."

His words darken the mood a little, but it's soon forgotten when he sits forward and reaches behind him to pull his t-shirt over his head.

He drops it to the floor before wrapping his fingers around the lace at my hips and pulling my thong down my legs. Lifting my arse to help him, coldness surrounds me until his warm breath replaces it.

I moan before his lips even touch me. Just the sensation of the stream of air he blows across me is enough to have me racing towards my release.

His tongue licks from my entrance all the way to my clit, my hips lift, and his arm rests across my lower stomach to keep me in place.

"Oh God, Ben," I moan as he teases around my clit and then lower, circling my entrance but never giving me quite what I need.

"Please, please," I chant, threading my fingers in his hair and trying to force him deeper.

"All in good time, baby," he says, pulling away and wiping his mouth with the back of his hand.

Standing to full height, my eyes drop to his sculpted chest and then down to his waist when he starts undoing his jeans.

Biting down on my bottom lip, I impatiently wait for what I want, what I need.

He doesn't bother removing his jeans and boxers. Instead, he just pushes both down his thighs once he's pulled a condom from his pocket.

My muscles clench as I watch him rip the packet and roll it down his length. "Ben," I moan impatiently.

When he turns his eyes on me, they're dark, hungry, and possessive.

Everything about what we're doing right now is wrong, but it doesn't feel that way. What we're doing feels like the most natural thing in the world.

I whimper when he rubs the tip of his cock between my folds. I fall down onto the cold desk when he starts pushing inside me. The sensation takes over and I go limp as I enjoy everything he gives me.

My hips burn where his fingers grip tightly and the edge of the desk digs into my arse, but I don't care. I don't care about anything when he's touching me.

Needing more, his hands skim up my body. One tangles in my hair, lifting me from the desk to find his lips. His tongue invades my mouth and mimics what his cock's doing lower down in my body.

My hands run up his back before my nails scratch all the way back down. He growls and, if it's possible, thrusts deeper inside me.

"Holy shit, Lauren," he groans when he pulls back from my lips. "Let me feel you. Let me feel you milking my cock."

"Oh God," I whimper as the first tingles of my orgasm erupt within me. "Oh God, Ben!" My body thrashes about in his arms as I give myself over to the pleasure. My head drops back as wave after wave rolls through me. It's only seconds until Ben swells inside me and I feel the first twitch of his release.

Ben pulls me tight against his chest, and we stay locked in our embrace as our heart rates decrease and our breathing slows.

I've no idea how much time passes, but eventually I pull my face from his neck and look up into his bright eyes. "So, was fucking me on Dad's desk everything you thought it'd be?"

He chuckles, and his semi-hard cock stirs inside me once again. "It was everything and more, baby."

THE REST of the week continues in a similar fashion, but I keep a closer eye on everything at work after Ben's words. I haven't seen or heard from him, and I miss him like crazy. By the time Friday rolls around, I'm receiving sympathetic looks from everyone in the office—bar Dad, of course. He seems totally unaware of my ever-souring mood as the hours pass by.

I'm just about ready to give up hope of seeing Ben tonight until I walk towards my bed. The sight of the Post-It note on my pillow has excitement racing through me. I forget about any frustration I have from not seeing enough of him and pluck it from its resting place.

*I'll pick you up from the end of the street at 7pm. Wear something hot!*

Glancing back at the clock, I see it's already gone six. I've got my work cut out for me if I'm going to be ready for a night out.

Rushing to my wardrobe, I thank God for the fact that I washed my favourite dress earlier in the week, and pull it from its hanger. I place my shoes next to it on my bed and rummage through my drawers to find the other set of lingerie I bought for the weekend but never wore.

I have the quickest shower of my life before standing in the mirror, trying to get my hair dry and my make-up applied in record time.

I'm flustered but ready by five-to-seven. Grabbing my bag from the sideboard, I tuck my phone inside and go to leave the house.

"Lauren, you look beautiful. Hot date?" Jenny asks when I bump into her at the bottom of the stairs.

"J—just meeting a friend," I stutter. She hasn't said anything about us, but I've still got a nagging feeling that she knows what's going on. Maybe she's equally as scared of Dad's reaction if—when—he finds out.

"That sounds like fun. I'm home alone tonight," she says sadly. "Well, have a wonderful night."

"You, too." The second the words have passed my lips, I rush out of the house, not wanting to waste a second of my time with Ben.

I come to a stop at the end of the street when I hear the deep rumble of his engine pull up behind me.

"Hey, beautiful." The smile he gives me takes my breath away, and I realise just how much I've missed him.

My arse has barely touched the leather when his fingers slide into my hair and he pulls me over to his lips.

"Fucking missed you, baby." A deep ache forms in my lower stomach at his words.

"I thought maybe…"

"What?" he asks, staring deep into my eyes. I swear he can see every single one of my insecurities.

"That you'd changed your mind about us." It comes out as a whisper because, when he's looking at me the way he is right now, I know it's not true. I can see everything he feels for me—it's written all over his face. It's equally as terrifying as it is relieving.

"Never," he states. "You're mine, Lauren. You're not getting rid of me. No matter what happens, I'll always come back for you."

I didn't realise I wasn't breathing, but when he stops talking I release a long breath.

"Come on, let's get out of here."

"Where are we going?"

"It's a surprise."

Sitting back, I get comfortable for the drive. Ben's hand stays firmly attached to mine as we head towards our destination.

"So...where have you been?"

"Keeping my distance. But I've not been too far away." Glancing over, he winks at me.

"What?"

"You're a really heavy sleeper, aren't you?"

"I guess. Are you telling me you've been with me and I didn't know?"

"Might be," he chuckles. "Did you also know that you talk in your sleep?"

"Yeah, Mum used to tell me that. Did I say anything interesting?" The muscles in his neck tighten and his teeth clench. "Ben, what did I say?"

"Everything I needed to hear to know all of this is worth the risk."

"You're most definitely worth the risk." Lifting our joined hands, he presses a kiss to my knuckles.

"What is this place?" I ask as Ben pulls the car to a stop in front of an expensive-looking restaurant on the other side of the city.

"Somewhere I can treat you, knowing we're safe from prying eyes." My heart flips over at his thoughtfulness. After spending a weekend hidden inside the house and then the office, it'll be nice to have a normal night out with him without having to look over our shoulders in case we see anyone we know. "It's won a ton of awards for its food, so I thought it would be a good choice."

"I'd eat anything as long as it means I get to spend a night with you," I admit, but I instantly feel ridiculous at how cheesy it sounds.

"Stay there," he instructs, and I watch as he jumps from the car and races around to my side. I unbuckle myself as he pulls the door open and, the second he reaches in for me, I slide my hand into his and allow him to pull me from the car. His actions are so far from the Ben I used to know—the angry, brooding teenager who hated the world around him. The man in front of me is all gentleman.

He pulls me up so I'm pressed against his chest. His breath tickles my ear as he leans in. "I think that might be the nicest thing anyone's ever said to me."

It takes me a moment to recall what I said, and I can't help laugh when I do. That is, until I realise he's not laughing with me. Lifting my head, I'm surprised by the serious look on his face. Shit, he's not joking.

"Ben, I—"

"Stop." I'm forced to do as he says when his fingers land on my lips. "Let's not go there. Tonight is about enjoying ourselves, not worrying about reality." Taking my hand, he leads me inside the restaurant.

It's exactly as I imagined it would be. The lighting is soft and candles flicker from the centre of the tables. There are a handful of couples enjoying their meals together, and mellow music fills the space. It is by far the most lavish and romantic restaurant I've ever stepped foot in. I feel totally out of place.

"What's wrong?" Ben asks when I don't immediately fall into place behind him and the maître d'.

"It's just so fancy."

"It's no less than you deserve." Looking at all the mature couples dining around us, I feel every bit my eighteen years and totally in over my head. "We can go somewhere else if you'd feel more comfortable."

"No. I'm just being silly. This will be amazing." I feel ridiculous making a fuss after he's gone to the effort of organising it. The second I saw him wearing a white dress shirt and trousers I knew I'd made the right choice with my dress, but never in a million years was I expecting something like this.

We're seated in a cosy corner of the room, and we order our

drinks. It feels like no sooner has the waiter left, then he's back, placing glasses down in front of both of us and reeling off tonight's specials. I try my best to focus, but other than remembering that one involves chicken and another fish, I've no clue what they are. I'm still too stunned with how my Friday night is shaping up.

"I feel way too young for this," I whisper to Ben.

"Age is only a number. You couldn't look more at home, or any more beautiful." Sliding my chair over so that it's closer to his, he leans in and places a kiss at the corner of my lips. "I've been waiting all week for this."

"Me, too, I just didn't know it was coming."

Sadness washes through him once again but he doesn't say anything.

"What's the matter?" I prompt, hoping he'll open up.

"I hate this. I hate having to hide. I hate having to treat you like a dirty little secret."

"Me, too. But there's not much else we can do."

"How drunk were you on Sunday night?"

"Uh..." I stutter, a little shocked by his sudden topic change. "Pretty drunk, why?"

"Drunk enough to not remember what you said to me?"

I run what I can remember of that night through my head. I almost say that I don't remember, until something hits me. *Fuck, did I say that out loud? Did I really tell him I was falling in love with him?* I don't need to say any more. He sees the moment the realisation hits.

"Did you mean it, or was it the drink talking?" Casting my gaze over his shoulder, I try to figure out how to vocalise my feelings. "Don't hide from me," he demands softly, his fingers touching my cheek and bringing my eyes back to his. The hope in his eyes is enough to pull an honest answer out of me.

"Yes. I meant every word."

His eyes flash with emotion before he nods like he's made some big decision. I go to ask, but he beats me to it. "I'm going to talk to your dad."

"You're going to what? You can't. He'll...he'll..."

"He'll what? Really, what's he going to do? We're both adults. He can't really stop us from seeing each other. Technically, we're not doing anything wrong."

My heart races and my hands tremble with the force of the sheer panic that rushes through me. I've witnessed arguments between Dad and Ben, and they're not pretty at the best of times. I can only imagine what will happen if he does this.

"No, it should come from me."

Ben's face hardens. "No. I won't let you do that."

"What? Why?"

"I don't trust him."

"What are you talking about? I'm his daughter, he won't do anything to me. It's safer coming from me. I might be able to calm him down about it."

"I doubt that very much. He's going to lose his shit."

"Then we won't tell him yet. Let's just enjoy ourselves."

Ben's face twists with uncertainty, and I know exactly how he feels. This fight between what we want and what we know is right is exhausting. "It'll be worse if he finds out before we tell him."

"Then we just have to be really careful." I can tell he's not happy about it. Neither am I, but there's no way I'm giving up on us.

Leaning into my ear, he whispers, "You'll have to stop screaming my name so loud."

My face is burning red when the waiter comes over with our starters. Ben just sits and chuckles at me. It's infectious as well as a relief to move on from our serious conversation. As much as it warms my heart that he seems to be thinking about a future for us, it also fills me with dread because I know that, as much as we might want to be together, doing so is going to involve a lot of pain.

I'M aware of new diners coming and going but I'm too consumed with the man beside me and the incredible food we're being served to take too much notice. That is, until a shiver runs down my spine. Untangling my fingers from Ben's across the table, I look up, but the ball of dread that's formed in my belly already knows what—or rather, who—I'm about to find.

I try to swallow down my panic as I look up into the angry eyes of my father with another woman on his arm. But he's not focused on me. His death stare is on the person next to me, who is currently totally unaware of the situation unfolding in front of him.

"Ben," I whisper, not taking my eyes from my dad for a second for fear of what he might do.

"Yeah, baby? What's—" His stare follows mine until he finds the reason for my concern. "It'll be fine." I'm sure he's trying to reassure me, but it's not working.

Silence descends as the tension grows. Dad's anger is palpable, and I start to think he's going to fly at Ben at any second.

"Nick, this is a surprise. I bet Mum loves this place. Oh, you don't seem to have brought her."

"What the fuck are you doing?" I whisper through gritted teeth. Surely, pointing out that he's here with a woman who isn't my stepmum is not the thing to say right now. Ben ignores me, instead continuing his stare-off with my dad while the waiter stands with his eyes flicking between the two of them, not knowing what the hell is going on.

"What I'm doing isn't any of your concern, boy. Unfortunately for you, what *you* are doing seems to have everything to do with me. Care to explain what you're doing here with my daughter?"

"We're—" Ben starts, but Dad's having none of it. Marching forward, he lifts Ben from his seat and pushes him back until he's up against the wall.

"What the fuck are you doing with her?" Dad growls in Ben's face. "If you've fucking touched her..."

Every person in the restaurant turns to take in the evening's entertainment, and my own anger bubbles over.

"Get off him." I pull at the arm holding Ben up against the wall. I've no doubt that Ben could overpower him, yet he just stands there.

"Lauren, go home," Dad demands, and it only adds fuel to my fire.

"Not a fucking chance. Get your hands off him. He wasn't doing anything wrong."

"I warned him what would happen if he so much as touched you."

"Dad, please." The waiter flits about behind me, clearly not used to this kind of situation, and I try to come up with something. "I love him."

"You *what?*" It's the first time Dad looks at me. When our eyes connect, fear races through me.

Letting go of Ben, he steps back like he's been winded. I breathe a sigh of relief that it's over, but I soon realise it's only the start. Dad pulls his fist back, his eyes locked on Ben, who's still staring at me.

"No!" I shriek, running to get between them. I'm too slow. Dad's already committed to throwing the punch, only instead of landing on the person he was intending to hit, it connects with my cheek.

"You motherfucker!" Ben roars, pushing himself off the wall and forcefully shoving my Dad out of the way so he can get to me. Unfortunately, Dad's so pumped up that he ignores me, still clutching my face while on the floor, and he goes for Ben. The noise that comes from Dad's throat is something I'd expect to hear from an animal, not a human—and certainly not my fucking father.

"I've called the police," someone shouts, and my Dad stops.

Blood drips from Ben's lip and his eye swells, but he doesn't cower away from Dad. "This whole restaurant just witnessed you assaulting both me and your own daughter. I suggest you get the hell out of here," he spits. "And take that cheap slut with you." His lip curls in disgust as he glances at the woman over Dad's shoulder.

"This isn't over," he warns. "Lauren, come on."

"No fucking way. I'm not letting you anywhere near her." The two of them stare at each other until the sound of sirens filters through the restaurant. Dad turns on his heel and marches towards the door, the woman hot on his heels.

"Fucking hell, are you okay?" Ben drops to his knees beside me and gently takes my face in his hands. His eyes run over every inch of my face, looking for injuries. His hands tremble, making the tears in my eyes finally drop. "Fuck."

His thumbs wipe the moisture away and I'm lifted into his arms. Somehow, he manages to pull out a wad of cash from his pocket and, after apologising to the poor waiter who's still standing there looking shell-shocked, he carries me from the restaurant.

The police car comes to a stop outside just as Ben pulls away from the curb. "Shouldn't we have stayed to speak to them?"

"Do you think sending the cops after your dad is going to make this any better?"

"No, probably not. I'm so sorry, I—"

"Lauren, none of this is your fault. You have nothing to apologise for."

"But your face."

"Trust me, it's looked a hell of a lot worse. He's right about one thing, though. I never should have touched you. You're way too good for an arsehole like me. I deserved a solid punch for that."

"Stop talking about yourself like that." He quickly glances over at me and my heart breaks at the look on his face. "I meant it, Ben. I love you."

His grip on the wheel tightens, turning his knuckles white. He blows out a long breath and stares ahead. I can't help feeling like my words just hurt more than my dad's fists, but I've no clue why.

"Stay here," he demands, pulling up in front of a shop. I have little choice but to do as he says, so I sit in the dark and wait. My phone vibrates in my bag but I don't have the energy to find out who it is. It's probably Dad ready to fire some more fucks into me for my stupid actions. Rolling my eyes at his childish behaviour, I rest my head back and close my eyes. My cheek throbs and ruins any chance I might have had of forgetting the last hour of my life.

My mind replays this evening over and over, trying to figure out how it all went so wrong. What were the chances of him being in the same restaurant on the other side of London? The shock I saw on his face when I first looked up, before his anger took over, told me that he hadn't followed us.

It really was just a horrific coincidence.

The image of the red-headed woman standing behind him pops up, and I feel like I'm going to puke. I didn't believe Ben all those weeks ago when he first found me in their kitchen and accused me of being my dad's bit on the side. I was aware it was his wandering ways that broke him and Mum up, but I really thought he was serious about Jenny. Knowing the only reason he was in that restaurant in the first place was because he was also hiding a dirty secret ensures that my stomach continues to turn over. I guess it gives us some ammunition when we go home and confront him about all of this.

"Don't fall asleep," Ben says the second he pulls the door open.

"I wasn't."

"You might have a concussion."

"I'm fine. Honestly. I didn't hit my head."

Dropping a couple of bags at my feet, he starts the car and pulls away from the curb. Silence descends around us. I hate the uncertainty I'm suddenly feeling. I knew Dad finding out was going to change things, but I wasn't expecting what happened.

"A hotel?" I ask when Ben pulls up into the underground car park.

"What? You wanted to go home?" The laugh that falls from him holds no amusement.

"No. I'd quite happily never go back there again."

"Now you understand a little of how I feel about that place." He throws both our phones in the glove compartment after turning off the engine, and I couldn't be happier to be cut off from the rest of the world after everything that's happened tonight.

With my hand locked in his, we walk towards the entrance and book a room. The woman's face behind reception twists in concern the moment she sees the state of us, but she soon drags her gaze away and hands over a key.

Knowing that we're going to be able to at least enjoy the rest of our night together before we face reality does have me breathing a little easier, although it doesn't mean I forget everything we've got coming our way when we do eventually go home.

"Go lie down." Ben pushes me towards the bed, then goes into the bathroom briefly with the bags. I listen as he runs the tap before he reappears with a glass of water, a packet of painkillers, and a bag of frozen peas. "Here, take these."

"I really am fine. You're the one who needs taking care of." I wince as he presses the cold peas to my cheek. "Please, let me look after you."

Placing my hand over his, I look up into his eyes, pleading with him.

"Fine," he whispers. "But be warned, I'm not used to being looked after."

Getting up from the bed, I go in search of something to clean up his face with. I dampen some tissue with warm water and head back into the bedroom. I find Ben still sat where I left him on the edge of the bed.

I unfasten his shirt buttons and push the fabric from his shoulders. He watches me through sad, swollen eyes.

"Scoot back." He does as I say, and in seconds he's resting back against the headboard.

I pull my dress up my thighs and throw my leg over him. After running my eyes over his face, I press some tissue to his blood-stained chin and attempt to clean him up. He winces when I brush past the cut, but he allows me to continue.

"I'm so sorry for—"

"Stop apologising for him. His actions have nothing to do with you."

"I know. But—"

"No. No buts. I'll always fight for you, Lauren, whether that's with your dad or anyone else who disapproves of this." His hips flex and I feel his length against me. Warm fingers wrap around my wrist, stopping me. He plucks the tissue from my fingers and drops it to the bed before pulling me down to him. "Me and you, Lauren. I'll always fight for you...protect you. Always."

His hands push my dress higher up my thighs and fingers slip inside my knickers.

"Always so wet for me," he murmurs as he finds my clit.

Groaning in pleasure, I grind myself on his fingers. I need the release that only he can give me after the night we've had. He works me into a frenzy before pulling his fingers out of me and undoing his trousers.

"Pocket," he grunts, and I dig around until I find the condom.

He goes to take it from my fingers but I hold tight. "Can I?"

His eyes darken with desire. "Be my guest."

I help him free himself and push the fabric down his thighs before I roll the condom down over his length.

"Over to you, then, baby."

Lifting myself up, I pull my knickers to the side and slide down onto him. We both sigh in pleasure.

"I'll never get enough of this." His hands come up and squeeze my breasts, and it only makes my impending orgasm build faster.

All of the stress from tonight falls away as I focus on the sensations that fill my body. I keep my movements slow, enjoying the feeling of him filling me to the hilt.

Circling my hips when I'm fully seated, I gasp when he hits me so deep that it almost sends me spiralling into my release.

"Let go, baby. That's it." His eyes stay locked on mine, his hands on my hips, helping me move.

Rotating my hips once more, light explodes behind my eyes and my body twitches and pulsates around him. I fight to keep my eyes on his but I lose the battle, the pleasure surging through me too violently.

Falling down onto his chest, I'm vaguely aware of him thrusting up into me until he groans and stills before his cock twitches, releasing everything he has.

His hands run up and down my back. It's relaxing, but reality soon starts to creep back in.

I reach for the bag of frozen peas still on the bed. Lifting them takes all my energy, but I manage to press them against Ben's eye.

"It's fine." He tries to move them away but I'm not having it. I feel pretty useless right now, and this is the only thing I can think of that will hopefully make somewhat of a difference.

The rest of the night is mostly filled with silence. We're both too lost in our own thoughts—or nightmares—to want to chat much. When I discover the bath has a Jacuzzi, I get it going and fill it with the salts I find on the side.

Even with the warmth of the water and the relaxing scent filling the room, Ben's muscles are still pulled tight. I can only imagine how he's feeling.

"I can't stop seeing him hitting you," he whispers once we're curled up in bed. He pulls me even tighter to him. "Every time I close my eyes, his fist is flying to your face. No man should ever hit a woman. *Ever*."

"I was trying to stop him from hitting you. He didn't mean to hit me," I argue, but I know it's weak at best.

"It doesn't matter. He still hit you. I was meant to be protecting you. I *promised* I'd protect you, and yet that arsehole hit you. In front of me."

Running my hand up his chest, I wrap my fingers around his neck and make him look at me.

"None of what happened tonight was your fault, Ben. You need to stop blaming yourself. There was nothing you could have done."

"I never should have allowed myself to touch you. Your dad's right. I'm bad news."

"Shut up, right now. Do not believe a word that comes from his mouth. He doesn't know you. You're incredible, Ben."

He makes an unintelligible noise and tries to push me away.

"No. I won't let you do this. I won't let you pull away from me." Wrapping my arm around his waist and throwing my leg over his, I hold him as tightly as I possibly can. No more words are said between us—we're too lost in our own heads—but eventually we must drift off to sleep in each other's arms.

# CHAPTER TWELVE

No words need to be exchanged the next morning. Just one look at each other and we know everything's about to change. I can't imagine a situation where Dad allows us to be together, but I'm not letting Ben go. Screw the business and the education I've been promised.

Other things in life are more important.

"I'm not ready," I admit when Ben comes back from the bathroom and begins pulling his clothes on.

"What's the point in putting off the inevitable? We need to go and face the music."

"Just a little longer?" I plead, hoping to live in this little bubble we've created for just a few more hours.

"We'll have lunch, then we're going back." If I couldn't see Ben's face, I would think the words he's saying aren't affecting him. He seems so strong and sure of what we've got to do, but in reality, I can feel the fear the uncertainty radiating off him. It breaks my heart to know he's hurting because of my dad again. But what can I do?

I stand to the side while Ben hands the key over to the receptionist, fighting to keep in the tears stinging my eyes. I just want to curl up in a ball and cry. Through hazy eyes, I take him in, head to toe. I'm not ready for this to be over yet. We've got so much more to get to know about each other. We deserve more time.

His eyes widen when he turns and finds me staring at him, but he doesn't say anything. Nothing he can say can make this any better.

I get a bit of déjà vu when he pulls up in front of the same shop we stopped at last night and tells me to stay put.

I will my brain to stop, but it continues to race. It feels like no time has passed at all when he pulls the door open and climbs back in. The more I pray for our time together to last just a little bit longer, the faster it seems to go.

I expect him to take us to a café or restaurant for lunch, so I'm a little surprised when he pulls up in the same car park he brought me the first day we really spent any time together. That day feels like a million years ago, now.

"This is where it all started," he says sadly. "It seemed like a perfect place to—"

"Do not finish that sentence." If he says the words I fear are coming, I'm going to lose it. Instead he nods, grabs the bag of food he bought, and climbs out of the car. His shoulders hang like he's got the weight of the world on them. With a sigh, I follow his lead.

After retrieving a blanket from the boot, we walk hand in hand over to the oak tree and set up our little picnic. The sun might be shining, but it feels like we've got a giant black rain cloud hanging over us, and I realise that as much as I want to put off going home, right now is torture. Looking at Ben, knowing this could be the end is just too much to bear.

"Fancy a sausage roll?" A weak laugh passes my lips at his attempt at a joke. "Lauren, you need to eat something."

"I can't. I feel sick."

I expect him to argue, but once again he just nods.

"I GUESS we should get this over with, then?" I ask after we've been sitting on the blanket in silence for well over an hour.

"Just one more thing." Crawling over to me, Ben cups the back of my head and gently lowers me down. His lips tickle against mine and I just about manage to hold back a sob.

His kiss is so gentle and so full of emotion. My heart pounds like it's going to explode out of my chest. For some reason, this kiss feels final, like it could be a goodbye, and it has a lump forming in my throat at just the thought of this being the end for us.

Turning my head from his lips, my first tear falls.

"Lauren," he whispers, running his nose across my cheek until his lips are at my ears. "I love you, too."

The sob I was holding in erupts. I want to scream. I want to shout about the unfairness of all this, but I know it won't help. Even if Dad were to hear it, it wouldn't make one ounce of difference.

Silence hangs heavy between us during the drive home. Our phones continue to vibrate from where we stashed them in the glove box yesterday and it's just another reminder of what's waiting for us.

I'm surprised when Ben pulls into the driveway to find only my car parked in front of the house. I expected the most depressing welcome home party ever.

Reaching over, Ben pulls both phones from their hiding place and hands mine over before unlocking his and reading through messages. I don't bother looking. I've got plenty of time for that later.

"Come on. I really need to get out of these clothes."

I can only agree—we're both still wearing the outfits we chose for our meal last night.

No one's home and the house seems creepier than ever as we walk through it. I feel like I'm being watched, but as I look over my shoulder, it's only Ben who follows me up the stairs.

Every time I hear a noise, my heart jumps in my throat, thinking he's going to come barrelling through the door. But he never does. When a key does slide in the lock while we're on the sofa trying to watch TV, it's Jenny who appears in the doorway, looking her usual self. She's does a double take when she sees Ben's black eye and cut lip, but she doesn't ask. I know for a fact it's not the first time he's come home after fighting. After asking us if we're okay, she turns to leave.

"Where's Dad?" I ask before she disappears.

"A golf weekend with a client, sweetheart. He won't be back until tomorrow."

Ben's eyes burn into the back of my head, and when I turn around, he mouths, *Golf weekend?*

Shaking my head, I stand. I need to do something or I'm going to go stir-crazy waiting for him to appear.

"What are you doing?" Ben asks in a panic when I go to leave the room.

"Going for a walk."

"Wait. I'll come."

"No." He looks totally taken aback by my refusal, but I just need a few minutes to myself. "I just need—"

"It's okay. I get it. I'll be here when you get back."

"Promise?"

"Of course."

Sliding on a pair of trainers, I leave the house and head off down the street. I've no route in mind. All I know is that I need to move. Pulling my phone from my pocket, I look down at all the notifications. To my surprise, almost all of them are from Mum. Ignoring the missed calls and voicemails, I open my messages.

> Mum: Your dad just called. Are you okay?
>
> Mum: Honey, please just let me know you're safe.
>
> Mum: Lauren. I'm worried. Ring me back.

There's a whole stream of messages from her, and I feel awful that she's been dragged into this, and even worse that I've given her a reason to worry.

"Lauren, are you okay?" she asks in a rush the second she answers the phone.

"Yes, I'm fine. I'm so sorry. We left our phones in the car. If I knew he'd called you I never would have—"

"It's okay, as long as you're okay."

"I am." I ignore the throbbing that comes from the purple bruise on my temple. Bringing that up would only anger her more.

"What the hell happened?"

I recount everything from the night before, much to her horror, although I omit the bit about Dad's fist colliding with my head and focus on him attacking Ben.

"Don't say I didn't warn you, honey."

"I know, I know. It was inevitable. It's just what happens next that I'm freaking out about. If he's capable of doing that in the middle of a busy restaurant, what's he going to do in the solitude of his own home?" I hate to say the words aloud, but I'm scared for Ben. Something tells me that what we experienced last night was only the tip of the iceberg.

"It might not be as bad as you think." She's trying to be supportive, but I can hear the quiver in her voice loud and clear. "Now that he's had time to calm down, he might see things a little differently."

I have to bite down on my lip to stop myself from asking if she's joking or not.

By the time I walk back up the driveway, the sun's starting to set. Ben rushes from the kitchen, looking harassed as I toe my shoes off.

"Fucking hell, Lauren." The second he's in reaching distance, he pulls me into him. I stiffen the second I'm in his arms, aware that we're standing in the middle of the hallway for anyone to see. "It's okay. He's not here." His words do little to relax me.

No, he's not here right now.

But he's coming.

For the first time since I moved in, we spend the evening like a normal family. Jenny cooks and the three of us sit around the table, chatting. It's weirdly enjoyable, even with the huge elephant in the corner of the room. She shows no sign of knowing anything about us or last night, so I can only assume she really believes that Dad's on a golfing weekend and not banging the red-head from the restaurant. I feel for her, but my sympathy only goes so far because I've got enough of my own problems to worry about.

Once we've all cleaned up, we make our excuses and disappear off in different directions. I head up to my room, hoping that in a few minutes Ben will follow. I'm not disappointed. We spend the whole night on my bed watching crappy Saturday night quiz shows and continuing to ignore the inevitable.

After hearing Jenny come up to bed, Ben turns the TV up a couple of notches and sets about making me scream, albeit quietly.

I'm sure it's just everything fucking up my head, but I swear there's something different about him when he slides into me. His eyes lock with mine and it's like he's trying to tell me something that he's not brave enough to say out loud. It makes my heart constrict and I have to remind myself that he's here.

And I just pray that everything's going to be okay.

We fall asleep wrapped in each other's arms, just as it should be, but I can't shift the feeling that something's very wrong.

I wake up a couple of times in the night and snuggle tighter against Ben's warm body, knowing that as long as he's here with me, everything's going to be okay.

---

I WAKE WITH A START. Sitting up, my heart races from a nightmare that seemed so real only moments ago. The image of Ben's back as he walked away from me is burned into my mind. The look in his eyes that screamed that he didn't want this but had no choice has a lump growing in my throat.

Reaching out, I expect to find him sleeping next to me but all I find is a cold, empty bed. When I turn to look, dread settles in my stomach. *That was just a nightmare, right?* I soon get my answer though, when I find a Post-It note on his pillow.

*I promised to protect you, and this is the only way I know how.*

*Forever yours, Ben x*

A tear splashes against the paper, making the ink run.

*No, no, no.*

This must be a joke. My heart thunders in my chest as I drop the note and scramble from my bed. Pulling on one of his t-shirts, I open my door and race towards his.

I tell myself that he's going to be there. He'll just be in the shower and this is all one very bad dream. But as I push the door open, I'm greeted with silence and I know it's wishful thinking. All his stuff might still be here, but I know the truth.

I feel it in my heart.

He's gone.

Falling down on his bed, I pull his pillow to me and cry. I cry for what we had as well as for what we've both lost.

I've no idea how long I'm there for, but when I hear movement downstairs and a deep male voice, I know it's time to find out everything. The real truth. Wiping my swollen and sore eyes, I pull my hair away from my face and secure it in a bun with the band around my wrist, preparing to fight.

"What the hell did you do?" I roar as I run down the last few steps, seeing my dad putting his overnight bag down in the hallway. "What did you do?" I fly at him, my arms taking on a life of their own as I try to slap and punch him. My heart breaks all over again and tears stream down my cheeks. His arms come up to protect his face as I hear Jenny's footsteps behind me.

"Lauren, what on earth?" Her arms wrap around my waist, but she's too weak and I fight her off in my need to get to him.

To *hurt* him. I need to do something that's going to take away the agonising pain of my heart splitting in two.

My arms start to burn as I fight to drag in air between my wailing, and he must see I start to tire because he reaches out and wraps his fingers around my wrists to stop me.

"What the hell is wrong with you?"

"You. You are what's wrong with me," I seethe, staring up into his hard, cold eyes. "What did you do? What did you say to him?" My body's limp, exhausted, and drained from the emotion that's washed through it in the past few minutes.

"Lauren, I've no clue what you're talking about?"

"He's gone, Dad. Gone. I know it's because of you." All I feel is emptiness as I say those words out loud.

"Who's gone?" Jenny asks, but I can already tell by the flat tone of her voice that she knows.

"Ben. He's gone, and it's all his fault." I thrash to get out of his hold and this time he lets me go.

"Where's he gone?"

"I don't fucking know. But this arsehole here sent him away."

"Lauren," he warns, but I cut him off when he starts to say more.

"Don't even think of chastising me for my language because you deserve much, much worse. Were you not content with controlling my education and career? You also had to weigh in on my love life? You're a fucking joke as a father. A *fucking* joke."

"Enough!" he roars. His fists clench and I flinch away from him, afraid to be on the wrong end of them again. "I haven't done anything. I've been at golf all weekend. I—"

"You're a fucking liar," I scream.

"I went to golf *after* my business meeting on Friday night."

A laugh falls from my lips, but it's anything but amused. "Golf? Was that her name? There's no way he'd have left by choice. *You* sent him away."

"Trust me, Lauren. I wish I got the chance. I'd have done it years ago if I could." I don't miss Jenny's gasp behind me, but we both ignore her. "He's a fucking waste of space. Nothing but bad news. You're better off as far away from him as you can get. This just proves what kind of man he really is, don't you think? He's been caught out and he's run. All he was trying to do was piss me off, trying to show that he's better than me by doing something I forbade him to. I told him very specifically what I would do to him if he came anywhere near you, but he did it anyway. Now, he's running scared. You don't deserve someone like him, Lauren. You deserve a real man, someone who'll stand by you and fight for you. Not a pussy like him."

"No, no. You're lying. He wouldn't just leave. I don't believe you."

"I swear to you, Lauren. I haven't done anything. I was expecting to come home now to sort this whole mess out."

"This isn't a mess, Dad." I shout, shoving my palms at his chest. "It's my life and you're fucking ruining it. You're ruining everything."

"I haven't—"

"You're a fucking liar. You don't care about me and what I do. All you care about it keeping up appearances and making money. You don't care about me," I repeat. The reality of the situation hits me. Fresh tears spill from my eyes, my fight draining from my body.

"Of course I care. I only want the best for you, Lauren. What's he's done just proves he's not good enough for you. He should be standing here now fighting for you."

"No, he wouldn't just leave me. He wouldn't. What we have... it's...it's..."

Dad's face softens, and for the first time since he walked through the door, I see concern on his face. "I'm sorry you're hurting. Come here, sweetheart."

I'm too weak to do anything but what he suggests, and I fall into his arms. He holds me as I cry and rubs my back to try to calm me. I was so convinced that this was his doing. I never even considered that Ben didn't want this as much as I did. I took all his words as gospel, and it's only now that I doubt everything he ever said to me.

Dad guides me into the living room, stopping to kiss Jenny on the cheek as we move past her. "It's for the best," he says, but I don't know if he's talking to her or me.

———

EVERYTHING CONTINUES around me like my world hasn't shifted on its axis. The house feels even colder than it used to. Even the office feels different without his presence. Everything I used to enjoy or look forward to just seems dull. Or maybe it's just me who's dull and lifeless. The hurt won't leave. No matter what I try to do to distract myself, he's always there in my heart. It's just a constant reminder of what I thought I'd found.

It's been a month since Ben walked out of my life, but I still can't seem to pull myself out of the hole I've fallen into. My heart aches more with every day that passes, and my anger at him grows. After everything, how could he just walk away like I meant nothing to him?

His bedroom door stays closed, and I have to fight not to look at it every time I walk past. Dad and Jenny have both been incredible and allowed me the time I need to attempt to put myself back together, but I fear that I'm never going to be the same again. Even with them in the same house, I'm lonely. I'm lonelier than I've ever experienced despite everyone doing their best to distract me.

They say it's better to have loved and lost than to have never loved at all, but right now I call bullshit, because I'm pretty sure I'd take never meeting him over the daily agony of this broken heart.

Ben Johnson was my first love.

My first everything.

I'll never forget everything he gave me.

And I'll never forgive him for taking it all away.

# ACKNOWLEDGMENTS

Nothing about this book has really gone as planned. Knowing BJ, I guess I shouldn't be surprised. This first part of his and Lauren's story was meant to be short, but as I delved deeper and deeper into the beginning of their relationship, I just couldn't stop.

I've loved Ben since I first mentioned his character—in *Falling For Lucas*, I think. As I wrote each following book, it just became more and more obvious to me that he'd have to have his own story. He likes to make out that he's just a player and happy to have a revolving door on his bedroom, but he's keeping a lot hidden. Mostly his heart, as you've seen.

I really hope you enjoyed this first instalment of their story. I'm seriously excited to discover where they're going to take me next.

As far as thank-yous go, as always I need to start with Michelle, for alpha reading this as I typed it and putting up with the nonsense that comes from my fingertips. It's a good job we're mostly on the same wavelength or she'd have no idea what I was trying to say.

My betas, Deanna, Helen, Lindsay, Suzanne and Tracy. Where would I be without you? Thank you so much for all your honest feedback and your love of my characters and books.

Evelyn, once again, for digging your way through a million typos to make this book as good as it possibly can be. I'd be nowhere without you.

Michelle, thank you for proofreading for me once again. You must be getting bored of the amount of words of mine you've read recently!

And finally, my husband and daughter for supporting me through this journey, pushing me forward and inspiring me every day.

Until next time,

Tracy xo

# LOSING THE FORBIDDEN

# PROLOGUE



Glancing over my shoulder at the house I grew up in, at the home where the people I love live, I know I don't have a choice. Walking away is the right thing to do.

I knew Nick, my stepdad, finding out about us would only end one way, but I really thought it would be with me in the hospital.

I never imagined this.

That vindictive arsehole knows exactly how to get what he wants. It's no different to how he wormed his way into my life. He wanted money and status, and my fragile, grieving mum was the perfect target.

Fire burns through my veins and my hands tremble with my need to find the motherfucker who's intent on ruining my life, but I know it'll be pointless. He's probably already got a plan in place for that.

Shoving my hands in my pockets, I force myself to walk away, to do what I need to do to keep the two women I love safe.

I've no doubt that the threats he just dished out were true. I've watched him ruin people before. He doesn't care about anyone, whether that's an employee or his own wife and daughter. He'll crush anything that gets in his way.

With one last look at the house my dad built with his bare hands, I tell myself that this isn't over.

I'll be back one day.

It might not be tomorrow, or even next year, but I will be back, and I will take what's mine.

Lauren included.

# CHAPTER ONE



*Present...*

"You can leave now," I bark, sitting on the edge of my bed with my head in my hands. I wonder once again why I thought this was a good idea. Sex and alcohol have been the only things that help me forget. Even if it's just for an hour, or a night, the reprieve from my memories is worth it.

Only now, ever since receiving that phone call, nothing takes away the images of my old life running through my mind like a fucking movie.

"You know, you really are a fucking arsehole," the redhead says, snatching up her clothes from my bedroom floor and angrily pulling them on.

"I'm aware."

"I'm sure I could make it better, whatever it is," she purrs, sounding like a desperate slut. "I could release all that tension."

"Get. The. Fuck. Out." Normally I wouldn't be able to refuse an offer like that. I've used woman after woman in my attempt to forget, but none of them have even come close to *her*. None of them soothe

the ache or the hole in my heart that's only been getting worse as the years have passed. Everyone around me might buy my act, but it's getting harder and harder to hide the real me.

I left the house that night with nothing but the clothes on my back, my wallet, and my phone. I had no idea where I was going to go or what I was going to do. With the amount of money sitting in my bank account, the world was my oyster. It's such a shame that the only place I wanted to be was the one place I couldn't stay.

I walked away, leaving my heart and soul behind, but I knew I didn't have a choice. The most important thing to me was to protect the two most important people in my life. My happiness was something I could easily trade for theirs.

I walked to the closest train station and got on the first one that arrived at the platform, not giving two fucks as to where it was going. I just knew that I needed to get away. I needed to be as far away as possible by the time she realised I'd gone. I knew that if I was too close then the temptation to reach out to her would be too strong, but I couldn't risk putting her future in jeopardy like that.

My heart was already in pieces. I couldn't cope with seeing what my leaving was going to do to her. I truly believed that they'd be better off without me. It wasn't our time. I just had to hope that one day we'd have more luck.

That hope hung around for maybe a year at best. I found myself a new life and I was only living a lie to believe that we were meant to be. She'd have moved on. She'd be excelling at uni and making strides towards taking over the business that should have been mine. The thought of her moving on with someone else still makes my heart ache. It's been six years. She could be married with a couple of kids by now, but I can't shift the idea that it should be me. I should be the one she makes a future with.

I don't regret anything.

If I had my time again, I'm pretty sure I'd have done everything the same. I fell hard and fast for Lauren, and I wouldn't trade that experience for anything in the world.

"Fucking hell." Pulling on a clean pair of boxers, I go in search of something to help squash the memories. Kristy...Kirsty...Kristal... whatever the hell her name is sure isn't helping, so I go for the next best thing.

Whiskey.

I unscrew the top and launch it across the room. What I really want to do is get my hands on something breakable, like someone's face, so the lid ricocheting off the wall and sideboard doesn't really have the same result.

Falling down on to the sofa, I bring the bottle to my lips and swallow down a couple of shots. I hardly feel the burn. I'm too numb.

I didn't have any expectations for what my life might be, but I've managed to create something close to a home here in this sleepy Devonshire town.

The train I got on that day took me to Exeter. I'd never been there before, but the idea of spending time by the sea held some kind of appeal to me.

I found a shitty bedsit and drowned myself in alcohol as I tried to figure out how I could have fucked everything up quite so royally.

*All I did was fall in love.*

THE NEXT THING I KNOW, there's crashing coming from the kitchen. Dragging my eyelids open, I wince as pain shoots through my head. I try to prop myself up on my elbow, but my head bangs and my stomach churns. Glancing down, I see the empty bottle of whiskey on the floor and groan.

"Morning, pisshead," Liv sings, a little too loudly, and I wince. She marches into the room with a bright smile and two mugs in her hands. "Here. I made it extra strong."

"Thank you," I mutter, sitting up and taking the steaming mug from her.

Her eyes are full of sympathy. Everything I've been trying to bury hits me once again. My chest aches and I fight to keep my breathing steady.

I told her yesterday about the phone call. She's the first person I've confided in about my previous life. In six years, I've managed to keep everything buried so deep that even my best friends have no idea. Both Dec and Liam have asked in their own ways about my past and my family, but I never once opened up. We've lived practically as brothers the past few years, and I know it's hurt them that I've kept so much of myself private. I never intended not to talk about what happened, but every time I even think about saying her name, all those old feelings, the devastation I felt as I walked away, hit me like a fucking hammer and I force it all back inside the box I've shoved it in so that I can attempt to live my life.

"When's the funeral?" Liv asks, dragging me from my living nightmare.

"Next week sometime. My uncle said he'd call back with more details once he has them."

She nods at me, an empathetic expression on her face. "You're going back before that though, right?"

*Isn't that the million-dollar question!*

Uncle Chris is the only person from my past life I've spoken to since the day I left. He's not really my uncle, just my dad's best friend, but he's treated me like a son from as early as I can remember.

When I left, I knew I needed some way of at least making sure both Mum and Lauren were safe. I needed to know that, with me gone, he'd keep his promise and they'd be able to live the lives they deserved, so I got in contact with him. Since Mum remarried, he'd kept his distance, but I knew they still spoke on occasion. He was the only one I trusted. We chatted quite often to begin with, but as time's gone on, we've drifted apart more and more. The moment I saw his name come up on my phone yesterday, a ball of dread sat heavy in my stomach. I knew he wasn't just ringing for a catch-up.

*"Nick died last night."* Those words have been on repeat in my head since the moment they fell from his lips.

My first feeling was one of pure happiness. That motherfucker was no longer breathing the same air as me. The world would be a much better place without a manipulative control freak like him. For the first time in as long as I can remember, my shoulders lifted, and I felt a little lighter.

That was until my next thought hit me like a truck.

*Mum and Lauren.*

My stepdad did a much better job than I gave him credit for of hiding the man he really was, because all these years later, Mum's still married to the wanker and Lauren continues to be in his life. If she had any suspicion that he had something to do with me leaving, I've no doubt she wouldn't have stuck around either.

But they're both still there, playing happy families.

I'm probably the only one who knows just how fucked up that reality is for all of them.

"BJ?"

"Shit, sorry. Uh...I've no idea if I'm going."

I can see the questions that are right on the tip of Liv's tongue, and I silently beg her not to ask them.

Up until earlier this year, my life in this seaside town consisted of my two best friends, one-night stands, and surfing. Then, Dec got himself whipped by his childhood enemy, quickly followed by Liam when he found the woman he'd always been searching for in the cute blonde staring at me with concern filling every one of her features. Of course, I was interested the first time we met her, but it soon became obvious that she only had eyes for one of us. She's too good to be kicked to the curb the moment I'd finish with her, anyway. She deserves her forever with Liam. Since she moved in, we've become close; she can see something in me, I think, something that everyone else either misses, ignores, or isn't brave enough to ask about. She's slowly breaking down the walls I've built up, and I'm terrified of what she's going to find if she manages to bring them all down.

Liv reminds me of the girl who captured my heart. They've got the same nature and a similar sharp wit. I've no doubt that they'd get on like a house on fire if they were to ever meet.

Sadness washes through me. Lauren would love it down here.

"What about your mum?" she asks, pulling me from my thoughts once again. Putting my mug on the coffee table, I drop my head into my hands. "Siblings?" The mention of siblings has me looking up. "What?"

I try to keep my expression neutral, but I can only imagine my heartache is clear in my eyes. "It's..." I can't say any more. It feels like the walls are closing in on me at just considering talking about her.

"It's okay. I was thinking about going for a walk along the beach. You fancy joining me? You can talk if you want...or not. I'm here for whatever you need, Ben." I hate the pain that hits my chest when she calls me that. I couldn't have been more relieved when I met Dec at Exeter uni and he nicknamed me BJ; every time I heard my real name, all I could picture was it falling from Lauren's lips.

"Let me shower, and I'll join you." Grateful to have something else to think about, I jump up from the sofa and attempt to wash away the stench of last night's alcohol.

The hot water does little to ease the tension pulling at every one of my muscles. There's a war raging inside me, and I've no idea which side's going to win.

Do I go back, try to reclaim my place and go to the funeral? Or has too much time passed? Will I only cause more pain by going back? Deep down, I know what I want to do, what I need to do, but it's not just myself that I need to think about.

---

"I LOVE IT HERE," Liv says on a sigh when we stop by some rocks. Sitting herself down on one, she looks out to sea.

She might have sunglasses on, but I know the second her eyes flick to me. I try to ignore her attention, afraid she's going to try asking more questions.

"You said something to me once, and it stuck with me when I was going through all that shit with David and Griff."

"I did?" I ask with a laugh. I usually steer well clear of dishing out any kind of advice. I've already fucked up my own life; I don't need anyone else's on my conscience.

"'*Don't fuck it up. Life's a long time to live with regrets*'. And you're right. I'm not going to pester you about what you're going through. I know you'll talk when you're ready. Just think about those words. What will you regret more: going back or staying?"

"Fucking hell, Liv."

"You're welcome," is all she says before turning back towards the horizon, a small smile of victory playing on her lips.

# CHAPTER TWO

"Ben, it's Chris. The funeral's going to be Thursday at one pm at the crematorium, and the wake is at The Crown. I understand your reluctance to come, but like I said before, I think your mum and Lauren could you use your support right now."

"Motherfucker," I shout, throwing my phone down on my bed and watching it bounce and crash to the floor. I was in the fucking shower when he rang, and now I've got the time and day of that cunt's funeral on my fucking voicemail, taunting me.

I spent the last few days fighting with my need to get in my car and drive to London to be with them. I've picked up my keys to go more than once, but something stops me every time.

They hate me. I know they do. He would have made sure of it. He told me he'd kill me for touching his daughter, and although I may still be breathing, I'm as good as dead to the two women I'd give my life to protect.

MY SOUR MOOD has had everyone keeping their distance from me—I assume at Liv's request. I can see in their eyes that they're worried about me, but they all know that sitting me down and demanding answers is going to get them nowhere.

Since moving here, I've made looking happy a full-time job. I've learnt all the tricks I need to convince everyone around me that my life's one big party. It's so far from the truth that it's not even funny. For whatever reason, Liv sees straight through it and she's starting to point things out to the others. I hate the sympathy in their eyes. Fucking hate it. It's one of the many reasons I've kept my past a secret.

Dec and Liam used to look at me with admiration. I showed the world that I had the perfect life: I had the looks, the brains, the women and enough money to not have to worry about where my next pay check was coming from. I've no idea how I got away without them questioning me for so long, but my time hiding from the truth is running out.

"Jesus, BJ, who died?" Dec asks the second he finds me sitting on the sofa later that evening.

Looking up at his concerned face, I can't help feeling grateful for Liv's discretion. She could quite easily have shared my bad news with everyone, but it seems she's kept my secrets from Dec at least. I'm sure Liam is another story.

"My stepdad," I mutter, pulling my eyes away from him in an attempt to hide the pain I'm sure is filling them.

"Fuck. Shit. I'm sorry, I didn't know. Liam texted to say we were taking you out tonight; I didn't realise—"

"It's fine, Dec. You weren't to know."

Falling down beside me, he's lost in thought and a ball of dread grows in my stomach. *Here come the questions.* "You know, in all the years we've known each other, you've never once mentioned your family. I didn't even know you had a stepdad."

"I know." I hate the guilt that fills me for keeping my best friends at such a distance all these years.

"I just kind of assumed you didn't have any, or that they're not worth knowing."

The silence hangs out between us, but when Dec turns his gaze on me, I find the words just tumbling from my mouth.

"It's a bit of both. My dad died when I was a kid, but my mum married some arsehole who was intent on ruining my life." His eyes widen in surprise, but Liam's footsteps pounding down the stairs prevent him from asking any more questions.

Liam's eyes hold a sympathy that isn't usually there when he looks at me, and I can only assume that Liv has filled him in, hence the impromptu night out. "Are we ready? BJ hasn't had a shag in days. I'm worried it might fall off."

"You're a twat," I mumble, getting up and putting the cans I'd already drained into the kitchen. I can't really say too much; I deserve it after all the stick I've given him over the years.

"Aren't we going to Dec's?" I ask when I spot a taxi idling outside our house.

"We thought we'd be a little more adventurous."

Usually the prospect of a night out with my mates would excite me. They're getting fewer and fewer now that they're both loved up, but for the first time since meeting them, I think I'd rather spend the night at home alone as I continue to argue with myself about what I do.

Every time I've bumped into Liv in the house the last few days, she's tried to convince me to go home. She knows I'm torn, and I think she's hoping that by reiterating what Chris said about Mum and Lauren potentially needing me, it'll make me go. I understand what she's trying to do. She thinks it's for the best. But she doesn't understand the clusterfuck that I'd walk into. I'm pretty sure me turning up while Mum and Lauren try to deal with their grief is the last thing they need.

When the taxi pulls up in front of the strip club, I drag Dec and Liam to every year for my birthday, I almost refuse to go inside. My head's too full of my previous life and *her* to have any desire to be surrounded by naked women. The prospect of possibly seeing Lauren again in only a few days has old cravings that used to consume my entire being returning.

Since getting that first phone call from Chris, every single memory I have of our time together is on fucking repeat in my mind. I see her out on the decking, surrounded by twinkling fairy lights that first night we spent together. I picture her laid out on a picnic blanket with the sun lightening her already fair hair. It's fucking torture. It's been six years; how I can still want her this badly is beyond me. She's just a memory now, but fuck if my body doesn't react as if she's right in front of me once again.

"What's wrong? You want to celebrate that that arsehole's out of your life for good, right?" Liam asks. I've barely scratched the surface with the details of my past life, but Liv's clearly passed on what a cunt my stepdad was. Dec's mouth drops open in surprise. It's really not like Liam to talk ill of anyone. "What?" he asks, his brows drawing together. "Liv said—"

"She was right. I think I described him as a waste of good oxygen. Come on, let's do this," I say with more enthusiasm than I feel. I've become a master at plastering a smile on my face and giving the impression that I'm okay, so I should be able to manage it for a night out. With my two best friends trying to support me the only way they know how, I can't exactly walk away from them.

Dec and Liam lead me to a table right at the front of the stage. It's where I always drag them when I bring them here, but today, it's the last place I want to be. Glancing over my shoulder to the booths in the back corner, I let out a sigh and pull out a chair. I don't want to come across like an ungrateful arsehole, but if I have to spend a few hours here, I'd rather be hiding in the shadows.

A tray of shots magically appears on our table and I waste no time in reaching for one and downing it.

Other than visiting the toilet, my arse stays firmly in the chair while Dec and Liam look at me like I've grown an extra head. It's not like me not to partake in everything offered in a place like this, but I already know it's not going to have the effect I usually crave. Sex and alcohol were my escape until that phone call. Now, nothing seems to quash the ache inside me and my desire for the only woman who's ever had a place in my heart.

I can only put up with the club and the concerned looks on my best friends' faces for so long. I down my drink and excuse myself, making it look like I'm heading to the toilets. Instead, I slip out the exit when both Dec and Liam are preoccupied with the girl up on the stage.

Sucking in a lungful of fresh night air, I feel like a pussy. I never leave a party. Well, *BJ* never leaves a party. I seem to be Ben more and more these days, and I'm not sure how I feel about that. The protective layers I've put around myself are being peeled away faster than I know how to deal with.

I don't bother calling a taxi. Hoping the long, peaceful walk will do me some good, I set off towards home. *Home...*I might love this place, but it won't ever truly be home. Home is where the heart is, and I left that in London a long time ago.

"Whoa, you guys are back early," Liv says, reaching for the remote to pause whatever she's watching when I eventually get back. Looking behind me for her boyfriend, her brows knit together.

"I couldn't stick it."

"This really is getting to you, isn't it?"

Falling down on the sofa, I drop my head back and scrub my palms over my face.

"I don't know what to fucking do," I admit.

She's silent for so long that I don't think she's going to answer. Her stare burns my skin, so after a few more seconds, I drag my head up and look at her.

"I think we both know what you need to do, Ben." Her voice is soft and her eyes hopeful. "As much as I want to demand you stay here because it's where you belong, I think we both know it's a lie. You're just using this place to hide. Whatever really happened is in the past now. He's gone. Whatever happened between the two of you, it's over."

"It's not really about him."

She nods at me to continue, and I try to swallow down the lump in my throat.

"It's my..." I cast my eyes away because, for how supportive Liv is, I have no idea what she'll think to what I have to say next. "My stepsister. We...something happened between us." Blowing out a long breath, I continue to stare at the wall and will the tears that are starting to burn the backs of my eyes away.

Liv's quiet for the longest time. When she does eventually respond, my chest constricts painfully. "You really love her, don't you? Even after all these years."

I open my mouth to respond but no words come. The lump I was trying to get rid of returns as images of Lauren fill my mind.

"Jesus, BJ. You need to see her. You need to..." she trails off. She doesn't know enough about the situation to give advice, and I think she knows that. After casting her eyes away for a second in thought, she turns back to me and tries a different tack. "What's her name?"

"L...Lauren," I whisper. Pain twists my heart at just the sound.

"Pretty. I know you don't have to listen to me, and I don't really know what I'm talking about, but...don't waste any more time. I know you're scared, but what if she still feels as strongly about you as you do her? Don't regret not finding out the truth."

"You need to stop doing this," I complain when her words hit exactly where she intends them to.

"Just think about it, yeah?" she says quickly before there's a crashing at the front door and Dec and Liam both stumble into the room.

# CHAPTER THREE

The sun's streaming through the window when I wake. I'm hot, covered in a sheen of sweat, and I'm hard as fucking steel. It doesn't take much brainpower to know whom I was dreaming about. I woke up multiple times last night with the image of her in my head.

*Damn Liv for making me talk about her.*

Once I've had a very long and cold shower, I make my way down to the kitchen to get coffee. I told Dec I'd be at his surf shack first thing, but seeing as it's almost ten am already, I guess he knows I'm going to be late.

Not needing to get a job has been pretty great. It's meant I've been able to help Dec out when he started his business and with renovating this house when he first bought it, but right now I could really do with a distraction that a career could give me.

When I get to the kitchen, I find Liv sat with a mug in her hands, listening to Liam doing his morning radio show.

"You know you don't have to listen to him every morning, right?"

"Fuck off," she grunts, her cheeks heating with embarrassment from being caught. "How are you feeling?"

Shrugging, I set about filling my mug.

"Did you think about what I said?"

I bite back my initial response because *of course* I fucking thought about what she said. I can't get it—*her*—out of my damn head. I don't get to answer because ringing distracts both of us.

"Are you going to get that?"

Reaching into my pocket, I pull my phone out. I don't need to look at the screen to know who it is. I had two missed calls from Chris after my shower. The fact that he's chosen not to leave voicemails this time has dread knotting my stomach. As much as I might try to ignore what's happening in London, I know that I can't. I also know that Mum and Lauren might not be coping as well as I hope they might be. Just because I'm glad the fucker's dead, it doesn't mean everyone will feel that way.

"Well?" Liv prompts as I stand staring at it like it's about to explode.

Sucking in a breath, I swipe the screen and bring it to my ear.

"Hello."

"I thought you were ignoring me," is the first thing Chris says, but he doesn't allow me any time to respond before diving straight into the reason for his call. "I need you to do something for me."

"What?" The knot tightens and I find myself leaning forward against the counter, waiting for his next words.

"I need you to go to the office and find me a load of paperwork."

All the air rushes from my lungs. "Can't anyone else do it?" Liv's stare burns into my back but I refuse to turn and look at her.

"Your mum and Lauren have enough going on. Neither of them has been to the office since...and I don't want to make them. I don't want either of them hurting more than they need to be right now." The memories that have been haunting me hit me once again. Image after image of Lauren runs through my mind. My heart starts to race and my hands tremble. She's not going to want me there, but fuck if I don't need her.

Clenching the fist of my free hand, I try to get myself together.

"Ben, are you still there?"

"Yeah, yeah. I'm here. What is it you need?"

Lowering the phone from my ear, I rest both my palms on the counter and hang my head, trying to catch my breath. I've always hoped this moment would come. That I'd have to go back. That I'd get a chance to reclaim what's rightfully mine. But now the time's here, I'm more terrified than I ever expected to be.

"You're going," Liv states, the sound of her voice dragging me from my panic. Turning my head, I glance over my shoulder at her. Her eyes drill into me, her lips pressed into a hard line. "Whatever it is, the reason you're so scared, you need to get over yourself and be there for Lauren and your mum."

"It's been six years. Six long fucking years since *he* sent me away.

"Fuck, Ben." I wince at her use of my real name, and she doesn't miss it.

"I've had no contact with Mum or Lauren since that day. For all they know, I could be dead. I've no idea what'll happen when I show my face."

She nods as she thinks. "You know you don't have a choice, right? Do you want me to go with you?"

"Thank you, but if I'm doing this, I should do it alone."

Getting up, she walks over and throws her arms around my waist. Dropping my head, I press a kiss to her hair and allow her warmth to ground me.

"You've got this. Your mum needs you right now."

"And what about Lauren?"

Liv blows out a breath. "If she loved you back then, then I'm sure she'll love you even more now. Give yourself some credit—you're a pretty good catch."

A lump forms in my throat and I have to fight the tears that sting my eyes. "Is that right?" I love her positivity, but I have a feeling none of what's to come is going to be that easy.

"Now, stop standing here wasting time with me. Go and get your girl." After unwrapping her arms from me, she gives me a sweet, encouraging smile and pushes me in the direction of the stairs.

I know I should be packing something, but the second I'm in my room, I just stand there. After years of locking everything down, fear of going back floods me. I can't deny there isn't a little excitement mixed in though. I'm desperate to know if they're both okay, to just see them again and take in how much—or how little—has changed over the years.

Instead of reaching for a bag, I pull open the drawer beside my bed and dig out my old phone. I took the SIM out the second I got on the train when I walked away that day. I believed every word of Nick's threats, so I didn't want to be traced. It's why I left my car behind. I could never bring myself to get rid of the phone, though— not when it was full of photos of our short time together.

I'm amazed when it turns on. It's been quite a while since I caved to my need to see her face. I get the usual warning about not being able to connect to a network before I pull up the photos. My heart aches the second I look into her blue eyes. She looks so young and carefree, exactly how she should at eighteen. She only had the slightest inkling of what was going on around her, how much her dad was controlling every single part of her life. I knew she wanted to live in that house almost as much as I did, but also like me, she didn't have a choice. Only it was for a very different reason. I refused to move out because I needed to ensure Mum was safe. She didn't have a choice because her dad was an abusive, controlling wanker.

Eventually, I get my arse in gear and I pack a duffle full of clothes. My entire body vibrates with nervous energy as I leave my room and make my way down the stairs. I've already had my life shattered once, but for some reason I feel like this is the beginning of me having to start over once again. Just this time, it could well be in the place I wanted to be the whole time.

"Call me if you need anything," Liv calls from the front door just as I'm about to climb into my car.

"Thank you." I really mean it. I'm not sure what I'd have done this last few days without her.

---

I HOPED the journey would give me the time to figure out what I was going to do once I got to London, but as I sit in my car in the street where the Johnson & Son's office is, I'm no closer to knowing.

I've no idea why Chris thought I should do this. I've no idea if I even know anyone who still works here. They might all think I'm some stranger trying to rob the place when I walk inside and start rummaging through Nick's office.

Erica was probably my closest friend in the years before leaving, but if she's still here, she'll probably hate me just as much as Mum and Lauren for walking away like I did. I'd rather not be on the wrong end of her fiery temper.

Reading through the message Chris sent me earlier that lists everything he needs to get Nick's estate in order, I blow out a steadying breath. I'm not stupid; he could have asked any one of the Johnson & Son's employees to find this shit, but he knows me too well. He knew it would be the push I needed to get my arse up here.

It's now or never.

Throwing the door open, I step out and get my first taste of fresh air since I left Devon hours ago.

As I walk towards the building's entrance, it's like I'm twenty again. I'm suddenly struck with the memory of the night I surprised Lauren when her dad demanded she work late.

I'd had plenty of indecent thoughts about bending her over her dad's desk and fucking the life out of her, but fuck, the real thing was so much more than I ever could have imagined.

That desk should have been mine. It had my name etched into it from the day I was born, but that motherfucker appeared in my life and trampled over everything that was meant to be. If I didn't know that my dad had died of natural causes, I'd truly believe he'd had something to do with it just so he could step into his life and fill his shoes. Not that he'd ever been able to. Dad was a shrewd businessman; he loved this company almost as much as he loved Mum and me. Nick, on the other hand, was nothing but an untrustworthy scumbag. I didn't have the time to figure out what he was doing, but there were definitely dodgy dealings going on.

The hallways are empty and my footsteps echo as I walk along the tiled floor to the office entrance. I try to focus on what I need to do and push the lingering memories from my mind.

My plan is simple: go in, get what I need, and get out. I don't want to cause any drama. Ideally, I'd like to not even be noticed, but I know that's wishful thinking.

Standing in front of the office door, I clench and unclench my fists in an attempt to ease the tension in my body.

I push the door open, look ahead, and march into a space I know like the back of my hand. I basically grew up in this office. From as early as I can remember, I used to come to work with dad. I'd help him with his photocopying, shredding, and licking envelopes when I was a kid. I remember the hours I would spend listening to him and Mum talk about the goings on in the office and I'd soak it all up like a sponge, knowing that one day it was going to be mine. As the years went on, he showed me more and more, and by the time he died when I was fourteen, I already had a pretty good understanding of how the business worked. Knowing that in a few years I'd be able to keep his and my granddad's legacy alive by taking over helped get me through losing both of them in quick succession.

Then *he* swooped in and saved the day.

Or so Mum thought.

She looked at him like he was her knight in shining armour. As far as she could see, he dragged her from the dark pit of grief and depression she'd fallen into, and he'd rescued the business that was on the verge of collapse when she couldn't deal with it alone.

I saw through his façade. None of his actions were to help Mum or me; they were for his own benefit, his own gain. He was one selfish motherfucker.

I was just a kid. There wasn't all that much I could do about the tornado that was my stepdad, but Nick wasn't aware that the company basically ran through my veins. He didn't know that I was watching his every move and noting every questionable decision he made from a distance. I had every intention of bringing him down.

I just didn't get the chance.

As glad as I might be that he's gone, a little disappointment that I didn't get to expose his true colours makes my steps falter. I stumble on the threshold of the office and I immediately feel eyes on me.

When I look up, I find every member of staff staring in my direction with their chins dropped and their eyes so wide that some look on the verge of popping out...none more so than Erica.

# CHAPTER FOUR

Erica's eyes bore into mine and her features stiffen with anger. Her hurt at my sudden departure all those years ago is clear in her eyes. All my fears about what everyone must think of me come rushing to the forefront. It's not until someone moves at the back of the office that I manage to rip my gaze away from her, but the moment I look over, I find the one person I wasn't expecting. Staring back at me with furious, red-rimmed eyes is Lauren.

My breath catches and my heart twists painfully in my chest as I take in her exhausted face. Every part of me aches to move, to get close to her, to touch her, but even from here I can tell it's the last thing she wants.

"Lauren," I breathe, but there's no way she hears my whisper with the distance between us.

I stand, frozen to the spot, as she drags her bag across the desk. All the paperwork flutters to the floor followed by a loud bang as something more significant falls victim to her hasty escape.

"Lauren," I repeat, managing to find my voice this time.

"Don't." A tiny pair of hands slamming down on my chest makes me look down to the person in front of me. "Don't. You. Fucking. Dare," Erica seethes. She might only be small, but my chest stings by the time she's finished. "You've already done enough damage. You don't get to show up unannounced and throw her world into even more turmoil. She deserves more than that—*more than you*." Erica's lip curls in disgust. It's my first taste of the kind of mess I left behind when I was forced to leave.

Every set of eyes in the office is still on us. As I glance at each of them, there are a couple I recognise but many that I don't. I almost laugh when I see Betty standing with a mug of tea halfway to her lips. Of course she's still here.

I just about manage a little smile in Betty's direction before Erica's fingers wrap around my wrist and I'm pulled towards the office. For such a small person, she's got some serious strength. The door slams behind us and she turns her wrath back towards me.

"Erica," I sigh. "I just came for some paperwork. I don't need—"

"I don't give a fuck what you need, Ben. What the fuck are you doing here? You've had what...six years to show your fucking face. Were you so scared of him that you had to wait until he was dead to come back?"

"Scared?" I can't help but laugh. "You think I was scared of that motherfucker? Jesus, what bullshit did he spew to you lot?"

"The truth, by the looks of it." Her hand lands on her hips and her eyebrows rise almost to her hairline as she waits for my response.

"I haven't got time for this. I don't owe you anything. There are only two women who need to know the truth, and one of them just stormed out."

"Oh, well that's fucking lovely. I was here, picking up the pieces of the mess you left behind you, and you think you don't owe me anything. You're almost as bad as he was." She nods towards Nick's desk and I see red. How fucking dare she compare me to him.

"Fuck you, Erica. You've no idea what happened that day. No idea of the threats he made, of the reason I did what I did."

"Try me. We were friends—best friends, if you don't remember. Hit me with it."

"Not now. I just need—"

"Paperwork. You said." Spinning on the spot to collect her thoughts, she pins me with another harsh look. "This is bullshit, Ben. You think you're the only one with issues? You think you're the only one with secrets no one else will understand? Well, you're wrong. We might not know the whole truth about why you suddenly vanished in the middle of the night, but things haven't been all sweetness and fucking light while you've been away. We haven't all been sat around our fucking campfires singing Kumbay-fucking-a. And for your information, your mum and Lauren weren't the only ones who n-needed y-you." Her voice cracks and her lip trembles.

Guilt stronger than I've ever known engulfs me as I watch her body start to shake with emotion. Closing the distance between us, I realise for the first time that me leaving didn't just affect two women, but potentially everyone around me. I don't think I appreciated what I really had here.

I wrap my arms around her shoulders. She tries to fight to start with, but she soon gives up and allows me to comfort her.

Breathing in her familiar scent, I remember what a good friend she was to me. I'd cast her aside like she meant nothing.

"I'm so sorry. Things back then were...complicated. I did the only thing I could at the time. Nick wasn't..." I trail off, not really wanting to get into this now. "Let me just say that what happened in reality probably wasn't quite how he made it out to be. I didn't leave willingly; I can promise you that."

She nods like she understands and pulls back so she can look at me. "Trust me, I know how he operated better than most. I don't think you'll shock me with anything you tell me, but you should have fought for her. You should have done whatever it took, not just run at the first sign of trouble."

My heart twists and my stomach turns over as I watch her walk out of the office. Resting back on the edge of the desk behind me, I take a few steadying breaths.

I've told myself that same thing time and time again, but nothing will change what happened. At the time, leaving seemed like the best thing for Lauren. I wasn't going to do anything that might make her life worse, and I had no intention of being the one to ruin her relationship with her dad. She wasn't stupid; she knew he wasn't going to win Dad of the Year or anything, but if she knew the truth... I lost my dad way too early, and I'll be fucked if I'm the reason someone else loses theirs. Even if he was a monster.

Despite his arsehole ways, Nick loved Lauren the best way he knew how. If he wasn't such a wanker, I might have been jealous.

But maybe I was wrong. Maybe I should have stood my ground and fought for her. If I'm honest with myself, I knew some of the crap Nick spewed was true. I wasn't good enough for her. I was the bad boy and she was the princess. It never would have ended well. I was her dirty secret. She may have told me that she didn't want to keep what was between us hidden, but it was easy to say that when the outside world didn't know what was going on.

The murmuring of voices from outside the office eventually filters through and I'm reminded of why I'm here. Pushing myself from the desk, I set about rummaging through the filing cabinets until I find what I need.

Just like the moment I first walked in, when I open the door and look out over the office beyond, everyone stops what they're doing and looks up at me. A number of eyes narrow in anger; others just look confused. It's good to know my memory wasn't banished quite as quickly as I was.

Erica appears from the kitchen just as I take a step towards the exit. I've no interest in hanging around here and answering all their bullshit questions. There are only two people who deserve answers, and they're my next stop.

"Ben, wait," she calls, but I don't stop moving.

She runs to catch up with me, but I'm already in the hallway by then.

"Look," she says, placing her hand on my arm and attempting to spin me her way. "I'm sorry, okay?" Those words have me looking back at her. "You've no idea what it was like here after you left, and you turning up like that was just a bit of a shock."

"None of that was by choice, Erica. I had no intention of leaving."

"I...I know. Well, I don't know, but I can only imagine how things went down."

The depth of understanding I see reflected back at me both surprises and scares me in equal measures. But then, I guess she's worked closely with Nick for years. She must have some clue as to what a manipulative bastard he was.

I open my mouth to say something, but I don't get a chance.

"You don't have to explain right now. You've got more important things to deal with. Lauren's waited long enough to find out the truth, don't you think?"

Nodding, I give her a sad smile and walk away.

"We'll catch up soon, yeah? If you need anything, you know where I am." I give her a quick nod, but I'm too intent on getting out of there to respond.

Dumping the folder full of paperwork on my passenger seat, I rest my head back against the headrest. I don't really know how I was expecting that to go, but it certainly wasn't what happened. The image of Lauren's sad eyes and exhausted face fills my mind once again, and my fists clench. Even after death, that motherfucker manages to hurt her.

Erica's right. It's time she learnt the truth. Turning on the ignition, I start a journey that I've made a million times before, except so much is different now. The corner shop I used to buy lunch from is now a hairdresser's, there's a new supermarket, and as I get closer to home, I find that they've managed to somehow shoehorn in a load more houses.

I park in a space a little down the street when I see the main gates to the house are closed.

As a kid, this place was my haven. I loved being here as much as Mum and Dad did and knowing my dad and grandad both designed and built it meant it was even more special. No other kids at school had homes like that. I always hoped it would be mine one day to bring my own family up in, but as I walk up to the front door, none of those old feelings are there. Everything I loved about this place has been tainted by *him*.

After ringing the bell a few times and getting no response, I make my way around the rear of the house. I can't believe my luck when I get to the French doors. This house must be worth well over two million by now, yet no one's bothered to fix the dodgy back door. Exactly like when I was a teenager, if I twist the handle just right, the door slides open. It allowed me to sneak in and out hours past curfew many times over the years.

Mum and Dad were never really that strict. They didn't have to be; I was a good kid. But after Dad died and Mum moved Nick in, things changed. I was a teenager hell bent on ruining my life, and he was a dickhead who couldn't deal with an unruly teenage boy. I had to be in by ten at the latest every night, or he would lock the house down. Mum caught me sneaking in loads of times. She was well aware of the broken door, but it was never fixed.

Sadness runs through me. That could be the exact reason it's still not been fixed. She's holding out hope that one day I might just sneak back in. It was like she was giving me permission to do what I needed to do. She was drowning in grief after my father's death, but she couldn't have been blind enough not to see how Nick came in and basically took over our lives.

The second I step inside, the familiar scent of home fills my nose. Nostalgia hits me so strong that I stumble back against the door. Images of happy times with my parents, my grandparents, and Lauren play out like a movie in my mind. Innocent memories like childhood birthdays, family meals and Christmases; along with ones that have my temperature soaring like taking Lauren on the island after our failed attempt at cake making.

Walking over to the table, I fall down onto a chair and drop my head into my hands. In one sense, that weekend with her still feels like it was yesterday; but being back here now it feels like a lifetime ago. I can still vividly remember how she tasted mixed with icing sugar and cocoa powder.

My cock twitches as I relive that morning with her. Six years on and just the memory of her alone still affects me like she did back then.

Although there were three cars parked in the driveway, the house is in silence. After it being a loving family home filled with laughter for years, the silence and coldness became normal pretty quickly once Nick moved in. I guess nothing's changed. The place still looks like a show home.

After getting myself a glass of water, I sit back down at the table and pull my phone from my pocket. I find a message from Liv and a smile twitches the corners of my lips.

**Liv: Good luck. Call if you need anything x**

I just start to type a reply when the slam of the front door echoes around the empty house.

A lump jumps into my throat and, as footsteps get closer, my stomach threatens to bring up the water I just drank.

Sucking in a breath, I wait for someone to walk around the corner and into the kitchen to find me.

"Oh my god!" Mum squeals, at first in fright, but the second she registers it's me, her face softens and her knees buckle.

I'm out of my seat and about to reach for her when someone else steps into the room and beats me to it.

A pair of very cold and angry eyes find mine. My mouth goes dry.

Lauren supports Mum until she's found her strength again.

Rushing forward, her petite body slams into mine and she wraps her arms around my waist so tight it's hard to breathe.

"Oh my god, my baby," she sobs into my chest.

Tentatively, I lift my hands and rub them up and down her back as she cries. The whole time, my eyes hold Lauren's. Everything I feared is looking back at me. She hates me. Any hope I might have had that she'd be glad to see me is gone. I've never seen her look so furious, and I've no doubt she's not going to hold back once she gets the chance.

"Lauren," I breathe, desperate to connect with her somehow.

Narrowing her eyes at me once more, she drops them to Mum, who's still attached to me, and then turns and leaves.

The breath I didn't realise I was holding comes rushing out of me. My eyes sting and I struggle to catch my breath again as regret, guilt, hope and love assault me all at once.

I'm frozen to the spot, staring at where she was. It's only movement against my chest that drags me from my living nightmare.

Mum looks up at me through teary, devastated eyes, and a giant lump forms in my throat. Seeing the evidence of what my leaving did to her breaks my heart. I did what I did for them, but looking at her now, I fear I may have made the wrong decision.

# CHAPTER FIVE

"I'm sorry about your t-shirt," Mum says sadly when she pulls away from me and finds the fabric soaked through.

"It's nothing," I mumble, not really knowing what to say. It might have been obvious that she was happy to see me to begin with, but now I can't read her.

Placing her palms on my rough cheeks, she stares deep into my eyes before focusing on every single one of my features.

"There were days I convinced myself that you must have been dead." Hearing her admission makes my insides ache with regret. "I didn't understand any other reason why you'd just disappear like that. This was your home, Ben. You had people who loved you under this roof and you just upped and left in the middle of the night."

"It was complicated, Mum." My voice is deep and rough as I try to contain the emotions running rampant around my body.

She stares at me for a few more minutes before schooling her features and stepping away.

"I don't see how," she snaps. Her eyes darken and suddenly I'm a six-year-old boy who's been caught doing something he shouldn't be. "That girl was head over heels for you, and you disregarded her like she was a piece of shit on your shoe." Her anger seems to come from nowhere, the grieving widow from moments ago long gone.

"You think I did that by choice?" I bellow back. "You really believe this is all my fault? I'm your son. I thought you knew me better than that."

Her face drops. I hate to cause her more pain, but the little faith that she has in me hurts more.

"Did *he* really have you that convinced by his act that you truly think that of me?"

She sucks in a breath, tears filling her eyes. "Have some respect."

"Respect?" I ask with a laugh. "He doesn't deserve it. The man was a scumbag, Mum, and it's about time you acknowledged the truth."

The moment she slides down the wall she's backed up against and breaks down in sobs, I know I've gone too far. She's right. He's just died; I need to be a little more sensitive for her sake. She's already dealing with enough. I didn't come here with the intention of making things harder.

Getting down on my haunches in front of her, I pull her hands away from her face and look at her. I'm reminded of the fact that no matter how much of a monster I knew my stepdad to be, he managed to control everyone else around him to the point that they'd never question him. It never worked on me. It's one of the reasons we were never going to see eye to eye.

"I'm going to have a lie down," Mum whispers, casting her eyes over my shoulder.

Helping her stand, she leans on me enough to show she's not going to make it up the stairs alone. With my arm around her waist, I silently lead her towards the stairs and up to her room.

Her breath catches as we come to a stop beside the bed and her eyes land on two photographs. One of them I haven't seen for a very, very long time.

Sitting on her bedside table is not only a photograph from her and Nick's wedding day, but also one from the day she married my dad.

Dropping down onto the edge of the mattress, she stares at both of them, tears silently dropping from her eyes.

"I don't know what I did wrong. I lost the only three men I've ever loved." It's so quiet, I almost miss it, but knowing I'm one of those three is like a knife to the heart.

"You didn't do anything wrong. I'm not going anywhere, okay?"

She nods, but I don't think she believes a word of it. And why would she?

I leave the room with a heavy heart. She doesn't deserve any of this. It was bad enough she lost her first husband, the love of her life; she shouldn't have to lose another.

Closing the door quietly, I go to head back downstairs, but at the last minute, I continue forward towards *my side* of the house, as it was always known, with two en suite bedrooms. Coming to a stop at my closed bedroom door, I wonder what the inside's going to be like. Did they bin all my stuff? Did they throw me away like I never existed?

I'm just about to open the door to find out when a noise from behind stops me. The closer I get to her bedroom door, the louder the sobs become.

Running my hands over my now shaved hair, I fight with what I should do. Every inch of my body is screaming to go in and comfort her, but my head knows she won't accept it.

I don't deserve for her to accept it.

After a few seconds, I back away. If there's ever going to be any kind of relationship between us again, I need to allow her to come to me. I've already caused enough pain to last her a lifetime.

Walking back up to my door, I push it open and step inside. What I find shocks the hell out of me.

I was expecting it to be empty or maybe turned into another bland guest bedroom. What I wasn't expecting was to find it exactly the way I left it.

"Fucking hell," I mutter, walking farther into the room and taking in everything I left behind.

It's exactly as I remember. There are still piles of CDs next to the player, as if I'm about to return to play them. The TV remote is sitting on my bedside table where it always was, and my charger is next to it, waiting for my phone. There's even one of my hoodies draped over the chair by the window.

Sitting down on the edge of the bed, I fight to drag in a couple of deep breaths. I expected Nick to have skipped all my stuff the first chance he got.

Seeing my room as it always was has the first tingles of hope trying to nudge their way in. It makes me start to believe that maybe not all that much has changed and that I can fit back into the life I should have here. The place I've always belonged could be my home once again.

Falling back onto my bed, I breathe in the familiar scent. Feelings I hardly remember wash through me. Contentment, safety, true happiness. That's what this house used to be to me, and it can be again. With him gone and no longer controlling everyone's lives, I can finally have what I've always wanted.

I make a plan and stay where I am, enjoying the feeling of my bed beneath me and being surrounded by all my childhood things. That is, until a shiver of awareness runs down my spine.

Propping myself up on my elbows, I look to the door. My heart drops when I don't find who I was expecting—until I see movement of a shadow.

I don't waste any time. Jumping from the bed, I rush to the doorway. I'm desperate for time alone with her.

When I pull the door wide, her eyes fly up to mine in shock. Her mouth drops open, but I beat her to it.

"Lauren," I breathe. I love being able to say her name once again.

Her tired and bloodshot eyes hold mine. I can see fire burning behind them. She probably hopes her anger will scare me off.

Her face softens the longer we stare at each other, and to my surprise, when I reach for her hand and pull her closer, she follows my lead.

I gasp when her breasts gently press against my chest. My heart hammers as all the feelings that I've spent the last six years burying come rushing back.

"Fuck, I've missed you," I admit, staring deep into her light-blue eyes.

They visibly darken the second the words are out of my mouth.

"Fuck you, Ben. Fuck you!" she hisses, backing away and putting her arms up to keep me from coming after her. She bumps back against the wall at the same time as sobs rack her body. "Y-you d-don't get to d-do this," she stutters out through her tears. "You don't get to just turn back up and act like nothing happened. Like you didn't abandon us. Abandon *me*."

She looks at me, her lids lowered and her eyes full of water. There might only be a few feet between us, but it still feels like miles.

My fingers twitch to reach for her and pull her to me. My muscles ache with the need to comfort her.

As I take a step forward, her eyes flash with concern, but I push past it. The moment her warmth presses against my chest, I feel like I can breathe for the first time in years. My arms wrap tightly around her and I hold her as she cries and trembles against me.

I don't think she's aware as I move us from the hallway and into the privacy of my bedroom.

"I'm sorry," she says after many long, incredible minutes in my arms.

I know she doesn't need me to say anything. I bite down on my tongue to stop myself. I lower my eyes—it's the first time I take in what she's wearing.

"Is that your boyfriend's?"

"What?"

"Your hoodie. Is it your boyfriend's?" I know the moment she remembers because her eyes crinkle at the sides. I'm almost convinced I've got to her, but in a split second, they harden, and she jumps from my lap.

"No, Ben. You have no right to ask me those kinds of questions."

She goes to leave. I should allow her, but I'm a selfish bastard who's missed her more than I'm willing to admit right now.

"Wait. I've ordered dinner. Is Thai still your favourite?"

Stopping in the doorway, she looks over her shoulder. "Is it from Thai Emerald?"

"Of course. I wouldn't get it from anywhere else."

She narrows her eyes at me, she's trying to look angry, but she knows as well as I do that she'll do anything for their Phat Thai.

"This doesn't mean anything."

Following her down towards the kitchen, I stop briefly to tell Mum I've sorted dinner, but she doesn't respond. I'm desperate to do something to help, but aside from being here, I'm not really sure what else to do for her. I can still vividly remember the depression she fell into after Dad died; I can only hope it's not as bad this time.

The second my foot hits the bottom step, the doorbell rings. I answer it and thank the guy while Lauren crashes around in the kitchen. When I get there, the table is laid with plates and glasses.

"What would you like to drink?" she asks politely, but it's far from her usual kind tone.

"Water would be great, thanks."

"We have beer if you'd like one."

I've used alcohol more times than I can count to help me drown out the reality of my life for the past few years. Now I'm back, with the potential to finally make everything right, it's time I stopped using it as a crutch.

"No, thank you. Water's perfect."

She nods, but she still looks at me curiously. "Well, if you don't mind, my life's shit right now," she says, placing my drink down and filling herself a very large glass of wine and taking a sip.

She sighs as she savours the taste and my eyes drop to the smooth lines of her neck as she swallows. My insides clench and my cock twitches as I imagine dropping my lips to that soft skin.

Her glass slams down on the table and drags me from my

fantasies. I watch as she huffs out a frustrated breath before she digs inside the takeout bag for her beloved Phat Thai.

"I'm sorry about your dad, Lauren."

"Are you?" she snaps, her eyes finding mine.

"I'm sorry you've lost a parent. I know how hard that is." I keep any unpleasant words I might want to spew about him to myself. The time will come where I'm going to have to tell her everything, but tonight, I just want us to eat. I want to spend time with her. To just be able to look at her. I want to pretend for an hour or so that things aren't totally fucked up.

"I'm doing okay." Her voice is weak and unconvincing. I can tell by her tired eyes and sad expression that she's anything but okay, but I don't point it out.

We eat in silence, but it's not as awkward as it could be. Just being in her presence brings me a kind of peace I've not experienced in such a long time.

Mum eventually appears, looking worse for wear. She joins us at the table but forgoes the food in favour of the wine. I bite my tongue from chastising her for drinking on an empty stomach. Turning up unannounced following the death of her husband and proceeding to tell her what to do is sure to go down like a lead balloon.

"You two go and relax. I'll clean all this up," I offer, once Lauren and I have finished eating.

Mum immediately gets up, and after thanking me unconvincingly, takes herself and her wine into the living room. Lauren hangs around a little, watching me curiously as I start to tidy up.

"What?"

"N...nothing." Raising my eyebrows, I wait for her to elaborate. "It's just...you're different."

"Different? Is that meant to be a good or bad thing?" My physical changes since the last time she saw me are quite obvious. My annoying teenage floppy hair has been shaved off, and I've spent many, many hours in the gym as I fought to forget and put this place behind me. I'm probably double the size of the boy she remembers.

"That's yet to be determined." Her eyes drop from mine in favour of my body. She bites down on her bottom lip as they take me in. It's clear she's happy with this change at least.

Leaning my hip against the counter, I wait with a smirk playing on my lips while she takes her fill.

She stills the second she realises what's she's doing. When she finds the amusement covering my face, her eyes narrow and her lips press into a thin line. "Don't think about getting any crazy ideas." Stepping up to me, she pokes me in the chest. If it's meant to hurt, she needs to think again.

Wrapping my hand around her delicate one, I pull her against me and put my lips to her ear.

"I'm not getting any ideas, Lauren. I never forgot them."

She gasps and fights to get away from me. I'll allow her to take the space she needs.

For now.

# CHAPTER SIX

I hardly get a wink of sleep. Knowing she's just over the corridor is torture. My constant stream of thoughts wondering if she was in her own bed thinking about me and what we once had kept my dick rock-hard all night. It didn't seem to care how many times I came with thoughts of her in my head. The second I allowed my mind to drift once again, up it popped.

I'd like to think I'd become fairly skilled at keeping thoughts of her at bay, focusing on other aspects of my life and trying to distract myself with other women, but one look at her, and just like six years ago in the kitchen, she's the only thing I can see. The only thing I want.

My eyelids are heavy with exhaustion when I eventually get up the next morning. The house is silent, so even though it's long past what most people would call early, I open the curtains and windows in the hope of brightening the place up a little, then kick-start the coffee machine. It's not the one I remember, so it takes me a few minutes to figure out how it works, but soon the scent of the beans fills the room and I already start to feel a little more alert.

With my steaming mug in hand, I slide open the doors that cover the entire back wall of the house and step out into the morning sun. It's not quite the fresh sea air that I've become used to, but it's not city smog either.

Falling down onto the swing seat, I rest my head back and try to enjoy the peace and quiet. It doesn't work; my mind still runs at a mile a minute with images of Lauren. I'm desperate to take her pain away, to make all of this better for her. But I know that's not possible.

Holding her to me last night felt so incredible, but I'm not stupid enough to think she's going to allow that to happen again anytime soon. She's had years to build up her walls when it comes to me, and I'm going to have one hell of a fight on my hands to knock them down.

She thinks I betrayed the one promise I made to her by leaving. I told her I'd always protect her, and that was exactly what I was doing. Protecting her from the knowledge of who her dad really was. Protecting their relationship. That was the most important thing to me at the time.

"Why are you here, Ben?" The sound of her soft, sweet voice has my heart pounding and picks my head up from where it was resting. I didn't hear her join me, but when I look over, she's stood in the doorway staring down the garden.

I allow myself a moment to take her in. Her blonde hair is in a mess and piled on top of her head. Her face is fresh and clear of make-up, although when she turns I know I'll see pain and sadness in her eyes. She's wearing that damn man's hoodie she had on last night and what I assume is a tiny pair of pyjama shorts just poking out the bottom, leaving her mile-long, tanned legs on full display.

Shifting to a slightly more comfortable position, I clear my throat and try to remember what her question was.

She must get bored of waiting, because after a few seconds, she turns her stare on me, her hands coming up to rest on her hips. Her attempt at attitude makes me want to laugh, but the hardness of her features stops me.

Widening her eyes, she continues to impatiently wait while I battle with what to say.

None of my answers are going to go down very well.

"I..."

"You were brave enough to show your face now Dad's gone?"

I open my mouth to argue, but in a way what she's saying is correct.

"No, Lauren. It's more complicated than that."

"Is it? Because the way I see it..." She walks closer, but her angry eyes never leave me. "You got scared, you ran, and you continued running until you no longer had to. The risk of coming home has gone, and you are free to do whatever your selfish, pig-headed self wanted to do. You should just do us all a favour and crawl back to wherever it was you ran to."

When she runs out of steam, she's right in front of me, staring hate-filled daggers down at me.

Slowly standing, my eyes run up the front of her until I find hers. They're dark and angry, but I also see more in them. Our bodies are only a breath apart, and her heat seeps into me. I clench my fists to stop me reaching out and pulling her to me.

Her breath tickles over my face as her chest heaves with anger.

"Nothing's changed, has it?" I ask, searching her face and dropping my eyes to her full lips.

"Y-yes. Everything's changed. Everything has changed." Slamming her palms against my chest, I fall back onto the chair as she spins and storms away.

My lips twitch up into a smile. I've gotten to her. She might think her act is fooling me, but I see her. I can see underneath the façade she's trying to show the world.

---

"SON, it's so good to see you," Uncle Chris says, pulling his front door open later that day.

"You too," I grunt when I find myself dragged into a brief man hug.

"Thank you," he says taking the folder from my hands. "Did you manage to get everything?"

"I think so. All the bank details should be in there. I can always go back if need be. Is everything...as it should be?"

Chris knows I had concerns about Nick's business decisions, but like me, he never found any evidence of any wrongdoing. As our family solicitor for as long as I can remember, Chris has always known the ins and outs of the business, and he's always been in the best position to know if there was anything questionable happening. The fact that he never found anything makes me doubt myself.

"So far so good. We're yet to get the will, but I'm assuming your mum is to get everything. But someone's going to need to take over, and soon." He pins me with a look, and I don't need to ask what he means by that statement.

I always thought the business was my future; but standing here now with it once again in reach, I'm not sure it's what I really want. As much as I've wanted to be back here, I can't deny I'm missing my new life just a little bit.

"How are your mum and Lauren doing?" he asks, changing the subject when I keep my lips sealed.

"Mum's...lost." She didn't show her face this morning. The only reason I knew she was still in her room was the sounds of her cries as I got ready to come here. I knocked, tried to convince her to come down for food, but she ignored me. "And Lauren's...angry."

"You sound surprised."

"Not really. I expected it."

"You need to tell her the truth, you know."

"I will. I just want her to get the funeral done first. I think it's important that she says goodbye to him as she knew him."

"You've got a wise head on those shoulders, boy. Your dad would be proud of you."

The mention of my dad, as always, has a lump climbing up my throat.

Chris looks over when I don't respond, his face full of sympathy. "You know the only person he'd want to take over now is you, don't you?"

Nodding, I sip at the coffee he placed in front of me.

*Am I ready for this?*

"Are you planning on attending the funeral?"

Looking up over the rim of the mug, I consider his question. I've no intention of going to celebrate that arsehole's life, but it's not about me.

"I think you should, Ben," Chris says, interrupting my thoughts. "Your mum needs all the support she can get right now. God knows it's the only reason I'm going." Seeing the determination on his face warms my heart. I've always felt a little comfort in the fact that Mum had Chris here looking out for her; but seeing how important she is to him confirms that I was right in reaching out to him when I left. Chris was Dad's old school friend, but he and Mum have always been quite close. When they both lost their other halves too early in their lives, it only cemented their friendship.

I stay with Chris until I know the office will be empty, then I head straight there. I've always felt close to Dad in the place he spent so much time, building the business, creating his empire, and I need that kind of comfort right now.

I upheaved my life six years ago. Totally started over. Do I want to do that again? The little voice in my head screams that I'm not starting over—I'm coming home. The hesitation I feel about the whole thing doesn't seem to agree with that though.

I spend hours on the phone to the IT support desk as I attempt to log onto the system and see what kind of state everything's in. I have full confidence in the office staff—the ones I know, anyway. It's the late boss who has me desperate to dig around in the background of the business.

I eventually manage to get access, and by the time I look up from emails, quotes, and invoices, it's already dark out.

---

IT'S WELL gone midnight when I pull up outside Mum's house, so I'm not surprised to find it in darkness. It feels weird not driving my old BMW, but I'm guessing that's long gone after my disappearance. It's certainly not sitting here, waiting for my return.

Flashing from the living room catches my attention the second I open the front door. When I get to the doorway, I find the telly playing to itself and Lauren fast asleep on the sofa.

Switching it off, I crouch down in front of her. "Lauren, you need to go to bed," I whisper.

Her eyelashes flicker, but she's doesn't show any other sign of waking. Reaching forward, I place my hand on her shoulder. She's freezing.

Without thinking, I slide my arms under her body and pull her up against me. She immediately nuzzles into the warmth of my shoulder.

I don't move for a few seconds as I allow myself to enjoy the moment. Dropping my nose to her hair, I breathe her in. My heart races at just being able to hold her again.

"Ben," she whispers. My entire body aches with my need for her.

My arms start to burn by the time I get us up to her room. Kicking the door open, it immediately hits me that although my room was like a time warp when I walked in, hers is very different. Gone are all the girly things she used to try to make the place look like home when she first moved in, and in their place are generic ornaments and fake flowers. It almost looks like a guest bedroom, and it saddens me that part of our past has vanished.

Regretfully, I lower her to her bed. I'm desperate to crawl onto it with her, but I can't imagine that would go down too well when she wakes.

I'm just standing up when her eyes flutter open. The pain she's in makes the light-blue I'm used to so much darker.

"Ben?" My name is a whisper on her lips like she doesn't believe I'm really here. Tingles shoot up my arm when her fingers brush against mine. "Please."

Looking back at her open bedroom door, I hesitate. I want more than anything to crawl into bed with her, but I'm fairly positive that she'll regret it.

"Lauren...I..."

"Just lie with me. I don't want to be alone right now." The hollowness of her voice has my body moving before I've even thought about it. Not that I would ever deny her what she needs.

Toeing my shoes off, I pull my hoodie over my head and drop it to her floor, waiting for her to change her mind. When she doesn't say any more, I climb onto the bed and lie down beside her.

We're not touching, but the heat from her body burns into mine. Fisting the sheet beneath me, I fight not to roll over, not to touch her.

Tension crackles between us. The only sound surrounding us is our heavy breathing. It's the only clue I have that she's as affected by our closeness as I am.

I suck in a sharp breath and my muscles tense when she moves, her arm sliding across my stomach and wrapping around my body. She presses herself against me and holds tight.

"Make it stop. Please, just make it all stop."

"I'm so sorry, baby." She stills the second the last word falls from my lips, and I worry she's going to pull away. But after a moment or two, she relaxes again, and I wrap my arms around her. Silent sobs shake her body, her tears soaking my shirt.

I wish I could take it all away. I remember all too well the pain of losing my dad. Sadly, the only way I know how to make her forget is something she'll probably regret in the morning.

I must eventually fall asleep, because when I pull my eyes open the next morning, I'm alone in Lauren's room. Sitting up, I look around, hoping she'll still be here. I almost smile when the handle of the door on her en suite moves—that is, until I get a look at her. She looks incredible wrapped in a fitted black dress, and her new womanly curves make my mouth water, but the moment I get to her eyes, all my thoughts are forgotten.

"Fuck, Lauren." I rush to get off the bed and she bursts into tears.

"No," she demands the second I'm in front of her. I'm desperate to comfort her, to give her anything to make her feel just that little bit better, but she wraps her arms around herself and turns her face away, cutting me off. "You need to leave. Last night was…"

"Don't do this," I all but beg, reaching up to cup her cheek.

"No, Ben. It was a mistake. All of this is a mistake. You need to leave." She doesn't look at me as she pushes me towards her bedroom door. "Get out. Please, just get out."

The second I step foot in the hallway, her bedroom door slams behind me.

Her cries sound out around me as she falls back against the door. It breaks my heart that she won't allow me to support her through this, although I guess it's no less than I deserve.

Falling down onto the edge of my bed, I try to decide what to do. I really have no desire to go and listen to what an incredible man my stepdad was. How he was a doting husband and father and all the other bullshit I'm sure people will spew. He was nothing but a controlling arsehole, but I guess that's not really the kind of thing you can say at someone's funeral.

I know Chris was probably right yesterday when he said we need to be there for Mum and Lauren, but I'm not really sure what good I'll do.

In the end, it's the thought of the two of them dealing with this alone that has me rummaging through the small bag I brought with me for something suitable to wear to this damn thing.

# CHAPTER SEVEN

Everyone's already in the crematorium when I arrive, so it's easy to slip in at the back unnoticed. The room's packed; I can't help but wonder who everyone is. Other than immediate family, I never knew Nick had any real friends, and I can't imagine any of the women he used to spend time with would show up.

I find Mum, Lauren, and Chris in the front row with a couple of others I recognise, and I spot Erica and some work colleagues a few rows back. Guilt hits me that I haven't found time to see Erica since our first meeting the other day. Hopefully, once today is over, we'll be able to catch up properly and she'll be able to help me shed some light on what might or might not be going on with the business.

Hiding in the shadows, the music starts as a small commotion at the entrance causes people to look around. Moments later, a man walks in. Marching past the rows of seats, he makes a beeline for the front. Looking forward, my heart sinks when I find Lauren looking back at him as if she was waiting with a sad smile on her lips.

I can't take my eyes away from them as he steps up to her, pulls her into his arms and kisses the top of her head. He whispers something to her before resting his lips against her head and comforting her.

*Fuck.* That should be me.

Rubbing my hands over my face, I try to keep my stomach from turning over at the thought of some other guy touching her.

When they eventually part, he pulls her into his side and they take their places in the front row.

I fight the urge to walk out. I didn't want to be here in the first place, but now I've also got to watch as another man comforts the woman who should be mine.

They stay huddled together as he whispers in her ear. My fists clench as my imagination runs wild about what he could be saying.

Her demands that I leave her room this morning suddenly make more sense. I thought she just didn't want me there, but in reality, she spent the night in a bed with a man who's not her boyfriend.

My stomach clenches, and I suck in deep breaths to try to settle it. Thankfully, the vicar stands and starts the ceremony. It might be the last thing I want to listen to, but it's a welcome distraction from the man currently holding Lauren in his arms. I knew coming here was a bad fucking idea.

SENSING that the service is about to come to an end, I slip out of the side door. There's no way I'm giving that motherfucker any more of my time. It's bad enough he got that much—although he's probably up there laughing that I had to watch another man with Lauren the entire time. The image of him holding her while she cried is burned into my mind.

That should have been me.

I should be the one comforting and supporting her. Me. That motherfucker took that away from me the day he made me leave. He allowed an opening for another man to step in and sweep her off her feet.

But instead, I'm in my car, racing towards the one place I know I'll get some solace. Although it'll still be filled with memories of her. I can't seem to go anywhere in this city without reminders of our short time together.

Pulling up into the deserted car park, I turn off the engine and rest my head back. I don't shut my eyes for fear of seeing them again. Instead, I just stare up to the blue, cloudless sky above. It's too good a day for that arsehole. It should be dark and miserable to match his heart.

Fire continues to burn through my veins, and the muscle in my neck pulses with my need to release some tension.

My phone vibrating in my pocket drags me from my depressing thoughts. I intend on ignoring it, but when I see Liv's name looking back at me, I find myself swiping to answer.

"Hey." My voice comes out sounding weak and pathetic even to my own ears.

"Well, that pretty much answers my question about how you're doing." Blowing out a breath, I try to come up with something to say. Thankfully, Liv fills the silence. "It was the funeral this morning, right? Did you go?"

"She's got a boyfriend," is the answer that falls from my lips.

"Oh."

"I should have expected it, but when I found out she was still living at home, I just assumed..."

"I'm so sorry, Ben."

"I should just come back and get on with my life."

"Is that what you really want?" My response is a sigh, but it's all she needs to hear. "No, I didn't think so. As much as I hate to say it, that's your home, Ben. Your mum, the business...Lauren..."

"Lauren's not mine anymore."

"It doesn't mean she won't ever be. Not everything you want in life falls into your lap. Sometimes, you have to put a little work in. It's time to fight for what you want. For what you deserve."

Liv's words stay with me long after she ends the call. I'm once again left wondering if this is where I'm meant to be.

I avoid the wake. I've no patience for shitty small talk about a man I hated. Instead, I stop at a shop, pick up some beer and spend what's left of the day in the bastard's home office, trying to dig my way through the backlog of emails sitting in his Inbox.

When the front door opens, it's with Chris and Lauren attempting to carry my drunk mother into the house.

"She overdid it a little," Chris says, not that her state really needs any explanation.

"I've got her." Taking over from Lauren, I help Chris get her up to bed.

"She's really not handling this well. I'm worried about her," he says, turning to me once we've shut her bedroom door. "I'm so glad you're here to keep an eye on her."

"I'll do whatever I can." I immediately regret the thoughts I had earlier about heading back to Devon. How could I even consider it when Mum's falling apart?

I say goodbye to Chris, agreeing that he'll come back in a few days with paperwork and Nick's will, so everything can be sorted. I bite my tongue to stop myself demanding he gets everything together faster so we can put that dickhead behind us for good.

A little of the fire from earlier flows through me when I find Lauren staring out the sliding doors at the garden. She's still wearing the dress from the funeral and it hugs her curves and arse perfectly. My old desire burns through me, mixing with my anger and jealousy. It's a dangerous combination.

"How are you doing?" I ask, although I immediately feel stupid for it when Lauren turns her dark eyes on me.

They're cold. Her pain hits me. I'd give anything to take it away right now.

"Fucking peachy," she snaps. I watch from the doorway as she wrenches the fridge door open with more strength than I gave her credit for and pulls out a bottle of wine. I flinch when she slams it down on the marble counter and sets about finding a glass. I almost stop her and tell her to sit down, but if she's anything like me, then I know she needs the distraction of doing something right now.

I wait her out. She knows I'm watching her every move, because every few seconds her hard eyes flick over to me. After drinking half a glass, she turns her glare on me. "What?"

"I'm worried about you."

"Well, isn't that fucking good of you?"

"I...I never stopped caring about you."

"I don't care, Ben. All of...*that*...is in the past. You made your choice, and I was forced to deal with it."

Seeing the pain that I caused her staring back at me is too much. "What else is there to drink?"

Not being able to deal with the images of our time together on repeat in my head, I find myself a bottle of Nick's old vintage whiskey and pour myself a generous measure.

"To everything we lost." If she thinks for one second I mean her father, then she's very, very wrong. The only thing I lost in all of this is her.

She raises her glass and then places it to her lips. My own drink burns my throat, but it never distracts me from her. I take in every movement as she sips at the golden liquid and swallows, followed by her tongue sneaking out to lick her bottom lip.

Fire fills my veins and my cock swells. I need to stop the images in my head. Those from the past are mixing with the one from earlier with her in another man's arms. There's only one way I know for that to happen.

Her eyes darken further, but I fear it's with different emotions to those I'm feeling.

"What are you doing?" she asks in panic when I take a step towards her. Her body visibly tenses, anger vibrating off her.

"You lied to me." I run my eyes all over her face for any more signs that I'm right. Her lids lower, her cheeks heat and her lips part with her increased breathing. "All of that," I say, repeating her earlier words, "is far from in the past. This. Me and you. It'll never be in the past, and you know it just as well as I do."

I'm right in front of her, my hands resting on the cold counter at her back as I cage her against it. Her increased breaths mean her chest is heaving and her breasts are a whisper away from brushing against me.

Dropping my head lower, excitement explodes within me as I watch her eyes drop to my lips. But I don't give her what she wants. Instead, I move to her ear. "Nothing's changed. I can still see desire in your eyes. I can still read your body like it belongs to me. Let me take it away. Allow you to forget."

A needy whimper falls from her lips. I go to move back, but her hands fist my shirt, stopping me from going too far.

Her breath caresses my face as she stares into my eyes. I can practically smell her need for me. Moving forward as if I'm going to make the first move, I brush my cheek against hers. She sucks in a breath as my scruff scratches her soft skin. "Be careful what you wish for, baby. You might not be able to handle the man I've become."

A laugh falls from my lips when her tiny fists slam down on my solid chest.

"You arsehole. You think you can just turn up after all these years and that I'm going to fall at your fucking feet. You're fucking delusional." I allow her some space and take a step back. My eyes drop from hers and run over every one of her tempting curves.

"I can fuck you better than he can any day, and you know it." The corner of my lip curls up in a smirk as she growls and flies at me.

I always enjoyed riling her up, but this is different. Our time apart means the tension between us is explosive.

She punches and slaps wherever she can make contact, but it's only a few seconds before I capture her wrists and pin them both behind her back.

Her harsh breaths rush over my face as she stares at me like she wants to kill me.

"You know I'm right, ba—"

Reaching up on her tiptoes, her lips press against mine, cutting off my words. My fingers release her arms and I crush her body against me. Her lips part the moment I run my tongue along them, and I'm hungrily welcomed inside. Her taste explodes in my mouth. It's just as I remember.

Glass smashes at our feet as we collide with the island, sending our drinks crashing to the floor.

There's no style or finesse to our kiss. It's wet, dirty, teeth clashing and lip biting as we reconnect. My hands explore her new curves— they feel incredible. We still line up like we were made for each other. Her nails scratch at any bit of skin she can find as we fumble our way towards the door.

Grabbing onto her arse, I lift her from the floor. Her legs wrap around my waist and I begin walking us towards the stairs.

Ripping my lips from hers when my lungs burn for air, I focus on not falling with her in my arms.

She has other thoughts though, because no sooner have we broken apart than her lips are on my neck. She kisses and licks up to my ear. I lose my footing as she sucks hard on the sensitive skin, and together we tumble onto the stairs.

"Fuck," I grunt, trying to keep my weight off her.

Giggling, her hands run over my head and I'm pulled down to her lips.

Hitching her leg up around my hip, I grind myself against her. She moans into my mouth and arches her back against the stairs in her need for more.

Her hands find the bottom of my t-shirt and, with my help, she pulls it from my body. Her dainty hands run down my back as I hungrily take her lips once again.

Lifting her, I slip my hands around her back and find the zip of her dress. In seconds it's undone and I'm peeling the fabric from her shoulders. My lips skate down her neck and onto her chest.

I slip the lace covering her breast down at the same time she reaches for my waistband. Sucking her nipple into my mouth, I groan as her tiny hand slides into my boxers and she grips my length.

Not able to wait, I push my jeans and boxers down over my arse and pull her knickers aside, exposing exactly what I want.

Rubbing the head of my cock through her folds, she arches once again, trying to find more of what I have to offer.

I don't give her the chance to ask for it. The second I find her entrance, I slide into her heat. Her walls ripple around me and I swallow down the roar that threatens to tear from my lips.

Gripping onto her hips, my fingers dig in, leaving me no doubt that she'll have a nice reminder of this moment in the morning when she looks down.

I thrust up into her, and she cries out in pleasure, the first signs of her orgasm already showing.

Lifting her arse a little, I find the perfect position to get her off, my memory of what she likes front and centre of my mind. She cries out once again before she falls over the edge. The tightness of her muscles squeezing my cock has me falling with her and I release everything I have inside her.

"Bedroom," she breathes without even opening her eyes.

I'm still inside her as we crash against the wall at the top of the stairs and eventually make it to her bedroom door and tumble inside.

Dropping her to her bed, I make quick work of removing the clothing that's still on my body. If she thinks a quick, angry fuck is it for us, then she's got another think coming.

She's still laid out when I step up to her and pull her dress from around her waist. It's quickly followed by her underwear until there's nothing between us. Climbing on top of her, my hands land on her cheeks and I stare into her eyes as I try to convince myself that this is real. Our breaths mingle and our chests heave. Eventually, my need for her has me dropping my lips to hers. I trail my lips down her jaw and drop them to her breasts, continuing what we started on the stairs.

She whimpers above me and chants my name as I suck one and then the other into my mouth.

"Ben. Please," she begs.

Unable to deny her anything, I slide my hand down her body and circle her clit.

"Fucking hell," I mutter, finding her soaked with the evidence of our previous encounter.

She sucks in a breath when my finger teases her entrance. Her entire body trembles with her desperation for release. Hunger and want fills me with my desire to be the one to give her what she needs.

Finding her entrance, I push one and then two fingers inside her while still licking at her breast. Her breathing increases and her moans get louder.

Just before she's about to fall over the edge, I remove all contact.

Climbing down the bed, I force her thighs apart and stare at her.

She props herself up on her elbows and looks down her body at me. The sight alone almost makes the last six years worth it.

I already knew that I never stopped loving her, but in this moment, with my heart pounding in my chest, I'm surer than ever that she's the only one for me.

I open my mouth to say something, but obviously sensing it's going to be something she can't handle, she softly shakes her head.

Trying to put everything I need to say to her to the back of my mind, I focus on the task in hand.

With my hands on her thighs, keeping her legs wide, I lower my head and circle my tongue around her clit.

She moans when I start to add more pressure—I'm desperate to hear the noise she makes when I tip her over the edge.

The fact that we're not alone in the house is far from my mind as I slide two fingers inside her and find the place that will ensure an earth-shattering release.

"Oh god, oh god," she chants as I feel the beginnings of her orgasm.

Upping my efforts, I press my tongue harder against her until her entire body tenses under me.

My name is a cry on her lips as her body shatters into a million pieces. I continue stroking her, ensuring it lasts as long as possible. If she remembers one thing tomorrow about this day, then I want to make damn sure it's this.

Her eyes are dazed and glassy when I climb on top of her. Wasting no time, I shift her up higher and slam my lips down on hers. She moans the second her tongue slides against mine, and I know it's because she can taste herself on me.

With one hand holding the back of her head, the other explores her body. I tease her breast and nipple before finding her pussy once again. She's writhing against my fingers almost immediately.

She's been waiting for this moment for six years, just like I have. There's so much I want to say to her right now, but I keep the words inside, scared that one wrong move might be the end. I'm nowhere near ready to walk away from this, but I know it's going to happen. I just need to make the most of the time I have.

She might be fully on-board with this right now, but I've no doubt she's going to regret it. If I was less of an arsehole, I might stop, but I'm fucking powerless to walk away from this woman.

"I need you." I don't need to hear any more. In one move, I'm lined up at her entrance and gently pressing inside.

"Look at me," I demand, pulling back from her lips. She does as I say, and her eyelids flicker open until I'm staring down into her eyes, into her soul. "Me and you," I whisper as I thrust. "Always."

Everything falls into place the moment I'm inside her once again. This is where I'm meant to be. Where I belong.

"What's wrong?" Looking into her concerned eyes, I realise that I've stopped moving.

I can see that warning on her face once again, so I swallow down my words and resume what I started. I thrust into her, and her back arches from the bed and her eyes close.

Dropping my head to her neck, I set about making her scream once again.

# CHAPTER EIGHT

I roll us over so she's on top. With my hands on her hips, I help her move as she brings us both closer to our releases.

"Lauren," I grunt. I'm so close, but I need her to come first. I need to feel her squeezing my cock tight. "Let me feel you."

She moves her hands from where she was playing with her tits and runs one down her stomach. I watch its descent, desperate to see her bring herself to orgasm.

Her mouth drops open when she finds her clit and I feel the first signs of her impending release.

"That's it. Let go, Lauren." She throws her head back and screams at my demand as she clamps down on me so hard that it forces me into my own release.

I groan as I empty everything I have inside her. Six years of waiting, of imagining I'd get the chance again has a lump growing in my throat and tears stinging my eyes. I feel like a pussy, but I can't help it. I've never felt anything with the other women, and now I'm here, everything is starting to bubble over.

Looking forward, Lauren gazes down at me. Her emotions are

clear as day on her face. Thankfully, it isn't regret that is staring back at me. The sadness over what today held is too strong to allow anything else in.

Running my hands around her back, I encourage her to lie down on my chest.

The second our skin connects her body starts trembling. I've no idea what to do to help, other than just hold her.

We stay locked in our embrace for the longest time. The after-effects of my orgasm have long since faded, but having her naked body pressed up against mine ensures my arousal isn't too far away.

I start to think she's fallen asleep and wonder what I should do for the best when I feel her start to kiss the tattoo on my neck. Her lips move over the ink and goosebumps race across my skin.

"It says regret," I whisper, feeling the need to explain just a small part of the tattoo that wasn't there before.

She sucks in a breath and stills. I panic that I've said the wrong thing, that I've fucked up, but after a second, her fingertip tickles across the ink on my pec.

"You always said you'd get more. They're incredible."

I know the moment she finds it. She stops and every muscle in her body tenses as she sits up and stares down at me.

"Lauren?"

"W-why...why is that there?" She doesn't take her eyes away from the place where her name is inked onto my skin.

"I told you, I never forgot anything about you. Nothing's ever changed for me." Reaching out, I tuck a strand of hair behind her ear, and the gentle touch has her eyes finding mine.

"But—"

Placing my fingers over her lips, I whisper, "Not now. Not tonight."

Rolling her over, I go into her en suite to find a cloth to clean her up with.

My heart jumps into my throat when I return and find her still naked on the bed. Everything I'm desperate to say to her is on the tip of my tongue, but I know she'll never accept it. Not right now, anyway.

Climbing back on to the bed, I encourage her to open her legs and gently clean her up with the warm cloth.

"I didn't use—"

"I'm on the pill," she whispers, regret starting to creep into her tone.

I nod, not really giving a fuck if she wasn't. She's mine, and I'm going to make sure she damn well knows it.

Getting the sense she's about to send me away, I drop the cloth, pull her into my arms and press my lips to hers. I'm not ready to let her go yet.

OUR EXHAUSTION eventually drags us under because, before I know it, I'm opening my eyes to find the room full of sunlight.

Reaching out, I hope to find Lauren sleeping beside me. I need her soft skin pressed up against mine again to remind me that last night wasn't just one incredible dream. Finding the side of the bed next to me empty, my heart drops.

"You need to leave." Déjà vu hits me.

"You need to stop this, Lauren."

"Me?" she asks as if she wasn't a willing participant last night.

"You're the one who keeps inviting me here."

"I don't think I ever—" I raise an eyebrow at her, and she trails off. She knows as well as I do that she wanted it last night. The blush on her cheeks isn't the only evidence.

Throwing the covers off, I shift to the edge of the bed and then stand. Her eyes drop from my face to feast on my body. Hours in the gym as well as surfing means it's a little different to what she was used to. Her chin drops and her tongue licks across her bottom lip.

She can try to pretend all she likes that she's not interested anymore, but her body tells a different story.

After a few seconds, she realises what she's doing. "Jesus, Ben. Put it away." Putting her hand up to cover my junk, she casts her eye to the corner of the room.

"You weren't complaining last night." I take a step towards her and push her outstretched arm away. She takes one back, bumping against the door frame.

She swallows and her features harden. "Last night shouldn't have happened."

"But—"

"No buts, Ben. It shouldn't have happened. Our time together ended the moment you walked out. I'm over it...I've moved on."

Her words are the reminder I need. She's taken, yet she spent the night with me. My teeth grind and my fists clench at the thought of her being with someone else.

The cactus sitting on the sideboard beside her catches my eye and I take a few seconds to look around the room I no longer recognise because it looks like a guest room, not one that someone lives in.

When I find her eyes, she knows I've figured it out.

"No," I shout. "No, Lauren. This is bullshit."

"This *bullshit* is my life."

"Why the hell are you here if you don't live here?"

"To look after your mum. Someone had to do it, seeing as she was convinced her only child was dead."

Lifting my hands to my head, I take a step away and try to collect my thoughts. As true as her statement is, it seriously hurts.

"This isn't how it's meant to be, Lauren."

"You don't need to tell me that. I didn't choose any of this. I was happy. I knew exactly what I wanted and you...you shattered it."

"You think I chose this? You think I walked away without a second thought?"

"Well, didn't you?"

"No, Lauren. I never once chose to walk away from you. The only thing I wanted was you. The only thing I still want is you. I- I—"

"No. You can't do this. It's too late...*it's too late*," she repeats as she side-steps me and storms from the room.

I stare at the closed door she leaves behind her for the longest time. Last night, when she was in my arms, everything felt right again for the first time since I walked away from this house. I knew it wasn't going to last forever, but this right now hurts more than I was expecting it to. How I still feel about her was about to fall from my lips, and she walked away. I guess it's what I deserve, karma or some shit, but fuck if the ache in my chest isn't worse than it's ever been right now.

As much as I want to spend the rest of the day in what was her bed, where so many of my memories are, I collect up my clothes and head towards my own room.

I'm just closing her door when someone in the hallway makes me look up. I find Mum at the top of the stairs, staring at me. I'm grateful I went to the effort of putting my boxers on before leaving the room.

"Do you think that was the best idea?"

The last thing I need right now is having her questioning me and making me feel like a kid again. I haven't had to answer to anyone but myself for years, and I'm not intending to start now.

"Fuck knows, but it's happened now, hasn't it?"

Her chin drops at my harsh tone, and I make my escape. I'm thankful that she looked better than she did yesterday, but selfishly, she isn't my main priority right now.

---

HANGING around the house all day feeling sorry for myself isn't an option.

Once I'm showered and dressed, I make sure Mum's okay and apologise for snapping at her this morning before heading towards the office. There's plenty to do to keep me distracted.

I wasn't really expecting Lauren to be here, but I'm kind of relieved when I see that I'm right. She obviously needs time to get her head together after what happened. I might not feel guilty about us spending the night together, but I'm sure as shit that she does.

The moment I walk in, Erica is up from her chair and heading my way. She has a weird look on her face as she approaches. She shocks the shit out of me when she doesn't stop at a reasonable distance and instead slams into me and throws her arms around my waist.

I return the gesture and carefully guide her into the office, away from prying eyes.

"Erica, are you—"

I don't get to finish my question because she pulls away from me and looks up. "I'm sorry for going off on you like that the other day. It wasn't fair for me to blame everything on you. It's just...I missed you." She whispers the last bit, her cheeks heating with embarrassment.

"Aw, you missed me?" She laughs as I ruffle her hair like a little kid, but a strange tension continues to radiate from her. Falling down into the office chair behind the desk, I watch as she wrings her hands in front of her and shifts from foot to foot. "What's wrong?"

Her eyes find mine and I swallow when I sense the seriousness of whatever she's about to say.

"You slept with Lauren. What were you thinking?" My eyes widen. I was not expecting those words to fall from her lips. "If it was that she'd have one roll around in the sack with you and forget all about what happened, then you'll be bitterly disappointed, Ben."

"I know, it's just...I saw her with *him* yesterday and..."

"And?"

"I just couldn't fucking stand the thought of his hands on what's mine."

"She's not yours. She hasn't been for a long time. You gave that up the minute you walked away. Joe's been there for her when she needed someone the most. He's a good guy."

Guilt finally starts to niggle at me. I've no doubt that he's a good guy. If Lauren thinks he's good enough for her, then he probably is. "Is that meant to make me feel any better?"

"No. I'm just telling you how it is. She's been living with him for a while now. I haven't seen her so happy for a long time."

"This isn't helping."

She shrugs and watches as I power up the computer. "So what's the plan?"

"With Lauren? Fuck knows."

"No, I meant for this place."

"Business as usual, I guess. It shouldn't take me too long to get back into it, especially when I've got seasoned pros around like you, of course." The more I say, the paler Erica's face gets. "Now what?"

"How much do you know about the state of the business?"

"Not much, but there's more staff on the payroll than I ever knew and looking at some of the jobs running and the profit margins, things appear to be good...but I'm sensing that might not be the case?"

Erica looks like she's about to throw up. Dread fills my stomach for what's about to come. "Yeah, that's how it looks."

"Go on..."

She lets out a breath, then looks behind her to make sure the door's shut. "I don't think I need to spell out to you what kind of man Nick was." When I don't respond she lowers her voice and continues. "The business is in real trouble, Ben. There's no money."

"But—"

"I know. I know exactly how it looks, because he made me make it look that way."

The ball of dread explodes and my heart starts to race at the thought of him ruining part of my heritage. "You need to start explaining, Erica."

"He started investing the profits. It was fine to start with, but then a few went wrong. He borrowed some money to keep up with wages, but everything spiralled to the point that he couldn't cover it up anymore. So I questioned him when he started demanding that I fudge the numbers."

"I bet that went down well," I mutter, knowing all too well how much he hated to be questioned, even when he was in the wrong.

"I was in a rough place at the time. He knew it and used it to his advantage." Erica doesn't look at me as she says this and my stomach twists.

"Erica?" She falls down into the chair in front of me and drops her head into her hands. "Erica, what—"

Looking up at me through her fingers, she sucks in a breath. "You know full well what a manipulative cunt he can be."

"What did he do?" Fury starts to seep its way through my body. The vibes I'm getting from her aren't good, and I know that whatever happened is going to make me even more glad the fucker's dead.

"Let's just say he used my weakness at the time against me."

A low growl rumbles up my throat as I stand with my hands on the desk. My fingers grip onto the edge, turning my knuckles white as I try to keep my head together. Just the thought of him manipulating someone else I care about makes me want to do some damage. I pin her with a look that has her sitting up straight in the chair. Tears fill her eyes, but I can tell she's fighting to keep them from falling. Her bottom lip trembles as she continues twisting her hands together.

"I...I can't, Ben."

The sound of the office buzzer rings out as we stare at each other. My imagination is running wild right now. There's not a lot I wouldn't say Nick was capable of. I need her to tell me exactly what it is so I can stop thinking the worst.

"What did he do?" She flinches at my cold tone, and I regret it instantly. I don't want my anger at him to push her away, but I can't help it.

"I...I slept with him."

"You what?" I roar.

"I didn't have a choice." Her voice is quiet and weak. There's so much more to this than she's letting on. Walking around the desk, I pull her from the chair and wrap my arms around her trembling body.

"It's okay," I say softly when she fights to get away. She must realise she's got no chance of overpowering me, because she soon gives up and relaxes into me for a few seconds.

It's only the click of the door opening that has us breaking apart.

"He's just in here," Betty says, gesturing someone inside.

# CHAPTER NINE

My brows draw together as I briefly wonder who'd be looking for me, but I soon get my answer when four people I was not expecting appear from behind Betty. "Holy shit."

The realisation that my worlds are about to collide renders me speechless as I stare at my two best friends and their girls.

"Surprise." Liv comes over to give me a quick hug. "You must be Lauren." She says, pushing me aside when she spots Erica hiding behind me. "It's so good to finally meet you."

"Oh, what? No...no. I'm Erica."

Turning, I can't help but laugh at the look of disgust on Erica's face at the thought of her being Lauren. "No need to look so horrified. You know you'd love it." I give her a wink and she makes a show of pretending to throw up.

"There's not enough money in the world for me to go there, *mate.*"

Dec and Liam stifle a laugh while Liv looks between the two of us. "I think we're going to get on," she says to Erica.

I'm reminded of the similarities between the two women. Both have been my saviours at different points in my life. I'll never be able to repay them for the support they've given me.

"What the hell are you guys doing here?" I eventually manage to ask, once my shock has worn off.

"Liv thought you might need a night out."

"You came all this way for a night out?"

"Yeah, well...we might miss you," Liam says, looking a little awkward.

"It's not same without you crashing around the house. You sounded like you needed some fun on the phone the other day, so I've organised a surprise."

Raising an eyebrow, I wait for Liv to elaborate, but she makes a show of zipping her lips shut. "All I can say is that tomorrow night you're going to love us more than you already do. The only thing we need from you is the name of a club for after."

"No strip club, please."

Both Dec and Liam's eyes widen, reminding me that the guy they've known for the last six years isn't the one standing in front of them. "Shut up, you fucking love it, BJ."

"BJ?" Erica pipes up with a smirk playing at her lips.

Falling down onto the chair behind me, I realise for the first time just how different my two lives are. Bringing them together is going to be weird as fuck.

Dec and Liam's eyes burn into my skin. I can practically feel them trying to work all of this out while the soft whisper of plotting female voices at the other side of the room floats around.

"So, this is the family business then?" Dec asks, looking around the office. "It looks pretty flash for a builder's office."

"That's because it's not just any builder's office." I give them both a brief run-down of what we do...or at least what we did before I disappeared.

"Have you guys got somewhere to stay or..." I trail off. The thought of taking them home and immersing them in my life here makes me feel more on edge than I've experienced in a long time. I try not to think about why that might be, but I know all too well that I'm worried what they'll think about meeting the 'real' me. The act I've put on around them became second nature. I hate that I've lied to them about my past and where I came from, but it felt right at the time.

"No, we thought we'd sort something once we were here."

"Do you...uh...if you want, I'm sure Mum wouldn't mind...uh..."

"We'd love to meet your mum, Ben," Nicole says softly. "Then we can always find a hotel later, right?" She looks to the others, who all nod, and I breathe a sigh of relief.

"I'll meet you out the front," I say, as everyone files out of the office.

"Are you okay?" I bend down slightly so I can look into Erica's downcast eyes.

"I'm a fighter, Ben. I've had no choice."

"That doesn't make any of this okay." Seeing tears starting to swim in her eyes again, I pull her against my chest and squeeze tight. Probably a little too tightly I realise when she starts to complain.

"Go and spend some time with your friends."

"Come with us?"

"No. I've got loads to do here. Someone needs to keep this place from going under." Guilt hits me that it's been left to Erica to take the lead. "No, don't look at me like that. I didn't say it to make you feel bad. You go and do your thing. Me and the business will be here when you're ready." I'm hesitant, but she soon starts attempting to push me towards the door. "We've all got a lot of work on our hands, but we've got a little time. Go."

"Okay, but we'll be talking, Erica. Soon." She tries to cover her fear, but I can see it in her eyes. "Everything will be okay." With a small smile, I leave her in the doorway of the office. I'm not sure either of us believe the words that just came from my mouth.

After joining the others outside, we head for home. Liv insists on coming with me while Dec follows behind on the short drive to the house where I grew up.

I know she's only concerned, but when Liv starts asking about Lauren, I keep my answers as short as possible. She sees through it though.

"What are you hiding?"

Glancing over, I find her staring at me, trying to figure me out. Feeling uncomfortable, I shift in my seat and try to change the subject.

"Dec and Nic were able to get away from the shack then?"

"Stop it. Stop trying to distract me. I just want to help, and I can't do that if you won't talk to me."

I bite my tongue and refrain from telling her that I managed just fine before she turned up and insisted on trying to find out more about me.

"I slept with her. Happy now?"

Liv gasps. "But you said she had a—"

"I know. Trust me, I know. But it...it just happened."

"I told you she didn't hate you," she says with a laugh, trying to lighten the mood.

"No, I'm pretty sure she does. I'm also pretty sure she regrets every second with me last night." I let out a long sigh as I recall her words this morning.

Liv places her hand on my shoulder and squeezes gently. "Everything will be okay."

"How can you be so positive all the time?"

"I just have a feeling. Fucking hell, is this where you live?" Her tone suddenly changes as I pull up to the gates in front of the house I used to call home and they open slowly. "You're rich?"

"I'm not, no. My mum is though, I guess. The only money I have is that arsehole's dirty money."

A shiver runs down my spine as I'm reminded of some of the things Erica said to me earlier. The reality is that Mum might not have anything. My stomach twists and I feel sick at the thought of him leaving her and Lauren with nothing. After all the bullshit he pulled, that would just be the tip of the iceberg. I always suspected that he only married Mum to get his hands on the business and the money that came with it. Him leaving it on the edge of bankruptcy is only more evidence that I was right all along.

Mum's car is sitting in the drive as I expected, but I suck in a breath when I see another next to it.

"Shit."

"What's wrong?"

"Lauren's here. I thought she'd gone back home."

"We can go somewhere else. Find a hotel and meet later..."

She trails off and I look over at her. She's been nothing but incredible since we met. I'll feel even more of an arsehole than I usually do if I turn them all away now. They've come here because they want to help. It's time I stopped running and embraced the real me.

"No, it's fine. Come on."

I jump out of the car as Dec brings his van to a stop behind me. Liam nods and I give him a weak smile.

"What are you so worried about? The guys will love you whether you're surfing in Devon or running an empire in London. Just chill, yeah?"

"Well, this wasn't quite what I was expecting. It's practically a fucking mansion," Dec says, helping Nicole from the van.

"I guess," I mutter. I always knew we were well off; but having gone to private school with even more privileged and wealthy kids, my house never seemed all that impressive.

They all follow me in, stopping to take their shoes off, unlike me who just traipses through towards the kitchen.

"Are you sure that's the best way to go about it?" I hear Mum ask as I get to the doorway.

Lauren's mouth opens to respond, but before she gets a chance, she must sense my presence. Her eyes find mine and anger twists her features. "I need to leave."

"Lauren, this is your home."

"No, Jenny. It's your home." She flicks another look my way. "And his. It's best I get out of your way."

"Thank you, Lauren. For everything. I know your dad's no longer..." she trails off, sadness clouding her features. "Just...don't be a stranger."

I watch as they embrace while the others come to a stop behind me.

When Lauren turns, it's with tears filling her eyes. She keeps her head down as she walks my way, but at the very last minute, she looks up.

There are so many things I need to say to her, mostly apologies, but all the words stay on the end of my tongue as our eyes hold. She looks tired. Exhausted. I know it's not all my fault, but I feel the weight of it pressing down on my chest nonetheless.

The atmosphere is heavy around us as we stare at each other. Reaching my hand forward, I brush my fingers against hers gently. Her eyelids flicker as our connection hits her, but she rights herself all too quickly and pulls her hand away.

Someone behind me clears their throat, and I'm reminded that they're there.

"Shit. Mum, Lauren, these are my friends." Turning, I introduce each of them. It's not escaped me that I'm yet to fully explain to either Mum or Lauren where I've been and what I've been doing over the past few years.

"N-nice to meet you. I'm sorry, but I need to..." Lauren's voice cracks and she all but runs towards the front door.

"Lauren...wait," Liv calls, shocking the fuck out of me—and Lauren, too, if the look on her face when she turns is anything to go by.

Liv races over and leans in to have a private conversation with a woman she's never met before as if they're best friends.

Narrowing my eyes, I watch them for a few seconds before Mum welcomes everyone in and offers them drinks. Dec, Liam and Nicole just about manage to squeeze past me and into the room as I stand stock still, trying to figure out what Liv's saying.

I'm still staring when she gives Lauren a quick hug and watches her leave the house. She then turns to me and smiles like she was expecting me to be watching, but comes walking over as if nothing weird just happened.

Reaching out, I grab her forearm as she tries to walk past me.

"What the hell was that?"

"It was nothing for you to worry about." She gives me a wink before walking farther into the room and introducing herself to my mum.

I watch from the corner of the room as my friends and Mum sit around the table talking as if they've known each other for years.

I was a little worried what state we might find Mum in when we got here, but she looks good. Better than I've seen since I came home. She's abandoned her glass of wine in favour of coffee with everyone else, and her smile is wide and genuine as she listens to Dec talk about Devon and what I've been doing.

"Yeah, he's an incredible surfer."

"Is that right, Ben?" Her question drags me from my own head, and I walk over and pull a chair out.

"I'm okay. Dec and Liam are way better than me. I'm not really built for a board."

"Yeah, you have grown a little," Mum says with a laugh. "He's been back days and I know nothing. Tell me everything my baby's been up to."

"Everything?" Dec asks, looking over at me with an evil smile playing at his lips.

"No, she doesn't need to know everything."

I've no idea why I was so nervous about this. I might have thought I was putting on an act in Devon, but I think maybe my friends have always seen through it.

For the first time in a very, very long time, I actually enjoy spending a night in this house. It's filled with warmth and laughter.

It's something I'm sure hasn't really happened since my dad died, but suddenly it's a home again. It's just a shame one person is missing. The seat next to me at the table is empty, and so is a huge part of me, despite being surrounded by these incredible people.

"Have you already got accommodation sorted for the night?" Mum asks.

"No. It was all a little last minute. We—"

"Stay here," Mum says quickly, cutting Liv off.

"Oh no. We don't want to impose. We know you've got a lot going on right now."

"Don't be silly. I won't take no for an answer. It's been so wonderful having Ben's friends here and hearing about my boy. I couldn't possibly allow you to leave. Let me go and make sure the guest rooms are ready for visitors." Mum gets up and quickly leaves the room. I can't help but think her having people to look after is going to help pull her from the dark hole she was falling into.

"Your mum's lovely, B...Ben." Dec's lips twist weirdly as he tries to wrap them around my real name. "BJ was never your nickname was it?"

"No. Until you, I was always Ben."

"You should have said something."

"Honestly, I needed the separation from here." Guilt hits me again at hiding so much of myself from my best friends.

"Yeah, I think I'm starting to understand that. Why did you never tell us any of this?"

"I didn't leave under good circumstances. The less I had to think about it, the better."

"Why did you leave?"

I smile at Liv, who's kept my secret even without me being there. "My stepdad made me."

"Made you?" Nicole asks with her brows drawn together. "Why?"

"I fell in love with his daughter and he found out. He paid me to—"

"He what?" comes from behind us. Turning, I find Mum clinging onto the doorframe for support, her eyes wide as she stares at me, willing me to tell her that I'm lying. "Ben? Is that true?"

Letting out a breath, I look over at my mum's distressed face. "Of course it's true. Did you really think I'd leave you both willingly?"

She sags against the wall, and both Liam and I are up and off our chairs to catch her.

"He paid you?" she whispers, looking up at me with sad eyes once we've got her settled on a chair.

"He did. But it wasn't the money that forced me to go."

"W-what was it?"

Looking up to the ceiling, I battle with how much I want to tell her. I know she deserves the truth, but the last thing I want to do is hurt her. She's already suffered enough pain. I look around at all the sets of eyes staring at me, and I feel awful for her finding out this way. We should have had this conversation in private, not in front of people she hardly knows. But I can't help feel that it's better to get it all out in the open.

Looking away from her, I swallow and consider my words. "He threatened you and Lauren. He said he had enough evidence that you...hadn't been faithful. That he could take everything." Mum's face pales and she swallows nervously; it's all I need to know it's true. "If I didn't walk away, he was going to take the business, the house, everything, and leave you with nothing. Both of you. I couldn't risk it. After Dad, I just couldn't—"

"You really loved her, didn't you?" she manages to croak out, taking the focus away from her.

Feeling everyone's eyes turn on me, I swallow down the lump that's growing in my throat. "I still do."

"You need to fight for her, Ben."

Not able to look into Mum's heartbroken eyes any longer, I push the chair out behind me, swipe a beer from the fridge, and head out to the garden. Watching her reaction to the truth about her husband on top of Erica's confession this afternoon is just getting a bit much.

Knocking the cap off on the edge of the table, I fall back onto one of the chairs and tip the bottle to my lips. The cool liquid goes down too easily, making old habits to drown everything out so bloody tempting.

I've no idea how much time passes before the sound of the doors opening pulls me from my own head. When I look up, Dec and Liam are heading my way with more beer.

They both drop down beside me and pass me a new bottle. Nothing's said as we all open them and take a swig.

"The girls are with your mum," Liam says, and my stomach twists.

"Fuck. I should go—" I go to stand but a hand on my shoulder stops me.

"They've got it covered. Stop worrying about everyone else for a few minutes and just take a breath."

I do as he suggests and drag in a few good lungfuls of air. "The business is going under. This place could end up repossessed and—"

"And we're going to sort it. You won't lose any of this."

"No, no, you don't—"

"Enough," Dec snaps. "All you've done since the day we met is help me. You practically rebuilt my house from the ground up. You supported me starting the business. You were there for me with everything with Nicole. We will not allow you to do this alone, Ben."

The determination on their faces chokes me up. Fear that the tears stinging my eyes might just escape if I acknowledge their support means I tip my bottle to my lips instead.

"Thank you," I say eventually.

"Whatever you need," Liam agrees before silence surrounds us once again. We're guys, we don't really talk about feelings and shit, but I don't need it. They're here; that's all I need to know that they mean everything Dec just said.

We've almost drunk our way through the bottles the guys brought out when the sound of the doors opening floats around us. Nic and Liv step out and walk over to join us.

"Is she okay?"

"She's gone to bed. She's exhausted."

They both give me sad smiles—it's their way of saying that she's not okay. I really wish that conversation about Nick could have happened in private, but I guess it's too late now.

We stay out on the decking, drinking and chatting long into the night. Once we decide to hit the sack, I follow both the couples up the stairs and watch as they go into their rooms for the night.

There's a stabbing pain in my heart as I head towards my own room alone. Forgoing my bedroom door, I push down the handle on the one opposite. Nothing in this room is like I remember, but just knowing it's where she used to be brings me some kind of comfort. Sitting myself down on the edge of the bed, I think about how I could have handled all of this differently. I thought not telling Lauren about her dad the second I got here was for the best. Allow her to mourn the man she thought he was, to say goodbye to the father she believed she had, before I hit her with the truth. But after the way Mum found out tonight, I'm starting to question that decision.

Knowing that sitting here wallowing isn't helping anyone, I get up to leave, but the sound of giggling coming from one of the guest rooms stops me. Will any of this get any easier?

Knocking softly on Mum's door, I push it open and poke my head inside.

"It's okay, I'm awake," she says quietly.

Walking in, I make my way over to the bed and sit myself beside her.

"I'm so sorry, Mum. My intention wasn't to hurt anyone in all of this. I was trying to do what I thought was best for you."

"Shush, now," she soothes, placing her tiny hand on my forearm. "You should have stood up for yourself and what you wanted."

"I couldn't do that to you. The business and this house are the only bits of Dad you had left. I just—"

"They're just things, Ben. No matter where I live, or where I work, your dad will always be with me." Tears sting my eyes and she brings her hand to her chest. "Your dad was the love of my life. Even to this day he holds my heart in his hands. I don't need to be in this house to remember him. You should have fought. If I'd have known, I'd have told you the same thing back then. Nick was ruthless. Everyone seems to think I wasn't aware of the kind of man he was, but I experienced it better than anyone."

My fists clench as I vividly remember some of their more heated arguments. I used to hide just out of sight waiting for the hand he raised to come down on her. I never witnessed it, but I'd put money on the fact some of Mum's *illnesses* were due to his fists.

"I really fucking hate him. He took everything from me. I wasn't going to allow him to do that to both of you, too."

"Oh, baby." Mum tries to wrap her arms around my shoulders, but I'm not the baby she remembers, and her arms nowhere near meet. She ends up with her head resting on my chest as I hold her to me. "We did lose everything. We lost you."

Thank fuck she's looking down; it means she misses the fight I lose with my tears as she sobs her own.

I angrily wipe at my eyes, frustrated with myself that I've allowed him to break me.

When Mum does pull her head up and look at me, she doesn't miss the emotion written all over my face. She places her hand softly on my cheek and stares into my eyes. I suddenly feel like a little boy again.

"You and Lauren were made for each other. I knew that the first time I caught you together. There was something about the two of you when you were close, an unbreakable connection. It was just like your dad and I had. You've no idea how I feel, knowing I played a part in ruining that. I knew about the two of you, but I didn't do anything to help. There are so many things I could have done. I—"

"Don't, Mum. It's too late now. What's done is done. She has every right not to want anything to do with me after what I did."

"That's just it though, Ben. She's still angry. That's a good thing."

"How?"

"It means she still cares. It means it's not over, no matter what she might try to tell you." My heart starts to race as her words settle in. "Don't give up." Reaching up, she places a kiss to my cheek before settling herself back into bed. "*Never* give up, Ben."

I leave soon after, but Mum's words stay with me as I lie in my own bed, staring at the ceiling, waiting for sleep to claim me. I wonder if what she said is true. Would things have been different if she'd have said something? Somehow, I really doubt it. Nick still would have found a way to get what he wanted. He might have just gone about it differently.

# CHAPTER TEN

"Morning," I grunt, walking into the kitchen to find both Nic and Liv cooking up something that smells fantastic.

"I hope you don't mind. We raided the cupboards."

"Knock yourselves out."

I get myself a coffee before refilling Dec and Liam's, who are sitting at the table watching their girls. Both of them have freshly fucked smug smiles on their faces.

"Which one of your headboards was banging all night?"

"Ours," Dec and Liam say in unison as the girls deny everything while turning a nice shade of pink.

"Mum said you can stay, not that you could turn the place into a knocking shop," I say with a laugh, falling down onto a chair with the guys.

"Oh please, like you didn't get up to all sorts here when you were a teenager." Everyone falls silent and realisation dawns on Nicole as to what she just said. "Oh shit, I'm sorry. I didn't think."

"It's fine. You're right, though. I've done my fair share of sneaking around in this place."

"Is that right?" Mum asks with a wink as she joins us.

"It's probably best we change the conversation." Mum laughs, and it's the first time since I've been back that I've seen her smile meet her eyes.

She walks over and gives me a hug. "Everything's going to be okay. You'll see." I nod at her because I don't want to ruin her good mood, but right now I'm getting fed up of everyone telling me that.

We've just finished eating when my phone vibrates in my pocket. Pulling it out, my brows pull together at seeing Liv's name on the screen.

"What the hell is this?"

"It's your surprise."

"You got Rita fucking Ora tickets for tonight?"

"I did."

"How? It sold out months ago?" I ask, totally forgetting any attempt to cover up my slight addiction to the singer.

"It doesn't matter. All that matters is that I got them."

"You're a fucking legend." I jump from the chair and have her in my arms in seconds. I spin her around as she squeals and the others all laugh.

"So you want to go then?" she asks as she tries to stand steady once I've lowered her to her feet.

"Fucking right I do. I seriously can't fucking believe this." The smile splitting my face hurts as I stare down my phone once again. I'm going to the fucking O2 tonight to see Rita fucking Ora. What did I do to deserve friends like these?

"This is so fucking awesome."

"It's good to see you smile again, dude," Liam says, clapping me on the back.

I guess that's why the muscles in my face are aching so much; they haven't really been used a lot lately.

"So what's the plan, then? We've got hours until the concert. There's no way I can sit around here waiting."

The girls announce that they'd like to go shopping, so we end up spending the afternoon walking up and down Oxford Street while Dec and Liam carry their bags.

We have a great afternoon, but seeing the four of them together is only a massive reminder of what I don't have. I'd give just about anything to follow Lauren around each and every shop, holding her bags and giving her my advice, which of course would be that she always looked incredible.

I tried phoning Erica before we left the house this morning, but all my calls went straight to voicemail. I may be bouncing about what tonight is going to hold, but everything she told me yesterday isn't far from my mind. I intend on making the most of having my friends here, but I need to find out just how bad a shape the business is in, and even more, I need to find out what exactly Nick did to Erica.

Before I know it, Dec, Liam and I are all sitting in Mum's living room, waiting for the girls to appear.

"Seriously, how did Liv get those tickets?" I ask Liam.

"I think someone was selling them on or something. Cost us all a damn fortune."

Guilt twists my stomach that they're all out of pocket trying to cheer me up. "I can pay for them all."

"Don't be stupid. This is on us," Dec argues as we hear footsteps and giggling descending the stairs.

"I think I've changed my mind about going out," Liam announces the second Liv walks into the room wearing a little black dress.

He immediately sweeps her into his arms, followed by Dec who does the same to Nic. I once again feel like the gooseberry of the group. Awkwardly, I manage to squeeze past them and walk out to the driveway with my head down.

Mum's words from yesterday ring in my ears. Is it too late? Is what she said true? Are we over? Has she really moved on?

Once they've finished manhandling each other, they join me and we head towards the tube station to take us into the city centre. Liam and Dec are oblivious, but I get sympathetic smiles from the girls.

They seem to have a better understanding of how painful it is seeing them all loved up and happy.

Nicole and Liv choose a popular gastro pub for dinner before heading towards the O2.

As we stand outside waiting in line, I'm more grateful than I think I've ever been for a distraction. The prospect of spending an hour or two watching Rita up on stage is enough for me to push everything with Mum, Lauren, Erica, and the business to the back of my mind. I know as soon as tonight's over that I'll have to deal with them all once again, but for now, I'm just going to enjoy myself.

The seats are fucking incredible for last minute, second-hand tickets.

"You're something else, you know that?" I shout to Liv as the support act takes to the stage. "You've no idea how badly I need this."

"I think I do." She winks at me, and I'm reminded of everything she went through recently and how she knows better than anyone what a good distraction from reality can do.

Wrapping my arm around her shoulder, I kiss the top of her head. Liam smiles at me from next to her and I nod back. These guys have been my family for the past six years, and they mean more to me than I think they'll ever understand. They were exactly what I needed in those first few months after leaving London, and the fact that they're here now when I need them is everything to me.

Feeling a little choked up, I'm glad when the band leave the stage and the crowd erupts in excitement for the lady of the night.

Butterflies explode in my stomach as the anticipation builds. The only thing that would make tonight better would be if Lauren were here to experience it with me. I look to my left, at the random lady patiently staring at the stage, and my excitement wanes.

I missed her so fucking much when I was in Devon, but being here, with her practically in touching distance, is even worse.

The concert is more than I ever thought it might be. I've wanted to see her live ever since I first heard her voice on the radio a few years ago. My desire only got worse when I Googled her and discovered she looked as good as she sounded. I've taken plenty of stick over the years about my obsession, but I couldn't give a fuck. She's hot and her music is sweet, so what's not to love?

The whole time she's singing, I completely forget about all the bullshit surrounding me, all the unknowns about my life. I embrace every second of the freedom she provides me with. I breathe that little bit easier with her voice filling my ears.

"So?" Liv asks as we walk from the arena once the show is over. "Was it everything you always dreamed of?" I don't miss the little smirk on her lips.

"It was incredible. Thank you so much."

"You're welcome."

"Please tell me we're not heading home yet." I'm buzzing after that and really not ready to deal with reality.

"No, we're heading to a club."

Liv takes the lead and we follow her down to the tube station and further into the city.

The second we emerge from the underground, I know exactly where we're going. I remember the little chat she had with Erica yesterday, and I realise they were planning this night. Erica never wanted to go anywhere but Fire back in the day.

As we approach the club I used to know so well, I notice some obvious changes. The orange Fire signage is long gone, replaced with a more upmarket look. It's now called The Avenue, and everything's black and chrome. From the few people outside, it no longer looks to be filled with drunk students and has a slightly higher quality clientele, something I'm relieved about.

"This place looks nice," Nicole says from behind me as we queue up to get in.

They chat away, but I don't hear most of it. The anticipation that's running through me is the only thing I can focus on. If Erica had something to do with these plans, then there's a very good chance she's here...and Lauren could be too.

My heart thunders in my chest as the bouncer gestures for us to enter. I immediately take the stairs up to the second floor. I've no idea if it would still be Erica's choice, but it's the only thing I have to go on if we're going to find her.

Dec orders us all shots of whiskey and I quickly down mine, not wanting to take my eyes off my surroundings for a second.

Tingles run up and down my spine. I know she's here somewhere. I just need to find her. My mouth waters as my imagination runs wild. I vividly remember us dancing here, the way her body felt against mine. How badly I needed her that night.

It's only a few seconds before the sea of people in front of me parts just right and my eyes land on her. She's wearing a deep red dress that's wrapped around her perfect curves. My fingers twitch to feel them once again as my eyes run down her long, exposed legs to her black high heels.

*Fuck me.*

Making my way back up over every delicious curve that's moving in time with the music, I eventually get to her blonde hair that's pulled away from her slim neck and piled on top of her head.

I'm getting closer before my brain's even registered that my legs are moving. I'm only a few feet away when someone steps out from the crowd, places their hands on her hips, and pulls her backwards.

My fists clench as my temperature soars. I stare at where he's touching her and fight my need to rip his hands away.

Raising my eyes, I take in his perfectly pressed white shirt, braces, and then his overly gelled hair. If I didn't hate him when I saw him touching Lauren at the funeral, then I do now.

Every muscle in my body tenses as I watch their hips grind together.

"Whoa, dude, what's...oh!" Dec stands beside me, watching the same car crash that I am.

"I need more fucking whiskey for this." Turning, I walk back up to the bar and order another round of drinks.

"Hey, we didn't think you were coming," I hear a familiar voice say behind me.

Spinning around, I find a very happy Erica smiling at me, but when I lift my eyes over her shoulder, I find the same anger on Lauren's face that I'm sure was on mine not so long ago.

"I think I should leave."

"Don't you fucking dare," Erica warns. The vicious look in her eyes has me rooted to the spot. "Ben, you remember Danni, right?" she says when Lauren's friend comes to a stop beside her. A similar hatred fills her eyes as she looks me up and down.

"Danni," I say with a nod.

"Hmm, look what the cat dragged in," she slurs, curling her lip up in disgust. "You've got some nerve showing your face here, you know that?"

"Danni, stop, please," Lauren begs, coming to stand beside her best friend.

"And this is Joe," Erica interrupts.

I hold her stare for a few seconds, so she knows just how unhappy I am about this before I look up.

I find him staring down at me with pure hatred pouring from his eyes. I take a step forward, ready to do whatever it takes to show this douchebag that he has something that belongs to me.

"Don't even think about it," Lauren seethes, jumping between us.

I stop millimetres from her body. Her heat seeps into me. It's almost enough to make me forget about the man who thinks she's his. Mum was right last night. Lauren still cares, so everything is still to play for.

It's not until her hands land on my chest that I pull my eyes from her *boyfriend*. My lip curls at just the thought alone.

"Step away, Ben," she warns. With her shoes on, she's much taller than usual. It wouldn't take much for me to lean down and take her lips right now. The idea has my mouth watering for another taste of her.

Narrowing my eyes, I can't stop the words falling from my lips. "You know you want me to fight for you. I can sense it." Lowering my head to her ear, I whisper, "I can smell it. He doesn't make you scream like I do, and you fucking know it."

Her hand connects with my cheek, and it stings like a motherfucker. Pressing my palm to my burning skin, I look down at her. Her eyes are alight with anger and her chests heaves as she stares back at me.

"I fucking hate you," she spits.

"No, baby. You just hate that I'm not fucking you."

"That's enough, Ben," Erica shouts, grabbing my arm and trying to turn me away to stop me saying anything else.

"It's nowhere fucking near enough. He needs to realise she's mine before I make him regret ever touching her."

"Whoa, calm down, caveman. I know I told you to fight for her, but that wasn't quite what I meant."

I'm ushered over towards the bar and a glass of whiskey appears in front of me.

When I look up, I'm met by the concerned looks of my best friends. I don't need to meet their eyes to know I just fucked up.

"Are you going to play nice, or do I have to send you home?" Erica asks with a hard stare and her hands on her hips.

"I'm fine. I'm fine."

I can tell none of them believe me. Hell, I'm not sure I believe me, but I'm not walking out of here and leaving them to grind it up on the dance floor without a care in the world.

Downing my drink, I grab Erica's hand and pull her into the crowd. Lauren and that prick aren't the only ones who've got moves.

I know everyone's watching as I twist Erica around in front of me, but there's only one set of eyes that are burning hatred into me.

Erica's body is stiff when I force her against my chest and start dancing. "What the hell are you doing? If you want to make her jealous, using me probably isn't the best idea."

"You're right." Pushing her away, I glance around. It doesn't take long before I find a woman watching me. She's not my type in any way, but right now, that's the last thing that matters. I pull her stick thin body against mine and together we move in time with the music.

She's clearly drunk and more than willing. Guilt starts to eat at me that I'm taking advantage of her, but I tell myself that I have no intention of doing anything more than dance.

I pin her hips against mine and she moves easily with me. The others join me and lose themselves with their other halves. Joe pulls Lauren to the edge of our group and my teeth grind as I watch his hands run down her back until they land on her arse.

My fingers squeeze the woman pressed up against me and it gives her the wrong idea. Her hand slides up my chest and wraps around the back of my neck.

My eyes stay on Lauren as the woman presses her lips to mine. It takes a second or two, but the moment she notices, she stops moving. Joe stares down at her before following her eye line and also finding me.

He turns back to her, and I do the same, but it's too late. She's already gone.

Forcing the woman pressed against me away, I rush in the direction where Lauren disappeared.

"I don't think so." I'm toe-to-toe with Joe. We're a similar height and build, but I'm confident I could take him if need be. He looks like a fucking IT geek with his black-rimmed glasses and slicked back hair after all.

"What the fuck do you know about anything?"

"More than you fucking know. You've already caused her enough pain, don't you think?" he asks, but I've already pushed him away in my need to get to her. "Let her go, Ben. It's too late."

I hear other calls from behind me, but I pay them no attention.

Racing down the stairs, I search for her, but there's no sign of her blonde hair or red dress.

"Go in the toilets and find her," I demand when Erica follows me.

"She's gone, Ben. Come back and get a drink?" Hope fills her eyes that tonight might not be a total bust, but it's too late. The damage has already been done.

"I'm going home. Give this to the others for a taxi later."

She shoves the handful of cash back at me and turns away without saying anything. *Great, I've pissed someone else off.*

I don't manage to get a taxi before the others come rushing from the club.

"What the fuck are you doing?" Liam shouts as he walks over. He doesn't stop until he's right in my face. "You want to fight? You want to hit someone? Come on, then. Take what you need."

"I'm not going to fucking hit you."

"Why not?"

"You haven't done anything to deserve it."

"And *he* has?"

He stumbles back when I push his shoulders, but Dec manages to catch him before he hits the pavement.

"Fuck you. FUCK YOU!" I bellow at no one in particular. Running my hands over my face, I rest them on my head and look up to the dark, cloud filled sky. It's angry, like there could be a storm any moment.

I suck in a few breaths in the hope of calming my racing heart and raging temper.

When I finally get a hold of myself and turn to the others, they're standing on the pavement, looking totally lost. Guilt engulfs me. They came here to try to cheer me up, and this is what I subject them to.

I'm a joke.

My life is a fucking joke.

"Come on. Let's get you home," Liv says softly, lacing her fingers with mine and pulling me towards a taxi idling at the curb.

# CHAPTER ELEVEN

"How are you feeling? Your friends said you had a bit of an eventful night," Mum says when I eventually drag my hungover arse into the kitchen sometime after lunch the next day.

"Like shit."

"Sit down, I'll get you a coffee. The others have gone into the city for the day. They didn't want to disturb you."

I watch as Mum faffs about. She looks better again today. I'm hoping that finding out the truth, although painful, has done her some good.

"Here. Chris is coming around in a little bit with Nick's will. Lauren's coming too." Dread sits heavily in my stomach. I was such a dick to her in the club. Mum must be able to read my thoughts, because after regarding me for a few seconds, she asks, "What did you do?"

"I wasn't very nice to her last night. She was at the club with Joe and—"

"Oh. I think you and Joe would get on, you know. You're really quite similar."

"Yeah, it seems we have similar tastes," I mutter.

Mum bites down on her bottom lip and considers her next words carefully. "Not all that similar," she says eventually. I don't get a chance to question what she means, because the doorbell rings.

Mum gets up, stops at the mirror in the hallway to smooth down her hair, and answers the door.

Chris' deep voice filters down to me along with Mum's laughter. The sound warms my heart.

"Afternoon, Ben," Chris calls as he enters the room, and I wince. "Good night?"

"Something like that," I mutter, regretting the amount of whiskey I consumed before finally crashing out.

"We're just waiting for Lauren and then we can get to it. What's that look for?" Mum asks Chris when concern washes over his face.

"It's just...not what I was expecting."

Mum swallows before turning to make Chris a coffee. "Whatever it is, we can deal with it, Chris. He didn't break us when he was alive, and he sure won't do it when he's dead."

It's the first time I've ever heard Mum say anything less than positive about her late husband. Maybe she was right with what she said the other day, and she was more aware of his ways than she let on.

Mum's just put Chris' coffee down when the sound of the front door slamming echoes through the house.

I hold my breath as her footsteps echo down the hallway. It all comes out in a rush when she finally appears in the doorway. She's wearing a pair of skinny jeans and an oversized hoodie, her hair's pulled back from her make-up free, tired face, but it's her eyes that make my body ache to get up. Her usual light-blue is dark and rimmed with redness that only comes from hours of crying.

My fingers grip the bottom of the chair to keep me in place. She's staring daggers at me. Getting up and giving her a hug is the last thing she wants right now.

"Good afternoon, sweetheart. Would you like tea?"

"Please."

"Take a seat. I'll be right with you all."

Lauren takes the farthest seat away from me and I almost laugh. If she thinks that's going to keep me away, she's got another think coming.

The wood of my chair legs screeches against the tiled floor. Her eyes fly up to me and hold a warning—one I'm about to ignore.

She tenses as I pull a chair out next to her and drop down. Resting my arm over her backrest, she sits bolt upright so we don't touch.

Leaning forward so Mum and Chris can't eavesdrop, I whisper in her ear, "I'm sorry about last night. It was uncalled for. It taught me something though." Turning to me, she narrows her eyes in question. "You still want me."

Standing, she goes to leave, but I'm faster. Wrapping my hand around her forearm, I hold her in place.

"Ben? Lauren? Is everything okay?"

"Please can we just get this over with?"

"Sure. Chris, are you ready?"

"Yes," he says hesitantly.

After ripping her arm from my grasp, Lauren sits back down beside me, folds her arms over her chest and waits for what Chris has to say.

He talks through all the waffle and formalities. He seems to really drag out the inevitable, that Mum will get everything. I assume he's left something for Lauren, but why Chris can't just come out and say it is beyond me.

"So, Nick has requested that in the case of his passing, this house and the business are left to...Ben."

"What?" both Lauren and I say at the same time.

"He's left everything to the man who walked away when things got too hard? What the fuck?" Anger vibrates from her as she stands. "What about Jenny and me?"

"I'm sorry, sweetheart. Ben is the only person named."

"This is bullshit." We all stare at her as she turns on her heel and storms from the room, and soon after, the house.

"Well, that went well," Chris mutters sadly.

"He really left everything to Ben?" Mum asks, her face twisted in confusion. It's in that moment that realisation hits.

"Well, he wouldn't leave that kind of disaster to someone he actually likes, would he?"

"What do you mean?"

"The business is about to go under, and this place has been re-mortgaged to the hilt. It's clearly his idea of a sick joke. He's left all his debt and dirty dealings for me to attempt to sort out."

"What are you talking about? The business is doing fine. Lauren does the accounts; she would have said if something was wrong."

"I don't think it's that simple, Mum. He's been cooking the books along with fuck knows what else."

"How do you know this?"

"I don't know the details, but he's been using Erica to hide what he's been up to."

"Motherfucker," Chris grunts.

Mum just sits there in total shock. "Am I going to lose the house?" she asks eventually. I expect her to break down, but there's no emotion.

"Not if I have anything to do with it. Is that it, Chris?"

"For now, yes. We'll need to sort out paperwork soon though."

"Okay, well, you've got my number." Draining my coffee, I stand from the table and head in the direction Lauren went not so long ago. My hangover is suddenly forgotten. I've got more important things to worry about, like keeping a roof over Mum's head.

The anger that had erupted within me at learning what that motherfucker had left me is raging by the time I pull up outside Johnson & Son's office.

My granddad started the business from his spare bedroom. It was my dad who moved everything here. He started with just a small corner of the floor, but as the business grew, so did the office space.

We now take up the entire second floor of the building—although, I doubt that's going to continue, depending on what I find when I start digging into my inheritance.

The crisp early autumn air chills my skin as I walk the short distance from where I manage to find a parking space to the office building.

I'm expecting it to be empty seeing as it's a Sunday, so I'm surprised when I push the door open and find the lights on.

"I just don't get it. Dad hated Ben—why would he leave it all to him?" The sound of her soft, emotional voice has goosebumps erupting across my skin. There's so much she doesn't know. So much that prick hid from her.

Pushing the door open wider, I walk towards them, ready to get everything out in the open.

I'm not surprised to see it's Erica she's talking to. Lauren's leaning back against her desk, totally oblivious that they have company. Erica, on the other hand, spots me immediately over Lauren's shoulder. Her eyes widen in surprise.

"I just don't understand why he'd do this to Jenny."

"Lauren...I..." Erica stutters, her eyes still on me.

"We need to explain a few things to you." Lauren's body visibly tenses as my voice fills the space around us.

"We?" Erica asks, fear draining the colour from her face.

"Yes, Erica. It's time."

"I don't want to listen to anything you have to say," she spits.

"Tough. You need to hear it." It's only the harsh tone of my voice that has her turning to look at me.

Her face is even paler than it was when I first saw her earlier, her eyes redder and now bloodshot from the tears she's shed. Guilt clenches my stomach that I've had a hand in her pain.

"You lost any right you might have had to tell me what to do the moment you decided to walk out of my life." She pushes away from Erica's desk and steps a little closer to me. My body reacts to her as it always does when we're in touching distance.

"That's just it though, Lauren. The only place I wanted to be that night was in bed with you. The only thing I've ever wanted is you."

"You had me, Ben. I gave you everything and you just stomped all over it."

"I didn't have any other choice."

"It's been six years. I don't care." She waves her hand in front of me and goes to turn away.

Reaching out, I grab her hand and pull her back so she's facing me. Staring down into her eyes, I prepare to say the words that are going to throw her world into a tailspin once again.

"He made me go, Lauren. He threatened your future, your happiness. Both of those things are more important to me than what I wanted."

"Oh that's rich, even for you," she says with a bitter laugh. "I thought it was a huge coincidence that you only showed your face after Dad died, but this is proof that you really were just waiting for him to die to take over."

"I've been waiting for him to rot in hell for a long time, Lauren, trust me." Even her shocked gasp isn't enough for me to regret the words I probably shouldn't have said. But they're true. "He didn't stay away on a golf weekend. He came back. He was waiting for me. Waiting for me to make me leave you."

"You're lying." Wrapping her arms around herself, her body's visibly shaking as she tries to reject the words I'm saying to her.

"I wish. I wish he'd have just accepted how I felt—how I feel—about you. I wish he'd allowed you the happiness you deserve, but just like every other part of his life, he waded in and took control of the situation. It's no different to what he's done here."

"Okay...say everything you're telling me is true. Then why the fuck would he leave this place and the house to you? You're trying to tell me that he hated you to the point that he made you walk out of my life, yet you're the only one listed in his will. What the fuck, Ben?"

She paces up and down in front of me, her fists clenching and unclenching as she tries to process and make sense of what I'm telling her.

"There's nothing here, Lauren. The business is on the verge of going under."

"Bullshit. I do the accounts, the profits are better than they've ever been."

"That's what he makes you believe," Erica says, chipping in for the first time.

"What? You're in on this too?"

"Lauren, trust me when I tell you that I understand how hard all of this is to swallow, but your dad wasn't the kind of man you thought he was."

Lauren looks between the two of us like we've just slapped her. "I don't know what to think. I see all the figures. I see exactly—"

"What he wants you to see."

"How? And why are you only telling me this now?"

"You might want to sit down," Erica says, gesturing to the chair behind Lauren.

"I'm fine. Just tell me what's going on."

"Okay, well...you know how things were for me after Matt and I split up?" Lauren's brows draw together in confusion, but she doesn't interrupt. "Nick knew I was in trouble financially, and he knew I'd do just about anything not to lose my home. So..."

"So?"

"Fucking hell, Lauren." Erica drops her head into her hands and blows out a few slow breaths. "Just remember that I was in a really bad place, okay? He started being really nice, helping me out, giving me lifts home after I sold my car, just little things. He helped me out financially so I wouldn't miss a mortgage payment."

"Right..."

"I slept with him."

"What?" As if Erica's words are like a physical blow to her chest, Lauren stumbles back and crashes into a chair. "Fucking hell. This is a joke, right? This isn't fucking happening," Lauren fumes, walking to the other end of the office. "You slept with my fucking dad?"

"I know how bad this sounds, Lauren. Believe me, none of this was by choice."

"I'm hearing that word a lot today." The laugh that falls from her lips is anything but amused.

"He blackmailed me, Lauren. He made me fall for his charms. He made me need him, and then he made me do exactly what he wanted for fear of the truth coming out and losing my home."

"And what did he make you do? Other than...the obvious." Lauren shivers at the thought while Erica looks like she could puke any second.

"He had me doctoring the figures. Intercepting documents after you'd filed them. Ben's right, there's nothing here. I'm so sorry, Lauren."

"Why the hell didn't you say anything?"

"I couldn't. I was—I *am*—humiliated that I allowed it to happen, but I was drowning and he gave me an out."

"So what you're both trying to tell me is that he made you leave," she says, looking at me, "and he made you sleep with him and cook the books?"

"Jesus, I'm so sorry, Lauren," Erica repeats, but Lauren's already turned away from her.

"This is all your fault. All of it." Her fists slam down on my chest, but I'm faster than her and I capture her wrists. "If you hadn't let him manipulate you. If you hadn't left. If you'd just fought for what you wanted; none of this would have happened. *That* is your fault," she says, pointing back at Erica, who's wiping away the tears on her cheeks. "All. Of. This. Is. Your. Fault," she says as she fights against her restraints. "And I fucking hate you," she screams. The shock has me releasing her arms, and she runs before I get a chance to stop her.

# CHAPTER TWELVE

"Well, that went well," Erica manages through her tears.

"Fucking hell," I shout, rubbing my hands over my head and down my face. "Now what?"

"Do what you should have done six years ago. Fight for her, Ben."

"What about you?"

"I'm a big girl."

Pulling her into my arms, I drop a kiss to the top of her head. "I'm so sorry you got dragged into this."

"It's my fault. I should have stopped it before it started."

"You weren't to know he was using you."

"Maybe not, but I knew nothing good could come of it. I need to talk to Jenny."

"I think that's a good idea."

"Really?" she asks, pulling back so she can look at me.

"Yeah. If we've got any hope of keeping any of this, we all need to be on the same page. No more lies. No more deception and bullshit."

"I couldn't agree more. She's going to hate me."

"I think she'll be more understanding than you expect. After all, how do you think he managed to worm his way in here in the first place?"

"Motherfucker."

I was only a kid when they got together. I have no idea how it all happened and what Nick's intentions were. They could have been totally honourable and he could have loved her, but knowing him now, I highly doubt it.

"I need to find Lauren."

"She said she was meant to be seeing Danni this afternoon. She's probably gone there."

"Where's there?" After getting the address, I go to leave but stop at the main door to the office. "Erica?"

"Yeah?"

"Why are you here on a Sunday?"

"Someone's got to try to keep this place from going under."

"Has anyone told you that you're a little bit awesome?"

"Yeah, every now and then." She tries to make it sound light, but I hear the sadness in her tone. Somehow, I think every now and then might be pushing it.

"Well, you are. I'll be back to help, promise."

"Just go and get your girl, Ben."

***

"SHE'S NOT FUCKING HERE. How many times?" Danni asks, standing her ground at her front door.

"You're lying."

"I'd do anything for Lauren. I'd lie for her time and again if I needed to, but seriously, she's not here." Not buying her excuses, I barge past her. "Come in, why don't you?"

I find two people sitting on her sofa, but other than that her flat is empty and my stomach drops.

"Happy now?" Danni asks when I join her and her friends back in the living room.

"I'm sorry," I mutter, regretfully.

"What's happened?"

"She's finally learnt the truth."

"What? That you're a weak fucking pussy?"

"Whoa. Who's bent your knickers out of shape?"

"None of your fucking business. Just like Lauren is none of yours. You need to stay away from her. You've already done enough damage."

"Whatever. Do you have any idea where she is?" Her eyebrows rise and she defiantly puts her hands on her hips. "Okay, well...it was nice seeing you."

I let myself out of her fancy basement flat and find my car where I left it half parked on the kerb, thankfully without a ticket.

Resting back, I wonder what I should do now, but the only thing I can see is the dejected look on Lauren's face as she walked away from me. I know she probably doesn't want me chasing her down right now, but we just dropped two huge bombs on her. I need to know she's okay.

Fighting my need to go back to the office and find her address, I drive to my favourite place. By the time I'm pulling up to the deserted car park that overlooks the city below, the sun is starting to set. Soft orange hues make the hustle and bustle in the distance look almost inviting. This place is the escape from reality that I need.

Disappointment hits me when I turn the corner and spot another car at the far end—that is, until I take it in properly.

She's here.

Pulling up next to her car, I look inside and find it empty. Where the fuck is she?

Quickly getting out without shutting off the engine, the music continues playing behind me as I go in search of the woman who still holds my heart in my hands.

The moment I walk to the edge of the car park, I see her. She's laid out on a blanket on the grass bank.

Walking over, I drop down beside her and stare at her peaceful face. Her eyelashes are resting down on her tear-stained cheeks. Her lips are slightly parted as she blows out shallow breaths.

She's so fucking beautiful, my heart aches for her.

"I'm so sorry, Lauren," I whisper. She can't hear me, but the need to say it gets the better of me.

Reaching forward, I brush a loose strand of hair from her face, but I'm not gentle enough.

Her eyes fly open as she scrambles to sit up. "Jesus fucking Christ, Ben."

"Sorry, I didn't mean to scare you. You shouldn't fall asleep out here. Anything could happen to you."

"Like being scared to death by you?"

"I'm the last person you should be scared of."

"I'm not so sure about that." Everything that's happened in the last few days seems to hit her all at once because her soft, sleepy eyes suddenly turn hard. She looks away from me, cutting herself off.

"Lauren, please don't do that. Can we just talk?"

"Talk? What would you like to talk about exactly? How you broke my heart? About how my dad apparently was intent on ruining my life along with everyone else's that I care about? About how you promised to protect me and you just fucking left?"

I pause and stare at her for a few seconds. After imagining her for so long, being able to sit beside her, to breathe the same air as her, feels surreal.

When I don't respond, she turns her blue eyes on me.

"The weather?" I ask, remembering that she asked me a question.

The skin around her eyes crinkles before the most amazing sound fills my ears. Laughter.

I can't help but laugh along with her as she lets out some of the tension she's been carrying around with her.

She laughs for the longest time. I really hope it helps her as much as it does me. Once she's calmed down, she looks up at me and smiles. "Thanks. I needed that."

"Glad I could help."

"It doesn't fix anything though."

Reaching out, I tuck the same stray piece of hair back behind her ear. "Doesn't it?"

Slapping my arm away, she puts a little more distance between us. "Why do you keep doing this?"

"Doing what?"

"Acting like nothing's changed. It's been six years, Ben. Everything's changed. I've changed. What I want has changed."

"Has it? Because from where I'm sitting, you still have the same passion and desire in your eyes as you did back then. Your body reacts in exactly the same way. You're just too scared to admit that nothing's really changed at all." Closing the space between us, I whisper, "Not where we're concerned."

"Stop it. I've moved on."

"See, there you go again. Pretending that's true."

"It is true. You've met him." She can't hold my eyes as she says this and turns to look over the city.

"Hmm...so I have. Look at me and tell me you love him. That you love him like you did me."

Anger fills her eyes when she looks back. "How dare you ask me that?"

"What? It's a simple question. Do you love him?"

"Of course."

"Like you did me?"

Her silence says everything I need to hear.

"No, I didn't think so."

"I'm leaving." Lauren jumps up from the blanket and goes to march towards her car. Unfortunately for her, I'm faster.

"No, you're not." Wrapping my arm around her waist, I pull her back until she's pressed up against my chest.

"Tell me you don't fall asleep at night wishing it was me next to you. Tell me it's not me you imagine when he's getting you off."

"He doesn't—" She slams her lips together to stop herself saying more. Her reaction soothes the sting of even suggesting another man might have touched her. "No, Ben. No."

"You're lying."

Our eye contact holds, our breaths mingling, our chests heaving. As much as I want to make the first move, as desperate as I am to feel her soft lips against mine, I know I need to wait for her to do it.

"Fuck you, Ben. Fuck you." Lifting up, her lips press against mine.

I wait a second for her to regret it, but when she doesn't pull back, I make the move I'm desperate for.

My fingers slide into her hair, while my other arm continues to hold her around the waist and I lower her back down onto the blanket.

Sliding my hand over her neck, I find the zip on the front of her hoodie and pull it down. We both know who it belongs to, and it needs to go. The second it's undone, I find the hem of her top and slip my hand underneath. I need more of her. I need to feel her soft skin against mine.

"Fuck, Ben. We can't—"

"Shhh." Kissing down the sensitive skin of her neck, I lick across her collarbone and pull the fabric of her vest down to reveal her full breast.

"We're out in the open."

"I've never seen anyone else here. It's safe. Take a risk with me, Lauren." I flick my eyes up to hers and they're met with burning passion. There's no way she's stopping this right now.

Pulling the cup of her bra down, I suck her puckered nipple into my mouth.

"Fuuuck, Ben," she moans, arching to give me more.

"I fucking love it when you're desperate for me."

"I'm always desperate for you." The second she registers that she said the words aloud, she sucks in a breath and bites down on her bottom lip.

"I know. I can see it every time you look at me. It's like you're begging me to find out just how badly you need me." Popping the button on her jeans, I slip my hand inside and beneath the lace covering her. "You're soaked for me, aren't you?"

She doesn't respond, so I dip my head and bite down on her exposed nipple.

"All you can think about is how I'll feel inside you again, isn't it?"

I don't get a chance to take her in my mouth again because she nods. "Yes, yes. Please."

Satisfied that she's admitting what she really wants, I slide my fingers lower and find her exactly as I was expecting.

"Fucking hell, Lauren." Taking her lips again, I tease her clit and dip my fingers inside her just enough to drive her fucking crazy with need.

I kiss her until I'm breathless and she's writhing beneath me, desperate for more.

Pulling my hand from her jeans, I sit her up and pull her hoodie, vest, and bra off. I need more. Squeezing both her breasts in my hands, she moans and bucks her hips against me. My cock presses against the fly of my jeans, desperate to be released.

Pulling her trainers from her feet, I slide her jeans and knickers down her legs.

Reaching back, I pull my t-shirt over my head. Her eyes immediately drop to my exposed skin and she runs her tongue along her bottom lip.

"It's yours whenever you like. You just gotta say the word, Lauren."

Her eyes focus a little more, and I worry that I just said the wrong thing, but instead of shying away, she reaches out for my fly.

Her delicate fingers make light work of undoing the button and zip and parting the fabric. Running her hands around the sensitive skin under my waistband, she slides them into the back of my jeans and grabs onto my arse. Her nails dig into my skin and I find her lips, pulling her bottom one into my mouth and biting down until I hear her soft gasp of surprise.

Forcing the fabric down my thighs, my cock springs free. She rips her lips away from mine and looks down. My cock twitches under her stare. I'm lost in my imagination for what's coming next, so I'm caught totally off-guard as she shoves my shoulders and I fall backwards onto the blanket ungracefully. Lauren wastes no time. Throwing her leg over my waist, she lines herself up exactly where I need her.

She grinds down on my cock and a growl rumbles up my throat.

"This is fucking everything," I manage to get out as she takes me in her hand and slowly lowers herself.

"Fuck." She throws her head back as the sensation washes through her.

She comes to a stop when she's fully seated, but it's not enough for me. Grabbing onto her hips, I lift her and then slam her back down.

I hit her so deep that her head flies forward and her shocked eyes find mine.

"Just reminding you who you belong to, baby."

"Fuck you." It comes out as a gasp as I slam up into her once again. Her walls ripple around me; she's already close to finding her release.

Needing to feel her clamping down on me, I release one of her hips in favour of teasing her clit.

"Fuck, Ben," she moans, grinding her hips against me.

"Come, Lauren. Remind yourself what it's like, because you know as well as I do that no one else makes you feel this good."

"Fucking. Hate. You," she shouts, her body tensing as her orgasm claims her. Every muscle in her body convulses with the pleasure that races through her. I continue thrusting up into her and allow her to ride out every second of her release.

Drained of energy, she falls onto my chest.

"This is how it's meant to be, Lauren."

Unable to find her voice, she instead sinks her teeth into my pec.

The sensation shoots straight to my cock and I explode on a roar, emptying everything I have inside her.

Once my body's come down from its high, I shift us and roll Lauren onto her back. If she believes I'm done with her for tonight, she's going to have a shock.

I settle myself between her thighs and take her lips in a wet and dirty kiss.

"I don't know how it's possible, but we're even more explosive than we were back then, baby."

Her nails scratch down my back as I suck one of her nipples into my mouth and release it with a pop.

The lyrics of Avicii and Rita Ora's *Lonely Together* float around the otherwise silent night around us, and I can't help thinking that it's perfect for right now.

I pepper kisses down her stomach, pausing when I hit her belly button. Looking up, I find her watching my every move.

The words start falling from my lips before I've realised. I can't help myself. "Lauren, I never stopped lo—"

"Don't." No sooner has she barked the word than she's scrambling out from beneath me and snatching up her discarded clothes.

"No, stop." I try grabbing at the fabric of her jeans as she shoves her leg in, but she manages to pull it from my grasp. Standing, I pull my own jeans up and watch as she quickly puts on the rest of her clothes.

"Enough, Ben. This was a mistake."

"No, it really wasn't. This was meant to happen. *We* are meant to happen, Lauren."

"No, we're not."

She may as well have just stabbed a knife through my heart.

"How can you say that?" My voice sounds just as defeated as I feel. I take a step towards her, but she takes two back.

"All of this was a mistake. I never should have gone anywhere near you. It was wrong, and we both knew it."

"There's nothing wrong with how I feel about you." I try reaching for her again, but she's backing up too quickly.

"You ruined my life, Ben. This is done. *We* are done."

I fight to breathe as she turns and runs towards her car.

"Lauren," I cry as her tyres kick up the stones covering the car park. But it's too late.

She's gone.

# CHAPTER THIRTEEN

Once the sound of her engine disappears, I fall back down on the blanket. At some point over the last hour or so, night descended around us and the only light is coming from the moon that's shining brightly above me.

I stare up at the star-filled sky as emotion clogs my throat and stings my eyes.

I tell myself that she didn't mean any of those words. She can't. I can see how she really feels when we're together. It's no different to our first few times all those years ago. I know it's not just me who still feels the connection between us. Hell, she's fucked me twice in the past week. There's definitely still something between us. There has to be.

Lauren's the only girl ever to own my heart, and I'm not letting her go because she's too stubborn to admit what we could be. I know I hurt her. I feel the guilt and pain of that day every waking moment. She's not the only one who had her heart broken.

The night chill eventually gets to me and I find myself back in my car. Rita's still singing away, but even her voice doesn't have the effect it usually does.

Not feeling strong enough to return to the house where so much has happened with Lauren, I head back to the office.

This time, all the lights are off and the place is deserted. I walk through the darkness until I'm in what was once my dad's office. I flick the desk lamp on and power up the computer.

I'm determined to give this business the lease of life it needs to stop it from going under, and in order for that to happen I need to start getting my head around what's going on.

I get so lost in everything that before I know it, the sun's starting to come up and the sound of someone entering drags my eyes up from the screen.

"Have you been here all night?" Erica correctly guesses when she finds me probably looking a little worse for wear.

"Looks that way."

"Are you okay? You seem…"

"I'm fine. Just trying to get my head around everything."

"Did you find Lauren yesterday?" I make a noise in agreement and Erica's eyebrow pops up in question. "I'll go make coffee and you can tell me all about it."

"Nothing to tell." The pain I felt as she drove away from me last night once again tugs at my heart.

"Try telling your face that."

I manage to distract Erica with a million work-related questions when she reappears thankfully with a steaming mug of coffee. I know she hasn't forgotten though. I can see it in the sympathetic looks I get while she thinks I'm doing something else. I know she wants to help, but quite honestly, I've no idea if anyone can do anything to help right now. Lauren made her thoughts very clear last night. I now just need to decide what I'm going to do about it.

Once the others start arriving for the day, Erica leaves me to it. I need to go home and get some sleep really, but now I've started getting to grips with this place once again, I'm desperate to continue. This might be the only thing I have here now, so I've no choice but to make a success of it.

I'm looking over a set of drawings when someone knocks on the office door.

"Come in," I call without looking up, because I assume it's either Erica or Betty with more coffee.

"We need to talk," an unfamiliar male voice says, dragging my eyes up from the desk.

"What the—" He might look like a different person from the first time I met him, but I know immediately that the man standing in front of me is Joe. *The boyfriend.* But this time, there's no crisp white shirt, braces, or slicked-back hair. Instead, he's wearing a skin-tight black t-shirt, tattoos on full display, and a Johnson & Son's high visibility jacket. "You've got to be shitting me."

Closing the door behind him, cutting off any prying eyes, he walks over to my desk and places his palms down. If he's trying to intimidate me with his muscles and ink, it's failing miserably.

My muscles twitch to stand toe-to-toe with him but I resist, not wanting to look like he affects me in any way. Instead, I rest back in my chair and plaster a neutral expression on my face.

"You need to stay away from her."

"Not happening. Did you need anything else?" Fire flicks through his eyes and I just about manage to contain my smile. Going a round or two with this guy might be the exact thing I need to ease the tension coursing through me, but I want it to be a challenge. When I beat him, I want it to be known that it's because I'm the better man.

"Do you have any idea what you're doing to her?"

"I know exactly what I did to her last night," I taunt. His jaw pops and the muscles in his neck tense. "Didn't she tell you?"

"Of course she fucking told me. Lauren's not a liar." My eyes widen slightly at his admission. "I know everything, Ben. I know every bit of pain you've caused her. I also know that it's time for you to disappear off to wherever it was you went before and to leave her the fuck alone."

"Make me," I state, deciding now's the perfect time to properly get in his face. There's about an inch between us when the door swings open and Lauren rushes in.

"For fuck's sake." She grabs Joe's arm and attempts to pull him away. "I told you to leave it."

"This needs fucking sorting, sweets."

*Sweets?* Who the fuck does this guy think he is?

"Just get your arse to site like you promised you would." Lauren's anger is palpable, and it makes me weirdly happy to know that it's not directed at me for once.

"If he so much as touches you again, I'll fucking kill him," Joe seethes.

"He won't." Lauren's words seem a little too confident for my liking. I know for a fact that if I got her in the right situation, she'd be like putty in my hands once again. The spark between us is too strong for her to deny, and she knows it just as well as I do. It's about time that this fucker realised it as well and got out of my fucking way.

"I'm serious," he says, turning his dark stare on me. A weaker man might cower to him, but that's not who I am. Standing taller, I tip my chin up to him. "You fucking touch her—"

"*And you'll kill me.* Yeah, I got that memo thanks. Are we done here? I've got a business to run, and I'm sure you've got some bricks to move or something."

"Actually, Joe's one of our site agents," Lauren says. "You might want to start being nice to him."

"Get out of my office," I growl. I've not had enough sleep or caffeine to deal with this right now.

"I'm fucking watching you," Joe warns.

"I'm real scared," I mutter as he turns and walks away. I don't see his reaction because my eyes are locked on Lauren as she tries to contain a smile.

"You need to start fighting your own battles, baby. You don't need a henchman to do it for you."

"You and I both know what happens when we fight. I think it's best we stay out of each other's way. I'll be working from home if anyone needs me." Spinning on her heel, she walks out of the office and, after a very brief chat with Erica, she leaves the building.

---

"YOU SLEPT WITH HER AGAIN, didn't you?"

"Sorry, I'm working," I say over my shoulder, feeling Erica's eyes burning into the back of my head.

"You need to stop playing games, Ben."

Spinning on my chair, I find her with her hands on her hips, staring daggers at me.

"What?"

"Lauren's one of my best friends, and you're hurting her. You need to stop."

"I thought I was your friend?"

"You are. But you're the one doing all of this. Just do as she asks and leave her be. She's moved on with her life, and you need to do the same."

"You're serious?"

"I want nothing more than for both of you to be happy, but at the moment you're ripping each other apart."

"We're meant to be together."

"Maybe so, but not right now. Just give her some time. Give her some space to breathe."

"So he can get his claws in even deeper?"

"Just trust her, Ben. Trust that she knows what she's doing."

"How can I when she's been sleeping with me?"

---

ERICA EVENTUALLY LEAVES THE OFFICE, but I only get a few minutes of peace before four others descend on me.

"Here he is!" Dec announces as he swings the door open. "Shit, you look rough, mate."

"Nice to see you, too."

"We've been waiting at the house for you. We need to head back home."

Guilt washes through me that I've basically abandoned them after they came all this way to try to cheer me up. "Shit, guys. I'm—"

"Don't even think about it. We came here to support you, not to make you feel guilty for doing your thing," Liv says, giving me a stern look.

I smile at her, but I don't feel any better about any of this. "This place is about to go under, and my darling stepdaddy left it all to me."

"Yeah, your mum mentioned something along those lines. Is there anything we can do?" Dec asks.

"Got a few hundred grand to spare?" Dec looks a little too serious. "I'm joking, I'm joking. I'm sure it'll all be fine once I get back into the swing of it."

"Well, you know where we are if there is anything."

"I hate leaving you like this," Liv whispers in my ear when I pull her in for a hug.

"I'll be fine. You don't need to worry about me."

"Keep me informed about everything."

"I will."

Saying goodbye to the people who've basically been my family for the past few years is more emotional than I expected it to be. When I left Devon, I wasn't expecting my life there to come to an end, but looking at how things have turned out here, it seems that might just be the case.

Walking back into the office once they've left, I'm met with a sea of concerned faces, and it reminds me that I haven't slept.

"Are you going to be okay holding the fort?" I ask Erica when I come to a stop by her desk.

"Of course. Who do you think's been running this place for the last two weeks?"

"I'll never be able to thank you enough."

"Ben, I caused half of this. It's my job to try to help put it right. I'm just grateful I still have a job."

"Don't be stupid. You're not going anywhere. Call if you need me, but there's a good chance I'll be sleeping."

"I've got it covered. Go look after yourself."

Laughter fills the house when I get home. Poking my head into the living room, I find Mum and Chris laughing at something on the TV. I can't help but smile at them both. Maybe what everyone has been saying is true, and things will all be okay in the end. An image of Lauren pops into my head, but I push it to the back of my mind—for now, at least. I just need to be happy that Mum's able to move past the disaster that was her late husband and the legacy he's left behind.

Memories of my time with Lauren last night fill my mind as I shower. The scent of her perfume has lingered around me since the moment she left. I'm not all that happy about washing it away.

My body's just about ready to crash when I drag my feet towards my bed. Crawling under the covers, I fall asleep the second my head hits the pillow.

# CHAPTER FOURTEEN

I wake with a start and one thought running through my mind.

*Joe knows we slept together, yet he didn't take my head off.*

I don't stop to question my decision. Instead, I jump out of bed and drag on some fresh clothes.

"Ben?" Mum calls from the kitchen as I race towards the front door. "Is everything okay?

"Yeah. What's Lauren's address?"

"I can't...I promised..."

"Don't worry. I'll find it."

"What are you doing?"

"Going to claim what's mine." Pride fills her face, but I don't miss the slight concern that's also present. It makes my determination to get this sorted right now falter slightly.

"Are you sure this is a good idea? She's already been through so much."

"I need her, Mum. I can't sit around and watch her with someone else when she's shown that she needs me too."

"You just need to give her time, Ben. She'll figure it all out when she's ready. You pushing her into it isn't going to help."

That doubt niggles at me again, but my need for her is stronger. "I can't stand by and watch her make a huge mistake with him. I won't do it. Wish me luck," I say, reaching for the door handle and pulling it open.

"Good luck," she calls out, but I'm already getting in my car.

The drive to the office takes longer than I think it ever has before, but the second I pull up, I race through to my office and power up the computer. Finding the folder full of all our employees' personal details, I find Lauren's and note down her address.

I don't bother taking the time to shut it back down again. I'm too intent on finding her and sorting this out once and for all.

She lives farther out of the city than I was expecting. I manage to get stuck at every set of traffic lights on the way, but before long, I'm jogging up the stairs towards the flat listed as hers and Joe's after a young mum with a little boy helpfully held the main door open for me.

Knocking on the door, I hear movement inside the flat. My heart thunders in my chest as I impatiently wait for it to open.

Finally, there's a click, and a slither of light from inside shines around the wooden door. But when it's pulled back enough to see the person at the other side, what I find isn't what I was expecting. Lauren's standing there, and her hair's a mess, sticking up in all directions. She's just wearing a man's t-shirt.

Her eyes harden as she watches me take in her appearance. "What are you doing here?" She's slightly out of breath, and it only ignites my anger.

"Who is it, sweets?" a male voice rumbles, before the door opens even wider to reveal Joe coming to a stop behind her in just his boxers. "Oh, it's you," he spits, sliding his arm around Lauren's waist and pulling her to him before dropping his lips to her exposed neck.

Something inside me explodes. My nostrils flare and my teeth grind as I try to keep myself from ripping his fucking limbs from his body.

"Did you want something?" he asks while Lauren stands stock still in his arms.

"I came for what's mine."

"Nothing here is yours, mate."

"Don't fucking ma—"

"He's right," Lauren says. Her eyes find mine, and I see a determination in them that wasn't there moments ago. "There's nothing here for you anymore."

"But—"

"There are no buts, Ben. I told you last night. I'm done. This is over. Stay if you want, for your business, but I won't be there. You'll find my resignation in your Inbox already. I. Am. Done."

"I'm proud of you, sweets," Joe whispers in her ear, holding her tight.

A lump the size of a fucking basketball climbs up my throat. I have no choice but to turn and walk away. I'd give everything to Lauren, but she won't see my tears.

# ACKNOWLEDGMENTS

Writing this part of Lauren and Ben's story just about broke me. It was hard going and so incredibly emotional, but the heartache had to happen.

I'm not desperate to dive straight into the third and final part of their story to attempt to soothe their broken hearts and to find out a little more about what happened in the long six years they were apart. But don't worry, I'm not going to make it easy for them. There's still plenty of anger and betrayal to come.

Once again, I need to say a HUGE thank you to my alpha reader, Michelle. You've been there with me word for word, egging me on and listening to me talk myself in circles over how all of this was going to play out. Oh, and of course you were the one who demanded that I break Ben and make him cry. I hope you're happy with yourself!

My beta team, Deanna, Helen, Lindsay, Suzanne and Tracy. Thank you so much for dropping everything to find out more about Lauren and Ben, and for now being too mean when I left you hanging once again with no date for a follow up. Your feedback as always is priceless and all your words and theories are still spinning in my mind as I plan book three.

Evelyn, once again thank you so much for working your magic and making my words as pretty as they can be. I seriously couldn't do this without you.

And as always, last but never least, my husband and daughter for supporting me and allowing me to follow this crazy dream.

Until next time,

Tracy xo

# FIGHTING FOR THE FORBIDDEN

# PROLOGUE

Lauren

The second the door slams shut, I turn into Joe's chest. Squeezing my eyes shut, I fight my need to break down, but the devastation running through my body is too strong.

I just did the one thing I never thought I'd be strong enough to do.

I sent the only man I've ever loved away.

Joe's strong arms wrap around my body and he whispers 'everything's okay' in my ear. I don't believe a word of it. How can anything be okay when it hurts this fucking much?

With my heart in pieces, I give myself over to my tears. I suck in deep lungfuls of air as I sob into the hot skin of his chest.

His hands softly rub my back, but it does nothing to soothe the pain. Nothing in the world can make what I just did any better.

The hurt in Ben's eyes as he looked at the two of us is going to be forever in my mind. I'd always hoped that I'd get the chance to do to him what he did to me the day he left. I hoped in some fucked up way that it would make it all right, but the crack in my heart that I've been living with for the past six years is now bigger than ever.

I'd convinced myself that he obviously didn't love me back then; that in the long run, him walking away was the best thing that could have happened. I'd fallen head over heels so fast that the longer it lasted, the more it was going to hurt when it ended.

But the man I just sent away isn't one who doesn't care. He's a man who loves me just as much now as he did back then. His feelings were written all over his face; they have been since the day he walked back into the office like no time had passed.

Everything I thought I knew has been smashed to pieces over the last couple of days, and right now, I don't know which way is fucking up.

It's not until Joe's warmth leaves me that I realise he's moved us to the sofa.

"You did the right thing there, sweets," he says, wrapping his hand around the back of my head and kissing my forehead. He rests his lips there for a few seconds, and I'm reminded of everything this man has given me.

He appeared in my life just at the right time. If it weren't for him, I've no idea how I'd have got my life back on track after Ben left. Somehow he managed to pick me up and point me in the right direction, something everyone else around me failed to achieve.

Fate brought us together, and I'll forever be grateful that he turned up looking for a job when he did. He's been my rock this week. He's done every single thing I've asked of him, which is why he's the one drying my tears right now. My body trembles once again as memories from only moments ago at our door hit me.

My head might tell me that it was the right thing to do, but it seems my heart has another opinion.

# CHAPTER ONE

Ben

"Ben?" Mum calls, following my footsteps from only seconds ago. "Ben, what the hell are you…" She trails off when she takes in the scene in front of her. "No. No, you're not going." Reaching out, she snatches my bag from the bed and frantically turns it over so she can shake out everything I'd just shoved inside. She doesn't stop until the bag's completely empty.

Her face twists with emotion and panic. "You're not doing this. You're not leaving."

"It's over."

"No, it's not. It's just the beginning. Please, Ben. Please." Her voice cracks, and the sound is like another knife to my heart.

All my life, I've only ever wanted to protect the two women I love, but at every turn, the only thing I seem to do is hurt them.

"It's best for everyone if I just leave. I'm causing too much pain."

She watches as I throw all the clothes I have back into my small holdall. She's deep in thought, presumably trying to come up with a way to make me stay, but I think we both know she's not going to win this fight.

"You're not. I love having you back. It's been an emotional week. We all just need a little time to find a new rhythm and get back to some kind of normal. Everything will be fine."

"I'm so fed up of everyone saying that. How is everything going to be okay, Mum? Huh? The business is one bad job away from going under. This place...well," I throw my arms out in defeat. "And Lauren. She's moved on. She doesn't want me."

"She's scared, Ben."

"She didn't look that scared in *his* arms."

Mum opens her mouth to say something but changes her mind at the last minute. "Put yourself in her shoes. Just give her time."

"Fuck time," I spit. "It's been *six years*. It's now or never."

"You don't mean that."

"Don't I?"

"This is my fault," she mutters, spinning on the spot and pulling her hair back from her face. Stopping what I'm doing, I stare at her, waiting for her to say more. When her eyes find mine again, guilt oozes from them.

"What did you do?"

"I..." She hesitates and my pulse picks up speed. "You need to remember that I'm trying to support both of you here."

"What. Did. You. Do?" I spit, my frustration building with her bullshit stalling tactics.

"I warned Lauren that you were on your way."

The fear on Lauren's face when she first opened the door earlier fills my mind; her hesitance to say or do anything as I stared back at her.

"*You* set that up? *You* put me through that?" I roar, not really believing what I'm hearing. "I had to stand there and watch him with his hands all over her because of *you*? Whose side exactly are you on here?"

"I'm not on anyone's side, Ben."

"Bullshit. I'm your son. You're meant to be helping *me*." I know I'm being irrational, but the image of them barely dressed at their front door is burned into my eyes.

"I am, I am. But Lauren's—"

"Lauren's what? More important?"

"No, no. She's like a daughter to me, Ben. Over the past six years we've become close. I don't want to see her hurt either."

"So it's okay for *me* to be the one hurt? This is fucking bullshit. I knew coming back here was a bad idea. I'm done." Storming past Mum, I knock into her shoulder and she stumbles back into the door.

"Ben, please," she wails. "You can't leave. What about your stuff?"

"I left with nothing once before. I can do it again."

The sound of her cries hardly filters through the anger racing around my body as I storm from the house and jump in my car.

The roar of the engine does little to settle me, but the knowledge that I'm escaping helps a little. Running is probably the coward's way out, but right now I don't really give a fuck.

I drive around the city for the longest time, taking in the sights I grew up with as my anger slowly starts to simmer down. I intend on this being the last time I'm here for the foreseeable future. Once I've had my fill, I head towards the motorway that will take me home.

The ringing of my phone cuts through the silence in the car.

Erica's name flashes on the dashboard. I want to ignore it, but at the last minute my thumb hits the accept button.

"Ben, are you there?" she asks after a few seconds of silence.

"Yeah."

"Is everything okay? You sound weird."

"I'm leaving."

"You're what?" she shouts, the volume making me jump and swerve the car. "You can't leave. What's happened?"

Looking up, I spot a sign for a place I haven't been in a really, really long time. "Hang on, I'm just pulling over."

Bringing the car to a stop in the almost deserted car park, I rest my head back.

"It's over, Erica. I was stupid to think I could turn up here and everything would just fall into place. I'm not needed here anymore."

"Stop talking shit, of course you're needed. *I* need you. I know I don't deserve it after what I did, but I need your help fixing everything I've done wrong. Your mum needs you. You've no idea how hard it's been for her without you. And she might not show it, but Lauren needs you. She—"

"She's got him. She said it herself, she's moved on."

"Do you truly believe that, Ben?"

After tonight, I want to say yes, but then I think about the small amount of time we've spend together over the last few days. The look in her eyes as she gazed up at me, the gentleness of her touch, her genuine smile when I caught her off guard. "I don't know," I admit quietly.

"I never thought you were the kind of guy who'd run the moment things got hard. I always thought you'd fight for what you really wanted, especially now you've got this second chance."

My lips press into a thin line as her words hit exactly where she intended.

"You'll regret leaving like this, and you know it."

"I...I need to go." I force the words out through the lump in my throat and hang up. She's right; I would regret not knowing what could have been, but does that mean I've got the strength to stay and fight this out?

With my eyes tightly shut, I blow a long stream of air past my lips. Everything that's happened in the last few days plays out like a movie in my mind. The arguments, the sorrow, the desire, the despair. Lauren's face as she asked me to just lie with her the other night when she was so lost. Mum's haunted eyes when she learnt the truth about her late husband. Can I walk away right now knowing how much they're both hurting? Even if I caused some of it?

My thoughts are warring in my head as I push the door open and head out into the late summer evening. The sun's just starting to set, casting everything in a soft orange glow. It almost makes this place look inviting.

I pass a couple of other people on the way, but no one pays me any attention, all too consumed by their own grief.

I've only been here once before, but that doesn't mean I don't know exactly where he is. I might have just been a kid, but every second of that devastating day is etched into my mind.

Mum tried convincing me to come here in the months after we lost him, but I always refused, not really understanding how standing and staring at a headstone could possibly help me.

As I come to stand in front of the place we laid my dad to rest twelve years ago, the same emptiness engulfs me like the first time I was standing in this exact place. I don't think I'll ever really come to terms with losing him the way I did.

Dad was my best friend, my hero, my idol. He was there playing football with me in the back garden one day, and then the next I was forced to say my final goodbye to him.

I guess I shouldn't be surprised to find a bunch of fresh flowers placed next to his headstone. I knew Mum used to come here on a weekly basis, but I kind of assumed that had stopped after marrying Nick. I guess I was wrong. It's not unusual these days.

Sitting myself on the patch of grass in front of the stone, I think back over my memories with Dad. All of them are happy. I can't help but wonder how my life might be different right now if he hadn't passed so early.

I probably wouldn't have met Lauren.

My breath catches as the thought really hits me. Lauren has been by far the best thing that ever happened to me. Our story might be full of pain and heartache, but still, she gave me something that I've not found anywhere else. She showed me what love really is and why it's worth risking everything for.

My fists clench as what I was about to walk away from really hits me. If I leave now, all of our past is for nothing. If I walk away now, then it's my choice. *I'm* the one putting the final nail in the coffin where our relationship is concerned. What we had all those years ago is worth more than me walking away.

Standing, a new lease of determination runs through me.

I've dealt with worse than this.

I've perfected the skill of pulling on a mask to get through the hard times, and if I have to revert to old tactics as I wait Lauren out, then I will.

I can put Ben and all his feelings back inside the box he's been shoved in for the past six years.

It's time for London to meet BJ.

# CHAPTER TWO

Lauren

"See, I told you this was a good idea," Joe says as we walk toward the entrance of Sixty4, our go-to bar a couple of streets away.

Once my tears started to dry up, Joe announced that we were going out for cocktails. To say I wasn't really in the mood was an understatement, but he was insistent that I would feel better for it.

I hate to admit it, but with a ton of concealer around my eyes, my favourite dress and my cute peep-toe heels, I do feel just a little bit better.

Someone waving from just inside the door catches my eye, and my face splits into a wide smile when I find Danni, my best friend, waiting for me.

"I thought you had loads of uni work to do?" I say, throwing my arms around her shoulders.

"I do, but Joe said you needed to get out of the house. Is everything okay?"

Joe pipes up before I get a chance. I'm grateful because I don't really want to think about what happened tonight, let alone talk about it. "Ben's just being a little overbearing."

The image of him standing at our front door earlier has my eyes stinging, but thankfully no tears come. I think I've probably run out.

"What are we waiting for then? Let's get a drink down us."

"Thank you," I whisper, terrified of breaking down while surrounded by strangers.

"It's two-for-one night." With my arms linked with my friends, they drag me towards the bar and order our first drinks.

The alcohol and the sweetness of the fruit juice definitely does help to cheer me up a little, but at no point does the image of his devastated face leave me. I swear it's going to be there forever, always making me wonder if I made the worst decision of my life by sending him away.

"Earth to Lauren," Joe sings, waving a fresh vodka martini in front of me.

"Sorry," I mutter. I hate the sympathetic eyes I get from both of them, but I've no idea how to attempt to convince them that I'm fine.

"So, any guys taking your fancy?" I ask Danni, trying to take the heat off me and my disastrous love life.

She glances around briefly before turning back and shaking her head. "Is your dry spell that bad?" Joe asks before Danni launches into explaining the handful of disastrous dates she's been on recently. I totally zone out, and it's not until my phone starts vibrating in my bag that I come back to myself.

"If that's him, don't answer," Joe warns when he sees me pull my phone out.

"It's not. I'm sorry," I say, excusing myself when I see Jenny's name on the screen. I know I should probably ignore her for the night as well, but I can't. She seems to be coping with everything better now that Ben's here, but I still worry about her.

"Hello."

"Hello. Lauren? Are you there? Hello?" I walk to the bar entrance as fast as I can so she can hear me over the commotion behind me.

"Yeah, I'm here. Sorry, I'm out with friends."

"Oh...uh...sorry, I'll leave you, then."

The sadness in her tone has me encouraging her to talk. "No, it's fine. What's up?"

"It's...Ben."

All the air rushes from my lungs. Of course it bloody is.

"What about him?"

"I told him that I'd warned you he was coming. He was furious."

"Right?"

"He left. I think he's really gone this time, and it's all m-my f-fault," she sobs.

I bite back the response that's on the tip of my tongue, because the guilt I feel for being responsible fills me.

"I can't lose him again, Lauren. I can't. He's all I've got." Her sobs get louder, and the words are out of my mouth before I've really considered the consequences.

"I'll find him."

Jenny might not be my mum, but living in her house for the past six years meant that we'd bonded and I'd do almost anything to ensure that she's happy. It's more than my dad did for her in the years they were together.

"You will?"

"I'll do my best."

Hanging up, I glance back into the bar at Danni and Joe, who are laughing away like they've not got a care in the world. It would probably make my life easier if I asked for their help, but I've got a pretty good idea what their opinion on all of this would be. They both agree that I need to stay as far away from Ben as I can. Most of the time I agree with them—well, my head does. But this isn't about me. This is about Jenny. She's already been through more pain and heartache than most people should have to deal with in their lifetime.

Squaring my shoulders, I look back one last time before walking away from the bar and going in search of a taxi. Once I'm settled, I send a quick text to Joe and Danni to explain my disappearance before putting my phone back in my bag and staring out the window.

When the taxi pulls into the car park, I'm convinced that his car is going to be parked in the far corner. It's his favourite place; the place he comes when he needs some peace and to get away from the world.

But it's empty.

Not knowing what my next move will be, I ask the driver to pull up and wait. I get out and the low evening sun immediately warms my skin. Walking to the edge of the gravel, I look out at the city beyond. So much has happened between us in this deserted car park. It makes me feel closer to him just by being here. I've no idea how he ever found this place, but I'll forever be grateful that he introduced me to it. It took me a few months after he left before I was brave enough to come here, but once I did, I found it to be my safe haven.

No one was watching my every move while I was here. No one was judging while I was still fighting to get over him. I could allow myself to grieve for what I'd lost without worrying what everyone else thought.

I had no idea that I was completely in the dark as to what was going on around me back then. I truly believed that Ben had left of his own accord. Naïve? Maybe, but it was what I was led to believe and I didn't really have any reason to question it. I knew the kind of man my dad was. I knew he liked to have everything and everyone under his control, but the little girl inside me who desperately craved for her daddy to be her hero wouldn't allow me to see the severity of it. The evidence was all around me, but I chose to ignore the majority of the warning signs. I truly wanted to believe he had my best interests at heart.

Jenny was devastated that her only son had upped and vanished, and Dad seemed to play the part of the concerned husband and father so well that I never questioned his involvement after I first accused him. I was too broken and lost to question it. Then Joe walked into the office, and he helped put me back together.

As the sun descends, it reflects off something at the bottom of the hill. Squinting my eyes, my stomach jumps into my throat when I see what I assume is Ben's car. I almost laughed when I first saw the bright orange Mitsubishi Warrior parked on Jenny's drive. It's not something I ever would have imagined him driving, but then I remembered it had been six years since I thought I knew him. A lot can change in that time.

Everything about this place starts to make sense.

I never noticed the graveyard below before, but it should have been obvious because I knew where his dad was buried. Ben comes here to be close to him. A giant lump forms in my throat at the thought.

Movement off to the side of the car drags my focus back, and I watch a man who can only be Ben walking towards his car. He stands with his hand on the handle, looking back over his shoulder at where he came from for a few seconds before climbing in.

My heart races. What do I do now? We're too far away to follow him, to do something to try to stop him. Pulling my phone from my pocket, I hesitate for a second but I find his number and put it to my ear, casting aside my concerns and focusing on what Jenny needs.

It doesn't even ring; the automated voice on the other end just tells me that the phone's turned off. Not knowing what else to do, I stand and watch as his car pulls out of the car park. If Jenny's right and he's leaving, then he'll head right out towards the motorway.

I wait for the indicator to flash, and when it does, I'm surprised to see the left one. After a second or two, he pulls away again and heads back into the city.

Blowing out a breath, knowing there's not a lot else to do, I walk back to the taxi. Without thinking, my mum's address falls from my lips when the driver asks me where I'd like to go.

Not feeling up to talking to Jenny, especially if she's still crying, I opt to send her a text explaining that I think he's still about. Hopefully, he'll just head home and they can sort everything out before focusing on the business.

It's dark by the time we get back into the city and pull up outside Mum's building. She still lives in the flat we used to share before I was moved into the show home.

Not knowing I would end up here means that I don't have any keys. I wince as I hit the buzzer, not knowing whether I'll wake her or not. I probably should just go home, but I don't want to be alone and I know that Joe will be out until the early hours.

"Hello?" Mum asks groggily.

"Mum, it's me. Can I come up?" My voice cracks at the end, and I have to fight the entire way up to Mum's flat not to break down.

The second my foot hits the top step and I see her waiting at her front door, I run towards her. She immediately engulfs me in her arms and pulls me inside. The stress, exhaustion and confusion all pour out of me as she walks us towards her living room.

I haven't seen Mum since the funeral.

I guess I've been putting off having this conversation and admitting the truth about what I've done. She knows Ben's back, and she's tried dragging information out of me on the phone, but I've kept my lips sealed. She knows something's going on though. She can read me better than I can myself. She *always* knows.

"Should I go and get us a glass of wine?"

"Yeah," I agree.

While she's busy doing that, I make use of her bathroom, and after splashing my face with water, I feel a little more with it once again.

When I get back, Mum's waiting for me with two giant glasses of wine on the coffee table. "I got the feeling we'd need big ones," she explains with a sympathetic smile, and I can't help but laugh.

Slipping my shoes off, I settle myself into the corner of the sofa and sip at my wine, trying to figure out where the hell to start.

"I'll sit here all night if you need me to, Lauren, but I should warn you that I have work in the morning."

"Sorry," I whisper, a smile twitching at my lips. God, I love my mum. She always manages to say something to lighten the mood.

"It's Dad."

"Oh," Mum says, her eyebrows rising in surprise. I know she was probably expecting me to say Ben's name, and maybe I should start there, but dealing with Dad first seems like the easier option.

"Apparently, he paid Ben off. Dad made him leave." The pain those words cause must be obvious in my voice, but Mum just nods, as if sensing there's more to come. "He'd been blackmailing Erica into cooking the books, and the business is on the verge of bankruptcy. Jenny could lose the house."

"Jesus, Lauren. I really want to tell you that I'm surprised by that but...I was married to your dad for almost ten years."

"I don't even know what to think, Mum. Everything I thought I knew has just been shattered. I thought he left because I was just some kind of twisted fuck-you to Dad. I never expected..." My bottom lip trembles as the reality of how much my dad messed with my life hits me once again. "We could have been happy. We could have..." I don't really want to think of all the things we could have been by now. It's too hard to even consider. "And then there's Erica. He was sleeping with her, Mum. She was at rock bottom after her ex left her, and he took total advantage. She's young enough to be his daughter." My lip curls in disgust. "How could he?"

"I'm so sorry, sweetheart. I always hoped you'd never have to experience that side of your dad."

"Why were you with him?"

"I fell in love, baby. I was young, and he offered me everything I thought I wanted in life. Like I've said many times before, we can't help who we fall in love with. What about Ben? If he didn't leave willingly, where does that leave the two of you? Is he single?"

I open my mouth to respond, but I don't know the answer to that last question. I want to say yes, but knowing that I haven't been entirely honest with him since his reappearance makes me question his own status. "I...uh...I don't know."

"To which question?"

"Either."

"But you're still in love with him. What's the issue?"

"He left me, Mum."

"Yeah, but not by choice, it seems."

"Does it matter? He still went. He could have fought for me. He didn't have to take Dad's money and run. He could have stayed. He could have stayed with me. Hell, he could have taken me *with* him. Anything but leave."

"Has anything happened?" My face flushes bright red, answering her question, and I cast my eyes away, embarrassed.

"What?"

Blowing out a breath, I prepare to tell her what I've done. "He thinks I'm with Joe."

"Why?"

"Because I made it out that way."

"Lauren," she says on a sigh. "What are you doing?"

"I've no fucking clue. I thought I had everything how I wanted it. I was finally in a place where I was enjoying life, and then he turns up and throws everything into chaos. Dad dies, I fall straight back into bed with my stepbrother, and I end up quitting my job." I can't help but laugh at how ridiculous it all sounds.

"You quit? Why?"

I'm silent for a few seconds as I consider how to answer that question. I want to say it's because I don't want to work with Ben, but she'd know that's a lie.

"Look, it's totally your decision, but don't you think you owe it to everyone to stick it out, whether the business makes it or not? If not for Ben or your dad, for Jenny?"

"Us working together isn't a good idea."

"Because you still love him?"

"Yes, okay? Yes, I still love him," I admit, a little louder and more forcefully than I was expecting. "But he left me. He walked out of my life and didn't reappear until my dad died. And what? I'm meant to just carry on like it's six years ago because it's what my heart wants? What about what I deserve?"

"What about what Ben deserves?"

"I'm sorry, what?"

"He hasn't had it easy in all of this either, Lauren."

"Hang on, whose side are you on here?"

"Yours, baby. Always yours. I'm just trying to look at things from both sides. He was forced from the only life he'd known because he fell in love. How easy do you think the last six years have been for him? While you've been here, trying to carry on, he had to totally rebuild his life. You told me before that he left with nothing."

"Nothing but the dirty money Dad gave him."

"That means nothing, and you know it. What's he even been doing for the past six years?"

"I've no idea," I admit quietly. Mum looks at me with disapproval in her eyes. "It hasn't really come up in conversation," I say, trying to defend myself.

"Have you even *had* a conversation?"

My silence says it all. It's true, I guess. When we've been together, we've either been arguing or fucking. I have no clue what his life's been like other than he has what seem to be good friends.

"Do you think maybe you need to sit down with him, get everything out in the open?" I don't respond, because my phone buzzes in my bag. Pulling it out, I smile when I see a picture message from Joe. I quickly swipe to see what he's sent me. It's usually something to show me how much fun he's having, trying to convince me to come and join him. However when the photo loads, my smile drops and my hand trembles.

"Lauren? What's wrong?" Mum's voice sounds a million miles away as I stare down at an image of Ben with a practically naked stripper wrapped around him.

"Motherfucker," I growl, throwing my phone down on the sofa and marching to the other side of the room.

The only thing I can hear is my blood rushing through my ears—that is, until Mum's voice breaks through.

"What's the problem? You're with Joe as far as he's concerned."

# CHAPTER THREE

Ben

"Ben." The volume of her calls only intensifies the pounding in my head. "Ben." This time, she accompanies it with knocking.

"Yeah, I'm here," I grate out. My throat's as dry as the fucking Sahara.

"We're meeting Erica at nine. We're going to be late if you don't hurry up."

Rolling over, I drag my eyes open, the morning light burning my sockets, and I have to fight not to pull the duvet over my head and go back to sleep.

Heading to that strip club last night probably wasn't the best idea, but drowning things out with alcohol and women is the only way I know how.

I've no idea what time I eventually made it home last night, and I only have very vague memories of the journey. Thankfully, I was sensible enough to get in a taxi.

"Ben?" Mum shouts again, correctly assuming that I'm trying to ignore her. "I know you're angry, and I'm sorry, but please, we need to get to the office. There's a lot that needs to be discussed before it's too late."

"Give me ten," I call out.

"Don't forget all your ID for Chris later either," she says, reminding me about our meeting to start the process of getting everything changed over to my name. The prospect of having the weight of not only the business and all its issues but this place on my head is more daunting than I've let anyone see. If I screw this up, it's going to impact a lot of lives.

Sucking in a few deep breaths once I've managed to sit myself on the edge of the bed, I will my stomach to settle. I haven't drunk that much in a long time, but unlike all the previous times I've drunk my problems away, Lauren's face never left me. The image of her in Joe's arms is still right there in front of my eyes, taunting me.

After a few seconds, I pull myself to my feet and stumble towards the en suite. I'm in desperate need of a shower before I grace other humans with my presence.

Mum's at the bottom of the stairs waiting for me. The second my foot hits the ground floor, she walks up to me and throws her arms around my shoulders. I tense. I'm still angry with her for interfering, but I don't have it in me to turn her away right now.

"I'm so glad you didn't leave."

"Trust me, it was close."

"Where did you go?"

"It doesn't matter." Placing my hands on her shoulders, I prise her away from me. There's no way I'm telling her about going to see Dad; it'll only make her ask questions that I'm not prepared to answer. "Come on, Erica will be waiting."

"Where's your car?" Mum asks when she notices it's missing.

"Outside the strip club," I mutter to her surprise, if her gasp is anything to go by.

"You went to a strip club?" The line between her brows deepens, disapproval written all over her face.

"Yes, Mum. I went to a strip club. I found the woman I'm in love with in another man's arms, and I needed a distraction. Do you have a problem with that?" I regret snapping the moment tears pool in her eyes, but I'm really not in the mood to have my bad decisions questioned right now.

Everyone's busy when we get to the office, but it doesn't stop Betty from dropping whatever she's doing and running towards the kitchen to make us coffee the second we enter.

"Give us ten minutes, yeah?" Mum says to Erica as we pass, then she shuts the door behind both of us once we're in the office.

I don't bother waiting to see where she's going to sit. I go straight for the chair behind the desk...my chair. What I don't expect is for Mum to turn her determined stare on me.

"What?"

"I need to know that you're in this for the long haul, Ben. This business needs someone who's going to be serious, not someone who's going to want to run at the first sign of trouble. Hell knows, we've already had enough of that. What we need to do here isn't going to be easy. It's going to take hard work and dedication, and if you're not the man for the job, then I have no problem with finding someone who is."

My eyebrows rise in surprise. It's been years since I've heard Mum talk with such conviction. She and Dad ran this place like a tight ship when I was a kid, but after he died and Nick took over, it was like all her fight just disappeared. If she'd kept just a little of her tenacity, maybe we wouldn't be in this position right now.

"I can do it," I say, spinning on the chair to power up the computer.

"What was that?" Her eyebrow quirks and her hand lands on her hip.

"I can do it."

"I know you can, but do you *want* to?"

It might have been inevitable that I end up here, but all my life it truly was the only thing I wanted. I never considered any other career options. I'd watched my granddad and dad build this business, and from as early as I could remember, I was hungry to join them. I always expected that I'd get to work beside Dad, for a few years at least. I never would have imagined that I'd be taking over at such a crucial time for the business, but that's even more reason for me to give this my all. This is where I need to be, because there's not a chance in hell that I'm going to allow what the men before me built to disappear as if it never existed.

I glance over Mum's shoulder at where all the office staff are behind the wall. It's the reminder I need that this isn't just about me. This is about them, their families, their futures.

"I want to. I always have," I admit.

"Good. Just remember that, because what's coming your way is going to be hard." I nod and our eye contact holds. "If we're going to dig our way out of the mess he left behind, you've got some tough decisions to make."

"We, you mean?"

"No. I mean *you*. This place is yours now. You're the boss. You say jump, and we all ask how high. The success of this place is yours to create."

"Jesus." The weight of what's been placed on my shoulders suddenly feels heavier than anything else I've dealt with in my life.

"Ready?"

"Can't wait." It might sound sarcastic, but Mum knows I'm taking this seriously—or at least I hope she does.

Mum turns when there's a knock at the door and Betty comes walking in with two mugs in her hands.

"Thank you, Betty." She smiles politely at us before scurrying from the room again. "Erica?"

Getting up from my seat, I walk over and join Mum at the meeting desk at the other end of the room.

Erica takes the seat next to me, her face tight with the stress of keeping this place going.

"Where's Lauren?" Erica asks, pointing out the obvious.

All eyes turn to me, and I hesitate to answer because it's my fault she's not here. "She's...uh..."

"She handed in her notice last night, effective immediately."

"What?" Erica shrieks. "She can't do that. We need her."

"I think Ben's got his work cut out for him to get her back." Mum's stare turns on me, and I groan in response.

"That's a work in progress, but it's not our most vital issue right now." Eyes widen at my quick dismissal of Lauren's position here, but I can't dwell on the fact that she'd rather not be here right now. "We need to nail down what work we've got, what we've got coming up, and we seriously need to look at staffing. I hate to say it, but we're going to need to cut costs, and getting rid of any dead wood seems like the best place to start."

"So it's probably a good thing then that Steve's retiring at the end of the month?"

"Seriously? No, that's not a good thing. We need someone to run the jobs we've got." Steve has been the main contracts manager at Johnson & Son's as long as I can remember. He's absolutely not one of the people I was considering that needed to go.

"Okay, right... We're going to need to sit down separately then, and make a plan of action. For now, though, let's look at the jobs."

We spend hours strategizing and trying to come up with a plan to save as much money and as many jobs as possible. The last thing I want to do is take over and make a load of people redundant, but with our financial situation, I'm not sure what else to do.

"There's one more thing I wanted to talk to you about," Mum says once Erica's gone back to her desk.

"Shoot."

"I think it might be worth looking at different premises. Maybe move a little farther out of the city. This place is quite a cost every month."

"No."

"Ben," she says with a sigh. "I know how important this place is to you. Trust me, I understand. It's like a second home to me, but we need to think with our heads, not our hearts, if we want to turn this around."

Ripping my eyes from hers, I look around the office. I've got so many happy memories of Dad in this place. I can't imagine moving the business somewhere else, but I know Mum's right. Now's not the time to be sentimental.

"I'll start looking for options."

"I've got faith in you, baby."

I nod, not wanting to get into that kind of conversation right now. My head is still pounding from last night's whiskey, and now it's spinning with everything I need to do here. Add the fact that I've just agreed to visit our biggest site right now to see how it's going, into the mix, and I'm ready to call it a day. It's not that I don't want to go to the site—I'm actually quite excited to see it as the project sounds incredible—but the problem is who's running it.

Pulling up to the old factory on the outskirts of Kensington, I sit back and appreciate the Victorian architecture hiding behind the cage of scaffolding. This building is going to be stunning once its restoration is complete. The luxury apartments inside are going to be worth a pretty penny. This is our most lucrative project currently running, so it's vital that we pull as much out of it as possible. That means I need to be on top of everything, as well as working closely with the site manager...Joe.

Reaching behind me, I grab my high-visibility jacket and hardhat from the van I borrowed, as my car's still parked somewhere by the strip club. Telling myself that I need to be civil and polite, I head off to find the man in charge.

There are people everywhere, both inside and outside the

building. I know from looking at the schedule back in the office that they're on a tight timeline to get the works complete, but still, it seems a little crazy.

Hearing from a couple of our guys that Joe had gone up to the roof, I find a ladder and start climbing.

When I eventually get to the top of the scaffolding, I find him talking to a couple of others by a broken section of tiles.

I've only taken a couple of steps towards them when his head snaps up and his eyes find mine. His expression hardens and only gets angrier the closer I get. It takes a few seconds for the guys he's with to notice, but when they do, they stop talking and turn my way.

"Ben, mate, it's so good to see you. I heard you were back."

"Will," I say, nodding to a guy I used to consider my friend. "How's it going?"

"Good, good. This one's a bit of a hard taskmaster though," he says, nodding to Joe.

"I'm glad he's keeping you on your toes. Do you mind? Joe and I have some things to discuss."

"Sure thing, boss man...you are the boss now, right?"

"I am, so I suggest you get to work."

"He used to be fun, you know," Will calls over his shoulder as he and the other guy I don't recognise head towards the ladder.

Every muscle in my body is tense as we stand in silence, waiting to see who's going to speak.

In the end, I break first. "I don't know how much you know about the current situation with the company," I say, assuming that Lauren will have filled him in, "but needless to say, this is our biggest job right now and it's imperative that it's as successful as possible. That means you and I will be working closely together in the coming weeks. So unless you intend on finding a new job, I suggest you get used to the fact that I'm going to be in your life whether you like it or not."

"Until things get too hard and you run again," he mutters.

"Excuse me?" I want to believe I misheard that, but I know I didn't.

"You heard. You don't belong here, and you know it. You made your bed six years ago, so I'd recommend you go back to wherever it is and lie in it."

"I'm not here to discuss my life with you or to argue over what's mine."

"That's good, because nothing here is yours," he spits. Red-hot anger races through my veins and my teeth grind in an attempt not to put my hands on him.

Stepping up to me, his fists clench at his sides. A smug grin twitches at my lips. Good, I'm getting to him. "You and I both know that's not true. There's only ever been one man for Lauren, and that man's me. Just give it time. You'll see." I know I shouldn't be rising to this, but the look on his fucking face is too much to deny. He thinks he's winning here, but he has no understanding of the thing between Lauren and I. Hell, most of the time I don't understand it. But it's there and it's very real, even after all these years.

"Remind yourself of that when you're lying in a cold and empty bed tonight and her hot little body is wrapped around mine."

"Fuck you," I spit, wrapping the fabric of his shirt in my hand and pushing him back against the scaffolding. My chest heaves as I stare deep into his eyes, trying to rid the image of the two of them together once again. "She doesn't want you. Not really. You were just a filler." His eyes narrow slightly at my blatant disregard for their relationship. It's obvious he cares for her, loves her even, but it will never be a match for what the two of us have, and I'm pretty sure that, deep down, he must know that. He knows she's been fucking sleeping with me for fuck's sake—of course he knows.

"Like the strippers are to you?"

"What?" My stomach knots and my hand loosens in surprise. Stepping back, he manages to put some space between us.

"That's right. She knows all about what you got up to last night, so don't try the fucking innocent act with me. You were all over those women. How do you think that made her feel when you say you only want her?"

"Motherfucker." I launch myself at him, but before we connect, there's an almighty crash below us, and the world falls out from under me.

# CHAPTER FOUR

Lauren

I ended up staying at Mum's last night. By the time we'd analysed the situation with Ben from every angle possible, I'd had too much wine and it was too late to faff around getting a taxi when I could just stay in my old room.

I stayed in bed long after Mum got up and left for work. The rollercoaster of emotions over the last few days have left me exhausted, so I made the most of the peace and quiet, and of course the fact that I'm now unemployed.

I've had a job since the week I turned sixteen, so not having somewhere to go, something to do or anyone waiting on me is the weirdest feeling. Emailing Ben my resignation was a bit of a spur of the moment decision, but after what happened out in the car park, I just knew it wasn't a good idea for us to spend time together. Was resigning from my job crazy? Maybe. But I couldn't—I still can't—see any other way. Seeing him after all this time is so hard. Seeing the longing in his eyes every time he so much as glances my way damn near rips my heart out.

I desperately want to believe the words I keep telling everyone, that we're over, that I don't care about him anymore. But they're all lies. I always knew I'd never stopped loving him, but seeing him again made it so fucking obvious.

Feeling lost, I drive to a spa in the hope that treating myself might make me feel slightly better. I book myself in for a facial, back massage and mani-pedi. I might feel like I'm dying inside with everything that's going on, so I guess I should at least try to look like I'm surviving on the outside.

Resting back in the relaxation room in my white fluffy robe after my first two treatments, I allow the soothing music and the soft scent of the candles to wash through me and try to push out all the stress.

It's all going well until my phone starts vibrating in my pocket. Seeing Erica's name, I pause before answering, knowing that she's probably only ringing to bend my ear about leaving.

The call rings off, but no sooner has the screen gone dark than it lights up again. My curiosity gets the better of me and I swipe to answer.

"Lauren?" Erica asks in a rush before it's even to my ear.

"Yeah, what's up?"

"There's been an accident." My heart drops into my stomach hearing those words.

"Ben?"

"Ben and Joe. They're on their way to Chelsea and Westminster Hospital."

Jumping from the chair, I rush towards the changing room. My robe's been discarded before I've got anywhere near my locker in my need to get to them. "I'm on my way."

My entire body trembles in fear as I try to get myself dressed. It takes me longer than it usually would, and I get more and more frustrated at myself for my inability to keep a cool head right now.

*I don't know anything. They could be fine. They are fine*, I repeat, trying to stay relaxed and focused on what I need to do.

The drive to the hospital is a total blur. I've no idea how I got here in one piece. For all I know, I jumped every red light and cut up every car I came in contact with.

It's the longest twenty minutes of my life before I walk through to the accident and emergency waiting room.

"Lauren," a female voice calls the second I step towards the reception desk, but everything's a blur. I've no idea what happened or if they're alive. My heart starts to race, and I fight to suck in breaths as the reality of the situation starts to hit me. "Lauren."

Everything around me fades to black. Hands touch me, but I've no idea what they're doing. The only thing I feel is sheer panic. My heart races and my chest heaves to drag in the oxygen it needs.

He has to be okay. This can't really be it for us. He has to be okay.

"Lauren, it's okay, sweetheart." The sound of Jenny's soothing voice eventually breaks through the haze. When I come back to myself, I realise that I'm sitting on one of the reception chairs with Jenny, the woman from reception, and a kind looking nurse all staring at me.

My heart is still racing, but I feel like I can actually breathe again.

"It's okay, love. You just had a wee panic attack," the nurse says like it's nothing to worry about. "Call if you need anything."

Nodding at her, I continue to focus on my breathing as she and the receptionist head back to work.

"What's happened?"

"There was an accident on site. A lorry hit the scaffolding and Ben and Joe were at the top."

"At the top?" I screech. "Are they...Are they...?" I can't bring myself to say the words.

"I've no idea." It's only now that I see the fear in Jenny's eyes.

Jenny takes my hand in hers, and we sit back in silence, both lost in our own thoughts and prayers. I've never been even slightly religious, but I'll do whatever it takes right now to ensure that I see them both again. I've already lost six years with Ben. I can't even comprehend—

"Are they okay?" Erica asks, rushing into reception a while later followed by Betty, who's trying her best to keep up.

"We don't know."

Betty pulls Jenny into her arms, and it's the final straw because she sobs on her shoulder. I know she was trying to be strong for me, and I appreciate it, but I'd rather she didn't keep it all inside.

I watch, feeling totally useless as Erica marches up to the reception desk and demands to know what's going on. The receptionist is busy trying to calm her down when a familiar figure walks through the door.

"Joe," I cry, racing towards him and throwing my arms around his shoulders. He winces and sucks in a sharp breath.

"Shit, I'm sorry. Are you okay? What Happened? Where's Ben?"

Gently pulling me back to him, he slowly walks us towards where the others are not so patiently waiting to hear more. It's only once we've sat down that I get a good look at him. He's got a black eye and swelling down the side of his face. He's clutching onto his ribs with a scratched and bruised arm.

"Shouldn't you be in there?" Jenny asks, concern filling her voice.

"I'm fine," he says, but he looks anything but. "It looks worse than it is. Ben broke my fall."

"Is he...?"

"I don't know, sweets. He was taken in a different ambulance, but he looked to be in a bad way." A sob bubbles up my throat and Joe pulls me into him as Jenny cries behind me.

"You look like you've gone a few rounds with Mike Tyson. What the hell happened?"

"Ben happened."

"Ben did this?" I ask, pointing at his bruised and swollen face.

"I confronted him about the strip club, and he lost it. The next thing I knew, we were both falling towards the ground."

Anger licks at my insides that Ben would allow his emotions to get in the middle of work like that.

"It'll be okay, sweets," Joe whispers, but it does little to stop the fury raging inside me.

It's well over an hour before a doctor walks out from the same doors Joe did and asks for Mrs Davis. All of us stand as he heads our way. The expression on his face is neutral; I can't tell if he's about to give us good or bad news. My body trembles and Joe once again tucks me against him.

"Mrs Davis?" he asks again once he's in front of us.

"Yes, yes. Is my boy okay? Please tell me he's okay," she begs.

"Would you like to come through to the relatives' room, and I'll talk to you about his condition."

"Condition. He's alive?"

"Yes. I'm sorry, I really can only talk to immediate family."

"I'm his...sister," I say with a wince. It's the first and only time I've ever referred to myself as that, and it feels wrong.

"Okay, well both of you come through then."

Joe reluctantly lets me go and I thread my arm through Jenny's as we follow the doctor through the doors.

We sit together as the doctor explains how Ben fell from the top of the scaffolding. Thankfully, the panels below broke their fall, but Ben had a potentially critical blow to the head as well as fracturing his arm and four ribs. He was unconscious when he arrived and they've now got him sedated until they can get him a MRI scan to assess any swelling on the brain. My hands tremble with fear. Although he's stable right now, things can change very quickly with brain injuries.

"Can we see him?" Jenny asks.

"Of course. But just the two of you. Follow me, I'll take you through."

My heart races as the doctor opens the door and the end of a hospital bed is revealed. Tears burn my eyes and I swallow down the giant lump in my throat as I prepare to see Ben lying there, totally helpless.

"Oh my god," I sob the second his body comes into view.

Jenny rushes forward to him, but I stay frozen to the spot, just staring at his lifeless body. My vision starts to blur again and I reach out to the doorframe for support as my heart races too fast. The anger that's been simmering within me since seeing the photo of him in the strip club last night collides with my panic.

The only time I've really spent in a hospital before today was the day Dad died, and that was only to collect his stuff. His heart attack hit him while he was driving. Thankfully, he knew something wasn't right, pulled over and called for an ambulance. But he never made it to the hospital. He crashed in the ambulance and they weren't able to revive him. I knew at the time that I wouldn't be able to cope seeing him hooked up to machines, but I think that might have been easier than what I'm witnessing right now.

"Lauren," Jenny breathes, racing over and helping me towards one of the chairs next to Ben's bed.

"I don't think I can do this. I don't think I can do this," I chant as she lowers me down.

"Yes you can. You can do this because Ben needs you to." Her voice is strong and steady and shows me that she's more capable in a crisis that I think I ever gave her credit for. I never realised how smothered she was by Dad, but it's only in the days since he's been gone that I'm starting to see the real woman that was hiding behind his control.

"He's quite heavily sedated, but you can talk to him. Hearing your voices might help," the doctor says from the corner of the room.

Once Jenny's happy that I'm okay, she turns to her son.

"Ben, baby, Lauren and I are here. Everything's going to be okay."

A sob erupts from my throat at her words. Standing, I turn to leave. I'm not strong enough for this.

"Lauren, he needs you." Jenny's words stop my progress to the door. "If you still care about him at all, you won't walk out that door."

Like a movie, images of our time together play out in my mind. The fun we had before he was ripped away from me. I remember the way he used to look at me with such awe in his eyes, the gentleness of his touch, his thoughtfulness. But then I'm once again filled with the emptiness that almost engulfed me when he left, and the anger from knowing what he was doing last night while I was breaking once again.

Letting out a sigh, I know what I need to do. This isn't about me and my fears or anger. This is about Ben and his fight.

Turning back, I take the seat closest to him and slide my hand into his. The callus that used to feel rough against my skin is gone, reminding me that I've no idea what he's been doing for work—or anything, really—since he's been gone.

Jenny nods, and a very small smile quirks the corner of her lips. She moves the second chair to his other side, and I sit in silence as she talks nonsense to him.

"We should probably let the others know what's going on."

"I'll go. You should stay with him. When he wakes, you're the one he's going to want."

"No, I—" One look from Jenny and all arguments leave me.

Leaning forward, she presses a kiss to Ben's forehead and silently leaves the room. The only sounds are that of the machines Ben's hooked up to and my racing heart.

My head's such a mess that I have no clue what I should be feeling right now. He threw me for a loop with his reappearance, but I never expected any of it to be this hard. I really thought Ben had gone for good, and when I got the call to tell me that Dad had passed away, I pushed any thoughts of him reappearing to the back of my mind.

The changes in him were obvious: his hair had gone, his muscles had grown and his tattoos were everywhere. I didn't stand a chance with his good looks all those years ago, and I knew if he was sticking around that I was going to have a fight on my hands. It's not just what's on the outside though, and I can try to convince myself that it is until I'm blue in the face. There's something inside him that just calls to me on a level I've never experienced with anyone else. Six years might have passed, but when he stared at me that first day, that feeling, that connection...it was still there, and it was stronger than ever.

I don't think I've ever been this scared. I barely made it through the heartache of him leaving before. I know for a fact that, if I open my heart to him again, I will not survive the consequences when he changes his mind.

I stare down at my hand in his as I think about everything that's happened since he reappeared...all the mistakes I've made. I told myself that I wouldn't go there again, that I wouldn't allow him to touch me, but I did. I broke every single fucking rule I made when he walked out of my life. I broke every fucking promise I made to Joe, and I can see his disappointment every time I look into his eyes. As angry as I am at him for breaking down the barriers I'd put up, I'm angrier at myself. I never thought of myself as weak, but knowing now how quickly I caved to him makes me think that I just might be.

That's why it won't happen again. I need to think about myself and my future. I want one where I'm not constantly either nursing the broken heart he's so good at leaving me with, or wondering if today's the day that he's going to leave again. I deserve better than that. I deserve someone who loves and protects me the way he promised all those years ago.

"You promised," I sob, my emotions getting the better of me. "You promised that, no matter what, you'd protect me. But you walked away and caused me more pain than anyone else had the power to cause. I fucking loved you, Ben, with all my heart, and you just stomped all over it like it meant nothing to you." Dropping my head into my hands, I continue to cry for everything I've lost.

Now knowing he left because of my dad doesn't make any of it any better. Ben didn't have to do what he was told. He could have stayed and fought, but he chose to follow orders and leave.

Sitting back when my tears have subsided, I refuse to look at him.

I'm angry with him for so much that I don't even know which bit to start analysing. All I know is that, right now, I love and hate him in equal measures. No matter how much I might want to walk out that door right now, I can't. I can't leave him here to fight this alone.

I tell myself that I'll stay by his side until he's pulled through, but then I'm gone, and whatever there might be between us is done. I can walk away knowing that he's okay, and I can properly make a fresh start this time.

# CHAPTER FIVE

Ben

Whispered voices fill my mind, but I can't make out who they belong to or even what they're saying.

I fight to open my eyes, to find out where I am, but it's like I'm in a dream and everything's just out of reach. Like I'm running towards a never-ending goal.

Just when the voices start to sound familiar somehow, everything goes black again.

The next time I hear something, it's just one soft and familiar voice...but although it's soft, there's unmistakable anger within it.

*What's going on? Where am I?*

I fight to focus, to hear just a couple of the words that are being said, but everything's a haze. Before long, everything's gone again.

"You should go home and get some rest. It's been almost twenty-four hours." It's the first time I've heard a voice I haven't recognised.

Panic starts to build, not knowing where I am or what's going on, but no matter how hard I try, I can't open my damn eyes.

"No, I want to be here just in case." My heart jumps. That's Lauren. Wherever I am, she's here.

"He's going to be fine. The MRI showed very little swelling. It's just a case of waiting for him to wake up."

I want to tell them that I'm here, that I'm awake, but I can't force my throat to work, and I can't feel my limbs move.

"Once he's awake, I'll leave."

*No,* I try to scream but nothing happens. I don't want her to leave. She's exactly where she should be. I just need to tell her.

Then, everything's gone once again.

"Are you sure that's a good idea?" That's Mum's voice. I'd know it anywhere.

"Yes. I just need a break, Jenny. This week has been..." Lauren trails off. *This week has been what? What am I missing?*

"I know, sweetheart, but he's going to need you when he wakes up."

"He'll be fine. The doctors have said so."

"Lauren, don't be like that."

"Like what? He made it very clear that he doesn't need me. He's coped for the last six years, so I'm sure he'll be fine after this."

Mum sighs but she doesn't say any more, and everything falls silent.

---

"HAVE YOU BOOKED IT? Awesome. What time's the flight? Heathrow? Can you forward me the details?" It takes a while, but I figure Lauren must be on the phone. "Yeah, they're going to wake him up if he hasn't already. Yeah, it'll be fine. Yes, I'm sure." Frustration starts to fill her voice at whatever the person she's talking to is saying. "Yeah. Okay. Yeah. See you soon, bye."

Lauren groans before the side of the bed dips. "Why is this so hard?" she complains. I'm desperate to do something to make it better for her.

Then, the most incredible thing happens. Tingles run up my arm as she slips her hand into mine. If I were able to, I might cry with delight, but it seems my body is still utterly useless.

I put everything I have into it, and eventually I swear my fingers move.

"Ben? Ben, can you hear me?" I'm so desperate to reply, but nothing happens. "Squeeze my hand if you can hear me." The effort it takes just to move my fingers is exhausting, but I manage it. "Oh my god, you can." She's silent for a few seconds before she speaks again, and as glad as I am to hear her voice, the words aren't what I'd like.

"This is fucking karma for all the bullshit you've caused. You know that, right? Do you have any idea what you've put us through? Maybe you should have left the other day. You might have made it easier on all of us."

I've no clue what she's talking about, and I rack my brain for memories, but there's nothing there. No reason why I might be lying here like a fucking vegetable with her shouting at me.

I've no idea if she says any more, because I fade away again.

"I swear he could hear me. He squeezed my hand," Lauren explains.

"It could still be hours yet. Please, come home, sweets." The sound of Joe's voice brings a memory of us to the surface. We were outside somewhere, and I was getting in his face. I remember being angry and wanting nothing more than to wipe the smirk off his face.

"Not until he wakes."

"You do know that if he wakes up with you here, he's going to get the wrong idea? Do you really want to encourage him after you only just got rid of him?"

He really thinks their little stunt was enough for me to forget about Lauren?

As they continue bickering, more and more of my body starts to come back to me. Being able to wiggle my toes is the best feeling in the world after being numb for fuck knows how long.

Her hand is in mine once again, and my lips threaten to break into a smile. I bet Joe's fucking pissed with his girl sitting beside my bed and holding my hand.

"I told Jenny I would get you to leave and at least have a shower."

"How many times? I'm not leaving until he's awake."

"Fine. Well...call me if you need anything."

"I will." The sound of him giving her a kiss has every muscle in my body tightening, but then the door shuts and silence descends.

"Ben, come on." She sounds exhausted. "It's time for you to wake up, baby." Warmth fills my insides. "Let me see those beautiful blue eyes. Show me that you're okay." Her words are sincere.

I give it everything I've got, and eventually I manage to drag my eyelids open so just the tiniest bit of light seeps in.

"Oh my god. Ben? Ben, come on, baby, look at me."

The light is so bright that my eyes start running the moment I manage to open them further. I want to see her more than anything, but right now she's just a blur of blonde hair.

"Can you see me?"

I manage to shake my head slightly and, after blinking a few times, my vision clears and I'm blessed with the most incredible sight.

Lauren.

She might look pale and exhausted, but I don't care because she's right here.

I stare at her, taking in every feature and committing it to memory just in case my eyes don't work again.

I open my mouth to say something, but nothing comes out. It's like I've been on a week-long bender with how dry it is. Although, to be fair, my head hurts pretty bad so maybe that's what happened. Did I drink myself into oblivion?

The warmth of her palm against my rough cheek feels like heaven. "It's okay. I'm here. My god, it's so good to be able to look into your eyes." The relief she's feeling is evident in her voice, and it makes me think that maybe this isn't the hangover from hell. She genuinely looks terrified. "What do you need? Can I get you anything?" I try to speak again to tell her that that she's the only thing I need, but it doesn't work.

"Here, sip this." A straw is placed between my lips and I manage to sip a little water. It does the trick, because I can swallow again.

"W-where am I?" It comes out as a hoarse whisper, but at least it came out.

"In the hospital." Her voice has lost the concern that was there only moments ago. It's hard, like I remember from when she was talking to Mum.

"Why?"

"Because you reappeared and turned everything to shit," she snaps. "What the fuck were you thinking, going after Joe like that? He's done nothing to you. He didn't deserve that. I'm so fucking mad at you," she fumes, getting up and pacing the room. I'm a little whiplashed from her sudden mood change.

"You just turn up and flip my world upside down. Do you have any idea how long it took me to get my life back on track after you left? No, how could you, because you just fucked off without looking back. You were a fucking pussy, you know that? One little threat and you fucking ran. I thought I meant more to you than that. I thought you loved me. I sure as shit know I did you.

"Look what good that did me." She throws her arms up as she continues pacing.

I watch her every move, more confused than ever.

"I said I'd stay until you were awake." She grabs her jacket from the chair, and I panic.

"No. No, please, don't go." I'm fucking exhausted but that doesn't mean I won't do whatever it takes to make her stay with me right now. "Please, Lauren." My exhaustion and emotions collide and my eyes fill with tears. I should be embarrassed about the fact that I'm about five seconds away from crying like a baby, but I don't give a fuck. Lauren is the one person on the planet I can truly be myself with, and if that means she sees me at my worst right now, then so be it. "Please." It comes out as a whisper this time, and it's enough to stop her.

She turns her tired eyes on me, and the sight is enough for guilt to flow through me at asking her to do this. What everyone else has been saying to her has been right. She needs to rest.

She stares at me for two seconds before she steps forward. I breathe a sigh of relief as she gently sits on the edge of my bed and takes my hand in hers.

"I'm...I'm sorry. That was...uncalled for. I was just so scared, Ben. I thought I was going to lose you. We had no idea if you were dead or alive, and I just couldn't even imagine what I would do if—"

"Hey, it's okay. I'm okay."

"And then Joe told me what happened, and I was so mad at you." My previous elation over her concern is clouded by confusion. "What did I do?"

"You don't remember?"

My eyelids get heavier and heavier as we stare at each other, and eventually I lose the fight. Everything goes black, and I've no idea if she stays or goes.

---

WHEN I COME BACK AROUND, I feel much more normal. I mean, my head pounds like a motherfucker, my throat's dry once again, and every muscle in my body aches, but I can open my eyes, feel every limb, and more importantly, I can move. A little sliver of positivity creeps in. Well, that is, until I look to the chair beside my bed and find it empty.

She's gone.

I shouldn't be surprised. It's what I deserve after what I've put her through, but I still hoped that she'd be here.

"Ah, he's awake," Mum says, walking in with a coffee.

"Where's Lauren?"

"Nice to see you too, son. You gave us quite a fright there."

"Where is she?"

"She's having some well deserved time to herself. She's been sitting by your side for the last twenty-four hours."

*I've been out for twenty-four hours?* I push the thought aside, because that isn't important right now. What is important is the fact that despite telling me she hates me and rubbing Joe in my face, she sat here with me the whole time.

"I need to find her."

Relief floods me when I go to swing my legs from the bed and they actually follow instruction. That is, until the searing pain from my ribs stops any further movement. I suck in a sharp breath. The agony is the only thing I can focus on, and its ferocity has tears stinging my eyes. "Fuck."

"Ben, you're in hospital. You can't just get up and walk out."

"Watch me," I wince through the pain.

"Ben, please. You need to be checked over before you do anything stupid."

"I'm fine," I lie. Moving right now is the hardest fucking thing I've ever done, but my need to get to Lauren is stronger. I go to move my hand to rip the cannula out, but my arm's heavy as fuck. When I look down, I understand why. It's wrapped in a solid white cast. Jesus, how much of me is broken?

"Ah, Mr. Johnson, it's nice to see you awake." A nurse and doctor come strolling in, looking delighted to see me. "Going somewhere?" the doctor asks, concern in his eyes.

"Yes. I need to see someone."

"How about we do our tests first, hey?"

"I haven't got ti—"

"Ben," Mum snaps. That, along with the looks in both the nurse and doctor's eyes, means I take a step back and sit on the edge of the bed.

"Just make it quick."

I watch the clock tick around as they check everything that needs checking and poke and prod me until they're happy with my progress. I told them I was fine and just needed some painkillers, but they wouldn't have it.

"We'd like to keep you in another night, just to monitor you."

"No," I say getting out of bed. "Do I have clothes here?"

"Ben, I really think you should—"

"Fighting me isn't going to work. I'm not sitting around in here. I'm fine."

"You've been unconscious for a day. You're anything but fine."

"I need her, Mum."

"I know you do, but now's not the time. She'll be gone–"

"Gone—" A memory hits me. Her one-sided conversation about flights and Heathrow airport. "Shit."

Jumping from the bed, pain from my ribs makes my breath catch and my head spins. I lift my arm, hoping to ease the pounding in my head, but the cast collides with my forehead, knocking me back to the bed.

None of this is going to stop me. I need to find her before it's too late.

Finding a little cupboard next to the bed, I pull the door open, not giving two shits that I'm flashing Mum in my open-back hospital gown.

"Ben, please be sensible. If the doctor says you should stay, then you should." Her warnings go unheard as I pull some fresh clothes from a bag and tug them on.

"Where's she going?" I demand.

Mum's face pales when she realises that I know. "I don't know."

"Don't give me that. Tell me. Make up for sabotaging me the other night."

"Honestly, I don't know. I told her not to tell me so I wouldn't be put in this position. All I know is that she and Danni are going away for a few days."

Fucking hell.

Grabbing the bag and the few belongings I have, I storm from the room and then the hospital.

The sun's setting when I drag my broken body out of the main entrance, and I realise for the first time that I lost a whole day of my life in a hospital bed. I eventually find a taxi idling at the entrance whose driver is willing to give me a lift. Fuck knows what I look like right now. If his wide eyes are anything to go by, probably like I've been hit by a truck.

*Scaffolding*...A memory of being on top of the scaffolding on site, talking to Joe, emerges. We were arguing, no surprise there.

The taxi pulls up beside my car, which is still parked up by the strip club, and the last piece of the puzzle falls into place. This is what we were arguing about. Joe knew I was here, which means so does Lauren. Christ only knows what kind of stories he made up after finding me there.

I pay the driver, dig my keys from the bottom of my bag, and climb into my car. Everything aches, and the pain in my ribs almost has me crying out.

I just about manage the short drive to the office. Thankfully, it's my right arm that's in a cast; I'd never manage this if it was my left. I practically drag my body up the last few stairs, desperate to rest. The thought of lying in that hospital bed suddenly seems appealing, but I know this is what I need to do.

Thankfully, the office is deserted when I stumble through the front door, pull out her chair and sit gingerly at her desk. I've no idea if this is going to give me the information I need, but it's my only chance of finding out.

Powering up her computer, I try a few possible passwords, but nothing lets me in. Groaning in frustration, I pick up the phone and call our IT support.

Twenty minutes later and I've got access to her account as well as her emails. Being the boss sure does have some perks.

She's got loads of unread emails, so the only one that's actually been read stands out like a sore thumb.

**Subject:** Rome, here we come!

Opening the email I discover that Danni's forwarded the itinerary as Lauren requested. Scanning through the information to find out when their flight leaves, my heart drops.

"Fuck."

Jumping from the seat, I cry out as pain shoots in all directions. Knowing that driving myself will take longer, I order a taxi. I don't know what I'm going to have to do when I get to the airport, but I somehow remember to grab my passport that I'd left in my desk ready for the meeting with Chris. Getting back down the stairs is a bigger challenge than I was expecting. I clutch my ribs, but every time I take a step down, my body feels like it's going to split in two.

The taxi's already waiting by the time I get to the front doors. I must look as pathetic as I feel, because the driver actually gets out to come and help me.

"I'm fine, thanks," I grunt.

After giving him my destination, I sit back and allow my head to drop to the headrest. I intend to just shut my eyes for a moment in the hope the painkillers will start kicking in, but when I open them again, we're pulling up to the drop-off area at Heathrow.

"You okay, mate?" the driver asks, looking back at me in the rear-view mirror.

I mumble a polite response as I dig some cash from my wallet and pass it over. "Thank you."

Standing in front of the colossal terminal, I'm not sure I can put another foot in front of the other. I knew this was a stupid idea the second I walked out of the hospital, but the magnitude of the challenge ahead of me now seems very real. There are thousands of people inside that building—what really are my chances of finding the one I want?

Deciding that she's worth the risk, I drag my foot from the ground and haul my aching body inside and towards the British Airways desks.

"I'm looking for someone who's scheduled to board your flight to Rome in thirty minutes."

The woman stares at me like I've got three heads. I know I probably look like a crazy man, but I don't care. I need to get to Lauren before it's too late.

"I'm sorry, Sir, but the gate has already been called."

I think for a second. "Give me a ticket."

"I'm sorry."

"Are there any seats available on the plane?"

"Uh...yes."

"Great, I'll have one."

The woman's eyes widen, but she clicks on her computer and, in a few seconds, she's asking for payment. I cough to cover my surprise when she tells me the cost. Lauren's worth it and then some, so I hand my card over willingly.

"It's departing from gate forty-three. You're going to need to hurry." She glances down at my cast and then to where I'm holding my ribs. "Would you like some assistance?

I hate the idea of being treated like an invalid, but the pain radiating through my body soon gives the answer I need. "That would be great, thank you."

She lifts the phone to her ear and is soon looking back up at me with sympathy filling her eyes. "Someone will be here to pick you up in just a second. Good luck, sir."

As promised, a guy on a golf buggy type thing pulls to a stop in front of me. "Your carriage awaits, sir. Where to?"

I rattle off the gate number and carefully climb on board. He wastes no time in putting his foot down and we speed off through the crowds at a fucking snails pace. The longer I sit there, the more my frustration grows. It probably would have been faster to fucking walk.

I breathe a sigh of relief when the gate number comes into view. I pray that she'll still be in there and that I'm not going to have to say what I need to on the plane with hundreds of witnesses.

The moment I turn to enter the gate, I see her. She's standing with Danni, just about to hand their tickets over to board.

"Lauren, wait."

# CHAPTER SIX

Lauren

As hard as it was to walk away from Ben, I knew it was what I needed to do. Danni had been talking about us getting away for a few days for weeks, and when the doctors confirmed that Ben would most probably make a full recovery and be fully awake within the next twelve hours, I knew it was time. It wasn't healthy for me to be sitting beside his bed, waiting for him to wake up. It was safe while he was asleep. I could cry and tell him all the things I was too scared to when he was awake. I could pretend that all the bullshit hadn't happened and that things were just like they once were between us as I held his hand and allowed his warmth to soothe me...see, unhealthy.

I told Danni I didn't care where we went, just that I needed some time away, and she came through within minutes, telling me that she'd booked us a few days in Rome. Of course I'm excited. I'm not only about to get to spend some much needed girl time with my best friend, but I'm going to be able to explore a new place while I attempt to push home and Ben to the back of my mind.

With Danni back at uni to do her Masters degree, we haven't spent much time together recently. There's so much that's happened in the last few weeks that she doesn't know about. My time has pretty much been taken up by family, Ben and Joe. I feel guilty that I haven't filled her in on all the huge revelations I've discovered. I'm also desperate to get her take on everything. She's always been the slightly more straight-headed one out of the two of us.

"Wait, so you're telling me that I shut myself in my flat for a few days to write an essay and missed all this? No wonder Joe demanded we go out the other night. Jesus, Lauren," Danni says when I finish explaining about what Dad did to both Ben and Erica. "So, where are things at with you and Ben? Please tell me you jumped him the second he reappeared, because if you don't mind me saying, that boy's only got hotter. He looked like sex on a stick when Joe pointed him out the other night at the stri—shit."

"It's okay. I was mortified when Joe sent the picture, but I've realised since that Ben wasn't really doing anything wrong. It's not like we're—"

"Joe sent a picture?"

"Yeah."

"Why?"

"I told Joe to do anything he had to keep me away from Ben. I guess that was his way of helping. He's done everything I've asked of him."

"I think you'd be better off sitting down with Ben and hashing it all out. Everything's changed now you know the truth."

"Has it? He still left, Danni. He took the easy way out. What's to say he won't do it again?"

"And what if he won't?"

Glancing over at my best friend as we head towards the airport, I narrow my eyes at how easily she's willing to forgive Ben after everything he put me through. "It doesn't matter, anyway. He thinks I'm with Joe."

Snorting out the coffee she just sipped, she turns her glare on me. "I'm sorry. What? Why?"

"Because we've made it look that way."

"Lauren, please don't tell me you've done what I think you've done," she warns, but the taxi pulls up in front of the airport and cuts off any further conversation. I'm grateful, because I can already tell that Danni's going to give me a serious ear bashing over this. For some reason, she seems to be on Team Ben all of a sudden, and it's pissing me off. Maybe this little trip wasn't such a good idea.

It's not until we're settled on a couple of tall bar stools with a cocktail each that Danni turns her disappointed stare on me.

"Start talking, Lauren." I look around at the happy people surrounding me and let out a sigh. "No point planning your escape. You're not going anywhere."

"Fine. I told Joe that under no circumstances was he to allow me to fall back into any kind of relationship with Ben. He witnessed the majority of the fallout after Ben left the first time, and he was only too happy to agree.

"I didn't think any more of it until Dad's funeral. Ben thought he was hiding in the shadows at the back, but I knew the moment he entered that room. I fought to keep my eyes from seeking him out, but when Joe arrived and pulled me into his arms, I managed to find him. He was staring daggers into Joe's back, and I realised then that the best thing to do to keep him at arm's length was to pretend I was taken."

"And how did that work out for you?" Amusement fills her voice.

"Oh, it was great for all of about six hours, because then I fell into bed with him."

"Lauren, what are you doing?"

"I don't know. That's the problem."

"You're still in love with him, aren't you?"

I look at her over the rim of my glass. She can read me like a book so I don't need to say the words aloud.

"Don't you think you should give him a second chance now you know the truth?" Just remember how good it was. You can always let me know if you don't want him, because I could sure use a little bit of that."

I know Danni's only messing, but still, the thought of her going after Ben has jealousy rising within me. "I'm trying not to think about the good stuff. I'm trying to focus on how much it hurt when he left and reminding myself that I don't ever want to feel that again."

"Lauren," she sighs, realising that she's not getting anywhere. "Hopefully a few days away will help give you some perspective."

"You really think I should forget everything that happened, what he did, and just dive back in?"

"No, I'm not suggesting you continue where you left off at all. I'm suggesting that you at least tell him the truth and spend some time with him...nowhere near a bed, ideally."

"Or a car park," I mutter, but it's not quiet enough.

"You screwed him in a *car park?*"

Groaning, I lift my glass to my lips and drain it. Danni doesn't need the details.

*Flight number BA439 to Rome is now boarding. Please make your way to the gate and have your ticket and passport ready.*

"Ready to run away?" Danni smiles at me innocently, but it's just another way of her showing me how she really feels about what I'm doing with Ben.

"I'm not running. I just need a few days."

"Sure, whatever you say."

"Danni," I breathe, already losing my enthusiasm for this trip.

"No, it's fine. If you say it's what you need, then I'll stop. Let's just go and enjoy ourselves."

A little of my previous excitement flutters in my belly as we finish our drinks and head towards the gate, ready to board our plane.

We've got seats booked, so we don't bother getting up to queue to get on board, instead favouring the uncomfortable seats and enjoying the coffees we stopped to pick up on the walk here.

"I've always wanted to go to Rome," Danni says, pulling out a travel guide. I can't help but groan at her. She's the same wherever we've gone. She's so organised it makes my brain hurt. She's even had an itinerary for the couple of beach holidays we've been on.

"What? I like to know what I'm going to be doing."

"Don't I know it! So what does our schedule look like for the next three days?" I ask with a laugh.

"Well..." She pulls out a list and I burst out laughing.

"You're something else, you know that?"

"You love it."

I sit and listen as Danni talks through our plans and how we're going to squeeze in as much of Rome as humanly possible in the next three days.

Once the queue has died down a little, Danni stuffs her guidebook and list into her bag and we head over.

I feel lighter knowing I'm about to get on a plane and disappear from everything for a few days. What Danni said earlier was wrong: I'm not running away. I'm just going to get my head together, to get some much needed sleep and to hopefully relax—not that I remember seeing that on Danni's schedule. I'm well aware that everything I'm about to leave behind will still be here when I get back. Joe wasn't all that happy about me going at short notice. He tried to convince me to wait until he could get the time off, but I knew I needed to go now. Jenny was equally as disappointed because she believed I should be there for Ben. I know she understood my reasons, and she's trying not to get in the middle of us after warning me about his arrival a few days ago, but she's got her hopes on us sorting everything out. I can only imagine Ben's reaction when he realises I've gone. I can still vividly remember the excitement and relief in his eyes when he first opened them yesterday and found me sitting there. I knew I was going to give him the wrong idea if I was still there when he woke up, but I couldn't find it in me to leave.

"Lauren, passport," Danni prompts when we're at the front of the queue.

"I'm sorry," I mutter.

I've just taken it and my ticket back when every muscle in my body stills and my stomach turns over.

"Lauren, wait."

"Holy shit. How did he..." Danni trails off as she looks over my shoulder.

His stare burns into my back as Danni's eyes flick between the two of us. I stare at the tunnel just in front of me that's going to take me away from here as my head and heart duel.

"You need to deal with this now, Lauren. Look at him; he should be in a hospital, yet he's here, chasing you down," Danni warns.

I know she's right, but the desire to run right now is so strong. Dragging in a deep breath, I prepare to turn around and see him. I keep my eyes on the floor, afraid of what'll happen if I look at him. I can only imagine the state he's in and how he's managed to get here.

When he was lying in that hospital bed, I prayed that I'd see him up on his feet again, but right now, I hate myself a little for wanting him to be incapable of chasing me.

"Please, don't leave me." My heart hammers against my chest. The attendant next to me gasps, along with a couple of the other passengers waiting to board.

"I'm just going for a few days. I'm not..." I trail off, not really wanting to explain in front of an audience.

"Look at me, Lauren."

My heart continues to pound, and the only sound I can hear is the blood whooshing past my ears. My hands tremble as I fight to keep my eyes from him, but after a few seconds, my need and concern for him gets too much. I drag my eyes up his ripped jeans, over one tattooed arm that's wrapped around his ribs and then the other that's covered in a pristine white cast. His shoulders are slumped, like it's a real effort to keep himself upright. But it's when I get to his face that tears start to burn my eyes and my fingers twitch to reach for him. His usual tanned skin is pale and grey, his eyes are dark, and the bruising down the side of his face is purple and angry.

Our eyes hold and our stare continues for the longest time. I can practically hear his voice begging me to give him a chance to just hear whatever it is he's made all this effort to say.

Eventually, he moves and closes the distance between us. The pain in doing so is clear in his eyes, but I'm frozen to the spot, unable to help in any way.

The stares of the others around us make my skin tingle. We really should be doing this in private, but I'm also aware of what happens the moment we're alone together—although his broken body might be enough to put paid to that right now.

I flinch when his warm palm covers my cheek. He steps right up to me until our foreheads are pressed together.

"Please don't go," he whispers, his eyes pleading with me. "I need you."

His words are like a baseball bat to my chest, and I fight to drag air into my lungs.

"Ben," I breathe, "I can't—"

"You can," he argues. "You can, and you know it. You know this is where you should be." I bite down on my bottom lip, knowing he doesn't mean this country or even this city, but in his arms.

I lose track of time as we stand connected, my body trembling as I try to decide the right thing to do.

*This is the final call for passengers travelling to Rome on flight BA439. Please make your way to the gate immediately.*

"I'm sorry, but are you getting on the plane?" one of the attendants at the desk asks, dragging my focus away from Ben.

"Uh…"

"You two go. You've got a ticket, right?" Danni asks Ben.

"Yeah," he responds, not taking his eyes from mine. "Up for it?"

Realisation of what Danni's just suggested has me pulling back from Ben to look at her. "But you've planned everything."

"I think you two spending some time together and sorting this shit out is more important than my itinerary, don't you think?"

"I—"

"I'm sorry, but if you're boarding, you really need to move," the attendant presses.

"Come on." Ben threads his fingers through mine and pulls me towards the tunnel I was so desperate to go down only moments ago.

I look back at Danni, who has a wide smile on her face. "Are you sure?" I ask, hating the idea of leaving her here.

"Of course. You two go. Just promise me you won't spend the whole time arguing and that you'll tell him the truth."

I know her words have Ben turning to look at me. My skin tingles with awareness, but I can't look at him. I daren't.

"Lauren?" he asks, prompting me to move.

"Okay," I say, but I'm not sure if it's for him or Danni. I guess it doesn't really matter because, in seconds, Ben moves and pulls me towards the aeroplane, albeit slowly.

All the other passengers are already seated and ready to go when we make our way up the aisle to find our seats. The two that were reserved for Danni and I are immediately obvious; the flight attendant pointing to them while looking a little harassed isn't necessary.

The doors were shut behind us the moment we boarded, and the second our bums are on the seats she scurries off to start her pre-flight checks. The engines roar and we start backing up. Any chance I had of changing my mind about this are long gone as I sit beside Ben, who has my hand clutched firmly in his.

He's staring at me, and my skin tingles with awareness, but I keep my focus out of the tiny window beside me at the airport we're about to leave. I've no idea if this was a good idea or not. The butterflies in my stomach won't abate, and my heart's still racing.

"You're going to have to acknowledge me at some point, you know?"

"This is insane, Ben," I admit, still keeping my eyes on outside.

"It is. But I also think it's pretty perfect." He leans in, his breath tickling the skin at the base of my neck, and he lowers his voice. "It means I get you all to myself for three whole days." Goosebumps prick my skin and heat floods my core. It's not the reaction I want, but it's no less than I expect when we're in close proximity.

"We're going to spend the time arguing," I state, but my voice comes out all breathy and needy. From the slight catch in his breath, I know he hasn't missed it.

"I could think of worse ways to spend my time. After all, you know what comes after the arguments." His nose runs around the shell of my ear and my entire body shudders.

"Ben, stop," I beg.

"You're going to need to say it with a little more conviction if you want me to believe you, baby."

"I'm all for talking and hashing everything out properly between us, but that's it. I've already made enough mistakes with you."

"Whatever you say." He chuckles, and his arrogance has me turning to him.

My breath catches once again when I get a look at his bruised face. "I'm deadly serious. Plus, it's not like you'd be able to anyway."

"Trust me, a couple of broken bones wouldn't stop me from giving you what you need."

*Christ*, this was such a bad idea.

Thankfully, my torture is paused when the flight attendants start doing their safety demonstrations.

I hold my breath once they've finished and wait for what's going to fall from his lips next. But I'm met with silence. When I glance over, I find out why. His head's resting back, and he's fast asleep.

# CHAPTER SEVEN

Ben

**D**anni's parting words repeat in my mind the whole way to Rome.

*Tell him the truth.*

I intended on asking her once we were in the air and she had nowhere to hide, but the moment I rested my head back, my exhaustion took over. The effort it took to find her wiped me out. It was only the relief that flooded me when I saw her at the gate that kept me going.

The second she turned and looked into my eyes, I knew I had her. She can tell me as much as she wants that there's no longer anything between us, but it's all lies. She needs to remember that although it's been six years, I know her. I know her like no one else, and I damn well know when she's lying.

"Ben. Ben." Her soft voice and warm hand on my forearm bring me around. "We're about to land."

Blinking a few times, it takes me a couple of seconds to register where I am and what's going on. The last time I woke up I was in a hospital bed, and this time I'm on an aeroplane.

Looking into her kind but tired eyes, something settles inside me. I was on edge from the moment I realised she'd left me in the hospital, but now, with her beside me, I feel right again.

"Thank you." Her brows draw together in confusion. "Thank you for agreeing to this. Thank you for sitting by my bedside and being there when I woke. You've no idea how much that meant to me. I could have done without the ear bashing you gave me moments later, but I can't deny I probably deserved it."

"Of course you did. You hit Joe."

"Uh...no I didn't."

"You did, right before you went down. He's got a black eye to prove it."

Twisting so I can look at her, I cry out as pain radiates from my ribs. Everyone around us turns to look and I hate the sympathy in their eyes when they take in the state of my face. I've yet to see it properly; I only got a hint of how bad I look in the reflection in the taxi's window.

I suck in a couple of deep breaths before reaching out and taking her hand in mine. She tries to fight me, but I feel so much better when I have some kind of contact with her, so I persist until she gives up.

"Lauren, my memory of what happened is still a little hazy, but I know for a fact that I didn't hit him. I damn well wanted to, but I'm his boss. I can't."

"But—"

"I swear to you, Lauren. I didn't hit him."

"So why would he tell me you did?"

"Because he doesn't want us together."

Lauren sits back, I can almost hear the cogs turning in her head where she's thinking so hard.

"What did Danni mean earlier when she said that you needed to tell me the truth?" Discovering whatever it might be moments before we disembark a plane isn't ideal, but the fact that she's been lying to me is eating at me.

"Not now. Let's get to the hotel, and then we can talk."

I don't want to, but I find myself agreeing because it's the right thing to do. She obviously doesn't want to talk about it, so I can't imagine having the conversation in front of a few hundred people in a small, enclosed space is the best idea.

---

"AT LAST," Lauren sighs as she moves towards the luggage belt to grab her case.

"Let me." Leaning forward, I wince in pain and totally miss her bag. Having predicted what was about to happen, Lauren is a few feet in front of me and easily reaches out and lifts it.

"I know you're trying to be all chivalrous, but I've got it," she says with a laugh. I watch as she pulls the little handle out and starts walking towards the exit.

Resting my head back in the taxi, I try to push aside the pain, but the throbbing is starting to get too much. My vision blurs a little, and it's aching all down my face.

"Are you in pain?" Lauren asks, looking over and seeing the tension on my face.

"I'm fine."

"You're lying." Leaning forwards, she asks the driver to stop at a pharmacy on the way to our hotel.

She picks me up the strongest painkillers they will allow her to buy over the counter. I'm not sure they'll quite cut it, but at this point, anything is better than nothing.

I swallow them down with the bottle of water she also picked up for me, and we continue our journey to the hotel.

"How did you know where to find me?" she asks, looking out the window at the passing city.

"Your emails." Turning back to me, she narrows her eyes in question. "I heard snippets of your conversation planning this trip. I knew whoever you were talking to had sent the confirmations over, so it wasn't all that hard to find out."

An unamused laugh falls from her lips. "I should have known I wouldn't be able to escape you."

"Oh, baby, you've no idea."

The taxi pulls to a stop outside a swanky looking hotel, and I'm reminded that Danni's family business is probably doing better right now than mine is. I really shouldn't be here chasing Lauren halfway around Europe. I should be a home fixing the business like I set out to do before my world came crashing down, quite literally.

"Are you okay? You've gone really pale."

"Yeah, I'm fine." She doesn't look convinced, but she lets it go and gets out of the car.

"Hi, we have a booking under Daniella Abbot." The receptionist clicks about on her computer for a few seconds before agreeing. "I was wondering if it's possible to make it two rooms instead of one?"

"You're shitting me?" The receptionist's eyes widen at my outburst, but she quickly rights herself.

"I'm sorry, Ms Abbot, but we're fully booked."

"Right, okay. Well, thank you for checking."

Lauren reaches out and swipes the key card from the marble counter, collects her things, and marches towards the lift after the woman has given her some brief instructions to find our *one* room.

"Do you need to look so smug?" Lauren asks once we're in the lift.

My lips twitch up at her frustration, and she huffs out another breath.

"Well, that's disappointing, although I reckon we could push them together. What do you think?" I ask when we step inside the room and find two single beds.

"I think they're staying exactly where they are, and you need to stop getting any ideas. Nothing like that is happening. And anyway, you need to rest." She drops her bags down on the first bed. "This one's mine. It's closer to the door in case I need to escape."

I stalk towards her, and she casts her eyes away. I don't stop until there are only millimetres between us.

"You're not going anywhere, and you know it," I say, breathing in her scent. My fingers twitch to reach out and pull her to me, and my cock swells. "You might tell yourself that you can say no, but we both know you can't. This thing between us...It's too powerful to deny. If it wasn't, we wouldn't be here right now. I wouldn't have been fucking you when you're meant to belong to someone else."

"Fuck you," she spits. Her hands land on my shoulders in an attempt to push me away. Unfortunately, all it achieves is to cause me pain. "Fucking hell. You need to rest."

"Wrong. What I need is you," I admit through gritted teeth as I will the ache in my ribs away.

"Ben, please. Just stop." The fight's left her voice, leaving her sounding tired. "I'm going to go and get us some dinner. You try to make yourself comfortable or something."

"Are you going to be my nurse? I hope you packed your uniform."

Her stare hardens and she slips away from me. "This is going to be a long three days," she mutters as she reaches for her handbag and quickly leaves the room.

Blowing out a long stream of breath, I gently climb on the bed she didn't claim and attempt to get comfortable. What I really need is a shower, but I know I haven't got the strength for that. I might tell Lauren that I'm okay, but it's far from the truth.

I must have drifted off again, because the next thing I know she's walking back through the hotel room door with two giant pizza boxes in her hands. My stomach grumbles right on cue and it reminds me that I've no idea how long ago it was that I actually ate something.

"Hungry?" she asks with a laugh and I delight in seeing a genuine smile on her face.

"Famished." I go to sit up, but every muscle in my body screams for me to stay still.

"Let me help." Rushing over, Lauren puts her hands under my arms and helps me to sit up. She's too tiny to do much, but if it makes her feel like she's helping, then I'm happy. Plus, it means I get her hands on me. It might not be exactly how I want them, but I'll take it. She finds some spare pillows in the wardrobe and uses them to prop me up before placing one of the boxes on my lap.

"That smells incredible."

"You can't beat authentic Italian pizza."

"I guess I'm about to find out."

I moan in ecstasy when I take a bite and the tomato sauce and mozzarella hit my tongue. Lauren's gaze snaps over and her eyes darken as she stares at me.

"Good?"

"So good. Much better than the shitty hospital food I probably would have been served tonight."

"You weren't meant to leave, were you?"

"I wasn't staying."

"That's not an answer."

I shrug and inhale another slice of pizza.

"You'd left, so I had no reason to stay."

"The broken bones weren't enough, huh?"

"Being away from you hurts more."

"Stop, Ben," she sighs.

"I'm only telling the truth."

Guilt floods her features as she realises that I now know she's hiding something from me. "Tomorrow. We'll talk tomorrow."

"Stop putting it off. We should have talked days ago."

"Don't blame all this on me. You're the one who showed up unexpectedly and turned my life upside down."

"I'm not blaming anyone. I just hate this. It should be me and you, baby." I try to fight my yawn, but I can't. Now that I've stopped and the adrenaline of finding Lauren has worn off, I'm exhausted.

"You need to sleep."

I'm too tired to argue, so I allow Lauren to take the empty box from my lap and then help me find a somewhat comfortable position to lie in. I think I fall asleep before my head hits the pillow.

---

I WAKE with a gentle breeze blowing across my face. Glancing to the side, I find Lauren's bed slept in but empty. The doors at the other side of the room are open, and the light curtains are blowing in the soft wind.

Taking a couple of deep breaths, I prepare to attempt to roll out of bed. The pain hits me like a truck, and any hope I had of it reducing overnight vanishes.

I see her the moment I get to the doors. She's sitting on one of the chairs with her feet propped up on the balcony and her head resting back with her eyes shut. She's bathed in sunlight, and my mouth waters for a taste of her flawless, tanned skin. She's much more breathtaking than the city before us.

I stand there for the longest time, just taking her in. She's even more beautiful than I remember from all those years ago. Her hair is just as blonde, and her curves are even more sinful than they were back then, but it's her eyes that fascinate me even more now. They hold so much inside them, a wisdom that wasn't there before. It kills me to know it was the pain I caused her that put it there, but I find it sexy as hell nonetheless.

I don't move or make any noise, but somehow she knows I'm here. She looks over her shoulder and her eyes find mine. The intensity in them almost knocks me on my arse.

"So it wasn't a drug-induced dream. I really am in Rome with you."

"So it seems." Her face is serious, but I can see in her eyes that she's at least a little bit happy about it. "How are you feeling?"

"Sore."

"I've got those painkillers in my bag, if you'd like some."

Getting up, she gives me an incredible view of her body wrapped in only a thin, white summer dress. It's cut low enough to give me just a hint of cleavage, and the obvious puckering of her nipples clues me in to the fact that she's not wearing a bra. My mouth waters as I take my time running my eyes over every curve, wishing it were my hands instead.

"Don't get any ideas."

"Oh, baby, I had those years ago. Now I know exactly what I want."

Sidestepping me, she heads back into the room. "Here, take these."

"Thank you."

"I went out first thing and got you some stuff."

Pulling my phone from my pocket, I blanch when I see it's lunchtime. "What did you want to do today? I don't want to ruin your time here."

Shrugging, she drags her eyes away from me. "I didn't come here for the sightseeing, Ben. I just came here to get away."

"You want to go and see stuff though, right?"

"I think it's probably better that you rest."

Nodding, I can't help but agree that a day out wandering around Rome is the last thing I need right now, but if it's what she wants, then I'd do it without question.

"You need to wash. You stink. There's a bath and shower; I don't know what will be easier," she says, pointing to the door at the other end of the room. "I'll be out there if you need me."

She's gone before I get to say anything else, but I can't argue with what she's saying. I can smell myself, and it's not pleasant.

Walking through to the bathroom, I weigh up my options as I have a pee and use the still packaged toothbrush to freshen my mouth up. I don't want to put too much thought to when the last time I did this was.

Thinking the bath might be my best bet if I want to keep my cast dry, I lower the plug, run the tap and pour in some of the bubbles sat on the side.

I manage to drop my jeans without too much fuss, and I discover that I can slip my socks off without wanting to scream in pain if I sit on the closed toilet seat. Attempting to remove my t-shirt, though, is another matter entirely. After a few minutes fighting, I give up after getting a much better idea. Pulling the door open, I poke my head around the corner. "Lauren, could I get some help?"

It's only seconds before she appears in the doorway. The sight of her in that white dress with the sun shining behind her confirms what a good idea this is. As she walks towards me, I can see every single curve of her body, and my cock swells.

"What's up?"

"I'm struggling. Could you help?" Pulling at the hem of my t-shirt, she drops her eyes.

"You're serious?"

"Deadly. Will you help get me naked?" Raising an eyebrow, she crosses her arms over her chest. "I'm serious. I can't get it off, it hurts too fucking much."

A little sympathy flashes through her eyes, and after letting out a sigh, she follows me into the bathroom, kicking the door shut behind her.

The tension crackles between us the second I turn my stare on her.

"I'm just helping with your shirt, and then I'm going back outside."

Her fingers grasp the fabric and she starts lifting. "Yeah, that's why you shut the door. So you could make a hasty escape."

"It was habit," she argues as I slip my non-broken arm free. Her presence helps to dull the ache in my ribs.

"Yeah, whatever you say, baby."

Lifting up on her tiptoes, she goes to push the fabric over my head. Her breasts brush against my chest, and I can't help my good arm reaching out and wrapping around her waist.

Her movements pause as she sucks in a breath, and when the

fabric clears my eyes, I find her staring up at me, desire flooding her features.

I know that if I were to drop my head now, I could take her lips, but some fucked up part of me is enjoying this game we're playing where she pretends she's not interested. I want to keep it going a little longer; that way, when I do break through the façade she's trying to maintain, it'll be explosive.

"All done." Her voice is a breathy whisper. Her obvious need has my cock almost at full mast.

When she steps back, she takes in the bruising covering my side. Her fingers reach out and she gently touches the purple and green skin. I suck in a breath at her contact.

"Shit, I'm sorry."

"It's okay. It doesn't hurt." It's a small white lie, because it always fucking hurts. My reaction was to the electric shock that shot through my body the moment she touched me. My hand wraps around her wrist to hold her in place, but she quickly tugs it away.

Tucking my thumb into the waistband of my boxers instead, I start pushing them down. I've got no qualms about getting naked in front of her; sadly, she seems to have other ideas.

Turning on her heel, she heads towards the door.

"Ow, fuck," I complain, slightly exaggerating, as I go to sit in the bath.

"Are you okay?" She's back in a flash, holding my good arm and helping to lower me into the water. I just about manage to keep the smile off my face. She's so easily played.

"Aw, that's good," I moan as the hot water surrounds my aching body. Lauren's cheeks burn red and she looks anywhere but directly at me.

"Are you okay...with the rest?" she asks, awkwardly standing above me.

"It would be easier if you stayed."

Her eyes find mine, and I'm convinced that she's going to tell me where to go and walk out, but to my surprise, she grabs her pink shower puff and a bottle of shower gel and settles herself on her knees beside me.

I watch as she dunks the puff in the water and then squeezes on a generous amount of soap before she gently starts washing across the top of my chest and shoulders.

My head falls back and my eyes close as I revel in the sensation of her taking care of me. She moves lower and very gently brushes my ribs.

"Is that okay?"

"So good," I moan.

Her movements still for a second. "What really happened up on that scaffolding?"

"We were just hashing out some issues."

"Issues?"

"Yeah. He seems to think he's got something that belongs to me." Cracking my eyes open, I glance over at her.

"I don't belong to anyone," she grumbles. "Not him, not you. I'm a person, not a *thing*."

I allow her to vent, because at the end of the day, we both know she's mine. I know for a fact that she's got me in the palm of her hands, and I'll willingly admit that to anyone.

"So there really were no punches thrown?" she asks again, like she didn't believe me the first time.

"No, although it was getting close and I'd have liked nothing better than to knock the smug fucking look off his face as he taunted me."

"Don't," she snaps.

"What? He can't mean all that much to you; I've been inside you twice since I've been back." I know my words are crass, but talking about that fucker riles me up.

"I'm done here," Lauren says, throwing the puff down on my chest, standing and going to storm out.

"Wait. I need you to help me out."

Her shoulders drop as she lets out a giant breath. "Of course you fucking do," she mutters, and I can't help but smile. "Come on then." She stands over me, waiting for me to shift so she can help.

Once I'm sitting, she puts her hands under my arms and does very little to help me, but it's not her help I really want.

I hold back the groan that wants to rumble up my throat as I try to stand, but knowing she's here helps.

"Slowly, Ben," she soothes when I go to step out and catch my toe on the edge of the bath. Her gaze drops, but I'm pretty sure she doesn't make it down to my toes, because my cock is still jutting out in front of me.

Once I'm back on two feet, I reach my good arm out and wrap it around her waist, pulling her up against me.

"Ew, Ben, you're wet."

"I bet you are too," I whisper in her ear. She fights gently to get away, aware that she might hurt me, but I hold tight. "See, you're not even denying it. You know as well as I do that if I were to run my fingers up your thighs, you'd be desperate for me." My cock twitches between us at the thought.

Lauren's eyes darken as she stares up at me, her breathing becoming heavy.

Slowly, I lower my hand. It runs over the curve of her arse until I find the bottom of her dress. My balls ache when my fingers connect with the hot and smooth skin of her legs. I just get to the juncture of her thighs when reality hits her.

"No," she says, jumping back, but she doesn't sound all that convinced.

"Spoilsport." Reaching for a towel, I make a show of rubbing it over my head and across my chest. I make no attempt to cover myself up, because even without looking at her, I can feel her eyes burn into my skin.

"I'm going to look at the room service menu. I'm hungry."

She leaves the room to the sound of my laughter. I'm getting to her, and she knows it. I fully intend on her being mine once again by the time we leave this hotel, and so far it seems to be going exactly as I'd hoped.

The moment she slips from the room, I lean forward against the basin and suck in a few deep breaths. Getting in and out of that bath was much more painful than I tried to let on, and it's still coursing through my body now.

Once everything's eased a little, I wrap a towel around my waist but fail to make it stay put, so I end up holding it.

"Where are you going?" Lauren's standing with her handbag over her shoulder when I walk out of the bathroom.

"I don't fancy anything on the menu. I saw a little deli down the street so I thought I go and get us some sandwiches."

"Okay, sounds good." Walking past her, I go to the bag she left on the sideboard earlier.

"A-are you going to be okay?" she stutters, a little taken back by my dismissal.

"I'm a fully grown man, Lauren. I think I'll be fine."

She hovers for a few seconds before eventually turning and disappearing.

I don't get a chance to pull out one of the new pairs of boxers she bought for me this morning, because my phone starts ringing on the bedside table. Shuffling over, I pick it up and smile when I see Liv's happy face looking back at me.

"Hello."

"Hey, how's it going up there?"

"I'm in Rome."

"Rome? As in Italy?"

"The one and only."

"What?"

"It's kind of a long story."

"I've got all day."

Walking out to the balcony, I try to sit myself down without groaning in pain, but I'm unsuccessful.

"Are you okay?"

"Yeah, just give me a few seconds."

"Ben, you're worrying me."

Once I've caught my breath, I give Liv the short version of the events of the past thirty-six hours.

"You should be in fucking hospital, not chasing Lauren to Rome."

"All right, Mum."

"I'm serious. You need to look after yourself."

"I'm hoping Lauren's going to do that for me."

"Ugh, you're such a pig."

"It's part of the reason why you love me."

"Hmm...yeah," she mumbles.

"Is everything okay down there? I miss the beach."

"Everything's pretty much as it always is, just without you. You should bring Lauren to visit."

"I intend to. If I ever make her see sense."

"That's kind of why I'm ringing."

"To make Lauren see sense?"

"No. Yes. Kind of."

"You're going to need to give me a little more than that, Liv."

"Okay, well, I've been looking into stuff, and I've found something you might find interesting."

"Go on."

"I'm going to send you some pictures over."

I pull the phone from my ear, put Liv on speaker and wait for her messages.

My phone vibrates and I open the first picture. It's a photo of a newspaper article about locals helping out to fix their community centre roof. Frowning, I zoom in and suddenly it makes sense. *Image above: Nick Davis and Joseph Kingsman (aged 6) after donating their time to fix the roof.*

Nick knew Joe prior to him being friends with Lauren? Questions start spinning around in my head as my phone buzzes again.

"I just thought that was interesting, but it's the next one you really need to see. Ready?"

The three little dots bounce and my impatience grows as I wait to see what's coming next.

It's fuzzy when it first comes through, and it takes a while to load, but when it does, my eyes widen and my chin drops. "Holy fucking shit."

# CHAPTER EIGHT

Lauren

I told myself when I agreed to this trip with him that I wouldn't do anything stupid. I've already made enough bad decisions when it comes to Ben to last a lifetime. But then I find myself arm-deep in his bath water, gently cleaning his broken and bruised body. I know he wants me; the evidence was pointing directly at me when I helped him step into the tub. I need to get my head together. We need to talk and find a way for us to continue to be around each other if he stays, which seems likely now he's taken over the business.

I'm not all that hungry after making the most of the continental breakfast the hotel had to offer this morning while Ben was still fast asleep, but it's the only excuse I can think of to get me out of that tiny hotel room and away from him before I do something I'm going to regret. He's not happy about it—he made that obvious when he appeared with bubbles and water droplets still running down his sculpted body and a towel barely covering his still erect cock. One glance at it and I knew I needed at least a few minutes break; it was calling to me like a fucking ice-lolly.

The second I step foot outside the room, I feel like I can breathe once again. I spend the short walk trying to come up with how I'm going to explain everything properly to him. Thanks to Danni dropping me in it yesterday, desperation to know the truth pours from his eyes every time I look at him. I'm amazed he's allowed me this long without demanding to know what I'm hiding, but I know that's soon to come to an end, and it's got to be better coming from me willingly than him having to drag it out of me, right?

I can't be gone any longer than twenty minutes, but as I walk towards our hotel room door my nerves get the better of me. Sucking in a few deep breaths, I prepare to tell him something that could change everything for us. Depending on how he takes it, I'm not sure if I'm going to be able to hold back. I know I should be stronger, should stand up for what I believe is right, but this is Ben I'm talking about. I've never been able to let my head lead the way where he's concerned.

The room's silent and deserted when I walk in. Dropping my handbag on my bed, I continue towards the open French doors with the bag from the deli in my hand. I find Ben sitting in the chair I was in earlier, staring down at his phone. He'd have heard the door shutting, so he knows I'm here, but he's yet to turn to me and that has the nerves that are fluttering in my belly exploding.

Something's wrong.

Eventually, he lowers his phone and slowly turns his face my way. Anger pulls at his features, his eyes hard with accusation.

"W-what is it?"

"I think you need to start explaining, don't you?"

"Shaking my head, I try to figure out what he's talking about, but I've no idea what could have possibly happened in the short time I was gone.

"I've no i-idea what—"

"Don't talk shit. You know exactly what I'm talking about. *Danni* knows exactly what I'm talking about. She already warned me."

My stomach drops and my hands tremble. I guess me wanting to get in there first has been shot to shit.

"I suggest you sit down."

"I...I'm good."

"Sit," he barks, and my body does as it's told.

"You remember Liv?" I nod briefly. She was the one who came over before I even knew who she was and told me that Ben still loved me. I kind of wanted to punch her in the face at the time, but I know she was only trying to help.

"Yeah."

"Did you know she's a journalist?" I shake my head, my heart racing. "Well, she is. And do you know what journalists are good at?" Shaking my head again, I wait for him to say the inevitable. "Would you like to be honest, or do I need to drag it out of you?"

Tears burn my eyes as he stares daggers at me. I knew he'd be angry if—when—he found out, but I didn't quite appreciate the level of anger I'm looking at right now.

"Joe and I..." I trail off, not really knowing how to put it.

"Yeah...?"

"We're not together," I admit, looking down at where my fingers are playing with the hem of my dress.

"Good. And why not?"

"Because he's...not interested in me," I whisper, feeling the weight of the lie I told pressing down on me.

"Now, that wasn't that hard was it?" he spits. I sniff as my emotions start to get the better of me, but his stare doesn't waver. "I fucked you, thinking we were betraying another man. You allowed me to believe that what we were doing was wrong. But the whole fucking time, you were mine to take."

"I'm sorry, I—"

"What?" he snaps.

"I thought it would keep you away." The laugh that falls from his mouth has a shiver running down my spine.

"Keep me away? Fucking hell, Lauren. You should know that nothing would have kept me away."

"But it did," I scream. "My dad kept you away for six fucking years. Six fucking years, Ben. You just disappeared and I had no fucking idea what to think. I had no choice but to get on with my life, and Joe was like a breath of fresh air when I met him. He listened to me in a way no one else did. He understood in a way that no one else could, and by some miracle he brought me back to life."

"He threatened me, Lauren. Threatened you. If I didn't leave, he was going to take everything from both of you. I did what I thought was the best thing for you at the time. I was young, naïve, and I thought I was doing you a favour. I don't give a fuck about Joe, Lauren. You lied to me." He stands, and I hate the feeling of him looking down on me like I could be less than him.

"You left me," I fume, standing, holding his stare. "I risked everything for you and you fucking left."

His jaw tenses, the muscles in his neck pulsing with anger, his increased breaths rushing over my face. Then I blink, and everything changes.

His fingers tangle in my hair and I'm pulled against his mouth. His tongue parts my lips and I accept him inside willingly. Our tongues tangle and duel as we pour our anger and frustrations into our kiss. Teeth clash and bite, but it only spurs me on. I step up to him, but his casted arm stops me from pressing myself against him and feeling the hardness of his muscles against me.

Reaching my hands around his back, I run my nails down until I hit the waistband of his boxers. A growl rumbles up his throat, sending my desire into overdrive. Slipping my hands into his underwear, I grab onto his arse and start walking him backwards into our room. I should be putting a stop to this. I told myself I wouldn't allow this to happen, but with his lips on mine and his hand on me,

I'm powerless to do anything but to give in to what my body craves. And right now, it wants what Ben can give me more than it wants air.

"I fucking need you, Lauren," he moans when he comes to a stop by his bed and rips his lips away from mine.

Dropping his face to my neck, he starts pulling at the strap over my shoulder with his one working arm, but it doesn't get him very far.

To help him out, I turn so he can find the zip. Pulling my hair to the side, I give him access to my bare skin. He wastes no time in dropping his lips to me, kissing and licking his way towards the fabric. Once he's there, he finds the zip and slowly drags it down. The sensation of the fabric tickling my skin has lust shooting to my core. I moan as it falls from my shoulders, catching on my peaked nipples.

Ben sucks in a breath as he steps back and takes in my bare skin. "I'll never get enough of you, baby." Turning me, he pushes me down on the bed and encourages me to lie back when he places his knee beside me. Pain twists his face and it's obvious that he's not able to take charge right now like he'd like to.

Slipping out from under him, I place my hands gently on his waist and push him towards the bed. His eyes widen as he stares down at me.

"Just do as you're told." His expression darkens. His eyes flick over my face before dropping down to my bare breasts.

"I think I can manage that."

Tucking my thumbs into the sides of my thong, I make a show of pushing it from my hips. Ben's cock twitches behind the fabric of his boxers, and it's all the encouragement I need. "Tell me if it hurts too much."

"Never." I give him a hard stare, but he doesn't waver.

"Lie back and take what I've got to give you."

"My pleasure." He slowly drops his back to the bed, his eyes never leaving me.

My heart hammers in my chest and my core throbs for what's to come.

Once he's settled, I grab onto the elastic of his boxers and pull them down his legs. His cock springs back against his stomach and my mouth waters. But as much as I may want to taste him right now, I'm too impatient for what I need. I need something to break the tension within, and Ben is the only way I know how.

Climbing up his body, I try not to move the mattress too much, but he still winces in pain. I know I should stop. There are a million reasons why I should, but I already know that none of them are enough to stop me right now.

I take him in my hand once I'm hovering over his waist. His body tenses with the sensation, and his eyelids flutter in pleasure. Lining myself up with him, I slowly sink down, gasping when he fills me to the point I swear I might burst.

"Fuck," I moan when my body gets exactly what it needs.

Dragging my eyes open, I stare down at Ben. Both pain and pleasure are etched onto his handsome face. His eyes are hard with anger still, and his teeth grind, making his jaw pop. He needs this release just as much as me.

Lifting up, I drop down on him, probably harder than I should, and we both cry out. But I don't stop. I pour every bit of anger, regret and remorse for what we both lost and what we could have been into my movements as I fuck him with everything I have. He lies lifeless below me, his fist clutching the sheets beneath him. I've no idea if it's because of pleasure or pain. A sadistic part of me hopes it's the latter, punishment for everything he put me through since the day he walked out of my life and now everything he's dragged back up since reappearing.

"Fuck, shit," I moan as my release starts to creep up on me. I can only feel the beginning tingles, but I know it's going to knock me for six. A few minutes of mind-numbing pleasure to forget is exactly what I need right now.

Grinding my hips down on him, I take everything I need to push myself over the edge.

"Shit, Lauren. Fuck, baby," he groans. The muscles in his neck are pulled tight, his eyes squeezed shut. I know he's getting close, I can feel him swelling within me.

I drop down on him one more time, and my body takes over as my orgasm slams into me. Light flashes behind my eyes as heat radiates through my body. My muscles convulse and I have to fight my need to collapse onto his body beneath me as I drag in lungfuls of air.

"Oh, shit."

He's just about to come; I know his tells like the back of my fucking hand. In a moment of madness—or weakness—I pull myself off him and climb off the bed.

"W-what? Lauren, what the—" Ben stutters as his body realises what's just happened. He cries out in pain as he tries to sit up to find out what's going on. By the time he opens his eyes, I've got my dress up my body and my bag and flip-flops in my hand.

Turning to look over my shoulder, I take in the panic on Ben's face. "Not a nice feeling, is it?" I pause for one second before marching from the room.

My heart pounds as the hotel room door slams shut behind me.

"Lauren," Ben roars and my stomach turns over.

*What the fuck did I just do?*

I quickly zip up my dress and drop my flip-flops to the floor so I can slide them on. Ben continues shouting before there's a loud bang and a cry sounds out. I instinctively turn and reach for the door handle, but at the last second, I change my mind and walk away.

# CHAPTER NINE

Ben

"Fuuuuck," I groan as the pain radiating from my ribs renders the rest of my body useless. In my need to get to her, I misjudge the width of the mattress and end up on the fucking tiled floor. My ribs scream in pain and my arm aches where I landed on the fucking cast.

"Lauren," I shout once again, but I know it's already too late. She's gone. Gone fuck only knows where in a foreign fucking city.

It takes me longer than I want to admit to get up off the floor, but I eventually manage to drag my aching, tense body back out to the balcony to find my phone. When I unlock it, the photo of Joe hovering over another man's lips lights up on my phone, and another wave of anger washes through me. She was fucking lying to me this whole time. Part of me knew something wasn't right. The warning signs have been there the whole time. He knew we'd slept together yet he didn't lay a finger on me. If someone else so much as looks at her the wrong way when she's mine, I'll break their fucking nose, so the fact he hardly even flinched should have been evidence enough. But the image of them both standing in their doorway looking all loved up when she sent me away still haunts me. They were so convincing. My fist clenches with my need to do something, to break something...or someone. I knew I should have fucking hit him on that scaffolding.

Finding Lauren's number, I lift my phone to my ear. It takes forever to connect, but when it does, it goes straight to voicemail.

"Fucking hell." Throwing it down on the table, I rest my head back and squeeze my eyes shut. My entire body is strung tight, desperate for the release that was so fucking close. My cock twitches at the memory of being inside of her and how tight she squeezed me as she got herself off. Lifting my head, I gaze down at my useless right arm. I might be right on the edge, but I already know that my left hand won't cut it.

I knew she was angry. Her eyes had pure hatred oozing from them as she climbed on top of me, but I'd no idea she was planning on leaving me high and dry.

Over the next few hours, I continue trying her phone, but at no point does it even ring. I've just about lost my fucking mind by the time I hear the click of the key card in the lock later that evening—hours after she walked out.

Moving as quickly as I can, I'm in the doorway when she comes into view. It takes her a few seconds to lift her eyes from the floor, but when she does, all I see is hurt.

"Fuck." Pushing my own pain aside, I walk up to her and pull her into me. The second she's in my arms, her body trembles and her cries take over. A lump forms in my throat and my eyes sting as my own tears threaten.

"I'm sorry," I whisper into her hair as the reality of how much we're hurting each other hits me. "I'm so sorry."

We cling onto each other for the longest time, but eventually her breathing evens out and her trembling subsides. She pulls back to look at me, her blue eyes swimming behind unshed tears.

"Where the hell have you been?" It comes out harsher than I intended, and her body stiffens before she forces herself from my arms.

"Where have I been?" she repeats, as if it's the most insane question she's ever been asked. "How fucking dare you." My eyes widen, taken back by her sudden anger. "I was gone for a few hours, and you were worried sick. How the fuck did you think I felt when you left for six fucking years, Ben?"

"I—" I swallow the emotion bubbling up my throat. She's right.

She blows out a long breath and I see her fight leave her. Her eyes drop from mine to where I'm holding my ribs. "Are you okay after..."

"After you fucked me half to death? Yeah, I'm good."

Her cheeks blush and she looks away. "Liar." She gives me a weak smile and I can't really argue because my ribs hurt like a motherfucker. "I picked you up some more painkillers. Here." She hands me a bag and heads out to the balcony. "We need to talk," she says, sensing me behind her. She's resting her palms on the railings, looking out at the ancient city in the distance. "We need to talk without shouting or fucking. We need to find a way to move past this...bullshit. I'm exhausted, Ben, and you've only been back a few days. We can't keep rehashing the same shit over and over."

"Here." At the sound of my voice, she turns and takes the bottle of water in my outstretched hand.

"Thank you." Our fingers touch as she takes it, and our eyes connect. There's no denying that the connection we had all those years ago is still there. If anything, it's stronger now. I know what I want to do about it; I've just no idea if Lauren's willing to give me the second chance I want. I know it's what she wants. I can see it in her eyes every time she looks at me. The question is, will she allow herself to go there again?

She watches as I carefully lower myself to the chair I've been sitting in, waiting for her to return. I wince in pain and she flinches like she can feel it too.

"We shouldn't have done that earlier. You need to be resting, healing."

"I'll never say no to you, Lauren. You should know that by now."

"Enough," she snaps, and my eyes fly to hers. "We're not doing this. We're just talking."

"You were the one who brought it up," I sulk, a smile playing at my lips. Thankfully, she takes it the way I intended and her lips twitch too.

"Ben...I—" She twists her hands in front of her.

"Hey, it's okay. Whatever it is, you can tell me." Taking her hand in mine, I squeeze gently, hoping to give her the strength she needs to talk.

"It's not that. It's just...revisiting that time is painful."

"I know, baby. I'm so, so—"

"No more apologies, okay? Let's forget all the blame and who did what and just talk." Nodding, she takes a few seconds to collect her thoughts. "Joe was...my guardian angel. He turned up looking for a job, and I found a best friend. I was drowning. You leaving like that... it fucking broke me, Ben. I can't even describe how I felt that morning or in the days and weeks that followed. I was like this hollow shell of a person just drifting between work and home, but not really being in either place. My head and my heart were stuck in my memories of us. It was the only way I could get up every morning and function. Dad played the perfect doting father. My first reaction was to accuse him for your disappearance, but he did such a good job of acting like he was concerned and trying to support me that I believed every fucking lie that fell from his lips. He picked out every tiny one of your flaws and used it to show me how untrustworthy you were, how you were never the kind of guy you pretended to be. Without you there, everything he was saying just made sense. I knew my dad wasn't perfect or even that good a human being, but I really never thought he'd have a hand in something that would cause me so much pain. So the naïve child that I was took everything he said as gospel.

"I honestly didn't think I'd see daylight the same as I once did ever again. My world was black, and there didn't seem to be a way out. I almost bailed on my place at uni, and I stopped turning up to work. Your mum tried to do what she could, but every time I looked at her, all I could see was you. It took me a long time to be able to form the kind of relationship we have now, despite the effort she put in. She was the only one who had some kind of understanding of how I felt. She came and laid with me in the dark in my room one night and told me all about your dad. She sobbed the whole way through, as if just telling the story felt like she was losing him all over again. Our relationship changed after that. We'd found some kind of common ground, and we were able to start again.

"It wasn't until Joe turned up that things started to change. To be honest, I thought Dad was going to take one look at him, see the similarities to you and send him back out where he came from. But he must have seen something in him, because he offered him a job labouring. Erica dragged us all out on her compulsory first day on the job drinks outing, and we became fast friends. He was having issues with his parents—they'd kicked him out and cut him off. We just kind of clicked. He understood what I was going through, and he just knew the right thing to say."

My stomach knots as I get a front row seat to the pain I caused her six years ago. I can see the shadows lingering in her eyes as she explains it. I'm desperate to make it all go away, to remind her of the good stuff and how incredible we are when we're together, but I know talking about this stuff has to happen. We can't put it off by arguing or fucking any longer.

"I think everyone expected us to get together. We were spending more and more time together, but there was always something missing for that to be possible. I love Joe, he means so much to me, but not once has there been anything more than friendship between us. It took him quite a long time to open up to me about his sexuality. It was ultimately what led to the breakdown of his relationship with his parents."

"With him in my life, I felt like I could actually move on. Uni was...fine. I made the best of it. Work was also okay. I loved working with Erica and Joe, and Dad was as overbearing as ever, but we all made it work. I even went on a few dates." My entire body tenses with her admission. "What?" she asks with a laugh. "You thought I'd been celibate all this time in the hope you'd come back?"

"I...uh..." Just the thought of her being with other men has my muscles tensing, ready to fight.

"Have you been? Celibate?"

An unamused laugh falls from my lips as the faces of the women I've spent time with over the past six years fill my mind. "Something like that," I mutter eventually.

"I'll take that as a no then. None of that matters though. I never met anyone who I could imagine spending more than one night with, let alone the rest of my life. You ruined me, Ben. No one else stood a chance after you."

My heart swells at her honesty. Leaning forward, I thread our fingers together, revelling in the feeling of her smooth skin against mine once again.

"I hadn't planned to use Joe to lie to you, but all of a sudden here you were, and I panicked. He knew everything about us, and I'd already told him numerous times over the years that, if you were ever to turn up again, he was to do anything in his power to stop me falling back into bed with you." My eyebrow rises in amusement; she knew that even after six years she wouldn't be able to resist me even before I turned back up. "You can wipe that smug look from your face," she warns, but she's fighting a smile.

"I thought that by pretending we were a couple, you might back off. I clearly didn't think it through properly."

"I think you underestimated me. Or us. Everyone else backed you up. I assume they all know you're not a couple."

Guilt twists her features. "I asked them all to play along. They weren't happy. Erica and your mum especially."

"I guess I should be slightly pleased that they weren't totally on board with the plan," I say sadly, thinking how quick everyone was to lie to me.

"You need to remember that it wasn't just me you hurt by leaving. Your mum and Erica were devastated too, and they had to watch me crumble. You shouldn't really be surprised that they were willing to back me up."

"I'm not." Although what she's saying hurts, I know it's true. I hurt a lot of people by disappearing like I did, a lot more than I intended to.

"Dad's death came out of the blue. He seemed fine in the days before he died. I had enough on my plate looking after your mum and knowing that someone was going to have to take over the business; I knew I wouldn't be able to cope. The last thing I expected the day I turned back up at work was to find you there, staring at me as if six years hadn't passed. I'd fought every day since you left to put you behind me, and there you were. I just...I didn't..."

Moving my chair closer, I put my arm around her shoulder. "It's okay. I didn't expect you to be there, either. Chris had asked me to get some paperwork and told me that you'd not been to the office since Nick had passed. I thought it was safe. I thought I had time to prepare for seeing you. I soon realised that nothing I did could have prepared me for that."

She looks up at me through watery eyes, and my heart aches for her, for everything I've put her through.

# CHAPTER TEN

Lauren

It feels good to finally tell Ben how it really felt when he left instead of just shouting at him. Being able to see his reaction reminds me that I'm not alone in this. I've been carrying around this anger and bitterness for so long that it's hard to accept that he's always felt the same. I'd no idea that when I was trying to get someone to understand how I felt, that the one person I'd swore I never wanted to see again was the only one who would truly get it. The longer I talk, the more I realise that my anger's been directed at the wrong person since finding out the truth. Yes, Ben was the one who walked out that night, but it wasn't of his own doing. And while I may always wonder what might have happened if he'd stayed and fought for us, I do understand why he thought he was doing the best thing. It might have been a little naïve and misguided, but his young heart was in the right place.

As he thinks back to the day he walked back into the office, pain and regret fill his eyes. "I'd convinced myself over the years that you'd hate me. It was no less than I deserved. But I knew your dad wouldn't have let me off lightly. I knew I was going to be the bad guy; he wasn't likely to admit his part in it. I told myself that you'd have moved on, found someone else. That you'd be happy. Then you glanced up from your desk and you looked at me exactly how I remember, and I knew. Nothing had really changed. I knew you were still mine."

I blow out a long breath as the realisation that he can read me so well after all this time settles within me. How is it possible that after six years, nothing can really change?

"Tell me about your life. What did you do when you left?"

"I got on the first train I found and ended up in Exeter. I was about as lost as you described earlier. I found a crappy bedsit and pretty much drank myself into oblivion for quite a long time.

"Then one day I saw an advert saying something about it not being too late to apply to university, and I thought why not. I had absolutely nothing else to fill my time with."

"You got a degree?"

"Yeah, you don't need to look so shocked. I'm actually kinda smart."

"I know you are. I just never imagined you studying."

"Me either," he admits. "But I had no idea what to do. I'd just walked away from everything that was important to me. I signed up to a business course, I still had hope then that it might come in useful if I ever got the chance to take over Johnson & Son's like I always planned to. I met Dec on the first day. We hit it off instantly and went out for drinks straight from our first lecture. He asked me about home and family, and I panicked. I put on this act from that very first day, and it became second nature."

"An act?" My brows draw together.

"I didn't want him or anyone digging into why I was there. I could barely think about it, let alone talk about you and the reason I had to leave, so I covered it up. I covered it by becoming the kind of guy I hoped the others would look up to. Who would appear so confident that they'd never need to ask about my past, because there's no way I could have any secrets hidden in my closet."

"I'm not sure I understand."

He blows out a breath and casts his eyes away. "I played up to my new nickname with alcohol and…" His face twists as if it's painful to admit.

"And?"

"Women."

My stomach drops. I knew there was no way he hadn't been with anyone else, but hearing him say it makes me feel a little sick.

The word seems to echo forever in the silent space around us. I want to ask more questions, find out more about what he did when we were apart, but my head's full of unwanted images of him with faceless women, treating them the way he does me.

"I'm sorry," I say in a rush and run to the bathroom, afraid I'm about to lose the contents of my stomach.

Slamming the door behind me, I come to a stop in front of the basin, rest my palms on the marble top and hang my head. I drag in a few deep breaths, hoping it'll help settle my stomach. My eyes burn, but I refuse to cry. What he did was perfectly acceptable given the circumstances. Plenty of people said I should have been doing the same thing, but I could never switch him off enough to really go through with it.

I'm surprised when he doesn't immediately chase me, but I'm grateful that he allows me a few seconds to process what he said and to attempt to deal with it in private. That said, it can't be five minutes later when a knock sounds on the door.

"Lauren, are you okay?"

"Yeah, I'm fine. I'll be out in a few seconds." My voice sounds pathetic, making me wish I were stronger.

As I stare at my pale face in the mirror, the movement of the door handle catches my attention. In a second, it's open and Ben's in the doorway, staring at my reflection.

"None of them ever meant anything. None of them ever

managed to make me forget you for even a second. It's only ever been you, baby."

The tears I was fighting so desperately hard to keep in drop onto my cheeks. The sincerity on his face doesn't falter as he says the words, and I believe every single one of them.

Turning on my heels, I run at him.

"Fuck," he grunts the second I collide with his body, and I immediately feel awful for not being more careful.

"I'm sorry, I'm sorry," I repeat, trying to pull away but he only holds onto me tighter. He must be in agony, but he doesn't loosen his grip until I stop fighting.

Running his hand up my back, he slips it into my hair and gently pulls so I have no choice but to look up at him. "Only ever you," he whispers before dropping his lips to mine for the sweetest kiss I think I've ever received. It's like my whole body sighs as his lips brush over mine. It's the first kiss we've shared since he's been back that isn't fuelled by anger and frustration. I wish it could go on forever. But as my body's gearing up for more, he pulls back. My head knows it's the right thing to do. The last thing I need is to fall back under his spell. His eyes are dark and full of emotion when he stares down at me. I can tell he wants to say more, but he's holding himself back. It's not the first time he's tried to open up about how he feels about me since reappearing, but I think it's the first time I'd be able to accept the words if he were to say them.

"Do you fancy getting out of this hotel room? I could really do with dinner."

"That sounds perfect. Let me just freshen up a little, and I'll help you get dressed."

---

WE WALK OUT of the hotel room hand in hand, and it's almost easy to believe that we're just a normal couple enjoying a few days away from the pressures of everyday life. But one look to my left to see his cast and bruised face and I realise once again that we're far from that.

We might have had a bit of a breakthrough in the last few hours, but we've still got a long way to go if we have any hope of a future, whether that's together or just as...family. I screw my nose up at the thought. Are we still even really that now? Dad's gone. Jenny will hopefully move on and find the happiness she deserves. Where does that leave us?

He must feel a change in me, because he looks over, his own eyes seeming brighter than they have in the last few days.

"You okay?"

"Yeah. I'm good, I think. How are you holding up?" He tried to put on a brave face as I helped him dress, but I could see the pain etched into his face every time he moved.

"I'll survive."

"Right, what do you fancy?" I ask when we step foot outside the hotel.

"You."

"I meant for dinner. I was thinking Italian," I say with a laugh. It feels so good not to be constantly arguing with him.

"Italian sounds perfect."

We've barely started our main, and Ben's already fighting back his exhaustion. It was easy to forget what he went through only days ago as we hashed out everything else, but he really needs to rest. I insisted on stopping at the first restaurant we found when it became obvious that navigating the cobblestones was causing him pain.

"Tell me about Devon," I say, hoping to perk him up a little. "You mentioned that you lived by the sea."

"Dec bought this old derelict house after we graduated. The place was a serious shithole, but he had a dream. He was originally going to tidy it up and pay to get it renovated as and when he could afford it. He was starting a new surfing business at the time, so money was tight. Then one night when I'd had a little too much to drink, I let slip that I knew my way around a building site and offered to help.

I didn't need a paying job, thanks to..." He trails off, but from the look on his face, he doesn't need to say more. "With the help of a few local tradesmen, we did the entire place. It's incredible. It looks right out onto the sea. You'd love it."

"I'd love to go one day."

He looks up with a forkful of pasta halfway to his mouth. "You really want to?"

"Of course. I want to see where you were living, what you were doing. I'd also like to meet your friends properly. Things were a little...stressed when they came to visit."

He studies me for the longest time. "Wha—" He clears his throat, anxious about what he wants to say to me. "What are we doing here?"

Thoughts of the future and trusting him again have my heart rate increasing, but a future without him in it would be even more panic attack inducing.

"We're just taking things one day at a time." I don't know how else to get across how I'm feeling. After all these years, he still means so much to me, but I'm terrified of being hurt again.

Nodding, he takes a sip of his water. "That sounds perfect."

It's nice to spend a few hours like a normal couple—not that we're either normal or a couple. But memories from the last time we were in a restaurant together aren't far from my mind. That night had promises of being incredible, but instead it was the beginning of the end.

"Stop thinking about it," he warns.

"How'd you know?"

"I can read you like a book. Plus, I was thinking the same thing. It's going to be different this time, baby. Just give us a chance." Stretching his hand across the table, he tangles our fingers together, rubbing my palm with his thumb.

The lump in my throat grows too big to be able to talk.

"What's wrong?"

"N-nothing," I stutter. "Just thinking about that night." It's an excuse, and I think he knows it but I'm not ready to put all my fears out on the table quite yet. Today has been draining enough already.

"Are you done?"

"Yeah. Let's get out of here. You need to rest."

"Rest wasn't exactly what I had in mind."

"That's a real shame, Ben, because that's all you're getting." I can't help but laugh as he sticks his bottom lip out in a childish pout. "One day at a time, remember?"

"If you say so," he mutters, gently tucking me against his side as we make our way back to the hotel. I want to relax into it like he wants me too, but I'm not ready to put all my trust in him again. He's going to have to fight for it.

The closer we get to the hotel, the slower he becomes, and it's just the reminder we both need that the only thing that's happening once we get inside the room is him sleeping. What started out as him holding me soon turns into me helping him along the corridor to our room.

"We're almost there."

"This is fucking ridiculous. I've hardly done anything all day."

"You're broken, Ben. It's going to take some time."

"Argh, fuck," he groans, lifting his arms so I can pull his t-shirt from his body. "I haven't got time. I've got things I want to do now." Dropping his head to my neck, his lips tickle against my sensitive skin.

"Not happening," I warn.

"Try saying that when you're not undoing my trousers." A laugh rumbles up his throat and the sound has butterflies erupting in my stomach.

"I meant what I said earlier. One day at a time. That means everything, Ben. I'm not ready to pick up where we left off like six years hasn't passed. So much has changed. We've both changed. We need time to get to know each other again. We might be totally incompatible now."

"You're kidding, right?" As he gently lowers himself to the bed, my eyes lose their fight and run down the length of him. Dark tattoos cover his arms and chest. His stomach is more defined than I remember it being, and my mouth waters to discover the ridges more intimately. Running my eyes down over the elastic of his boxers, I find the evidence of what me undressing him really did to him.

"It's been like that since you upped and left earlier. Fancy finishing the job?"

His eyes are dark and his jaw clenches with need. My mouth waters as the idea of giving him what he needs pops into my head, but it goes against everything I just told him I wanted.

When I glance back up, his eyes are half-closed, and it's not with desire. It's the reminder I need. Him in touching distance is too bloody tempting. It would be too easy to pretend that I'm a careless eighteen-year-old again. If we're going to do this properly and have any chance of rekindling what we had, then I truly believe taking things slowly is the way forward. Pulling the sheets from the bottom of the bed, I cover his body.

"I'm going to go and change. I'll be back in a few minutes. Shout if you need anything."

"Lauren," he calls, just before I disappear into the bathroom.

"Yeah?"

When I turn back, his eyes are closed, although the tension in his body means he's anything but relaxed.

"I never stopped loving you. I need you to know that."

"I know," I whisper.

# CHAPTER ELEVEN

Ben

I felt a little more like myself the next day, so Lauren and I spent a couple of hours in the city. We had a very slow walk around the Colosseum and threw coins in the Trevi Fountain. I tried to put on a brave face, but Lauren could tell I was struggling. The moment she spotted a sightseeing bus, she bought us both tickets and we enjoyed the rest of the city from the open top. I hoped she was trying to reserve my energy for when we got back to the hotel room, but I was bitterly disappointed when I once again fell asleep in my tiny single bed with her in her own only a few feet away.

I'm not sure if she's trying to torture me on purpose, but my balls are bluer than I thought possible after she walked out mid-sex the previous day. She's standing by her words and not taking things too far. I've no idea how long she intends to continue it; every time I ask, she just repeats the same words about taking each day as it comes.

Our alone time passes us by all too quickly, and before I know it, we're back at the airport, preparing to head back to whatever our lives might hold.

"Are you ready to head back and take the building world by storm?" she asks with a laugh, dragging her eyes away from the little aeroplane window beside her.

"No."

"It is what you want, though?"

"Right now, all I want is you. My wanking hand's in a cast, and you're all the way over here." Running my nose around the shell of her ear, her body shudders before she gently pushes me away.

"Behave," she warns, raising an eyebrow, prompting me to answer her original question.

"Honestly, taking over that business is the only thing I've ever wanted to do. But..."

"But?"

I sigh. "I never imagined it would be quite like this." A sad smile tugs at her lips.

"I feel like all of this is my fault." It's the first time she's said anything about work the whole trip. "I should have seen that something was wrong. I manage the accounts, for fuck's sake. I had no idea there was no money."

"Don't even think of shouldering the guilt for him, Lauren. Your dad was a scumbag, and he made sure he covered his tracks so you wouldn't find out." She visibly pales at hearing those harsh words, but they're true, and she's going to have to find a way to deal with it.

"I still should have known. How bad is it?"

"Bad. We're going to have to let people go. Mum suggested we look at moving offices to somewhere cheaper but—"

"That's where your dad chose for the business." Looking over, I reach out and take her hand in mine. She's always had this ability to know exactly what I'm thinking, what I'm feeling, and this is no exception.

"Yeah. I know it's the most sensible thing to do, but I can't help feeling like I'm betraying him."

"He would understand, Ben. He would want you to do whatever it takes to save the company, and if that means we run it from the double garage at Jenny's, then that's what we'll do."

"We?" I ask, my voice filled with hope. Her expression drops as she thinks over what she said.

"Oh...uh. I don't—"

"Just come back, please?"

"I don't think it's a good idea." I study her face for any sign she's lying, but I don't see anything.

"But we need you."

"No, you don't," she says sadly. "Erica's more than capable. You won't even notice I'm not there."

"Don't. You belong there just as much as I do."

"No, I don't. I was only there because of him. Everyone's going to think I was involved or whatever." She tries brushing the conversation off with a flick of her hand, turning back to the window and trying to cut me off.

"Lauren, I want you there with me."

"No," she barks, and I have no choice but to drop it—for now, at least.

"Have you spoken to Erica?" She shakes her head. "I think you should."

"You seem to have a lot of opinions on what I should do for someone who hardly knows me." Her words cut, but I can't really argue. I do feel like I've just been slapped with her change of attitude, mind you. "I'm sorry," she whispers. "I just...ugh. All this shit just happened all at once. I need to process one thing at a time, and you might be surprised to hear that *you* were more persistent."

"I don't know what you mean. Has she tried to talk to you?"

"Yeah. She's been texting me for days, but I just...she was sleeping with him, Ben"

"I know, but I really think you should hear her out. She said she was in a bad place after her ex and—"

"He was a dick."

"He manipulated her. She didn't willingly sleep with him."

"I know, I know. It's just…" She sighs and drops her head onto my shoulder. I want to feel happy about the fact that she's using me for comfort, but the truth is that she's just exhausted and overwhelmed. She's had so much to try to deal with and process in only a few days. It's no wonder she doesn't know what to deal with first.

"Just promise me you'll talk to her. Don't let him ruin your friendship."

"I promise."

The rest of the flight and the taxi drive into the city are pretty quiet. We've both got too much on our minds to do much talking.

"It's on the right here," Lauren says, twisting in her seat, getting ready to get out.

I was less than impressed when she immediately gave the driver her and Joe's address when we got in, but I'm not sure what I was really expecting. This is her home.

The taxi pulls to a stop outside her building and my heart falls into my stomach. I'm not ready for our time together to come to an end already. I don't really feel like I've achieved all that much, other than the fact that all our words are no longer shouted at each other.

"Well…uh…thanks for gate crashing, I guess."

I think back to my journey through the airport to find her, and it feels like a lifetime ago, not three days.

"You're welcome. I hope I didn't totally ruin your time away."

"Not entirely. There were a couple of good bits."

"A couple?" I try to make it sound light and playful, but I seriously miss the mark.

Her sympathetic eyes turn on me and she smiles.

"Thank you, I think."

"Wait," I call just before the door closes. "When can I see you again?" Her mouth opens to respond, but no words pass her lips. "I'm not giving up here, Lauren."

"I…I don't know. I'll call you in a couple of days, and we'll sort something out."

Before I get a chance to respond, the door's shut and she's walking away, tugging her small suitcase behind her.

"Fuck."

"Where to, mate?" the driver asks, ignoring my frustration. I rattle off Mum's address.

Resting my head back, my exhaustion takes over and I sleep the whole journey. The driver actually has to wake me up when he pulls up in front of the driveway.

"Shit, I'm sorry. How much do I owe you?"

I pay him and stagger out. I don't have anything; the few bits that Lauren picked up for me I either left behind or squeezed into her case.

Letting myself through the gates, I find both Mum and Chris' cars in the driveway. Thinking nothing of it, I unlock the front door and head towards the kitchen for a drink.

There's music playing somewhere in the house, but there are no voices, so the last thing I expect is to stumble upon two barely-dressed people locked in an embrace in the kitchen.

"Oh fuck. Shit. Sorry." Closing my eyes, I turn and walk away, trying to will the image of Chris' hands on my mum's body from my mind.

Flustered, panicked voices sound out from behind me before Mum's soft footsteps start getting closer.

"I'm so sorry. I didn't think you were back until tomorrow. I was—"

"Pre-occupied?"

She's clutching her silk robe tightly around her body in an attempt to cover up what she's wearing—or not—underneath. No grown man should have to see his mum in slutty lingerie; it's just wrong.

"Fuck," Mum whispers, looking up to the ceiling. "We... I...fuck—"

"It's okay, Mum."

"But—'

"But what?"

Back when Nick told me about her indiscretions when he was trying to get rid of me, I had no idea if she had cheated or whatever, but something told me that if it were true—and she's since pretty much confirmed that it was—it would be with Chris. They'd been friends for years, and although Mum fell in love with Dad, I always thought Chris was a little too attentive. "You're both consenting adults. I mean, I didn't need to witness...*that*. But what you do is up to you."

She lets out a giant breath. I don't understand why she was so worried, but then something Lauren said recently hits me. *I don't know who you are now.* Guilt sits heavy in my stomach that the reason Mum looks so relieved is my fault. It's true; they have no idea who I am now and how I'm going to react to things. Anger burns within me. I clench and unclench my working hand, trying to release some of the tension building.

"O-okay," Mum stutters, looking at me as if I might blow at any minute. "Did you have a good time with Lauren?"

"It was...good. Weird. But we talked. I think we've cleared the air at least."

"Good. That's good."

"I'm going to go." I point towards the stairs and turn to leave. "Keep the noise down, yeah?"

The sound of her light laughter behind me lifts my spirits a little. Chris sheepishly pokes his head from the kitchen just as I go to climb the stairs. One side of his mouth twitches up in a smile and I nod. "Just look after her." His smile grows as Mum tucks herself into his side, and I can't help my heart swelling a little. Has she moved on fast? Yeah, most people would probably say so, but then none of them knew the reality that was living with Nick. If Chris makes her smile, then who am I to criticise their choices? Fuck knows I've made enough bad ones over the years.

Undressing without Lauren to help me is a harsh reminder that she's across the city. At least I now know that she's not doing fuck knows what with her boyfriend. I still can't quite believe she lied to me, that she made me believe they were a couple, but looking back, I really should have seen the signs. I was too blindsided by her to see much else. Although, I could have sworn the look in his eyes every time he glanced at her went beyond friendship.

I'm just walking out of my en suite after attempting to shower while keeping my cast dry, when there's a light knock at my door.

"Come in."

"Hey," Mum says, poking her head inside. Thankfully, she's now fully dressed in her pyjamas. "Chris has just left."

"He didn't have to. I don't want to get in the way."

"No, it's fine. He was going anyway. Are you really okay with it?"

"Yes, I really am." She nods, but I don't think she believes me.

"Here," she says handing me a white paper bag. "I brought these home from the hospital for you. They might help with the pain." She nods to where I've got my arm wrapped around my ribs.

"Thanks." Ripping into the bag, I pop a couple of pills out of the packet and swallow them down, hoping they'll help me sleep tonight.

"Are you okay to talk, or do you need to rest?"

"We can talk." I slowly lower myself to my bed. Mum jumps up like she wants to help, but there's nothing she can really do. "What's up?"

Once I've found a somewhat comfortable position, I look over. She looks more concerned than she did after being walked in on earlier. "Word's got out at work that there are money issues."

"Shit." We were hoping to keep it quiet from the staff so they wouldn't panic unnecessarily. "What does that mean?"

"We've lost a few."

"Already?"

"The rumour's gone around that wages might not be paid, and a few of the newer ones have jumped ship."

"Christ."

"Bert's also handed his notice in."

"Are you shitting me?" Bert worked with Steve on the contracts. We'll be fucked with both him and Steve gone.

"I tried to convince him to stay, but his son's set up on his own and he said it was the perfect time to support him."

"Fabulous. He's helping the competition," I say with a strained laugh. "What are we going to do?"

"Chris said he might know someone who could help?" I bite my tongue from asking what he knows about the building industry. I soon realise that I've no idea how to fix this, so if Chris knows a guy, then it's more than I've got. "Plus, I guess it frees up office space so we can—"

"Are the garages still full of Dad's crap?" I ask, remembering something Lauren said to me on the way home.

"Yeah, why?"

"What do you think about converting it into offices? We could apply for planning to extend to the side, so we'd have stores. It wouldn't be perfect, and it might not be a long-term solution, but it would save us some serious cash in the long run."

"I think..." She trails off, walking over to the window to look out at the driveway and the garages I mentioned. "I think we've got enough space for a few vans out there. We could pave some of the grass if need be. I think it's perfect, Ben."

"Are you sure? I don't want to crash your home, but it might be the new lease of life the business needs."

"It's not my home anymore, Ben. This place belongs to you, remember?"

"I know, but—"

"No buts. If you want to move the business here, that's your call to make. Just give me some warning before you decide to kick me out as well."

"I won't do that. This is your home."

"It was. It was my home when your dad was here with me. It's only been a house since then." The honesty in her voice makes my heart ache. I had no idea she felt the same way about this place that I did. "It deserves to be a home once again. I'd love nothing more than for you to raise a family of your own here."

A giant lump climbs up my throat at the idea of living here with Lauren and starting a life together. I've no idea what she sees for her future and if I'm in it, but I know exactly what I want, and it seems Mum does too.

I nod, unable to speak around the lump blocking my throat.

"I'll leave you to sleep. I just needed to tell you what was going on."

"I appreciate it. Thank you," I manage to get out before she leaves the room.

"Jesus," I mutter, rubbing my hand over my face.

The prescription painkillers Mum gave me work like a charm, because as soon as I find a semi-comfortable position, I'm out like a light.

# CHAPTER TWELVE

Lauren

I didn't anticipate how empty I would feel as I walk away from Ben. Everything inside me screams to turn around and go back to him, but I know I can't. That's my heart talking, and it's already got me in enough trouble where Ben Johnson is concerned. Before I let it have its way, my head needs to be certain that he's in it for real this time. I already know I won't survive the heartache if he walks away again and I've allowed myself to fall.

It's late Friday night and I expect the flat to be empty, so I'm shocked when I hear water running from Joe's room. He's usually out getting drunk and having the time of his life by now. I'm definitely the quiet one in our friendship while he's the wild child.

Propping my suitcase up in the hallway, I step into his room. "Hey, I'm back," I call but get no response. Glancing around, I take in the mess that I've become used to. Thankfully, he keeps it all confined to his room.

A stack of papers on his desk catches my eye. I shouldn't be spying, but the giant red FINAL DEMAND stamp on the top is kind of hard to miss. Walking over, my heart pounds when I see the logo for our letting agent at the top of the letter.

"What the fuck?"

Picking up the paper, I read words I never thought I would. Pay our outstanding rent arrears or face eviction. Joe hasn't been paying the rent?

"Oh, hey, you're back. Did you have...fuck." Racing over, he snatches the paper from my hand and screws it up. "Did you have a good time?"

"What the fuck was that, Joe?"

"It's nothing. You don't need to worry about it."

"I don't need to worry that we're about to be evicted? What the hell?"

"It's just a mistake. I'll sort it."

"Look me in the eye and tell me that," I demand when I notice that he's looking everywhere but me.

He turns his dark eyes on me, guilt etched into every one of his features, and I already know that this isn't a mistake. "I...fuck."

"I give you half of the rent every month. What the hell have you done with it?" Anger starts to bubble through my veins. I really fucking want this to be a joke, because I'm not sure I can deal with anything else right now.

"I spent it."

"All of it?"

"It was never an issue before, because the rent was covered."

"What do you mean the rent was covered? Who was paying for it?" I don't know why I ask. The tight knot in my stomach already knows.

"Lauren, this isn't how it sounds," he pleads, concern filling his eyes.

"You'll need to tell me before I figure that out."

"Fuck." Lifting his hands to his hair he runs his fingers through and tugs hard. "Fuck." I jump at the volume he shouts it at.

"Just tell me." My hands tremble as I wait for the inevitable to fall from his lips. "Who paid our rent?"

"Your dad," he mutters, and although I knew it was coming, I still feel like the world just fell from under me.

I drop down onto the edge of Joe's bed as I try to figure out why.

"I didn't have any other option at the time, and your dad knew it." Frustrated with hearing the same words from so many people recently, I narrow my eyes and wait for him to continue. "My parents had disowned me. I had no money and nowhere to live. It was my only option if I didn't want to sleep on the streets."

My mind spins and blood rushes past my ears as what he's confessing registers. Sucking in a few deep breaths, I look up. Joe looks like hell when my eyes land on him, but it doesn't make me feel any better about all this.

"You're telling me what exactly? My dad paid you to be my friend?" My body trembles with anger as I wait for his response. Surely those words can't be true. Joe has been the kind of friend I could have only wished for, especially when we first became close. I'll be the first to admit that I wasn't in a great place back then...why would he want to spend time with me if he *weren't* being paid? A sob rumbles up my throat as I realise that it's true. He doesn't need to say the words; they're written all over his face.

"Lauren, it wasn't like that."

"Really? So what was it like?" Standing toe-to-toe with him, I wait. I wait for him to tell me that it's all a sick joke. But instead, he swallows and looks away. My eyes burn as the realisation that my relationship with my best friend is based on a lie really hits me. "I can't do this," I whisper, walking from his room and collecting my suitcase.

"Lauren, please. Let me explain. It's not as bad as it sounds," he begs.

"So my dad didn't pay you to be my friend?" I look back over my shoulder to find him in the doorway, guilt twisting his face. "Exactly."

"Lauren, please don't do this. I love you, please." His pained voice hits my ears as I wrench the front door open, but it doesn't stop me, and I storm through it. The lump in my throat is painful, and my eyes continue to burn, but I won't cry. Not until I'm in the safety of my car at least.

I didn't have a plan other than to get away, but when I find myself driving up the street where I know Ben is, I'm not surprised. The most sensible thing would be to go to Mum or Danni, but they're not who I want right now.

Before I change my mind, I pull up to the gates and slowly drive through once they're open. Looking up at the house and wiping the tears from my eyes, I realise I don't hate it like I once did. I don't really want to accept it, but since Dad passed, everything is just so... different. I'm not sure I can really explain it, but everyone is walking a little straighter, everyone's eyes are a little brighter. It's not that they're glad he's gone or anything...I don't think. It's more that the pressure he put on everyone has disappeared, and they're all feeling lighter. I can already see the difference in Jenny; she's becoming the woman I'm sure she always was; too busy hiding in Dad's shadows.

Turning off the engine, I start to question myself. I don't want to give him the wrong idea. He's desperate for us to re-start where we left off six years ago, but I need to protect my heart. That doesn't stop me needing his comfort after this latest revelation. The thought of having his strong arms wrapped around me right now is enough to have me pushing the car door open and heading towards the house.

Everything's quiet as I make my way up the stairs, but it's not an uncomfortable silence like I remember all too well.

Placing my hand on his door handle, I almost turn around and walk back out, but the image of Joe's guilt-ridden face has me pushing down instead.

The only light in the room is a small lamp on his bedside table. It allows me to clearly see him sleeping. I spot a box of painkillers beneath the lamp, and I realise that I shouldn't be here. Not just because I'm treading on dangerous ground with him, but also that he needs to sleep. He tried telling me that he slept fine in Rome, but I know he was lying. I heard him shuffling about and sucking in sharp, painful breaths as he tried to get comfortable. I need to walk out; but his peaceful, sleeping face has me lingering longer than I should. His bedroom is the same as I remember; the only difference is the man sleeping within it. I don't just mean physically. He always seemed so confident as a kid, but as we grew closer, I saw that most of that was a cover. He was hiding from the pain of losing his dad and acting out to make it seem like he'd dealt with it. He was lost back then. He didn't know his place in the world, and he just bumbled around, enjoying what he could. It's why I wasn't convinced that he really wanted me in the first place.

Ben the man seems much surer of himself. I know he's still got plenty of issues to deal with, my dad being one of them it seems, but to me at least, he's found where he needs to be. I know he's having a hard time leaving the life he's lived for the past six years and the friends he's made, but he knows as well as I do that he belongs here.

Letting out a sigh, I turn to leave.

"Lauren?" His voice is rough and gravelly, and it makes me stop in my tracks. I look back over my shoulder, and he stares at me like I can't possibly be standing here.

"I should go. This was a bad idea."

"No, wait." He gets up much more smoothly than I was expecting. The sight of the sheets slipping down his torso has me frozen in place. "Shit, what's wrong?"

Before I know it, he's in front of me, his thumbs wiping the tears from my cheeks.

"It's..." The security of his warmth seeping into me along with his scent filling my nose is too much. I lose the fight with my emotions, and a sob rumbles up my throat. "It's..."

I don't get a chance to say any more before I'm pulled against his hard body and his arms wrap around me. Dragging in a few deep breaths, I try to calm myself down. I'm fed up of falling apart and being such a mess, but it's just one thing after another right now. Every single thing is the result of one man's actions, and I'm really starting to dislike him.

I'm seeing a side to my dad that I should have seen when he was alive.

Some of this might not have happened if I didn't bury my head in the sand. I feel stupid and naïve for ever believing he was a man I could trust and who had my best interests at heart. All he wanted was to be in control. Another wave of tears hits, and Ben moves us over to his bed. His arms don't once leave me and the amount of comfort I find in that scares me.

"It's okay," he whispers, his lips in my hair. "I'm here for whatever you need."

"It's...Joe," I finally get out.

"What's happened? Is he okay?"

"Oh, he's fine. At the moment," I say, thinking that might not be the case when Ben catches up with him after this. Broken arm or not, I already know he's going to want to fight this battle for me.

Pulling his head back, he looks at me with his brows drawn. "What do you mean?"

"My dad paid Joe to be my friend. Everything between us has been based on a lie." My lips tremble as I say the words aloud.

Ben tenses beside me. "Motherfucker."

"I thought our relationship was just as important to him as it was me, but he was only there because he was getting paid for the privilege."

Ben vibrates with anger. His eyes are dark, his lips pressed into a thin line and his jaw pops as he fights to stay here with me. "I'm gonna fucking kill him," he growls. Lust shoots through me at the sound of his deep voice. I may still have a lot of reservations about re-starting a relationship with Ben, but one thing I do know for certain is that he will protect me, no matter what.

"No," I sigh, placing my hands on his chest. "I don't need you getting involved."

"What do you need?"

"I've no idea. Can I…" I trail off, not sure if I should be asking the question that's on the tip of my tongue.

"Can you what?"

"Can I stay?"

"This is your house too, Lauren. You don't need my permission."

"That isn't what I meant, and you know it. Can I stay?" I flick my eyes to his bed. "I don't want to be alone."

"You can have whatever you want, baby." His eyes darken, and I immediately regret asking. He wants more than I'm willing to give right now.

"Just hold me?" I look away, embarrassed by my request, but his fingers gently press into my chin and turn me back.

"Always."

Our eyes hold, and my mouth waters. It would be so fucking easy to lean into him right now. My fingers fist the sheet beneath me as I try to remind myself why I wanted to take this slow.

"I just need…" As I move, he releases his hold on me.

"Lauren," he calls just before I disappear into his bathroom. My breath catches when I look over my shoulder at him. His bruises are starting to fade and he looks incredible sitting there with the covers pooled at his waist. "Yeah?" I breathe.

"I mean it. Whatever you need. I'm here."

"I know." Ducking inside his bathroom, I close the door and take a breath. I was expecting to spend the evening at home alone as I dissected every second of our time together in Rome, but here I am, hiding in his bathroom. I couldn't even make two hours without him.

Shaking my head at my ridiculousness, I do what I need to do before splashing my face with cold water and attempting to brush my teeth with my finger.

Finding one of Ben's folded t-shirts on the side, I run my finger over the cotton. Lifting it from its place, I bring it to my nose and inhale his scent. Butterflies erupt in my stomach and I can't stop myself.

Stripping out of my own clothes, I leave them in a pile on the floor and slip his shirt over my head. Something within me settles the moment I'm surrounded by him.

I run my fingers through my knotted hair and stare at my red-rimmed, tired eyes in the mirror. I'm fed up of all the bullshit and drama. I thought it was over, but it seems that was just wishful thinking.

The second I pull the door open, I'm less confident about my decision to borrow Ben's shirt, but I soon realise that I needn't worry because one look at him and I know he's out cold. A smile twitches at my lips that he's finally able to get some good rest as I make my way across the room. Pulling the covers back, I slip in beside him and run my eyes over every inch of his face. He's not shaved since the accident, so he's got five days' worth of growth covering his chin; if anything, it only makes him more beautiful. His dark eyelashes rest down on his strong cheekbones and his lips are curled into the slightest smile. The thought that I could have something to do with that causes heat to bloom inside me.

Leaning forward, I gently place my lips to his forehead. "Thank you," I whisper. I'm not sure what exactly it's for, but it feels right. He might have turned my world upside down once again when he reappeared, but I can't imagine dealing with the fallout of Dad's death without him.

There's no sign he's awake, but suddenly his arm moves, and he wraps it around my waist and pulls me to him. It feels so incredibly good to be wrapped in his arms once again.

# CHAPTER THIRTEEN

Ben

I truly thought it was a drug-induced dream, so when I come to and hear the shower running in my en suite and the other side of the covers flicks back like I have company, I'm shocked.

The water stops and the sound of her light footsteps filters through the slightly ajar door. If I didn't know better, I'd think that was an invitation.

The moment her shadow fills the gap, my cock twitches to life. Propping myself up against the headboard, I wait. I'm not disappointed when she appears, because she's dressed in only my t-shirt.

"Fuck me. This is the best sight I've woken up to in a long time."

Her cheeks heat and she tugs at the hem. "Sorry, did I wake you?"

"No, not at all. I just wasn't expecting you to be here."

"You thought I'd run?" Confusion fills her voice.

"No. I thought it was a dream."

"I wish," she mutters sadly.

"Come here." To my surprise, when I open my arms for her, she comes willingly. Sitting on the edge of the bed beside me, she allows me to comfort her. Knowing she's accepting it—me, maybe even *us*—has some of the uncertainty within me settling. She came here to be with me last night. That means something. It means a lot, actually.

"Do you want to talk about it?"

She shakes her head, but after a few seconds, her soft voice fills the room. "I found a final demand letter for the rent. Dad was paying for it. I guess the payments stopped with all the financial issues. I had no idea. I was giving him my half every month. Christ knows what he's done with that. Unless we pay the outstanding debt, we're being evicted... next week." She shudders in my arms and I hold her a little tighter.

"I just can't quite get it into my head that after everything we've done together, how close I thought we were, he was only there for financial gain. It just doesn't make sense."

"You need to talk to him." She's silent in my arms, and it's clear she's got nothing to add. "It might make more sense if you found out more. I know for a fact that things aren't always that simple where your dad was concerned."

"I'm not ready. I can't cope with the fact that two of my best friends were manipulated by a man I used to love, who I thought, although controlling, was a good guy. I just don't know how to deal with it all. It's too much too soon."

"I know, baby. But I really think—"

"Take me away. Just for the weekend. Please. I need just a little time to try to process everything. Then I'll come back and talk to both Joe and Erica."

Placing my hand on her shoulder, I push her back so I can look in her eyes. I open my mouth to argue, but she beats me to it.

"Please, Ben. I've got my case from Rome in the car. We don't have to go far, just somewhere I know they're not going to find me.

Please," she begs. Her blue eyes stare into mine, and I can see all the beautiful but broken pieces her dad's left behind.

"Okay," I concede. I've never been able to say no to her. "Let me get dressed and we'll make a plan."

"I'm not planning. Just take me somewhere. Anywhere." An idea pops into my head, and I smile. "What?" she asks sceptically.

"I know just the place, and I can guarantee that you'll be distracted."

"Should I be worried?"

"Possibly," I admit with a laugh. "Now get dressed, unless you're planning on going in my t-shirt."

---

"WE'RE GOING AWAY for the night," I say to Mum, who's drinking coffee at the kitchen table and smiling down at her phone.

"But you just got back."

"I know, but—"

"It's my fault," Lauren says, walking around me and into the kitchen.

"Lauren? What are you doing here first thing in the morning?" Mum looks between the two of us with an amused expression plastered on her face.

"It's a long story. One that you'll probably not be surprised involves my dad."

"Now what?"

"Did you know that Dad and Joe knew each other prior to his employment?" I'd shown Lauren the other photos Liv sent me while we were away before leaving my room a few minutes ago. It only confirmed what she already knew.

"No, not that I know of. Why?"

"Dad paid him to be my friend. I guess to distract me from him," she says, nodding her head towards me.

"I'm sorry, he what?" Mum asks, spluttering coffee all over the table and down her chin.

"At some point, I might find someone in my life who hasn't been manipulated by my father."

Mum and I look at each other, and a knowing look passes between us at being two of those people.

"What's Joe got to say about all this?"

"I didn't hang around long enough to hear. It's just all too much. I just need a few hours to try to get my head straight. I thought dealing with his death would be hard, but all this other crap is just...ugh," Lauren complains. I can't help but feel for her. Losing a parent is one of the hardest things to deal with, even as an adult. I might not agree with her running away right now, but I do understand her need for time.

"Take whatever time you need, sweetheart. At a time like this, no one can tell you what you need. Only you know, so trust yourself and don't rush it. Grief is a bitch, and it can hit you when you least expect it. Things will get better though." Sadness fills Mum's eyes. She knows how true that is all too well.

"Thank you." I watch as Lauren walks over to give Mum a hug. It's the first time I really appreciate how close they became while I was gone.

They're only separated when the doorbell rings.

"Are you two expecting someone?" Mum asks, looking confused. We've never really had the kind of house that people just turn up to.

Shaking our heads, I leave them to find out who it is.

I'm pretty sure I already have a good idea. My muscles tense as I reach out to open the door. I might not be on top form right now, but I'm not opposed to kicking his arse.

"What?" I grunt the second my suspicions are confirmed.

"Can I see her?" Joe asks, looking tired and stressed.

Stepping out and closing the front door behind me, I focus my stare on him. "No, you fucking can't. What the fuck were you playing at? She fucking trusted you." My teeth grind as I fight the urge to punch the fucker. Sadly, I'd have to use my left hand, and I know it wouldn't hurt as much as I'd like it to.

"It's not like it seems," he pleads.

"Really. So Nick didn't pay you to be her friend? To distract her from me? I guess we can both see why he chose you. You're a weaker version of me. Wait...don't tell me. You're not gay either?" His eyebrows pinch together but he remains silent. "Yeah, I know."

"I don't...It's not..." With a sigh, he gives up. "She's my best friend; I love her. I couldn't give a fuck about her dad. Yeah, I needed him in the beginning. I was in a bad place, but it soon became clear that we had a connection."

"Then you should have fucking owned up. He's caused her enough pain trying to control her life over the years. You owed her the truth. It should have come from your own lips."

"Like you're one to give advice. At least he didn't run me out of London."

"Fuck you," I spit, lurching forward.

"Go on then. Fucking hit me."

"Enough," is called from behind us before Lauren's hands wrap around my upper arms to pull me back. "Ben, don't. He's not worth it." The pain that fills Joe's eyes at her words almost has me feeling bad for him. It's enough for me to know that what he just said is true. He does care about her. But it doesn't fix the fact he's lied to her for years.

"Joe, you need to leave."

"Lauren, please. Just hear me out."

"Not now."

"Please," he begs.

"Not. Now." Lauren spits, and Joe has no choice but to back away. "Are you okay?" she asks, turning her concerned eyes on me.

"Me? Yeah, I'm fine. Are you?" She shrugs before leading me back inside. "You really need to talk to him." I know she probably doesn't want to hear it, but I can't stop the words falling from my mouth. Why I'm defending the fucker is beyond me, but I truly believe he does care, and if he's done as good a job as I think he has of looking after her for the last few years then he deserves to be heard.

Mum's stood in the hallway waiting to see what's going on, concern written all over her face. "Just do what feels right," she says to Lauren with a small smile before heading up the stairs.

"Let's go." Turning, she locks her eyes on mine.

"You sure?"

"Yes. Now take me away, Ben."

"Fine, you're driving."

"Just point me in the right direction."

---

"WE'RE GOING TO DEVON, aren't we?" she asks the second we're on the motorway heading out of the city.

"Is that okay?"

"Stop questioning everything," she says with a chuckle. "I told you I didn't care where we went, and I meant it."

"I just want to make you happy."

"This is making me happy." She might not say that I'm the one making her happy in so many words, but hope explodes within me nonetheless. "I'm looking forward to meeting your friends properly."

The journey is fairly quiet, and I allow Lauren the time she needs to process everything that's whizzing around her head. It's late afternoon when I direct her to pull up on the driveway of Dec's house.

"Whoa, when you said you looked out on the beach, I wasn't quite expecting this. It's incredible."

"Dec was really lucky to get this place."

"I can't believe you wanted to leave in favour of London."

"It wasn't the place that was calling me back." She turns the engine off and shifts in her seat so she can look at me. "My home is wherever you are." Her breath catches and her eyes soften. I expect her to say something, but after a few seconds, she just smiles. "Are you ready? This lot can be a little crazy."

"Worse than those we left behind?"

"No, probably not," I admit with a laugh, thinking of Erica and a few of the others.

"Holy shit, Ben!" Liv cries the second I step foot into the living room. She jumps up and runs towards me. She's just about to collide with me when she takes in the cast. By some miracle, she manages to stop before she hits me and gently wraps her arms around my waist. "What's happened? Are you okay? What's going on with Lauren?" She fires the questions out without giving me a chance to answer any of them.

"Nothing, she's right here," Lauren says from behind me, causing Liv's eyes to go so wide I'm worried they might pop out.

"Oh my god!" Liv turns her attention to Lauren and gives her the overenthusiastic hug I was almost about to get. "Can I get you drinks?"

"Sure."

We follow Liv through to the kitchen. I can see Lauren looking around at everything out of the corner of my eye. It feels weird being back here, and even weirder having her with me. I never thought I'd ever have my two worlds become one, but it seems that it might just be happening.

Liv puts the kettle and coffee machine on and then turns her attention to us. "So are you two..."

"Friends," Lauren answers quickly.

"Friends?" Liv's eyes flick between the two of us before landing on me. "How's that working for you?"

"Fantastic, I love being Lauren's friend," I say through gritted teeth, which earns me a slap to the shoulder.

"Behave," Lauren chastises. "He's trying."

"You have some weird power over our BJ, that's for sure." Lauren stifles a laugh while Liv just looks amused. "I never thought I'd see him whipped."

"Enough. Don't make me regret bringing her here."

"No, please continue. I really want to learn more about the elusive BJ," Lauren encourages, and I groan.

"You really don't."

"Okay, no, I don't want to know about *that* side to BJ."

Liv and Lauren chat away like they're old friends. Neither seems to be even slightly concerned that I'm in the same room as they talk about me and compare notes.

"Babe, whose car is parked in the...BJ!" Liam exclaims as he rounds the corner. "Dude, it's good to see you. Lauren, hey, this is a surprise. Are you two...?"

Liv pierces him with a look while running her hand in front of her throat to get him to stop, and it works...eventually. "They're just friends. I'm going to make up the guest room for her."

"Wow, BJ has a woman here, and she's not going to share his bed. What a novelty."

"Shut up, dickhead."

"Ow," Liam complains, rubbing the sting my hand left behind on his head. "I had years of stick off you; it's time for payback."

"I was afraid of that," I mutter.

"So what's the plan? The shack to meet Dec and Nic?"

"Yes. Let me show Lauren to her room so she can get ready."

The girls disappear up the stairs. Liam and I watch them leave before I head up to my old room to shower and dress. The painkillers Mum got from the hospital mean I can move a little easier, and getting dressed isn't quite as agonising as it was in Rome.

I'm hit with a huge wave of nostalgia when I open my bedroom door and find it exactly as I left it the day I headed for London. I think back to the uncertainty I felt that day. I had no clue what I was about to walk into. In reality, I think it's worse than I was expecting— business-wise at least. But Lauren's single and mostly open to us again, even if she is trying to fight it.

As soon as I'm ready, I head back downstairs and find Liam at the table nursing a beer where I left him. The second he sees me heading his way, he grabs me a can so I can join him.

"So...friends? How's that working out for you?"

I groan in pain and a smug smile spreads across Liam's face. "Oh, just fuck off."

He laughs but his face soon turns serious. "She just needs time. You two are it, and you know it."

"Yeah." A sad laugh falls from my lips. "I know it. I'm just not sure she does."

"She does. I can see it in her eyes every time she looks at you." I narrow my eyes at my best friend, wondering when he turned into a love doctor. "What?"

"Nothing, nothing. So, how're things down here?"

"Quiet. This house just isn't the same without you. What are your plans now? Have you moved to London officially?"

I look around the house that I called home for years and realise that I can no longer call it that. "Yeah, I guess I have."

"This place was too small for you anyway."

"I guess," I say sadly. As much as starting over with the business and Lauren in London excites me, I'm also sad to say goodbye to this place. It might never have been where I was meant to be, and I never fitted in, not really, but I've got some amazing memories of my time here—not to mention some incredible friends.

"Distance doesn't mean shit when...fuck." Liam's distracted when footsteps hit the bottom step and he looks over to Liv. She looks good in a little playsuit thing, her legs going on for miles. I understand why he lost his train of thought.

He gets up and goes straight over to her, ruining her perfectly applied lipstick.

"Where's Lauren?"

"Coming," Liv mumbles against Liam's lips.

Exactly as she said, footsteps descend the stairs and I wait. A pair of sandals appears before a tanned pair of legs has my mouth watering. Slowly, the rest of her is revealed. She's wearing a sexy little floral dress that hugs her body in the most delicious way. I swallow and shift on my seat as I will my cock not to go full mast just from looking at her. Once she's down, I take in her loosely curled hair and simple make-up. She looks fucking stunning, and I realise that tonight's going to be torture. Her eyes find mine, and something crackles between us. I may be the other side of the room, but I can sense the hitch in her breathing as our connection holds.

"Okaaaay," Liv says, trying to break the tension. "Ready to go?"

Liam gestures for Lauren to head out and I expect him to grab onto Liv, but she manages to give him the slip so she can grab me. "You're welcome," she says with a wink, nodding towards Lauren.

"This is painful."

"Yeah, I noticed that cast was on your writing hand. I bet you're having a hell of a time right now." She tries to contain her amusement but fails miserably. "Sorry, I'm sorry. You're totally winning her over, just so you know. She might put you out of your misery soon." As she says that, Lauren looks over. Our eyes lock again and a bolt of lust hits me so strong it makes my knees buckle.

*Jesus Christ, I need her.*

# CHAPTER FOURTEEN

Lauren

Ben's eyes have been glued to me since the moment I stepped down the stairs. His stare had goosebumps covering my skin and tingles shooting around my body. Every time I'm away from him, I tell myself that the next time I see him will be different, that the crazy connection between us is just in my head. But then I step into the same room as him and all my good intentions go to shit, because just like when I was eighteen, he has this power over me.

Liam walks beside me as we head towards the beach, leaving Ben and Liv trailing behind. Their hushed voices just about carry to us, and I can only imagine that Ben's getting quizzed about me. Seeing Ben with his friends settles something inside me. Although I hated him when he left, and I still do a little now, it makes me happy to know that he had people looking out for him when he was without family. My thoughts turn back to Joe, and my shoulders sag. I'm having a hard time believing that our friendship is based on nothing but lies and deceit, but that seems to be the level my dad functioned on so I'm not sure why I'm surprised.

"So, what was he like as a kid?" Liam asks, dragging me from my thoughts.

"I uh...didn't know him as a kid. Our parents married when I was fifteen, and we never really spent any time together until I moved in at eighteen."

"I hear you spent quite a bit of time together then," he says, giving my arm a nudge.

"Yeah," I sigh.

"Shit, I'm sorry. I didn't mean—"

"It's fine, it's fine." It's really not, but I don't want to bring a downer on what should be a fun night. "He hasn't changed all that much since back then. He's just a little more focused, I guess. He was always a bit of a joker, but he's more determined now. It's like he knows what he wants and he'll do whatever it takes to make it happen."

"You're talking about yourself, right?" My cheeks heat under his stare. "You know he won't stop." I can see that Liam wants to say more, probably to ask me how long I'm going to string his mate along for, but thankfully, he keeps his mouth shut. "Here we are."

"This place is incredible." I look around, taking in the perfect sandy beach with the sun setting in the distance, casting everything in an orange glow.

"Lauren?" Ben's deep voice rolls through me. I turn to look at him, and concern covers his face—that is until I smile at him and it lights up. I'm reminded of everything he's done for me in the last few days, and it chips away a little more of my restraint.

Stepping into his side, he wraps his arm around my shoulder and drops a kiss to my head. Heat fills me and I snuggle in deeper.

"Is this okay?"

"It's perfect."

Together we walk into Dec's beach shack. It looks exactly as I would have imagined, if not better.

Dec and Nic get up from the sofa to greet us. Dec pulls Ben into a very gentle man hug while Nic comes over to me.

"It's so good to see you again."

Her wide smile makes guilt twist my stomach as I think back to the last time I saw them. It wasn't exactly an enjoyable experience as Ben and I squared up to each other in the club.

"I promise to cause less drama this time."

"We live in a sleepy little town; we love a bit of drama here."

I'm ushered over to the bar with Liv and Nic while the guys make themselves comfortable on the sofas, looking out at the beach beyond.

The three of us watch them catching up and laughing together.

"How's he really doing?" Liv asks.

"What, aside from the fact that he fell from the roof of a building?"

"Yeah, we can see how he's doing with that," she says with a laugh.

"He's okay, I think." I hate that I can't really answer with confidence. I've been so lost in my own head that I don't really know where his head is at. "He's got a lot of work on his hands with the business. My dad did a really good job screwing everything up."

"If anyone can do it, BJ can."

Pride swells within me at their words. "Yeah, he can." Looking over at him laughing and joking with his friends, friends who have been his family for the past six years, makes my heart ache. There's so much of his life and who he is that's a mystery to me, and I hate it. I want to know him like I did back in the beginning, not have this huge void between us.

He must be able to feel my stare because he looks over. Something crackles between us and my temperature rises.

Nic waits until he's turned away and joined back in with the guys' conversation before she speaks. "We've never seen BJ like he is with you. It's something we really never thought we'd see." I look between the two of them, urging them to continue. I'm desperate to know more about the Ben they know. "He was..." Nic pauses as she thinks. "A little...free and easy—"

"Manwhore," Liv chips in helpfully. "What?" she asks when Nic gives her a hard stare. "Lauren knows the basics, and I don't think she wants us sugar coating. Right?" she asks, turning to me.

"Right," I agree, even if the idea of discussing Ben with other women makes me want to throw up.

"I really didn't ever think I'd see him hung up on one woman. I think it looks good on him." I don't need to turn around to know that he's looking at me once again. My skin burns with his attention. "He really loves you, Lauren."

A giant lump forms in my throat. I nod because that's all I'm capable of before swiping my wine from the counter and swallowing a huge mouthful. I know how Ben feels. I can see it every time I look into his eyes. I just wish I wasn't so afraid to have my heart broken again.

"I know you both probably think I'm stringing him along but—" I let out a sigh as I try to find the right words.

"You don't have to explain anything to us. We know all too well how complicated these things can be," Liv says, placing a comforting hand on my arm.

I smile sadly at her. "He shattered my heart when he left. I know I won't survive if it happens again."

"None of us can predict the future, Lauren, but we can regret the past. Don't waste time if you think it's something you'll look back on later and regret."

Her words hit with the punch I think she intended.

"Are they playing nice?" Ben asks when the girls get distracted by their boyfriends and I find myself accompanied by him at the bar.

"Yeah, they're lovely. They were dishing the dirt on you. I've been learning what a dog you were." He swallows nervously. "I'm kidding, but I'm assuming from your reaction that it's not far from the truth."

"The less we discuss my antics here the better." The image of him touching faceless women once again pops into my head. "You want to get out of here?"

"Only if you're ready."

"I am. I don't want to share you anymore."

"Is that right?" Butterflies erupt in my stomach at the prospect of it just being the two of us. I try my best to put the little bit of lingering doubt I have aside.

After saying our goodbyes, Ben links his fingers with mine and we head out into the night.

"Isn't the house that way?" I ask when he tugs me in the opposite direction and then down onto the sand.

"I thought we could just walk for a bit."

"Okay, hang on." Coming to a stop, I lean against the wall and slip my shoes from my feet. The cool sand seeps between my toes as I gather my sandals and reach for Ben's hand.

It's the perfect night. The sky's filled with twinkling stars and the sea gently crashes against the sand.

"Are you warm enough?" Ben asks, pulling me into his side and wrapping his good arm around me.

"Uh huh," I mumble, too content right now to ruin it with words. It was a lovely late summer's day, and although it's getting cold fast, with him beside me I'm fine.

We seem to walk for the longest time in silence, enjoying each other's company. It feels so good to just be after all the arguments and bullshit.

"It's really beautiful here," I eventually say, breaking the quiet night. "Are you sure you're ready to leave?"

"I'm going to miss it, that's for sure. The beach, the peace and quiet, the sea air."

"You know you don't have to, right? Just because everything's been left to you, it doesn't mean you have to deal with it. If this is your home then…" I trail off, not really wanting to voice the rest of that sentence.

Ben slows to a stop and pulls me in front of him. Tucking a lock of hair behind my ear, he stares into my eyes. It's like he can see right inside me and read all my fears.

"My home is wherever you are, baby."

My heart pounds at his honesty. It might not be the first time he's said it, but I'm starting to really believe him now. It might be foolish, but Liv's words are still on repeat in my mind.

I try not to think about what I'm doing and reach up on my tiptoes and press my lips to his. He sucks in a breath of surprise but soon accepts my kiss. His arms wrap around my waist and I'm pulled tightly against him as his lips part and his tongue dances with mine.

We kiss like it's the first time in six years. It's exactly how our first one should have been, instead of the angry, punishing one we shared at the time. Suddenly his words about home being wherever I am make sense, because right now, wrapped in his arms, with his lips on mine, this is home. A contented moan rumbles up my throat as I cling onto him tighter and kiss him deeper.

When we eventually break apart, our chests are heaving and his eyes are glassy with lust.

"W-we should get back," Ben whispers, his forehead pressed against mine, our bodies still woven together.

I hate the moment he releases me. It leaves me cold and I immediately want to step back into him.

The walk back is just as silent as before, and my concerns and doubts about what he's thinking and feeling start running rampant.

"I can practically hear you worrying."

"I am not," I argue.

"Really?" he says with a laugh.

We come to a stop at my bedroom door for the night, and I see Ben look over to his own longingly.

"Thank you for bringing me here, for showing me this side to you."

"You're welcome. You still like me with this side?" The little hesitation in his voice has me stepping closer.

"I like all of you, Ben. You don't need to worry about that. We all have things we wish we'd done differently; but looking back doesn't achieve anything."

"I know. I'll never forgive myself for walking away from you."

Placing my palm on his rough cheek, I look up into his dark-blue eyes. "At some point you're going to have to accept it, Ben. What happened...happened. You came back, and we can still write our future."

"Yeah?" Hope blooms in his eyes and my desire gets the better of me. My lips find his and I pull him against me. His cock almost immediately hardens against my stomach as the intensity of his kiss deepens.

"Jesus," he moans when I start kissing across his jaw and down his neck. My hand slips around from his back and I rub him over the fabric of his jeans.

The moan that rips from his lips has the ache between my legs almost unbearable.

Warm fingers wrap around my wrist and stop my movements. Ben dips his head and I shiver as his breath tickles my ear. "Don't start something you can't finish, baby."

"I can—" His fingers press against my lips, stopping any more words.

"The next time we're together, it's because I've proved to you that I mean every word I say. I want it to be the start of us, of our future. I want it to be because you're in this for real and not because you feel like you have to."

"I don't—" His lips cut me off and I start to believe he's changed his mind.

"Goodnight, baby." He releases me and walks down the corridor. I might think he's happy about this if it's not for the pained look on his face when he stops and glances back at me.

"Ben, I—"

"Sleep tight."

A long breath leaves me when his door clicks shut, cutting us off from each other. I follow suit and close mine too before leaning back against it and wondering how the hell I'm meant to fall asleep after that.

# CHAPTER FIFTEEN

Ben

The tension in Lauren's body increases the closer we get to London. I know she doesn't want to go home and deal with everything, but I'm not letting her run away any longer. As much as I'd love to keep her all to myself, we've both got things that need to be done. I've got a business that really needs my attention, and she's got two friends to speak to and decisions to make about her future. I haven't said any more about her coming back to work since we were on the plane. As much as I'd love for her to come back and work beside me, I'm not about to force her. She had enough of that from her dad over the years. If she feels that now's the time for a fresh start, then so be it.

"This is you then," she says, pulling up in front of the house. Her voice is full of sadness and I'd do almost anything to help get rid of it, but she really needs to go home and get everything out in the open.

"Thank you for everything. Can I call you later?"

"Do you really need to ask that?"

"I guess not."

"If you need me, I'll be here, but no running away. You'll feel better once you've talked through everything."

Leaning over, I give her a quick kiss. It's nothing like what my body's craving, but it's all I can get away with right now. The memory of how her curves felt pressed up against my body last night is still at the forefront of my mind. I've no doubt that if I hadn't stopped her, I'd have ended up in her bed, but I knew it wasn't the right thing to do. I'd agreed to give her time to figure shit out, and I was determined to do the right thing...this time, at least.

"I'll see you soon." I try to sound positive as I get out of the car and grab my bag from the boot. I watch as she lets out a huge sigh before backing off the drive. She asked me to go with her, but I stand by my decision that she needs to do this alone. Me being there will only get Joe's back up.

"Hey, I'm home," I call once I'm in the house, hoping that it will stop a repeat of the last time I turned up unannounced.

"In the kitchen."

"Fully dressed?"

"It's safe," Mum shouts with a laugh. When I round the corner, I find Mum and Chris aren't alone—there's another man sitting with them, drinking coffee. "Hey, sweetheart, did you have a good time? Where's Lauren?" she asks peering around my shoulder, expecting her to appear.

"Gone home to deal with Joe."

"Oh...okay. Well, this is Trey, the man Chris suggested might be a good fit for us." It takes me a few seconds to catch up with what she's talking about. My drug-hazed brain had mostly forgotten the conversation I'd had with her when we got back from Rome about employees handing their notice in and finding someone new for the office.

"Hi. Your mum was just telling me all about you." Trey says, holding his hand out towards me. He's older than me, probably mid to late thirties, but he's a similar build, and I can see that we share a love of ink from the black intricate patterns poking out from his sleeves. His face is hard, his lips set in a slight scowl, and I can't help thinking he must be an arsehole of a boss. I'm not sure I'd want to be on the wrong side of his temper.

"All good I hope."

"Of course." I join them at the table while Mum faffs around getting more drinks. "So, I was just telling your mum a little about me..." he continues on to tell me his employment history within the building industry. I can't help find it odd that this man, who clearly looks capable, and I have every confidence that he is if Chris is vouching for him, is selling himself to me; the guy who's not held down a proper job since he walked out of this house over six years ago but suddenly finds himself in charge of a failing company. Everything sounds perfect; his experience is second to none, and I think he's got the attitude and determination it'll take to help me drag this company back from the dead.

"Sounds perfect. When can you start?" I ask with a laugh, but in reality I couldn't be any more serious. The prospect of being the boss is more daunting than I'm allowing anyone to see, but with the knowledge I have someone who knows what they're doing by my side with regards to running jobs and dealing with employees, the challenge suddenly seems a little more manageable.

Trey looks a little sceptical but eventually says, "Tomorrow?"

I'm too stunned to respond but Mum does it for me. "Done. Now, shall we have something a little more appropriate to celebrate? I feel like this could be the start of a new chapter for all of us."

When I fall into bed later that night, it's with hope filling my veins. Lauren seems to be softening to the idea of an 'us' again, and we've got some solid plans for how to save the business. I believe what Mum said earlier is true. This really is a turning point, and we're all about to find out if we're going to sink or swim.

# CHAPTER SIXTEEN

Lauren

My hand trembles as I lift it to slide the key in the lock. I really don't want to be forced to deal with all this bullshit and manipulation, but I know Ben's right. I need to get everything out in the open with both Erica and Joe and see where we go once all the truths are on the table. I'm terrified that my relationships with two of my closest friends are going to be forever tarnished by my dad's selfish actions, but I guess it's something we're all going to have to live with now.

Pushing the door open, I'm met by two shocked faces as they put photo frames and ornaments into boxes. "If I didn't know better, I'd think this was an ambush."

"We didn't know...shit," Joe says, looking down at the boxes at his feet.

"Moving out?"

"Erica offered me her spare room until I sort myself out. I didn't know when you'd be back, so we just started. You didn't answer any of our calls and—"

"It's fine, really. You need to do what you need to do. I guess I'll go pack too."

"Where will you go?"

I shrug. "Do you care?"

"Jesus, Lauren." His hands go to his head and he pulls at his hair. "Of course I care. You're my best friend."

"Am I? Because the last I heard, your position was a fully paid job."

"It's not like that. Please, just come and sit down and let me explain."

Knowing it's the reason I'm here, I do as he suggests.

"Shall I go or..." Erica says, standing awkwardly in the corner of the room.

"No, if we're going to do this, we should do it properly. Sit."

"I'll get the wine," Joe suggests, disappearing into the kitchen.

"Did you know?" I snap at Erica when she sits on the sofa opposite me.

"No, I had no clue until he turned up at my door on Friday night. I'm so sorry, Lauren. But he's a mess. He really loves you."

"This is so fucked up."

"You're telling me. But just hear him out. Hear *me* out. There's too much good here to allow *him* to ruin everything."

I agree, I do, but the last thing I want to do is spend my Sunday night hearing tales about what an arsehole my dead Dad was.

Joe comes back, and if it's possible, the atmosphere gets even heavier. We all take a sip of wine, putting off the inevitable, but it can only last so long.

"Nick was a friend of my parents. I've known him for as long as I can remember. But as the years went on they drifted apart as people do. Everything you know about the beginning of how we met is true. I really did turn up that day after seeing an ad online for a job. I was desperate. My parents had kicked me out and cut me off after I 'shamed' them. I was never expecting to find Nick sitting in the office. I hadn't seen or heard from him for years. He sat me down and interviewed me like he would any other employee before he started asking about my parents. I gave him a shortened version about what had happened and he offered to help. I thought he was just being friendly, but it turned out to be far from that. He told me he'd push me up through the ranks, pay me more and even put a roof over my head if I did one thing for him."

"Be my friend," I mutter.

"It wasn't even that." He lets out a sigh and casts his eyes to the ceiling. "He wanted me to distract you in any way I could."

"Distract me?"

"He was concerned that you were going to go running after Ben. I think he took one look at me, another bad boy with tattoos, and thought I could make you forget him. Nick knew my parents. He knew that although I was going through a rough patch, I had 'good blood' or whatever bullshit he spewed."

"I can't believe you agreed," I say, shaking my head at how ridiculous it all sounds.

"Why wouldn't I? I had no money and nowhere to live. I'd been sleeping on friends' sofas but the offers were drying up fast once they realised I could no longer fund the booze and drugs. Plus, Lauren's hot...why wouldn't I want to spend my time with her?" he adds with a laugh.

"You should have told me, Joe."

"I wanted to. I intended to. But I soon realised that I really liked you, despite you being a miserable bitch and pining after Ben."

"Thanks."

"Would you put it any differently?"

"No."

"You quickly became my best friend, Lauren. You truly did, and I didn't know how to tell you then. You'd already had your trust smashed, and I just couldn't do it to you."

"So you just kept up the façade?"

"Yeah. I kind of thought your dad would get fed up with paying for this place once he realised you'd moved on with your life, but he never did. So I continued spending my wages every month—and your rent," he adds with a wince, "and here we are."

"Didn't you think to do something when you started getting late payment notices?"

"I mentioned it to Nick and he said he'd sort it. I had no idea he had no money."

"Jesus, this is such a mess."

"I'm so sorry, Lauren. I never had any intention of hurting you. I was just in the right place at the right time. Maybe it was wrong of me to agree, but I don't regret it because it brought me you. I might have been there to support you as a distraction for you, but you were the same thing to me, and I'll forever be grateful for our friendship, even if you don't forgive me."

"Forgive you? Don't be stupid." Getting up, I sit myself down next to him. "You should have told me sooner. If I'd known what he was capable of, a lot of other things might have gone differently." I glance over at Erica and she gives me a sad smile.

The three of us talk for hours. Thankfully the topic of conversation steers away from my dad and it almost feels like old times. Sadly, one look at the boxes surrounding us and I'm brought back down to earth with a bang.

"So what now?" I ask.

"Now, we start over without the lies and secrets."

"That sounds like a plan, but you're moving in with Erica and I'm about to lose my home."

"We sort of assumed that you and Ben..." Erica trails off.

"We're not together."

"Why not? Lauren, he looks at you like you're the most amazing thing to ever grace the earth. He loves you so much; it's obvious every time he glances your way. It's been that way since you were eighteen. Put the poor boy out of his misery!"

Both Erica and Joe stare at me, waiting for my response. I open my mouth to say something, to argue, but nothing comes out.

"You know we're right," Joe adds, but I don't miss the sadness that darkens his eyes. "That man would move heaven and earth for you."

I can't fight the smile that twitches at the corners of my mouth. I can't argue with Joe, and I'm starting to realise that I need to be brave. I can hide all I like, but at the end of the day, I'll regret not having this time with him. Even if it all comes crashing down again, knowing my fears kept me from living life to the full with Ben would haunt me forever.

"Do you want some help packing?"

A few hours later, our flat is totally packed. It didn't take long to realise that we didn't have all that much stuff to begin with.

"I'm so sorry it came to this," Joe says, regret written all over his face.

"It is what it is. I think we could all use the fresh start, don't you?" Both Joe and Erica nod sadly as we each collect the last few things to carry down to our cars. The only thing left is furniture, which Joe says he'll collect tomorrow in a work van—as long as the boss agrees.

I tell myself I'm not going to cry as the three of us stand in the car park. Nothing's changing, not really. We're all still friends. Yes, our relationships might be a little more strained than they once were, but things will get better again with time.

"This is stupid," I say, my voice heavy with emotion as tears sting the backs of my eyes. "I'll see you both soon."

Two sets of arms wrap around me, and I lose the fight with my tears.

"I'm so sorry," they say simultaneously, and a sob bubbles up my throat.

In the space of only a couple of weeks, my life has completely changed. I lost a man I thought was a caring father, only to discover he was controlling my life every step of the way. The love of my life, who smashed my heart to smithereens, reappeared and turned my life upside down again, and I almost lost two of my best friends in the process. Things can only get better, right?

When I drive away from our building, it's with a heavy heart, but I can't deny there's a little bit of excitement for what's to come. Everyone I love gets a shot at a new start. I just hope they make the right choices this time around.

The logical part of my brain is screaming that I should be heading in the opposite direction—going to stay with Mum until I sort myself out would be the simplest and safest option—but I find myself heading towards a house I never thought I'd willingly want to live in again.

I hated that house when I was first forced to move in. I still hated it the day I moved out to live with Joe. Although it held some good memories of my time with Ben, seeing him everywhere I looked was so painful. Dad was totally out of order with what he did with Joe, but it was like he knew exactly what I needed. I guess in a way I was lucky that the guy he paid to be my friend was a decent guy who, despite the reason he was there, had a good heart.

Pulling up onto the driveway, images of the time I spent here with Ben run through my mind, from that very first night when he was an arsehole to me in the kitchen all the way to how he supported me on Friday night when I found out about Joe. A smile twitches my lips and I know I made the right decision coming here. It's time to start this new chapter in our lives, and I need to stop being so afraid and enjoy what's right in front of me.

Pushing the front door open, the sounds from the TV filter through to me. I slip my shoes off, drop my bag to the side and head into the house to find everyone.

As I round the corner into the living room, I find Jenny and Chris cuddled up on one sofa; the sight of them makes my breath catch. Ben had told me about their relationship when we were in Devon, and although I'm okay with Jenny moving on, I can't deny it doesn't sting a little that it's not my dad she's sat with.

"Oh, hey, sweetheart. Is everything okay?"

Her voice drags Ben's gaze away from whatever they're watching. His eyes burn into me the second they land on my body, and his brow creases with concern. He goes to get up but pauses when I speak.

"Yeah, yeah I'm fine. I was just wondering if I could ask you a favour?"

"Of course."

"Could I...uh...move back in?"

The skin around Jenny's eyes crinkles in delight as a wide smile spreads across her face. "I'm not sure, sweetheart." My stomach drops, and I suddenly feel stupid for even asking. This isn't my home anymore. Dad's gone, and I'm no longer part of this family. Tears sting my eyes and I'm about to turn when she speaks again. "This house no longer belongs to me. It should be Ben you're asking."

Turning my attention to him, I don't get a chance to say anything because his wide chest is in front of me. His arms wrap around my waist and I'm lifted off my feet. His lips find mine as he backs us out of the room.

"Turn the TV up," he shouts over his shoulder, and although my face flames red, I throw my head back and laugh. It feels so incredibly good to just let go and allow my heart to take the lead for the first time in six long years.

"I can walk," I offer. Ben must be regretting his decision to try to carry me up the stairs with one arm.

"I'm not letting you go." His words make me melt. I drop my face into the curve of his neck and start peppering kisses along the hem of his t-shirt. "That's not making it any easier," he chuckles.

By the time we get to his room, sweat is beginning to bead his brow, showing that carrying me up here isn't as easy and pain-free as he's making out.

"Put me down," I demand. The conviction in my tone is enough that he does as I say and slides me down his body. Taking his still unshaven cheeks in my hands, I stare up into his eyes. "You're in pain. We've got all the time in the world. You don't need to rush this."

"You've no idea how long I've waited for this."

"Don't I? I ask, quirking a brow up.

"Come on." Threading his fingers through mine, he starts tugging me forward. "You're aware that you moving in comes with one condition?"

"What's that?"

"You're moving into my room."

Pushing his door open, he hurries inside. The second the door slams shut, I'm pressed up against it.

His palm glides up my neck and to my cheek, his fingers tangling into my hair. "Is this it?" His eyes bore down into mine, their intensity has my insides quivering.

I nod once but it's all the confirmation he needs. "I won't let you regret it...me." Then his lips are on mine and his body is pressing mine into the door. A whimper rumbles up my throat as his tongue slides against mine, tasting me, reminding him how good we are together.

My body sags against his, but he senses it. His knee presses between my legs, and along with his hips, he keeps me upright as his kiss continues.

Pulling his lips from mine, he kisses across my jaw and down my neck. My chest heaves with my increased breaths and I hungrily suck in some deep lungfuls of air.

"I never thought I'd get this again. Jesus, Lauren. Fuck." His hand brushes down my body and slips inside my jumper. "I need more. I need everything."

His fingers skim across my stomach before he finds the button holding my jeans closed. He makes quick work of popping it open, and in seconds, he's sliding his fingers inside and past the lace covering what he wants.

"Fuck," he grunts when he finds me wet and ready for him.

His fingers circle my clit, and quiet whimpers and begs for more fall from my lips. "Ben, please," I moan as he circles my entrance, teasing me.

My orgasm is just in reaching distance when he stills and pulls his hand from my jeans.

"I need to be inside you right now." He undoes his own trousers and pushes them and his boxers down his thighs. His cock bobs in front of him, the head purple and already glistening at the tip. "Lauren," he growls, and I manage to come back to myself enough to shimmy out of my jeans and knickers.

"I don't think you should be—"

My words are cut off as he wraps his hand around my thigh and hitches it up to give him the space he needs. With his hand wrapped around his cock, he bends his knees and lines us up.

We both moan as he sinks into me. My walls ripple around him and the pleasure takes over my entire body. I've no idea if his moan was in pleasure or pain, or a little of both.

Dragging my eyelids open, I look up at him. All his muscles are pulled tight, his eyes locked on me as he starts to thrust in and out of me. I want to ask if he's okay, but he hits me deeper and I lose all train of thought. The only thing I can focus on is him and the sensations he's causing within me.

"So fucking good," he grunts, his movements never faltering. "I want to feel you, baby. Show me how good it feels having me inside you." His words, along with his thrusts, push me higher and higher, closer to my release.

Wrapping my arms tighter around his shoulders, I try to take a little more of my weight to help him. It changes our angle slightly and my orgasm hits, taking me by surprise. I cry out his name as he picks up the tempo a little. Dropping his head into the crook of my neck, I feel him swell inside me before he growls and releases everything he has.

We stay exactly as we are for the longest time, locked in our embrace and him softening inside me.

"Are you okay?" I whisper eventually.

Pulling his head up, he looks down at me. He's eyes are alight, and any tension that was on his face previously has gone. "I can honestly say I've never been better." The smile that splits his face melts my heart.

"That didn't hurt?"

"Like a motherfucker, but it was so fucking worth it."

I laugh but only briefly, my concern for him taking over. "You need to go and lie down."

"But I'm not finished with you yet." He pouts.

"I wasn't suggesting we'd finished, just that you need to lie down." Desire floods his face as realisation dawns, but something more serious soon dampens it down. "What? What's wrong?"

Stepping back from me, he takes my face in his hands. The look on his face has nerves racing through me, and I start to panic.

"Lauren," he breathes. "I fucking love you. Not a minute has gone by in which I haven't."

The breath I was holding comes rushing out of me. "I love you too, Ben. I always have."

Our eye contact holds, silent promises passing between us until he ruins the moment as only he can. "I think it's time you showed me. I'm an invalid, after all." Backing up, he awkwardly pulls his shirt over his head and kicks his jeans and boxers from his legs so he's standing in front of me, gloriously naked. "You're wondering how you resisted for so long, aren't you?"

"There's still time for me to change my mind."

"No fucking chance. Now, get naked and get over here."

I've no idea what time we eventually fall asleep, but when we do, it's wrapped in each other's arms. I sleep better than I have in about six years. Giving in to my feelings for him settled something inside me that's been restless all this time. I could have continued fighting, but I would have always ended up back here, in his arms. It's where I belong.

# EPILOGUE

Lauren

*One Month Later...*

*Go to our room x*

Plucking the post-it note from the mirror, I smile as memories assault me. Excitement has butterflies taking flight in my stomach as I run up the stairs to see what's waiting for me.

When I get to the top of the stairs, I turn the opposite way I'm used to. It's going to take a while for it to feel natural. A week after I moved back in, Jenny announced that she was moving out and in with Chris. They've still not made their relationship official; they're happy to just take things as they come and enjoy each other. I can understand that, after everything they've both been through. I'm happy for them. They deserve a happily ever after.

Pushing open the door to the master bedroom, I take in our freshly painted walls and new furniture. It's the only room of the house we've changed so far, but we've got big plans once things are stable with the business.

There's a box with a giant bow sitting in the middle of the bed with another post-it note on the top.

*Wear me x*

Slowly, I pull the silk ribbon, wanting to remember every second of this anticipation. A laugh falls from my lips when I pull the lid off and push the tissue paper aside. Lifting the new Johnson & Son's hoodie from the box, I place it down on the bed. Beneath is a stunning new maxi dress. It's not all that different from the one he bought me the last time he did this. That dress is still one of my favourites, and thankfully it still fits.

I have a quick shower before dressing and reapplying my make-up. Before heading out to find Ben, I rummage through my jewellery box and find the necklace he bought me, putting it back where it belongs.

I don't bother looking in any of the rooms; I already know he won't be inside. The glow from the fairy lights is obvious the second I step into the kitchen, making me even more anxious to find him than before. With the scent of the barbeque surrounding me, I walk out through the sliding doors, but I'm not prepared for what I find.

The decking area is even more beautiful than I imagined. Every single tree glows with lights and candles flicker on every surface. But the most breath-taking of all is Ben standing in the middle, dressed in a white shirt with the sleeves rolled up to his elbows and a pair of dark trousers, minus shoes. He looks incredible, and I'm once again reminded of how lucky I am that we were able to find our second chance. I still have moments where I worry about the future, but as each day passes, that fear gets less and less. Ben's not once given me a reason to worry. I've no doubt he's in this for the long haul now.

"Hey, baby," he whispers when I get closer. Stepping right up to him, I wrap my arms around his waist and hold him tight. It feels so good to be able to do this properly, knowing I'm not hurting him like I was before. His lips drop to my hair as his hands run down my back.

"Everything okay in the office?"

I laugh because he makes it sound like I've been far away at work when, in reality, I was just in what used to be the garages, making sure everything's ready for our first day in there tomorrow. "Yeah, we're all ready to go."

Tomorrow is our new start. Ben and Jenny sadly had to let a few more employees go, and we've had to do some serious negotiations with some of our merchants and sub-contractors, but things seem to be going in the right direction, and of course, saving on the extortionate rent as of now will be a huge help.

"Still glad you came back?" he asks for the millionth time. Even after moving back in, I wasn't sure I wanted my old job back, but Ben has a way of wording things, and a few days later, I found myself sitting at my old desk beside Erica once again. That's all changing with the new office, because Ben insisted that my desk be beside his. He's told me time and time again that this company isn't just his, but ours, and he wants me involved all the way. I'm terrified of missing something so huge again like I did with Dad, but I have total trust in Ben and his capabilities in running the company.

"You know I am. I want it to work as much as you do."

"Did IT get everything set up for Trey?" Although they joked about Trey starting immediately, things took a little longer in reality, so in the end they agreed on his start date being tomorrow.

"Yep, all good. Stop worrying."

"I'm not. I'm just excited to see how he fits in and how it all goes."

"Oh, I think he's going to fit in just fine."

"What's that look for?"

"Nothing. I just think he's already got a vested interest in what goes on in our office."

Ben's silent for a minute before the penny drops. "What the fuck has Erica done now?"

"Nothing you want to know about, I can assure you."

"Jesus, she's a pain in my arse."

"Aw, you love her really. Now, can we please stop talking about work?"

"Sure. Are you hungry?"

"Starved. But seeing as we're re-living the past tonight, I thought I needed to do something else before we eat."

We're laying out on the swing chair covered in a fluffy blanket and staring up at the star-filled sky after eating our way through the pile of food ben barbequed. Ben's eyes darken as memories hit him. "I can't argue with that. Six weeks ago, I really never thought this would be my future," Ben whispers beneath me.

"Me neither. I never wanted anything else though."

"Me neither, baby. This is it for us now. The beginning of forever. I want it all with you."

Turning in his arms, I reach up and press my lips to his. "Forever, baby."

The series continues with Erica and Trey's story in CRAVING REDEMPTION.

DOWNLOAD the duet now
or keep reading for a snippet.

# CRAVING REDEMPTION
## SNEAK PEAK

**Chapter One**

"You want the usual?" I watch as Joe gestures for the barman. Much to everyone else's annoyance, she takes one look at him and saunters over, ignoring her other customers who have been waiting longer.

"What can I get you, handsome?" She bats her very fake eyelashes at him, and he leans forward on his elbows, eating the attention right up.

Rolling my eyes at them, I glance around the bar. It's not unusual to bump into a couple of the guys from work here. This place might be a little classier than it was back in the day, but it's still our regular. It was called Fire back then and was full of drunken students. Now, it's a fancy bar called The Avenue and has chrome fittings everywhere and chandeliers hanging from the high ceilings. I'd like to think we've also grown and are a little more sophisticated, but I usually end up questioning that once we get a few drinks inside us.

"Here you go," Joe sings, sliding a prosecco towards me. "To your awesome new housemate." He clinks his glass to mine, his face deadly serious.

"You're an idiot." I can't help but laugh at his puppy dog eyes.

I haven't lived with anyone since my ex suddenly vanished on me a little over six months ago. I must admit that I'm looking forward to having someone else to talk to. Joe promised me it would be only a short-term fix for his little homeless problem, but I'm in no rush to get rid of him—well, not yet, anyway. We've only been living together for a few days. I've not had the chance to discover if he has any weird quirks I'm not going to be able to deal with.

If I start finding stray toenails littered over the bathroom floor, there are going to be issues.

"So, anyone catch your attention?" I shake myself from my nightmare and look up into his dark eyes.

"Huh?"

"Anyone catch your eye?"

"Oh no, I'm not really interested." I've been going through somewhat of a dry spell recently. When I admitted how long it had been since I'd had sex, Joe immediately demanded I put on my sluttiest dress and dragged me out of the flat.

I was excited in the taxi on the way here but now, looking around and finding absolutely no one who catches my eye, I kind of want to go home, put my pyjamas on, and snuggle up on the sofa.

Joe's brow rises before he turns to scout the perfect man for me himself. I know it's unlike me. I used to have a reputation for being the party girl, but, after my last two bad experiences with men, I'm more than happy keeping my distance for a while.

Sipping my drink, I keep my focus on the colourful bottles behind the bar. I used to live for this, for a night out and the thrill of meeting someone new, but with everything that's happened over the past few months, I've totally lost the enthusiasm.

"Erica, come on. You need to get yourself back out there. Hiding isn't healthy. It's not *you*."

"Maybe it's the new me," I mutter, sipping my drink. "Anyway, who are you to start dishing out advice? I hate to break it to you, mate, but your life isn't all that great right now."

"What makes you say that?"

"Oh, come on. You can't tell me you don't realise you've been moping around since the day you moved out of yours and Lauren's flat. I know you miss her. I'm trying not to let it affect me, being your new roommate and all." I wink to let him know I'm only winding him up. If he needs time to 'grieve' or whatever the fuck it is he's doing, he's more than welcome to it. I know he appreciates my offer of a place to stay.

"I just—"

"You can say it, you know, that you miss her. I know how tight you two were."

"Yeah, fine. I miss her, okay?" Something passes through his eyes, and it only feeds my earlier suspicion that there might be more to this than he's letting on.

I open my mouth to say more, but I don't get the chance. Joe is too keen to change the subject.

"Do not tell me you passed up the guy at ten o'clock?"

Following his instruction, I look to my left and immediately lock eyes with a handsome older man. A shiver runs down my spine as our eye contact holds. I can't tell from this distance what colour they are, but they're dark. Ripping my gaze away, my mouth waters when I take in his pristine white shirt covered with a sharp black waistcoat. *Fuck.* I'm a sucker for a man in a suit.

"He is *so* your type, and by the way he's staring at you like he wants to devour you, I'd say you're his, too."

"Nope, not interested. I am off men for the foreseeable future."

"Fuck off. You don't really expect me to believe that, do you? You're Erica Wilde, this is what you do: go out, have fun, pick up guys." I wince at his opinion of me.

"Well, if that's how you see me, it's even more reason for me to swear off men."

"I didn't mean it like that, and you know it. I just meant that... fuck, I'm screwing this up. You're not yourself right now, and I hate it. You've lost that sparkle in your eye. Your zest for life. *He* stole that from you."

"No," I spit. "We do not talk about him. *Ever.* You got that?"

"I know. I'm just...I'm worried about you."

"I could say the same thing."

"I'm fine. I just need a good fuck. You've been winding me up all week, walking around in those little fucking shorts and practically see through top—"

"That top is not see through."

"Maybe not, but I sure as shit know you don't wear a bra under it."

"Yeah, you really do need a fuck." I pull my eyes from his and look around, much like he did for me earlier. "Guy or girl?"

"A guy. Definitely a guy. I need him to—"

"Spare me."

Rolling his eyes, he moves to scan the room, looking for his target.

With Joe's attention averted, I risk another look at the suit. My skin's been burning the entire time we were talking, so I know he hasn't got bored and moved on. Our eyes lock once again, and I swear they fucking call to me. They drop to my lips and I watch as his tongue sneaks out and runs along his bottom one. My thighs clench and my fingers curl around the bar stool I'm perched on as my body temperature spikes.

I allow myself a minute to appreciate him.

His eyes are hard, and there are a few lines creasing his forehead. His lips are pressed into a thin line. From anger or desire? Only he knows, but damn if I don't want to go over there and find out. He's got the perfect amount of stubble on his jaw, just enough to enhance what I'm sure his mouth is capable of but not enough to leave a rash.

Biting down on my bottom lip, I try to imagine what it might be like to be with a man who looks as dominant and dangerous as him. I've experienced my fair share of demanding lovers, but he looks like he might be capable of taking it to the next level. Tingles ignite in my core as I think about how capable he probably is.

"I'd put one hundred quid on you leaving with him tonight," Joe says in my ear. I laugh but my eyes don't leave the suit's for even a second.

**DOWNLOAD the DUET NOW to keep reading!**

## ACKNOWLEDGMENTS

Wow! Writing Ben and Lauren's story has been one hell of an emotional ride. I knew it was going to be a little heavy, but I never expected quite what happened. It was meant to be one book, but only a few words in and I knew these two had a lot more to give. And it's not just them, because there are a few others I hope you'd like to discover a little more about. Yes, that's right, I have plans for more. Who do you think's coming next?!

A huge thank you once again to Michelle. She read every single word of all three of these books almost the moment they fell from my fingers. You lived every second of their pain, betrayals and joy right along with them. I really don't know what I'd do without you pointing out all my stupid mistakes and loving each of my characters as much as I do.

My betas: Deanna, Helen, Lindsay, Suzanne and Tracy. You waited so patiently for this final instalment and didn't harass me too much to find out if Ben and Lauren were going to get their happily ever after. Thank you for dropping everything to read their conclusion and messaging me with your every thought along the way.

Evelyn, thank you for falling for Ben and making his and Lauren's story as good as it can be and for falling for Ben right alongside me.

Andie, a massive thank you for managing to squeeze this into your unbelievably busy schedule for proofreading for me.

I also need to thank you, my readers. Thank you for being on this journey with me, for sharing, reviewing and recommending me to your friends. I really wouldn't be here without you.

I can't let this trilogy come to an end without taking a moment to appreciate the beauty of the cover and the incredibly talented James Critchley for taking such amazing shots of a man who just screams BJ to me. His real name is George RJ and for me he represents Ben perfectly. I hope you agree.

And finally, I have to thank my husband and daughter for supporting me through these emotional books and allowing me the time to write all the words.

So, until next time,

Tracy xo

# ABOUT THE AUTHOR

Tracy Lorraine is a *USA Today* and *Wall Street Journal* bestselling new adult and contemporary romance author. Tracy has recently turned thirty and lives in a cute Cotswold village in England with her husband, baby girl and lovable but slightly crazy dog. Having always been a bookaholic with her head stuck in her Kindle, Tracy decided to try her hand at a story idea she dreamt up and hasn't looked back since.

Be the first to find out about new releases and offers. Sign up to my newsletter here.

If you want to know what I'm up to and see teasers and snippets of what I'm working on, then you need to be in my Facebook group. Join Tracy's Angels here.

*Keep up to date with Tracy's books at*
www.tracylorraine.com

# ALSO BY TRACY LORRAINE

## **<u>Falling Series</u>**

<u>Falling for Ryan: Part One</u> #1

<u>Falling for Ryan: Part Two</u> #2

<u>Falling for Jax</u> #3

<u>Falling for Daniel</u> (A Falling Series Novella)

<u>Falling for Ruben</u> #4

<u>Falling for Ein</u> #5

<u>Falling for Lucas</u> #6

<u>Falling for Caleb</u> #7

<u>Falling for Declan</u> #8

<u>Falling For Liam</u> #9

## **<u>Forbidden Series</u>**

<u>Falling for the Forbidden</u> #1

<u>Losing the Forbidden</u> #2

<u>Fighting for the Forbidden</u> #3

<u>Craving Redemption</u> #4

<u>Demanding Redemption</u> #5

<u>Avoiding Temptation</u> #6

<u>Chasing Temptation</u> #7

## **<u>Rebel Ink Series</u>**

<u>Hate You</u> #1

<u>Trick You</u> #2

<u>Defy You</u> #3

<u>Play You</u> #4

<u>Inked</u> (A Rebel Ink/Driven Crossover)

**<u>Rosewood High Series</u>**

<u>Thorn</u> #1

<u>Paine</u> #2

<u>Savage</u> #3

<u>Fierce</u> #4

<u>Hunter</u> #5

Faze (#6 Prequel)

<u>Fury</u> #6

<u>Legend</u> #7

**<u>Maddison Kings University Series</u>**

T.M.Y.M: Prequel

<u>TRYS</u> #1

<u>TDYW</u> #2

<u>TBYS</u> #3

<u>TVYC</u> #4

<u>TDYD</u> #5

<u>TDYR</u> #6

<u>TRYD</u> #7

**<u>Knight's Ridge Empire Series</u>**

<u>Wicked Summer Knight</u>: Prequel (Stella & Seb)

<u>Wicked Knight</u> #1 (Stella & Seb)

<u>Wicked Princess</u> #2 (Stella & Seb)

<u>Wicked Empire</u> #3 (Stella & Seb)

<u>Deviant Knight</u> #4 (Emmie & Theo)

<u>Deviant Princess</u> #5 (Emmie & Theo

<u>Deviant Reign</u> #6 (Emmie & Theo)

<u>One Reckless Knight</u> (Jodie & Toby)

<u>Reckless Knight</u> #7 (Jodie & Toby)

<u>Reckless Princess</u> #8 (Jodie & Toby)

<u>Reckless Dynasty</u> #9 (Jodie & Toby)

Dark Halloween Knight (Calli & Batman)

Dark Knight #10 (Calli & Batman)

<u>Dark Princess</u> #11 (Calli & Batman)

Dark Legacy #12 (Calli & Batman)

<u>Corrupt Valentine Knight</u> (Nico & Siren)

Corrupt Knight #13 (Nico & Siren)

Corrupt Princess #14 (Nico & Siren)

Corrupt Union #15 (Nico & Siren)

Sinful Wild Knight (Alex & Vixen)

Sinful Stolen Knight: Prequel (Alex & Vixen)

Sinful Knight #16 (Alex & Vixen)

Sinful Princess #17 (Alex & Vixen)

Sinful Kingdom #18 (Alex & Vixen)

Knight's Ridge Destiny: Epilogue

**Harrow Creek Hawks Series**

Merciless #1

Relentless #2

Lawless #3

Fearless #4

## **<u>Ruined Series</u>**

<u>Ruined Plans</u> #1

<u>Ruined by Lies</u> #2

<u>Ruined Promises</u> #3

## **<u>Never Forget Series</u>**

<u>Never Forget Him</u> #1

<u>Never Forget Us</u> #2

<u>Everywhere & Nowhere</u> #3

## **<u>Chasing Series</u>**

<u>Chasing Logan</u>

## **<u>The Cocktail Girls</u>**

<u>His Manhattan</u>

<u>Her Kensington</u>

# SNEAK PEEK

*Falling for the Forbidden* is a spin off from my *Falling* series. If you've not read it then keep reading for a sneak peek at *Falling for Ryan,* my friends to lovers romance that kicks off the series.

# FALLING FOR RYAN: PART ONE
## CHAPTER ONE

Molly

*Present*

It's midnight, and I've been sat on Ryan's doorstep for nearly an hour. I've already started on one of the bottles of wine. Although it was a scorching summer's day, the heat has now worn off, the clouds have gathered, and it's lumping it down with rain. I'm trying to tuck myself into his little porch to stop from getting so wet, but with the wind direction, it's not doing much good. I'm soaked through. It was a silly idea to pick white t-shirts when I rebranded the coffee shop; thank God for padded bras!

By the time I'd cleaned and locked up, it was just gone ten. I love working at Cocoa's and have done so since I was sixteen. Hannah and Emma's parents own it. Susan started the business after she finished university. She came into some inheritance and, with the money, Cocoa's was born. The place was a huge part of my childhood.

Hannah, Emma, and I would go there after school to do homework or just chat about boys, and it pretty much stayed that way until we finished university. We still have a booth in the back corner dedicated to us.

I will forever be grateful for Susan and her husband, Pete, whom she actually met as a customer in Cocoa's. It was love at first sight for them. Not only did they give me a job, but they took me under their wing when I was much younger.

Megan, who works in the evenings, had a phone call from her boyfriend at eight o'clock saying their little boy was really sick. I let her go home to be with him and finished up the rest of the night on my own.

Once I got in my car, all I could think about was having a nice hot bath and snuggling into bed in my tiny one-bed flat with my boyfriend, Max. We've been together on and off for the past three years, but when Hannah, whom I'd lived with above the coffee shop, decided eight months ago that she wanted her own boyfriend to move into the flat, I decided it was time I moved out and left them to it. Max had suggested I move in with him. I wasn't thrilled by the idea, to be honest, but at the time I didn't have the money to find anywhere decent to live. I hate being alone. I would have had to find someone who was renting out a room anyway, so it seemed like a sensible suggestion and a logical step in our relationship.

A week later, we all moved. Me into Max's flat, and Hannah's boyfriend into the one we'd shared for the past six years.

The ten-minute drive to our home seemed to take forever. I pulled up out the front; it was weird to be parking next to Max's car. He had worked nights the whole time I'd known him.

I dragged my body up the stairs to the third floor and let myself in. I shut the door behind me; the only light was coming from the bedroom. My heart dropped into my stomach when I heard voices and strange noises coming from down the hallway. As quietly as I could, I tiptoed towards them.

When I got to the door, I couldn't believe my eyes. Now, I knew

Max was no angel, but I was under the impression that we had put the past behind us when we decided to live together and had become a monogamous couple. Yes, the past few months had been a strain, but still.

What was happening before my eyes on our bed showed me how wrong I was.

I numbly slipped back down the hallway and grabbed a couple of pairs of knickers that, luckily for me, were drying on the radiator, and left.

I tried to keep myself together as I made a pit stop at the shop on my way to Ryan's house. I didn't want to be one of those emotional women sobbing in the alcohol aisle, trying to decide which bottle would make me forget.

Once I'd paid for two bottles of my favourite wine and a crate of lager for Ryan, I made my way over to his new house. He'd only moved in two weeks ago, although it was months ago that he made the decision to buy the three-story townhouse in the new development on the outskirts of the city. It was basically a pile of bricks when he took me with him to see it for the first time, but I could see why he'd fallen in love with it. It was modern and spacious, with amazing views across fields from the back. From the front, you could see all the lights from the city in the distance. Because it was yet to be finished, it meant Ryan could choose a lot of the interior to suit his taste, and he didn't have to spend his whole summer re-decorating.

Grabbing my phone, I open up my messages to re-read the conversation I'd had with him earlier. He said he was going out tonight to celebrate the end of the school year but that he wasn't expecting to be home late. I guess that didn't really go as planned—not that he'd be expecting me to be sitting here waiting for him.

I'm starting to think I should have gone somewhere else. It's not that I don't have any other options, but out of all my friends and family, Ryan knows me the best.

What we've been through this year has made us close. I think I can safely say he's turned into my best friend somewhere in the last six months.

As I wait, images of what was happening on my bed flash though my head. I guess I should have seen it coming, really. A leopard never changes it spots, right?

Eventually, the tears come flooding out. To add to my misery, I now have black mascara streaks running down my cheeks and red puffy eyes.

Finally, I see headlights coming my way and Ryan's white Honda Civic pulling into his drive. At first, he looks shocked to see me. That changes to anger as he strides towards me.


Ryan


AS I COME TO A STOP, I can see that there's a very wet Molly huddled in my porch. She looks dreadful. I come to a very quick conclusion that it's because of her dickhead of a boyfriend. I knew it was coming; it was just a matter of when.

"Ryan," Molly sobs as I lift her tiny frame off the ground and into a hug. She shakes from both the cold and the sobs wracking her body.

Tucking her into my side, I grab her bags and let us in. On the ground floor, my townhouse has a large room with French doors looking out to the courtyard garden, and a bathroom. I thought it would make an excellent gym. The middle floor is an open-plan kitchen, living, and dining room with a small cloakroom, and the top floor has three bedrooms, one being the master with ensuite and the other a large family bathroom.

I love it.

From the moment I looked at the plans, I just knew it was going to be my little piece of heaven, and I'm still in awe that I was able to buy this place. I'll be forever grateful for the generous gift from Susan and Pete. Nothing will ever make up for what we all lost, but thanks to them, I've been able to attempt to move on with my life.

Currently, there are boxes everywhere. I haven't had much time to unpack with everything I had to do at school to end the year, but my first holiday job is to get this place sorted and looking like a home.

Anger fills my veins as I lead us up to the living room. "It's going to be okay. Let's get you warm and dry and you can tell me what the fucker did." My fists clench. I want to beat the shit out of him for treating her so badly for so long.

"How do you know he's done anything?" Molly asks in a quiet voice.

"I can read you like a book, Molly Carter. Plus, he's a massive dickhead. I think I've mentioned that before. Only Max can make you feel this bad about yourself."

"Why was I so fucking stupid? I had my doubts, everyone had their doubts, but he convinced me that it was what he wanted. I'm not really surprised, but what does shock me is how much it *hurts*."

"Come on, get your arse upstairs and in the shower. I'll find you a t-shirt to wear."

---

AS I ROOT through a suitcase in one of the spare bedrooms, the door to my ensuite shuts. I pull out my Oxford Brookes polo and leave it on my bed. I hope my choice will make her smile, remembering happier times.

I knock lightly on the door. "Have you got everything you need?"

There's silence for a few seconds, and I can imagine her checking out all the products in the shower, realising they're all for men. Eventually, I hear a quiet "Yes" from the other side of the door.

"Okay, I'll see you downstairs when you're done. Take your time."

I gather up her wet clothes and take them with me. They may be soaked, but I can still smell her vanilla scent on them. It makes me feel oddly warm inside. She's been my rock for the past six months. I don't know what I would have done without her.

As I put everything in the washing machine, I spot her bra poking out of the pile. "What the fuck do I do with this?" I mutter to myself. Something in me wonders if it needs some kind of special cycle in the machine, but fuck if I know. I decide to shove it all in and just put it on a cool, quick wash.

That shouldn't do it much damage, right?

DOWNLOAD NOW to continue reading